VOLUME 6

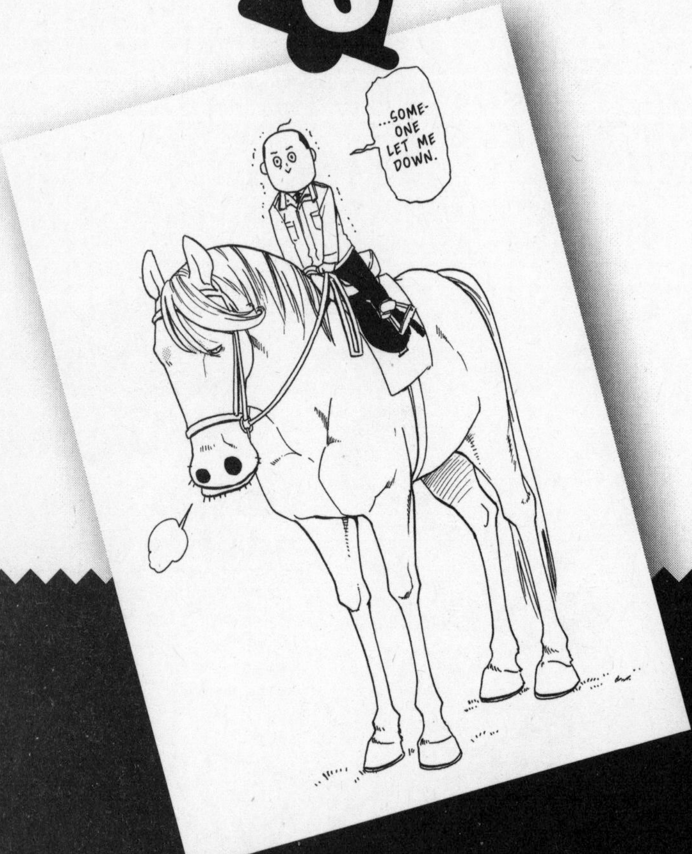
...SOME-ONE LET ME DOWN.

Silver Spoon

HIROMU ARAKAWA

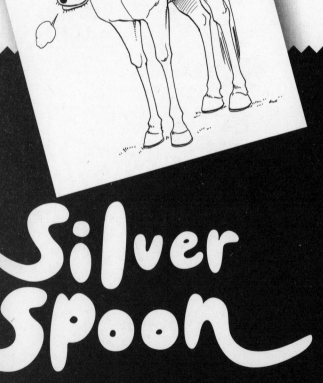

STORY & CHARACTERS

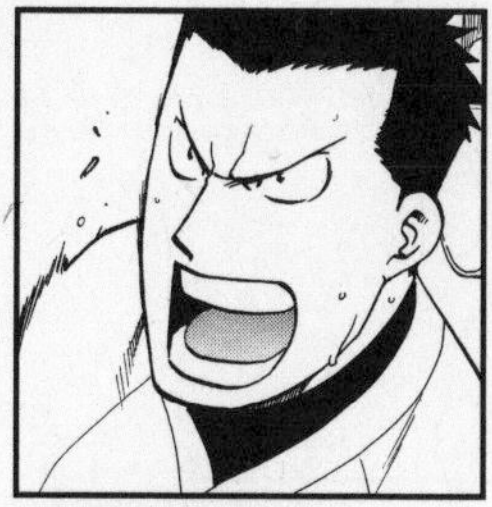

ICHIROU KOMABA

A first-year student at Ooezo Agricultural High School, enrolled in the Dairy Science Program. Pitcher for the baseball team with the potential to be their next ace player. Plans on taking over the family farm after graduation.

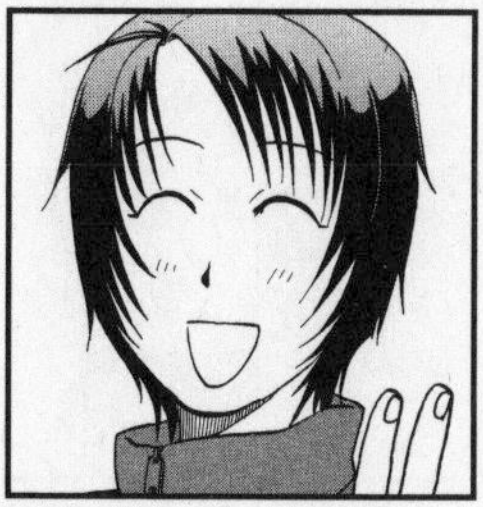

AKI MIKAGE

A first-year student at Ooezo Agricultural High School, enrolled in the Dairy Science Program. Her family keeps cows and horses, and she's expected to carry on the family business. Deep down, though, she wants to work with horses...but...

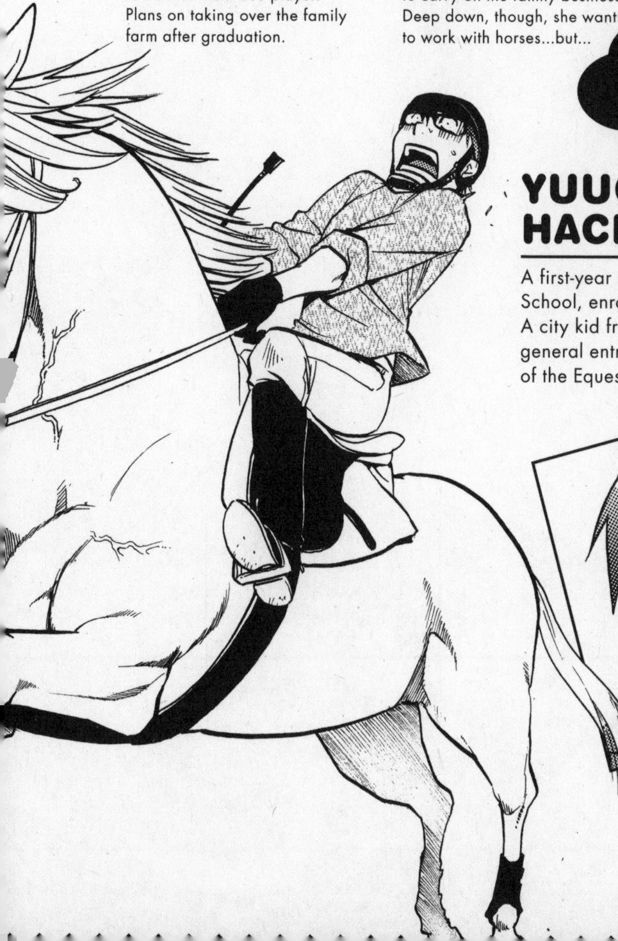

YUUGO HACHIKEN

A first-year student at Ooezo Agricultural High School, enrolled in the Dairy Science Program. A city kid from Sapporo who got in through the general entrance exam. Now he's vice president of the Equestrian Club.

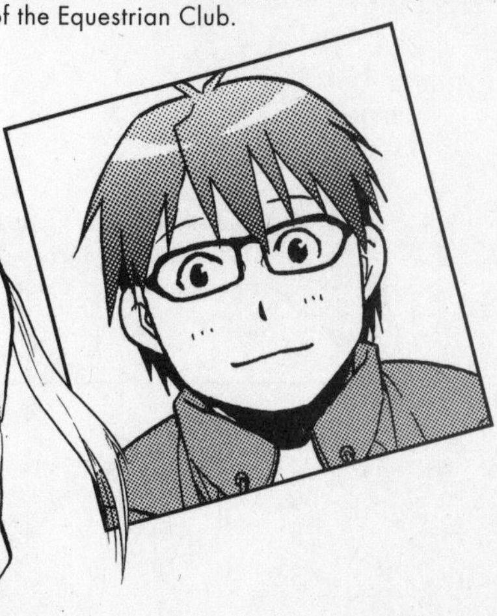

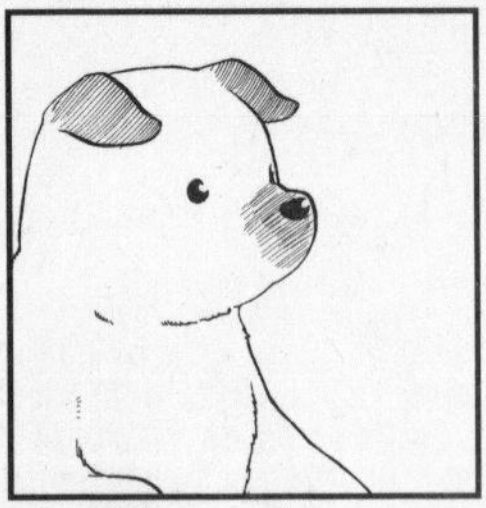

VICE PREZ

Hachiken found the abandoned pup during a campus cleanup. Now he's the Equestrian Club's guard dog (mascot).

The Story Thus Far:

Autumn: clear blue skies and horses growing stout... Hachiken has become vice president of the Equestrian Club. As always, he's busy with classes, club, and chores...but now he has a new problem. Of all the Equestrian Club first-years, he's the only person who hasn't done a jump. Hachiken spirals into embarrassment and panic—but Aki pulls him out of it. He eventually takes the lesson to heart, albeit clumsily. And the sky Hachiken leaps through with Chestnut is a spectacle unlike any other.

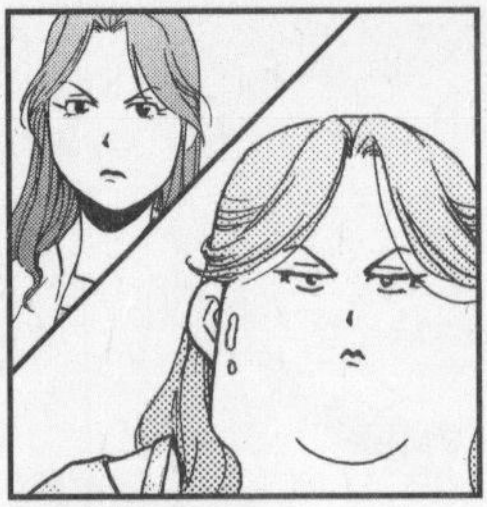

TAMAKO INADA

A first-year student at Ooezo Agricultural High School, enrolled in the Dairy Science Program. Her family runs the megafarm. A complete enigma.

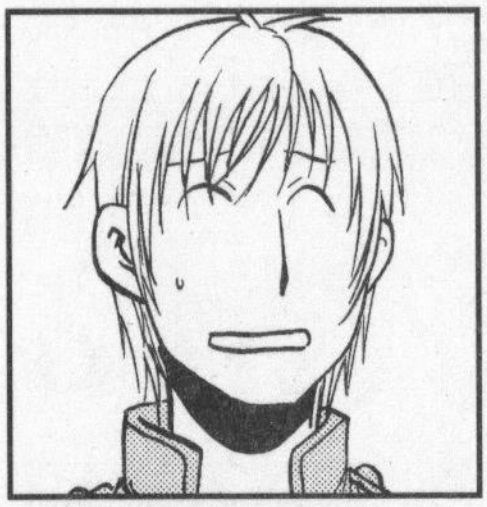

SHINNOSUKE AIKAWA

A first-year student at Ooezo Agricultural High School, enrolled in the Dairy Science Program. His dream is to become a veterinarian, but he can't handle blood.

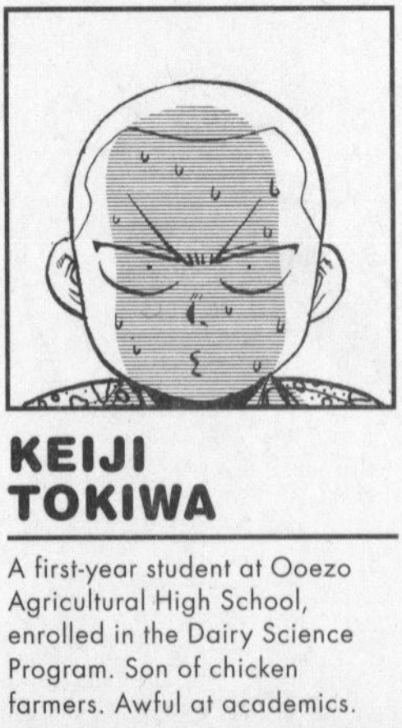

KEIJI TOKIWA

A first-year student at Ooezo Agricultural High School, enrolled in the Dairy Science Program. Son of chicken farmers. Awful at academics.

CONTENTS

Silver Spoon

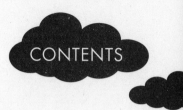

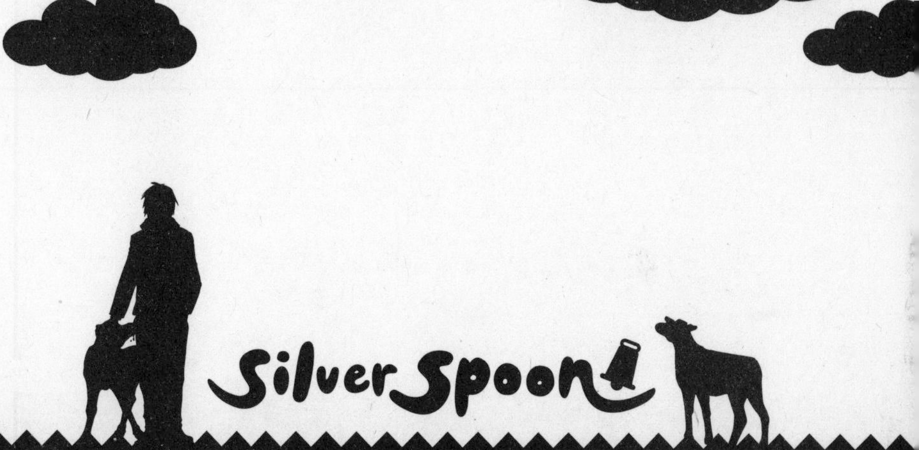

Chapter 45:
Tale of Autumn ⑭

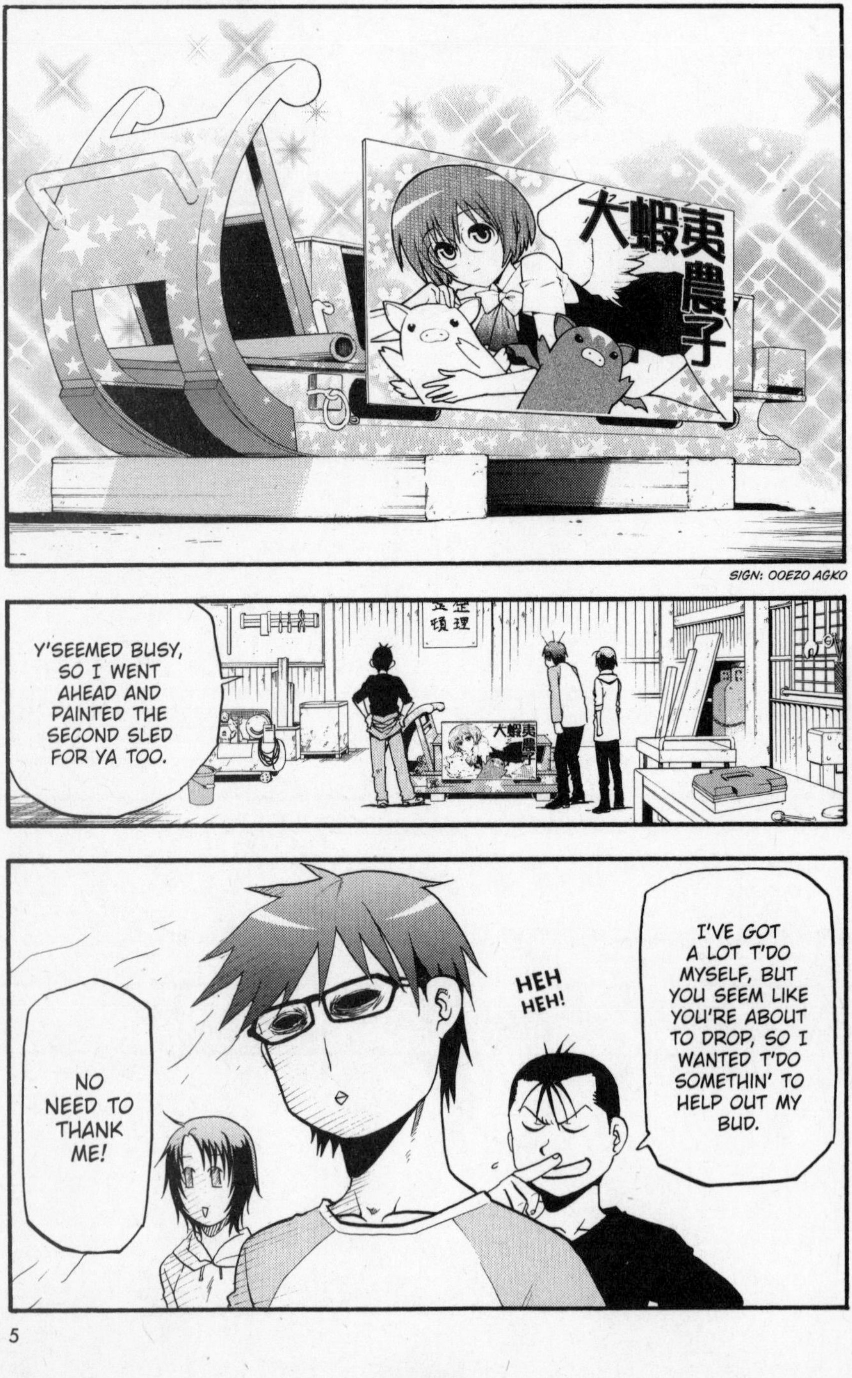
大蝦夷農子
SIGN: OOEZO AGKO
Y'SEEMED BUSY, SO I WENT AHEAD AND PAINTED THE SECOND SLED FOR YA TOO.
I'VE GOT A LOT T'DO MYSELF, BUT YOU SEEM LIKE YOU'RE ABOUT TO DROP, SO I WANTED T'DO SOMETHIN' TO HELP OUT MY BUD.
HEH HEH!
NO NEED TO THANK ME!

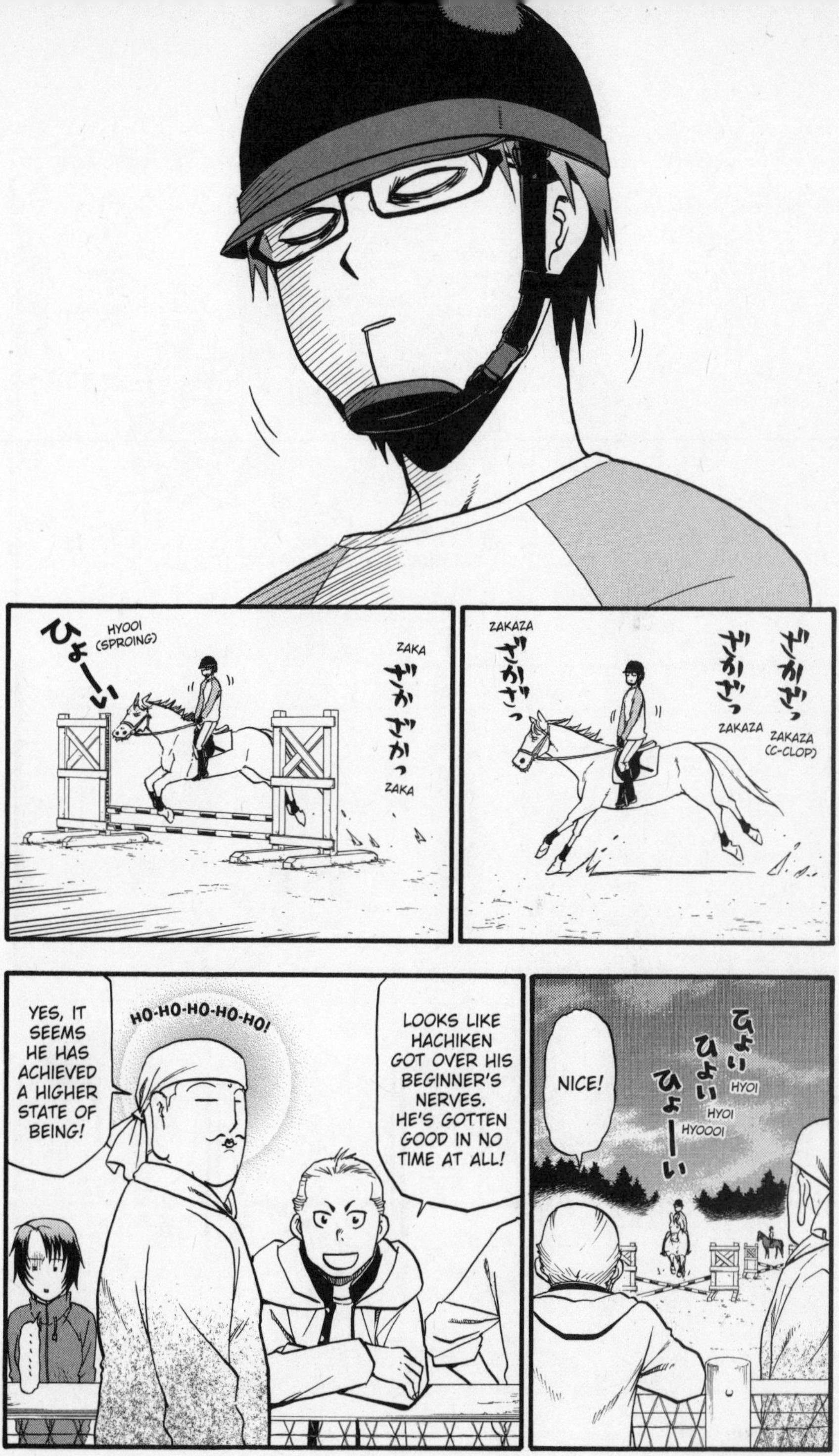
ざかざっ
ざかざっ
ZAKAZA
ZAKAZA (C-CLOP)
ざかざっ
ZAKAZA
ZAKA
ざかざかっ
ZAKA
ひょーい
HYOOI (SPROING)
NICE!
ひょい
ひょい
ひょーい
HYOI
HYOI
HYOOOI
LOOKS LIKE HACHIKEN GOT OVER HIS BEGINNER'S NERVES. HE'S GOTTEN GOOD IN NO TIME AT ALL!
HO-HO-HO-HO-HO!
YES, IT SEEMS HE HAS ACHIEVED A HIGHER STATE OF BEING!
......

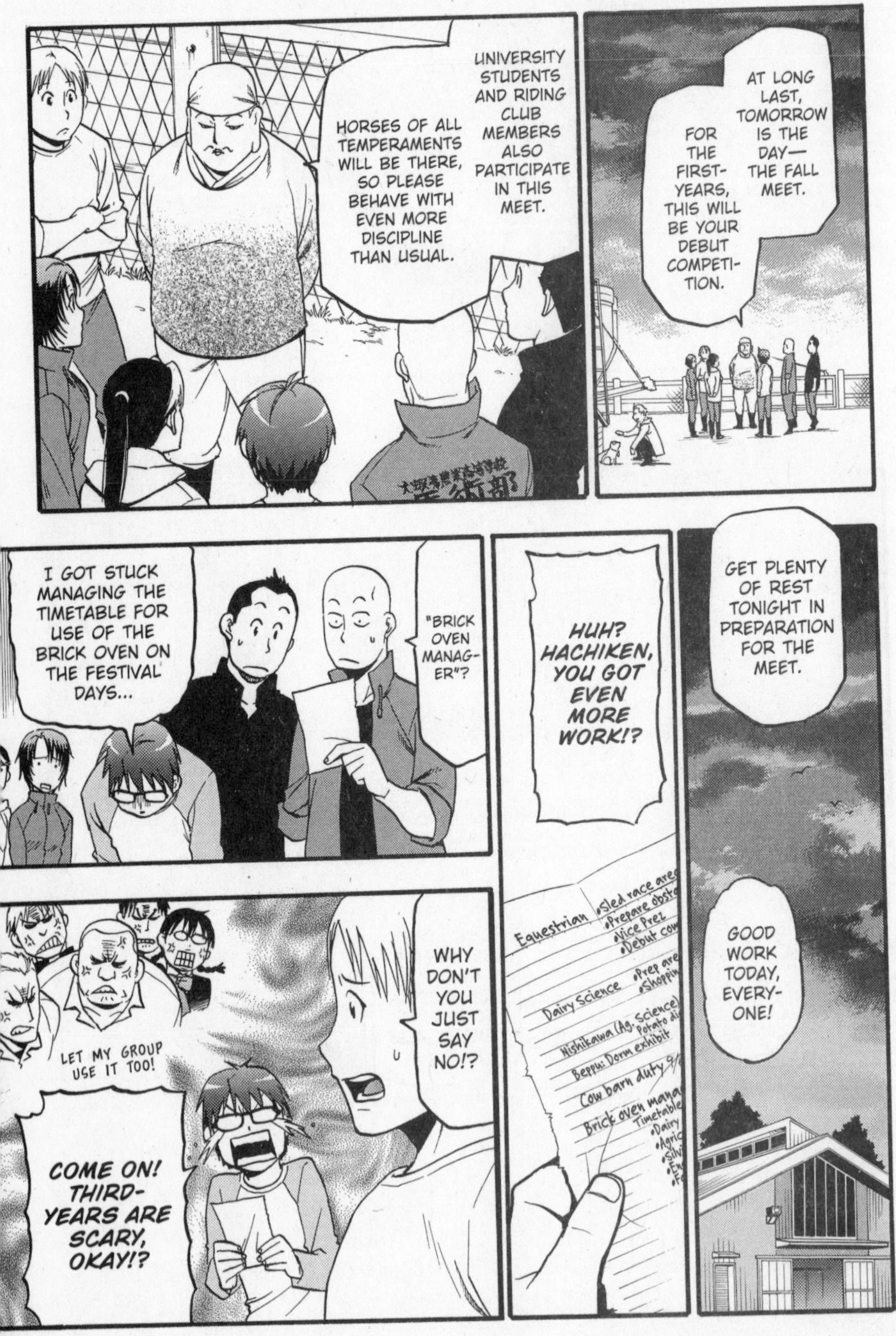
AT LONG LAST, TOMORROW IS THE DAY— THE FALL MEET.
FOR THE FIRST-YEARS, THIS WILL BE YOUR DEBUT COMPETITION.
UNIVERSITY STUDENTS AND RIDING CLUB MEMBERS ALSO PARTICIPATE IN THIS MEET.
HORSES OF ALL TEMPERAMENTS WILL BE THERE, SO PLEASE BEHAVE WITH EVEN MORE DISCIPLINE THAN USUAL.
GET PLENTY OF REST TONIGHT IN PREPARATION FOR THE MEET.
GOOD WORK TODAY, EVERYONE!
HUH? HACHIKEN, YOU GOT EVEN MORE WORK!?
Equestrian
Vice Prez
Dairy Science
Nishikawa (Ag. Science)
Beppu: Dorm exhibit
Cow barn duty
Timetable
"BRICK OVEN MANAGER"?
I GOT STUCK MANAGING THE TIMETABLE FOR USE OF THE BRICK OVEN ON THE FESTIVAL DAYS...
WHY DON'T YOU JUST SAY NO!?
LET MY GROUP USE IT TOO!
COME ON! THIRD-YEARS ARE SCARY, OKAY!?

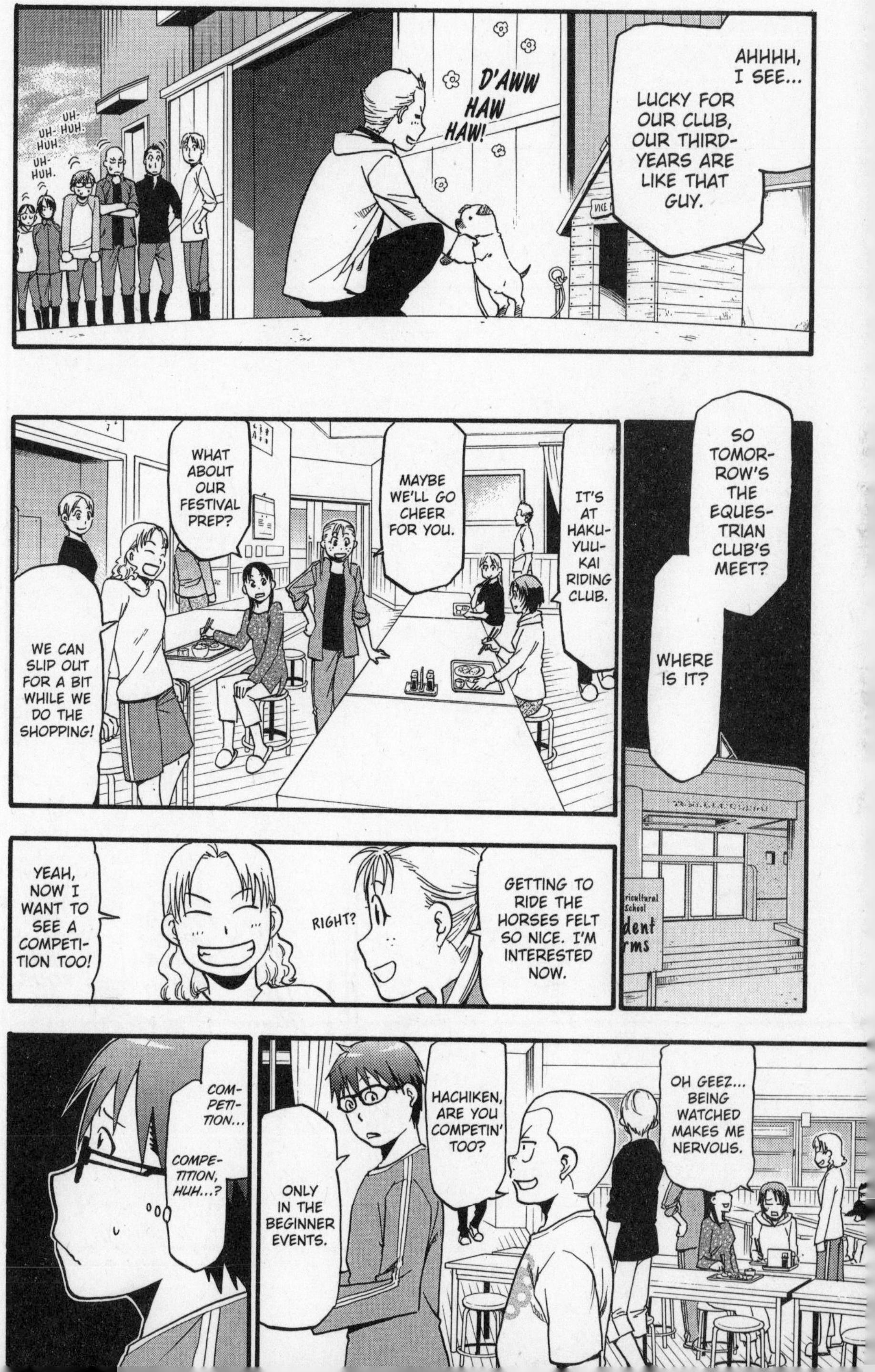
AHHHH, I SEE...
LUCKY FOR OUR CLUB, OUR THIRD-YEARS ARE LIKE THAT GUY.
D'AWW HAW HAW!
UH-HUH.
UH-HUH.
UH-HUH.
SO TOMORROW'S THE EQUESTRIAN CLUB'S MEET?
WHERE IS IT?
IT'S AT HAKUYUUKAI RIDING CLUB.
MAYBE WE'LL GO CHEER FOR YOU.
WHAT ABOUT OUR FESTIVAL PREP?
WE CAN SLIP OUT FOR A BIT WHILE WE DO THE SHOPPING!
GETTING TO RIDE THE HORSES FELT SO NICE. I'M INTERESTED NOW.
RIGHT?
YEAH, NOW I WANT TO SEE A COMPETITION TOO!
OH GEEZ... BEING WATCHED MAKES ME NERVOUS.
HACHIKEN, ARE YOU COMPETIN' TOO?
ONLY IN THE BEGINNER EVENTS.
COMPETITION...
COMPETITION, HUH...?

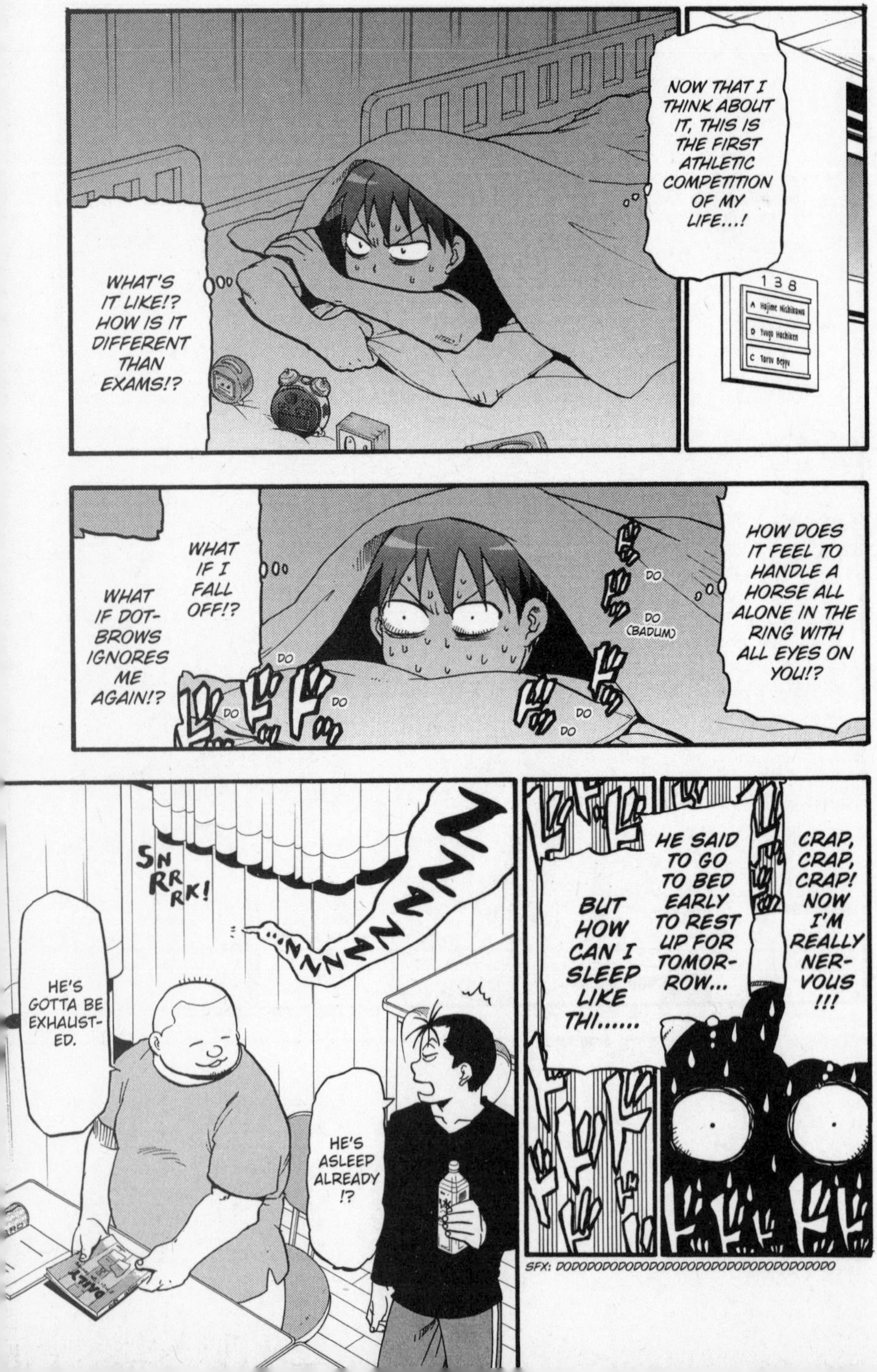
NOW THAT I THINK ABOUT IT, THIS IS THE FIRST ATHLETIC COMPETITION OF MY LIFE...!
138
A Hajime Nishikawa
D Yuugo Hachiken
C Tarou Beppu
WHAT'S IT LIKE!? HOW IS IT DIFFERENT THAN EXAMS!?
HOW DOES IT FEEL TO HANDLE A HORSE ALL ALONE IN THE RING WITH ALL EYES ON YOU!?
DO
DO (BADUM)
WHAT IF I FALL OFF!?
WHAT IF DOT-BROWS IGNORES ME AGAIN!?
DO DO DO DO DO
CRAP, CRAP, CRAP! NOW I'M REALLY NERVOUS!!!
HE SAID TO GO TO BED EARLY TO REST UP FOR TOMORROW...
BUT HOW CAN I SLEEP LIKE THI......
SNRRRK!
...NNNNNNNNNNN
HE'S ASLEEP ALREADY!?
HE'S GOTTA BE EXHAUSTED.
SFX: DODODODODODODODODODODODODODODODODODODO

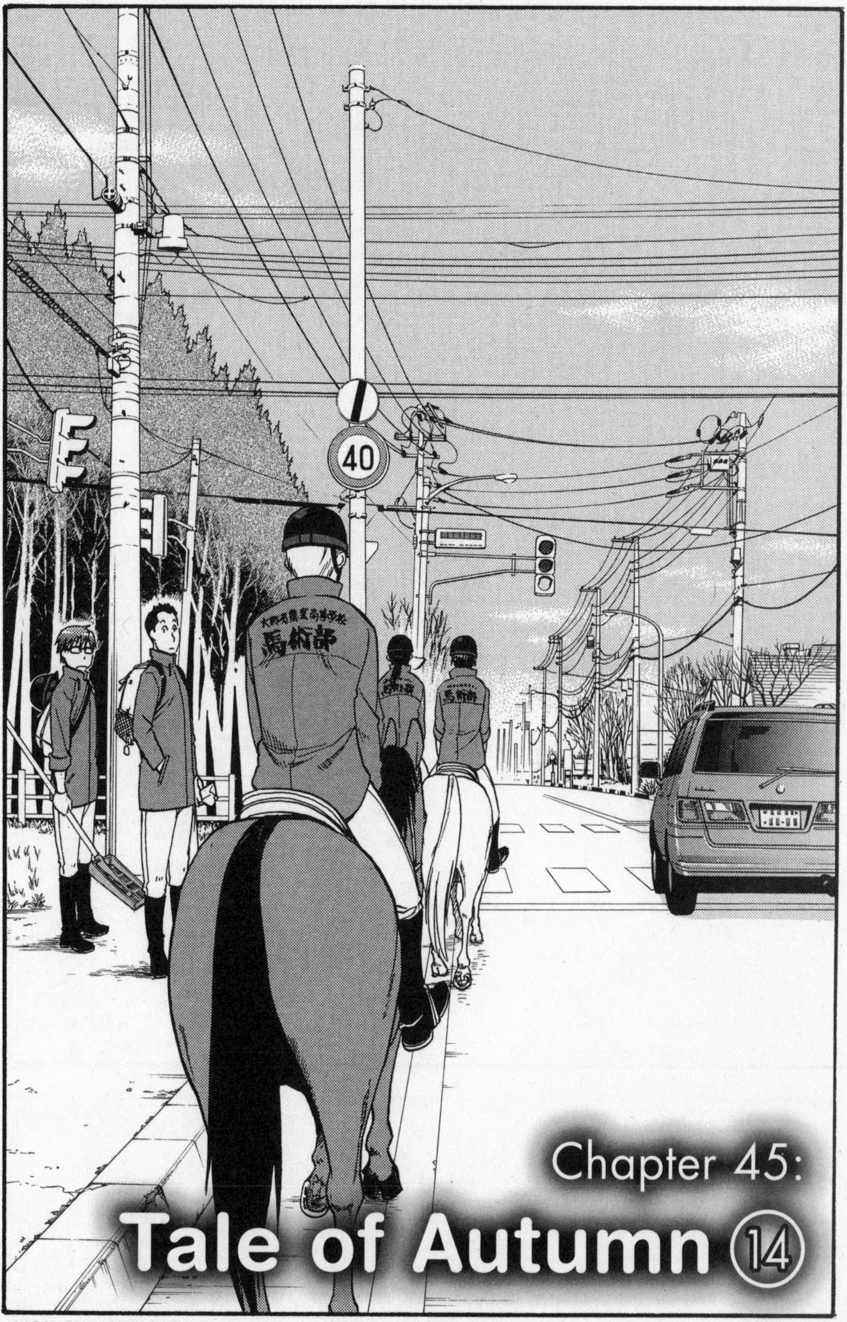
40
馬術部
Chapter 45:
Tale of Autumn ⑭

SHIRTS: EQUESTRIAN CLUB

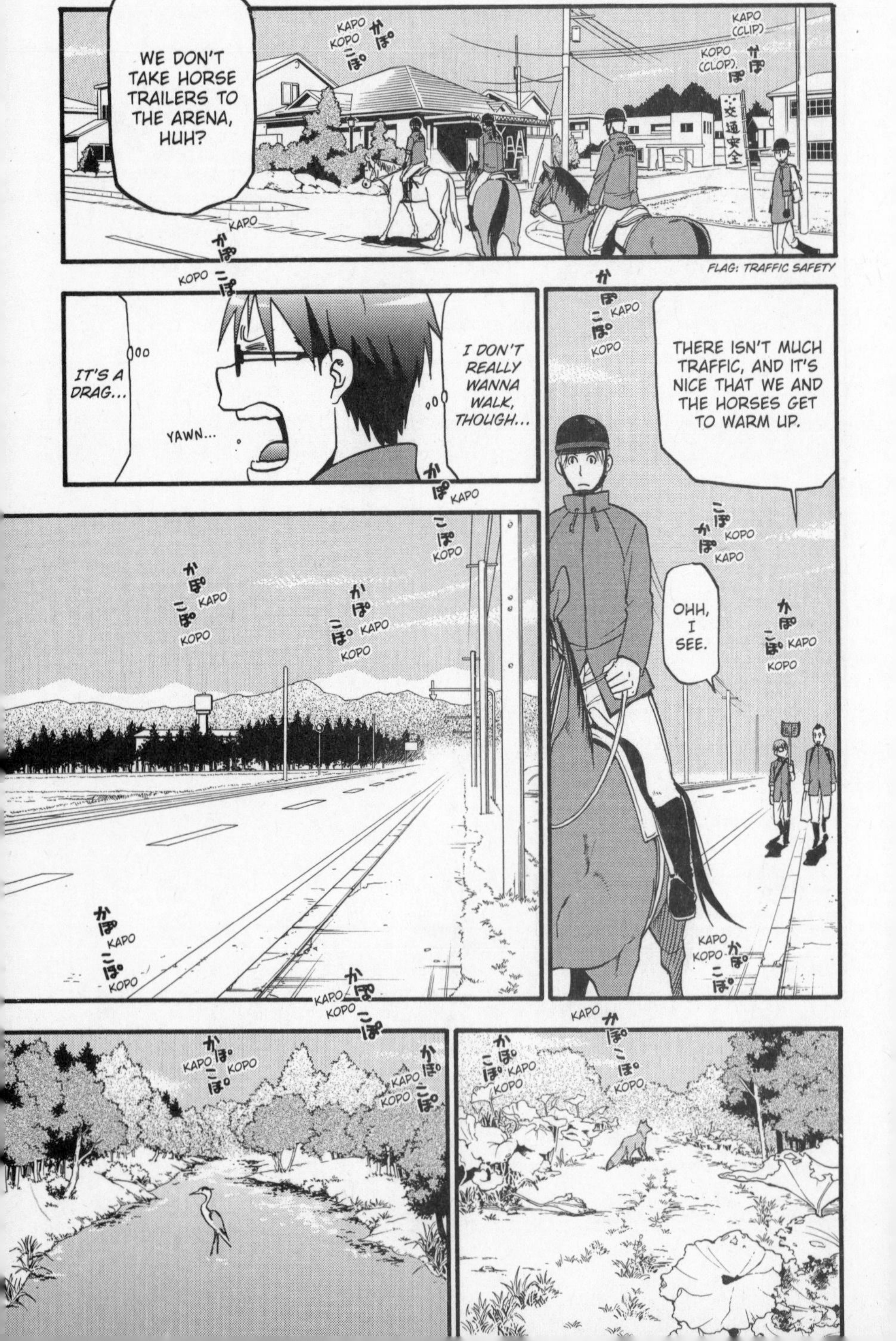
KAPO (CLIP)
KOPO (CLOP)
かぽ
こぽ
KAPO
KOPO
かぽ
こぽ
WE DON'T TAKE HORSE TRAILERS TO THE ARENA, HUH?
交通安全
KAPO
KOPO
かぽ
こぽ
FLAG: TRAFFIC SAFETY
かぽ
こぽ
KAPO
KOPO
THERE ISN'T MUCH TRAFFIC, AND IT'S NICE THAT WE AND THE HORSES GET TO WARM UP.
こぽ
かぽ
KOPO
KAPO
OHH, I SEE.
かぽ
こぽ
KAPO
KOPO
KAPO
KOPO
かぽ
こぽ
I DON'T REALLY WANNA WALK, THOUGH...
IT'S A DRAG...
YAWN...
かぽ
KAPO
こぽ
KOPO
かぽ
こぽ
KAPO
KOPO
かぽ
こぽ
KAPO
KOPO
かぽ
こぽ
KAPO
KOPO
KAPO
KOPO
かぽ
こぽ
KAPO
かぽ
こぽ
KOPO
かぽ
こぽ
KAPO
KOPO
かぽ
こぽ
KAPO
KOPO
かぽ
こぽ
KAPO
KOPO

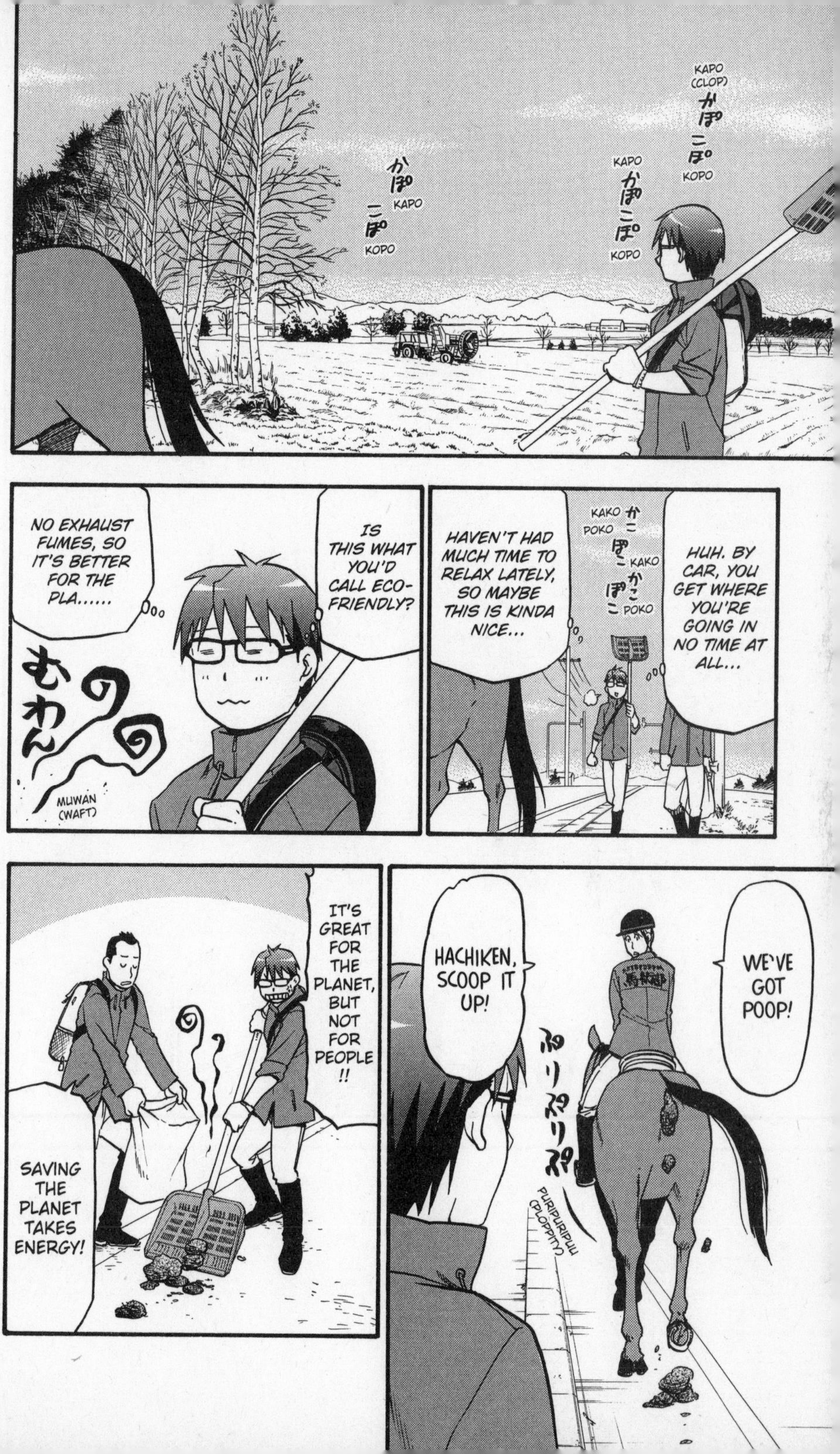
KAPO (CLOP)
かぽこぽ
KOPO
KAPO
かぽこぽ
KOPO
かぽこぽ
KAPO
KOPO
HUH. BY CAR, YOU GET WHERE YOU'RE GOING IN NO TIME AT ALL...
KAKO
かこぽこ
POKO
KAKO
かこぽこ
POKO
HAVEN'T HAD MUCH TIME TO RELAX LATELY, SO MAYBE THIS IS KINDA NICE...
IS THIS WHAT YOU'D CALL ECO-FRIENDLY?
NO EXHAUST FUMES, SO IT'S BETTER FOR THE PLA......
むわん
MUWAN (WAFT)
WE'VE GOT POOP!
HACHIKEN, SCOOP IT UP!
ぷりぷりぷり
PURIPURIPURI (PLOPPITY)
IT'S GREAT FOR THE PLANET, BUT NOT FOR PEOPLE!!
SAVING THE PLANET TAKES ENERGY!

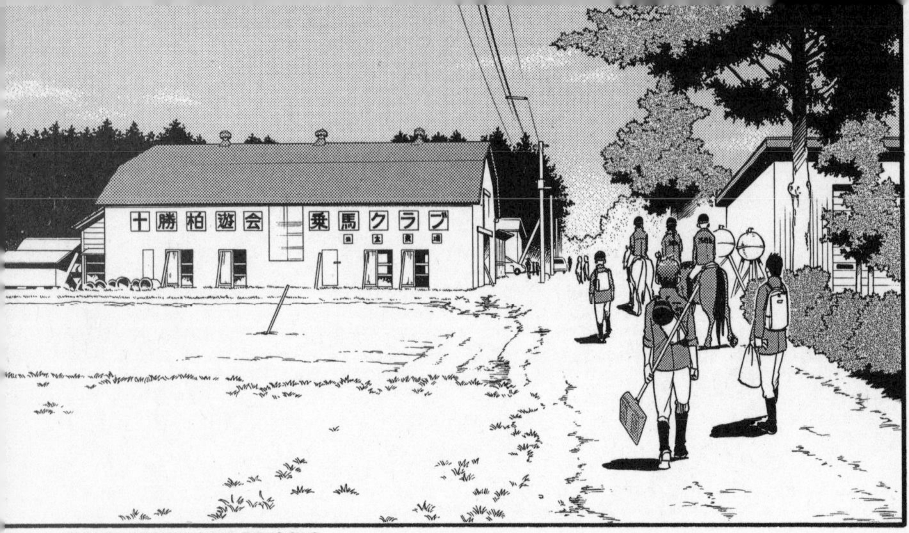
十勝柏遊会 乗馬クラブ

SIGN: TOKACHI HAKUYUUKAI RIDING CLUB

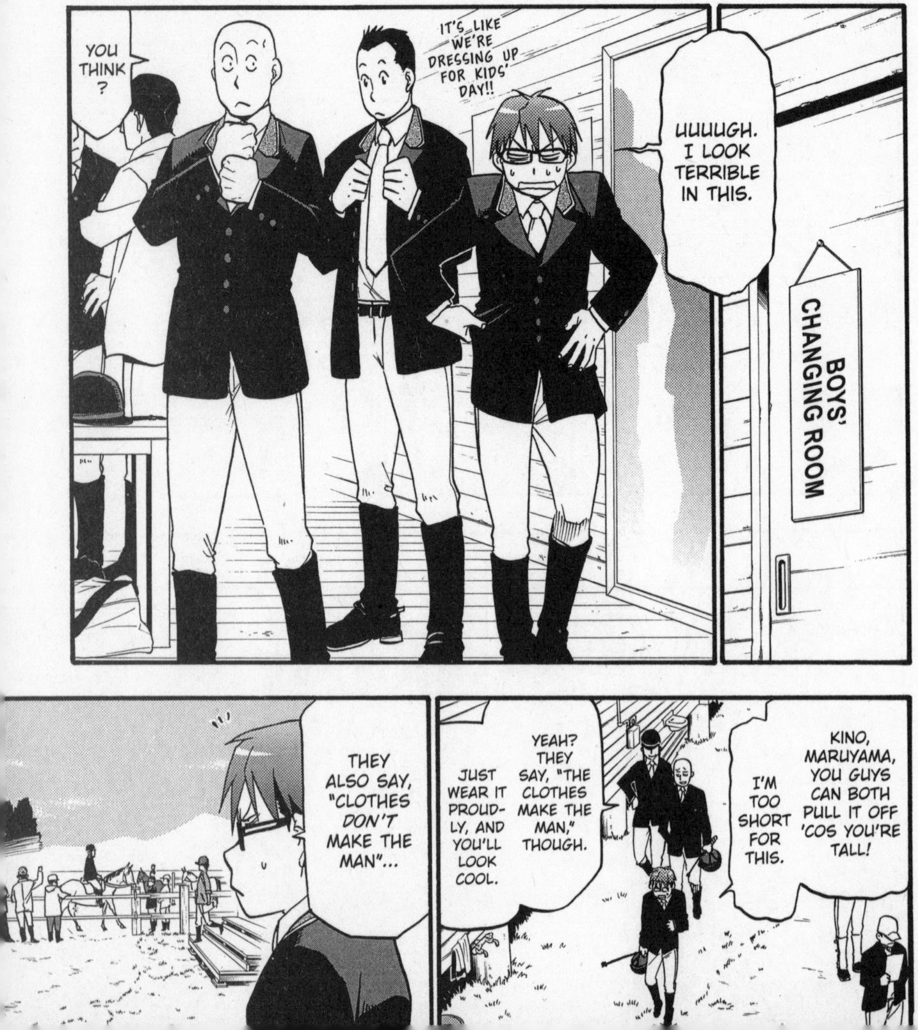
BOYS' CHANGING ROOM
UUUUGH. I LOOK TERRIBLE IN THIS.
IT'S LIKE WE'RE DRESSING UP FOR KIDS' DAY!!
YOU THINK?
KINO, MARUYAMA, YOU GUYS CAN BOTH PULL IT OFF 'COS YOU'RE TALL!
I'M TOO SHORT FOR THIS.
YEAH? THEY SAY, "THE CLOTHES MAKE THE MAN," THOUGH.
JUST WEAR IT PROUD-LY, AND YOU'LL LOOK COOL.
THEY ALSO SAY, "CLOTHES *DON'T* MAKE THE MAN"...

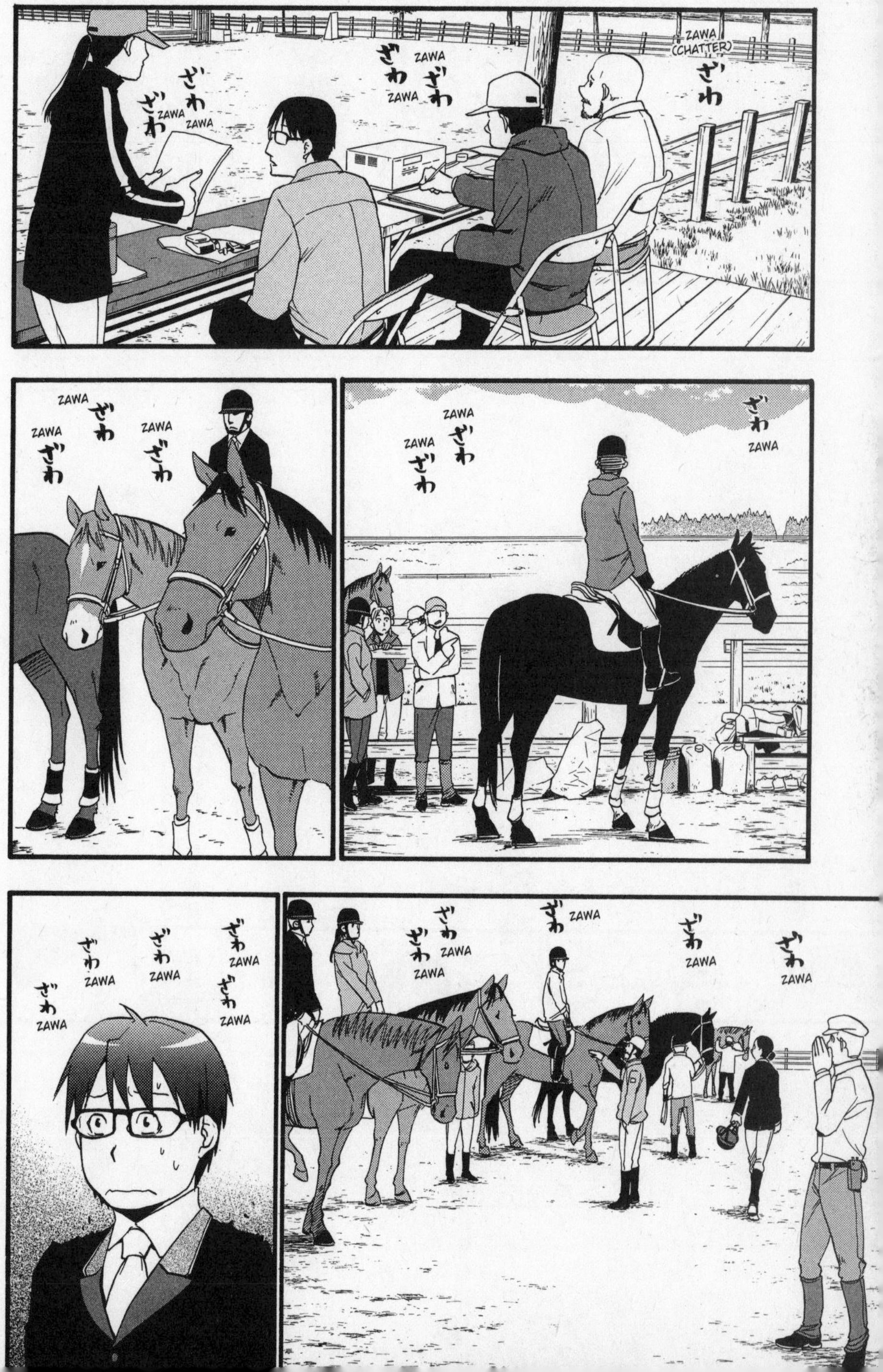
ZAWA (CHATTER)
ざわ
ざわ ZAWA
ざわ ZAWA
ざわ ZAWA
ざわ ZAWA
ざわ ZAWA
ざわ ZAWA
ざわ ZAWA
ざわ ZAWA
ざわ ZAWA
ざわ ZAWA
ざわ ZAWA
ざわ ZAWA
ざわ ZAWA
ざわ ZAWA
ざわ ZAWA
ざわ ZAWA
ざわ ZAWA
ざわ ZAWA
ざわ ZAWA
ざわ ZAWA

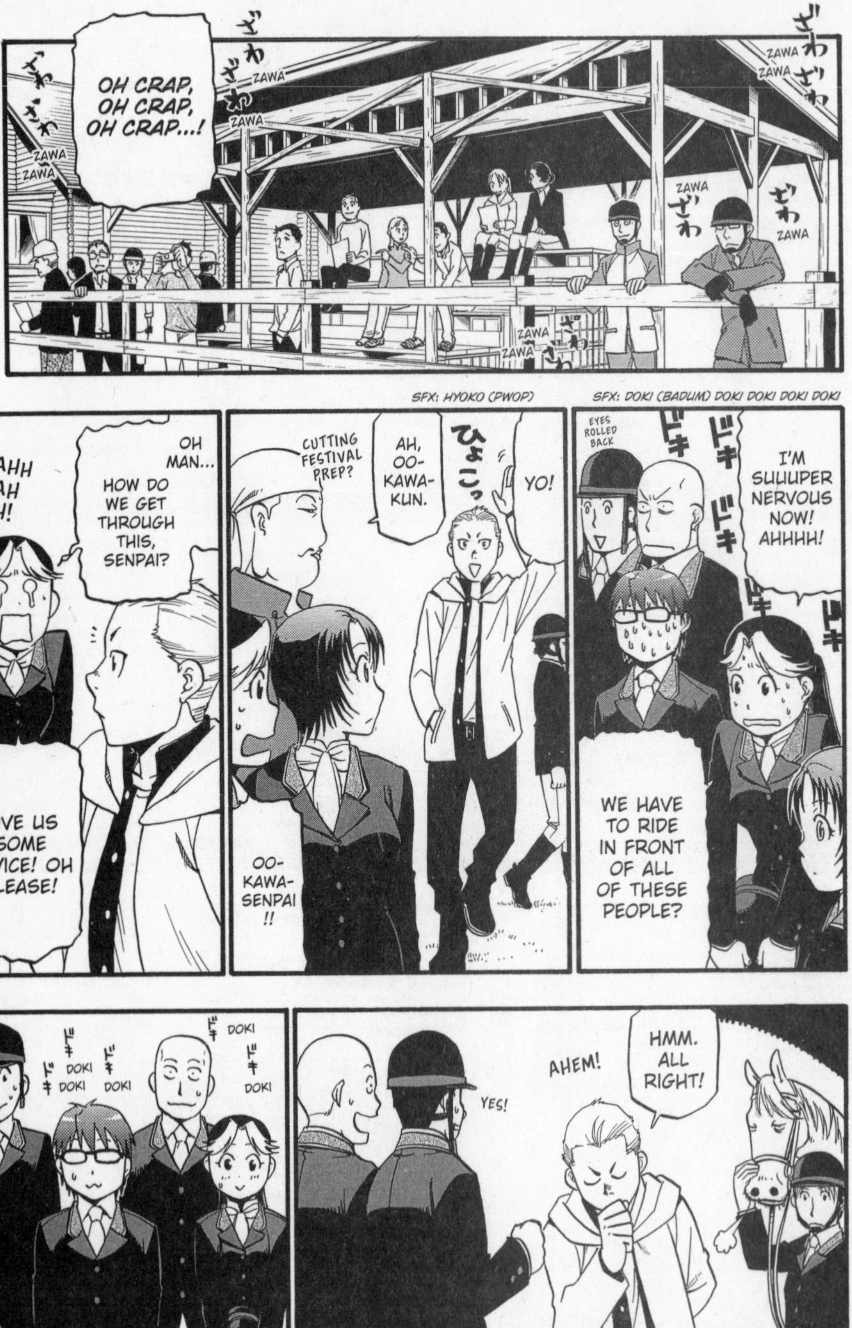
ZAWA ZAWA
ZAWA ZAWA
OH CRAP, OH CRAP, OH CRAP...!
ZAWA ZAWA
ZAWA
ZAWA
ZAWA ZAWA
SFX: DOKI (BADUM) DOKI DOKI DOKI DOKI
SFX: HYOKO (PWOP)
I'M SUUUPER NERVOUS NOW! AHHHH!
EYES ROLLED BACK
WE HAVE TO RIDE IN FRONT OF ALL OF THESE PEOPLE?
YO!
AH, OO-KAWA-KUN.
CUTTING FESTIVAL PREP?
OO-KAWA-SENPAI!!
OH MAN... HOW DO WE GET THROUGH THIS, SENPAI?
AHH WAH WAH!
GIVE US SOME ADVICE! OH PLEASE!
HMM. ALL RIGHT!
AHEM!
YES!
DOKI DOKI
DOKI
DOKI
DOKI

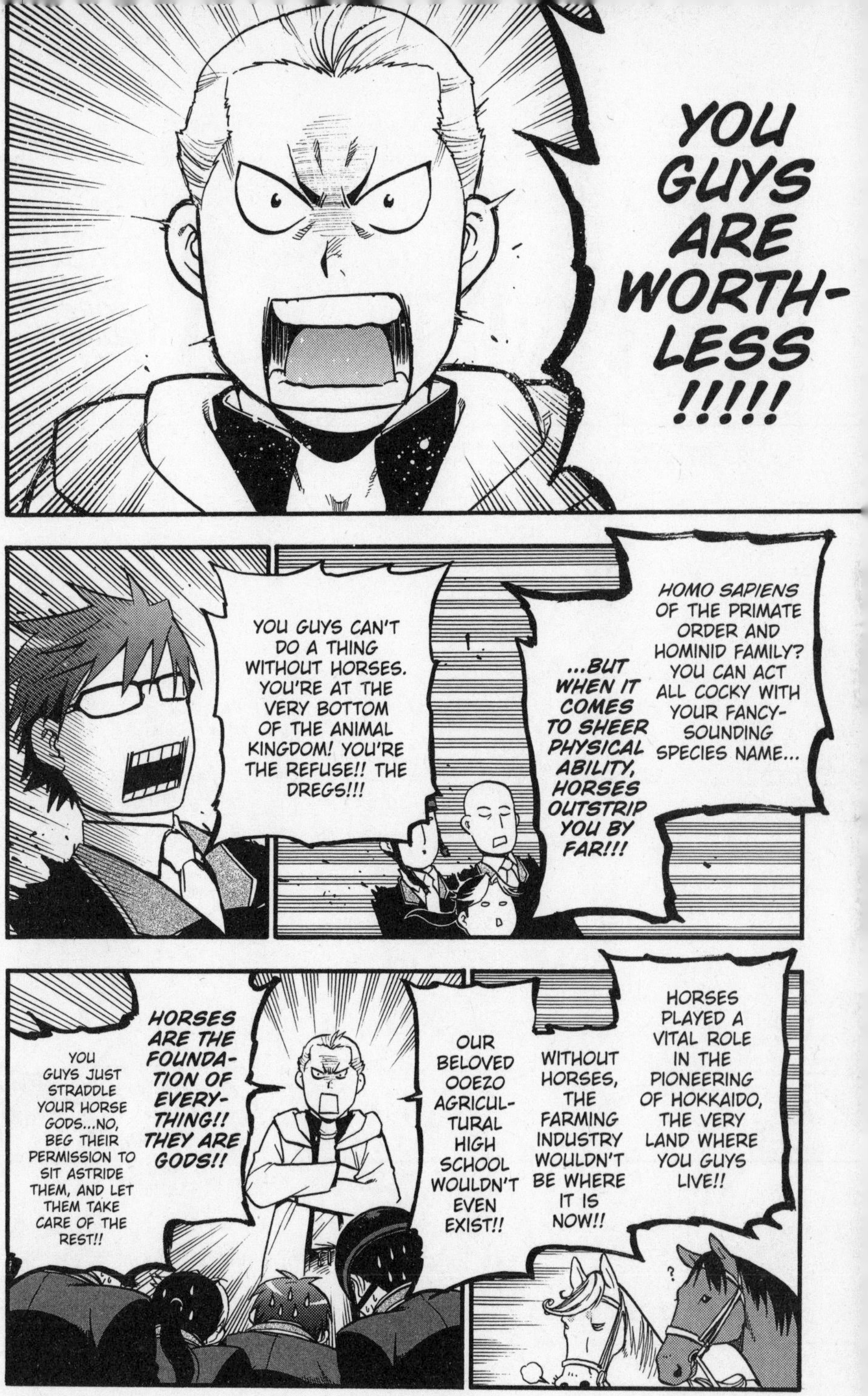
YOU GUYS ARE WORTH-LESS!!!!!
HOMO SAPIENS OF THE PRIMATE ORDER AND HOMINID FAMILY? YOU CAN ACT ALL COCKY WITH YOUR FANCY-SOUNDING SPECIES NAME...
...BUT WHEN IT COMES TO SHEER PHYSICAL ABILITY, HORSES OUTSTRIP YOU BY FAR!!!
YOU GUYS CAN'T DO A THING WITHOUT HORSES. YOU'RE AT THE VERY BOTTOM OF THE ANIMAL KINGDOM! YOU'RE THE REFUSE!! THE DREGS!!!
HORSES PLAYED A VITAL ROLE IN THE PIONEERING OF HOKKAIDO, THE VERY LAND WHERE YOU GUYS LIVE!!
WITHOUT HORSES, THE FARMING INDUSTRY WOULDN'T BE WHERE IT IS NOW!!
OUR BELOVED OOEZO AGRICUL-TURAL HIGH SCHOOL WOULDN'T EVEN EXIST!!
HORSES ARE THE FOUNDA-TION OF EVERY-THING!! THEY ARE GODS!!
YOU GUYS JUST STRADDLE YOUR HORSE GODS...NO, BEG THEIR PERMISSION TO SIT ASTRIDE THEM, AND LET THEM TAKE CARE OF THE REST!!
?

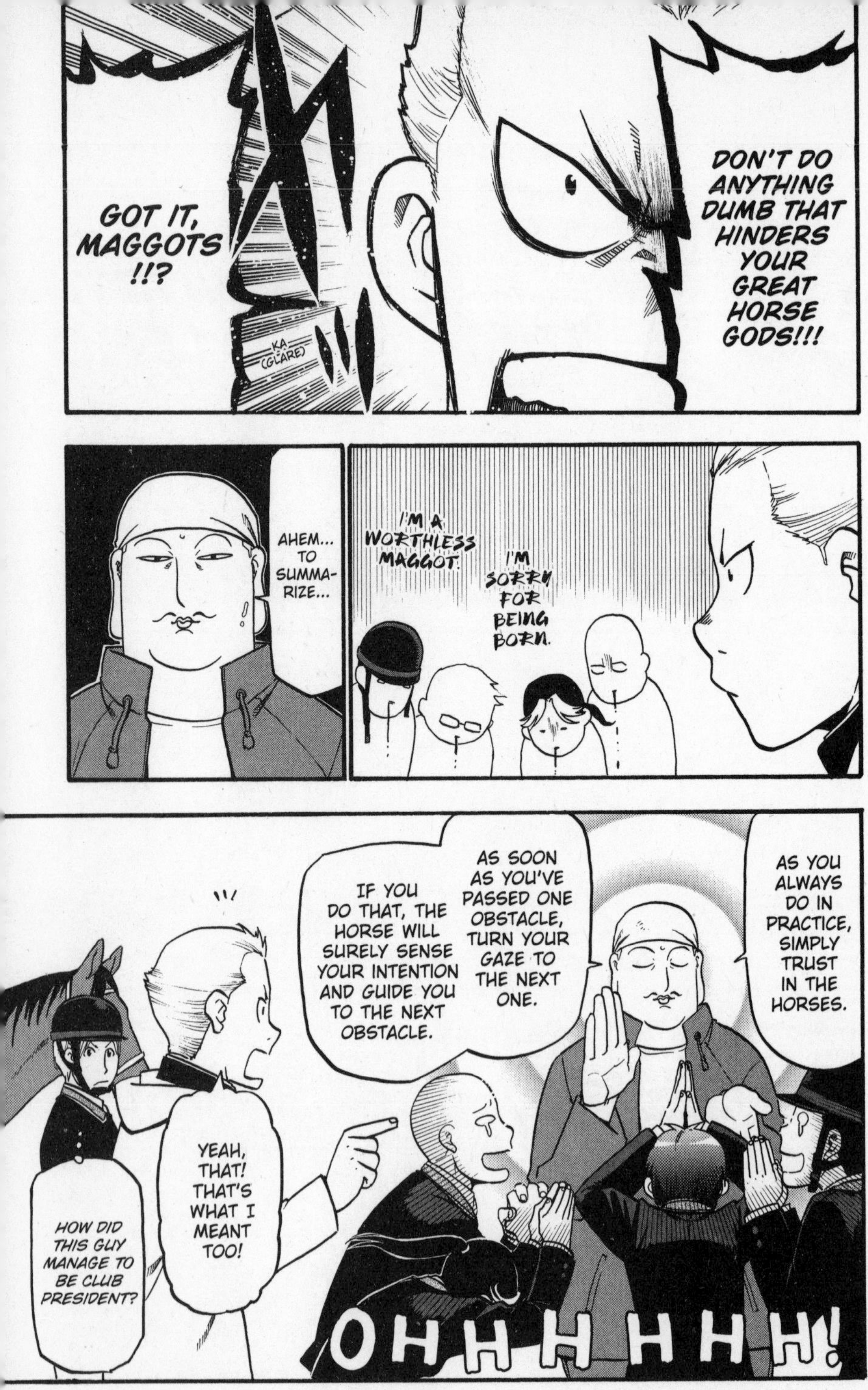
DON'T DO ANYTHING DUMB THAT HINDERS YOUR GREAT HORSE GODS!!!
GOT IT, MAGGOTS!!?
KA (GLARE)
I'M A WORTHLESS MAGGOT.
I'M SORRY FOR BEING BORN.
AHEM... TO SUMMARIZE...
AS YOU ALWAYS DO IN PRACTICE, SIMPLY TRUST IN THE HORSES.
AS SOON AS YOU'VE PASSED ONE OBSTACLE, TURN YOUR GAZE TO THE NEXT ONE.
IF YOU DO THAT, THE HORSE WILL SURELY SENSE YOUR INTENTION AND GUIDE YOU TO THE NEXT OBSTACLE.
OHHHHHH!
YEAH, THAT! THAT'S WHAT I MEANT TOO!
HOW DID THIS GUY MANAGE TO BE CLUB PRESIDENT?

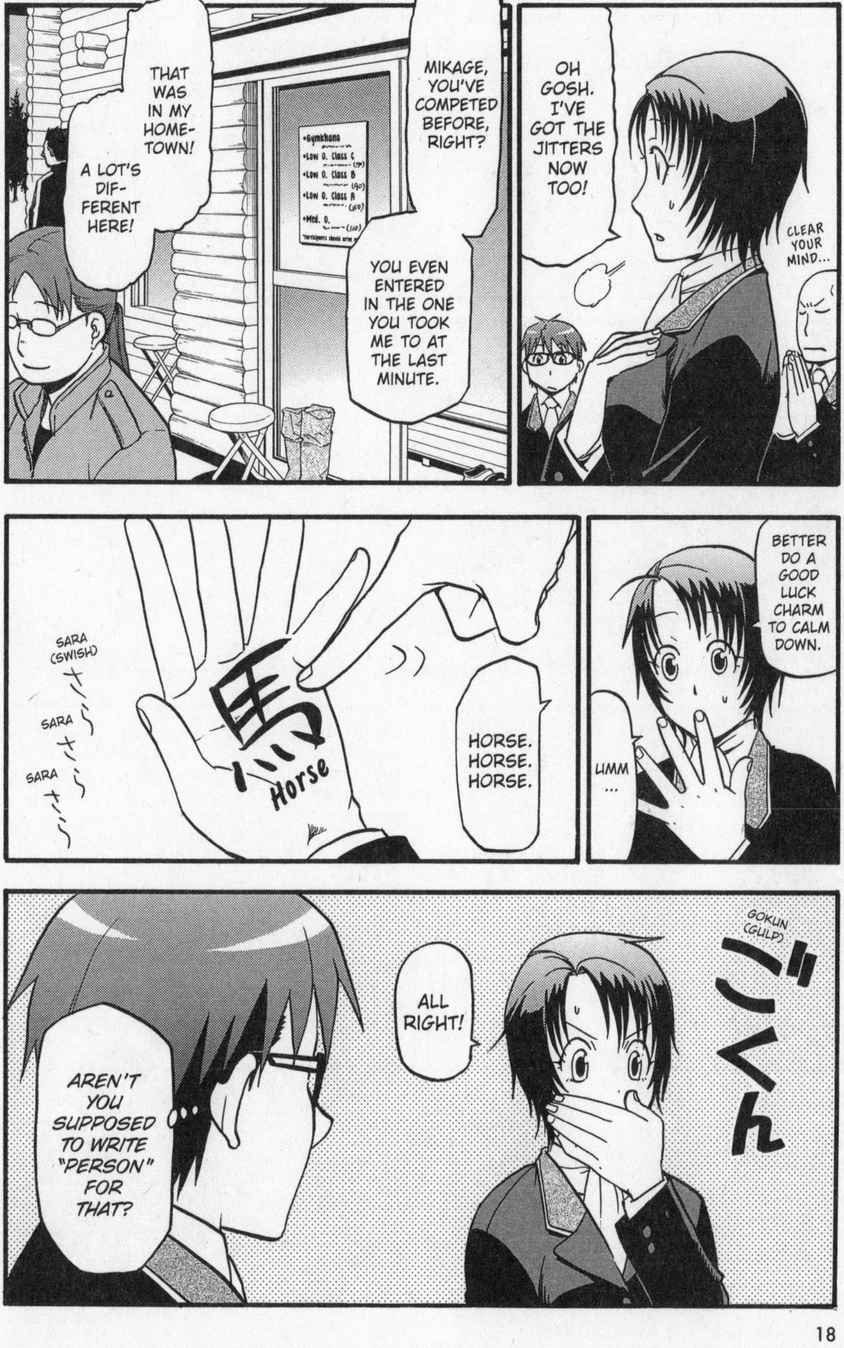
OH GOSH. I'VE GOT THE JITTERS NOW TOO!
CLEAR YOUR MIND...
MIKAGE, YOU'VE COMPETED BEFORE, RIGHT?
YOU EVEN ENTERED IN THE ONE YOU TOOK ME TO AT THE LAST MINUTE.
Gymkhana
Low O. Class C
Low O. Class B
Low O. Class A
Med. O.
THAT WAS IN MY HOME-TOWN!
A LOT'S DIF-FERENT HERE!
BETTER DO A GOOD LUCK CHARM TO CALM DOWN.
UMM ...
HORSE. HORSE. HORSE.
馬
Horse
SARA (SWISH) さら
SARA さら
SARA さら
GOKUN (GULP) ごくん
ALL RIGHT!
AREN'T YOU SUPPOSED TO WRITE "PERSON" FOR THAT?

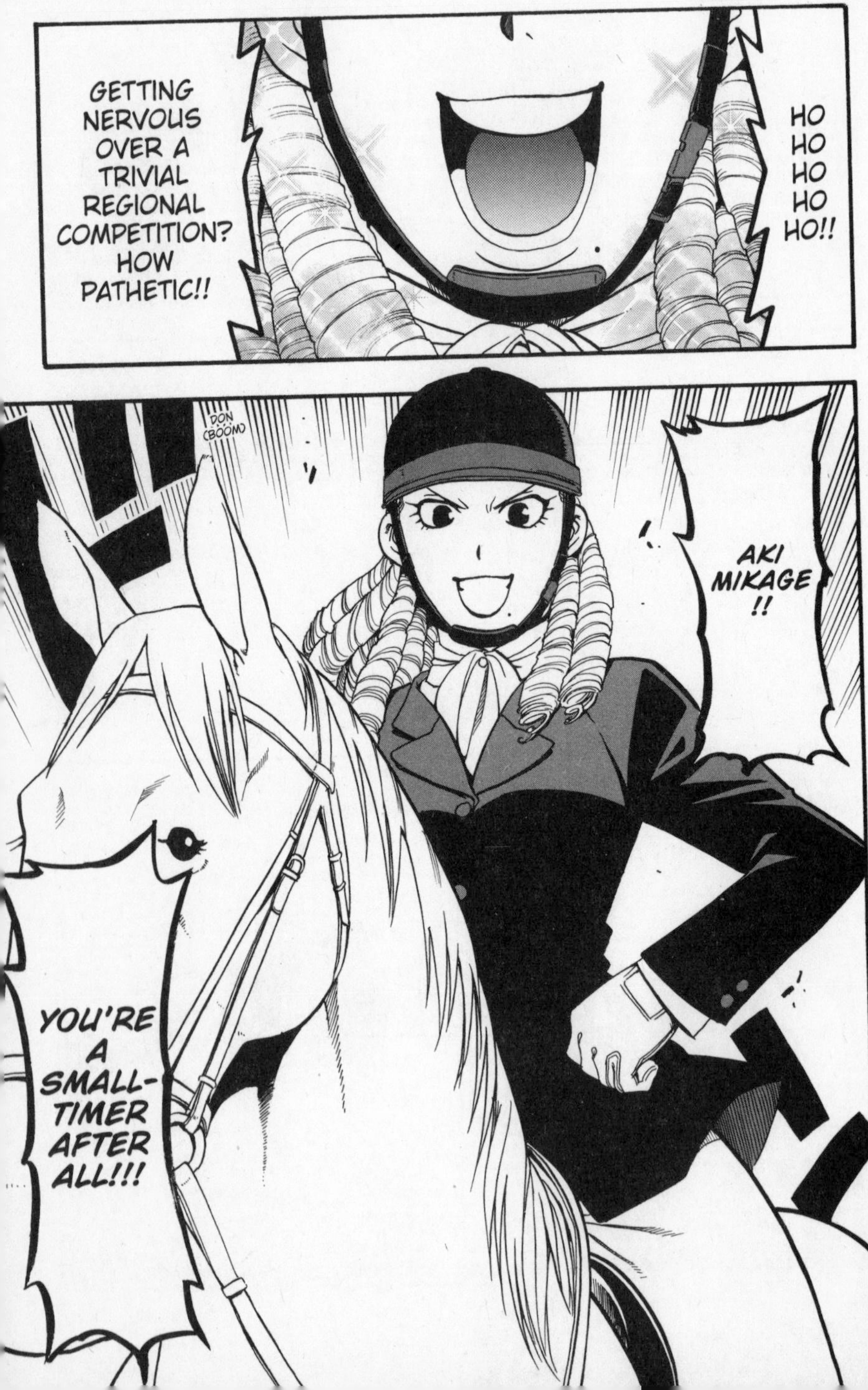
HO HO HO HO HO!!
GETTING NERVOUS OVER A TRIVIAL REGIONAL COMPETITION? HOW PATHETIC!!
AKI MIKAGE!!
DON (BOOM)
YOU'RE A SMALL-TIMER AFTER ALL!!!

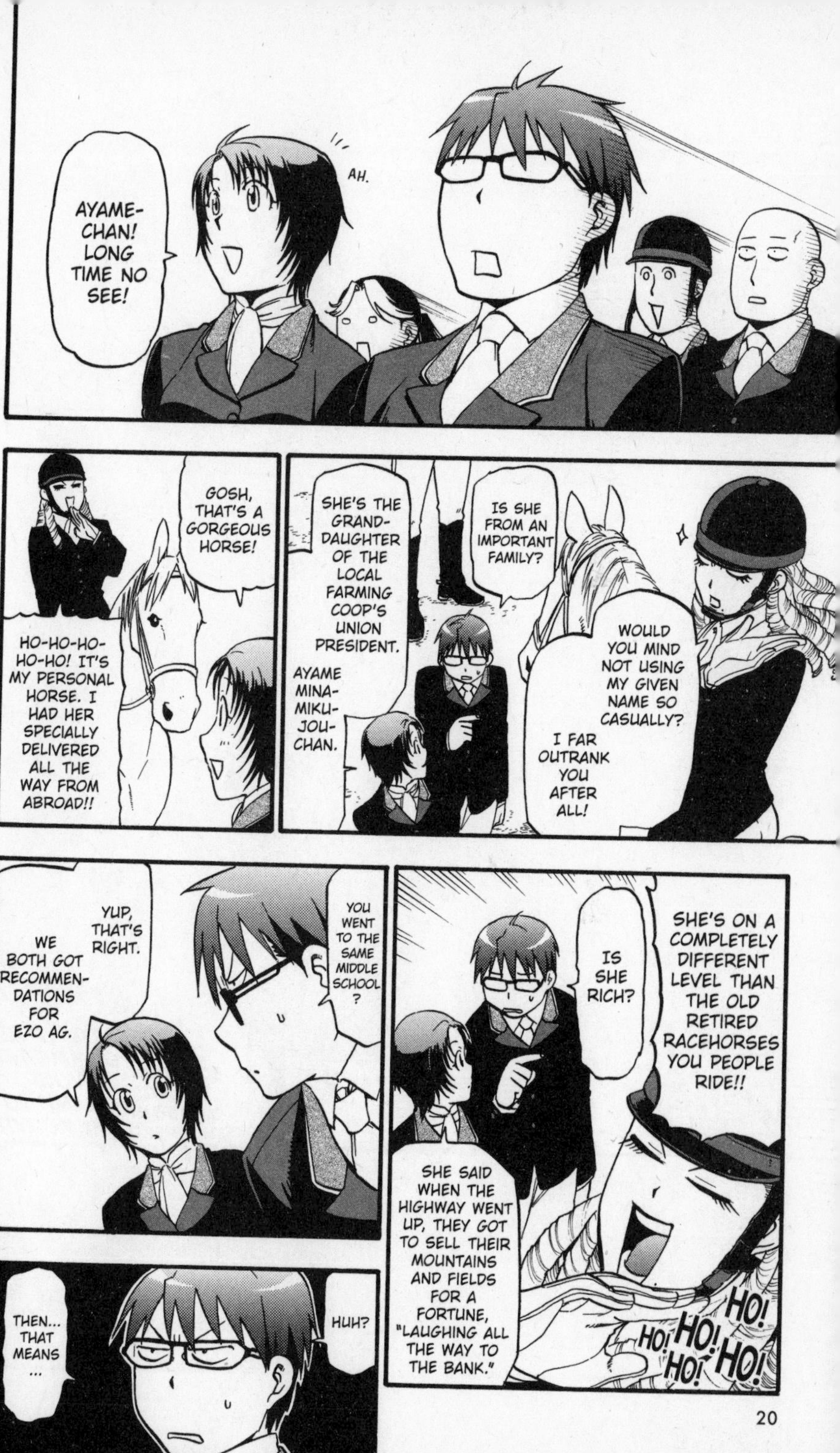
AH.
AYAME-CHAN! LONG TIME NO SEE!
IS SHE FROM AN IMPORTANT FAMILY?
SHE'S THE GRAND-DAUGHTER OF THE LOCAL FARMING COOP'S UNION PRESIDENT.
AYAME MINA-MIKU-JOU-CHAN.
WOULD YOU MIND NOT USING MY GIVEN NAME SO CASUALLY?
I FAR OUTRANK YOU AFTER ALL!
GOSH, THAT'S A GORGEOUS HORSE!
HO-HO-HO-HO-HO! IT'S MY PERSONAL HORSE. I HAD HER SPECIALLY DELIVERED ALL THE WAY FROM ABROAD!!
SHE'S ON A COMPLETELY DIFFERENT LEVEL THAN THE OLD RETIRED RACEHORSES YOU PEOPLE RIDE!!
IS SHE RICH?
SHE SAID WHEN THE HIGHWAY WENT UP, THEY GOT TO SELL THEIR MOUNTAINS AND FIELDS FOR A FORTUNE, "LAUGHING ALL THE WAY TO THE BANK."
HO! HO! HO! HO! HO!
YOU WENT TO THE SAME MIDDLE SCHOOL?
YUP, THAT'S RIGHT.
WE BOTH GOT RECOMMEN-DATIONS FOR EZO AG.
HUH?
THEN... THAT MEANS...

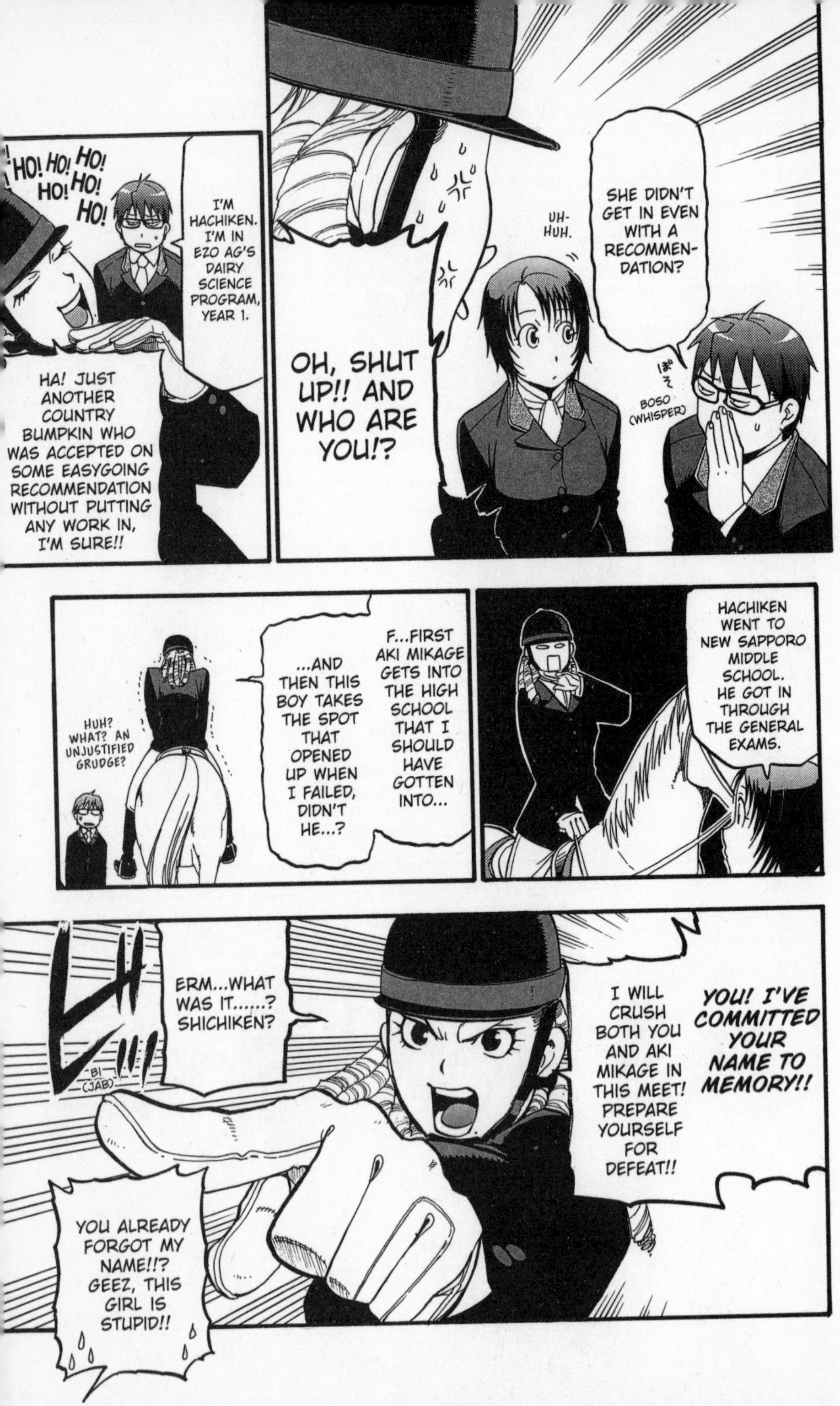
SHE DIDN'T GET IN EVEN WITH A RECOMMENDATION?
BOSO (WHISPER)
UH-HUH.
OH, SHUT UP!! AND WHO ARE YOU!?
I'M HACHIKEN. I'M IN EZO AG'S DAIRY SCIENCE PROGRAM, YEAR 1.
HO! HO! HO! HO! HO! HO!
HA! JUST ANOTHER COUNTRY BUMPKIN WHO WAS ACCEPTED ON SOME EASYGOING RECOMMENDATION WITHOUT PUTTING ANY WORK IN, I'M SURE!!
HACHIKEN WENT TO NEW SAPPORO MIDDLE SCHOOL. HE GOT IN THROUGH THE GENERAL EXAMS.
F...FIRST AKI MIKAGE GETS INTO THE HIGH SCHOOL THAT I SHOULD HAVE GOTTEN INTO...
...AND THEN THIS BOY TAKES THE SPOT THAT OPENED UP WHEN I FAILED, DIDN'T HE...?
HUH? WHAT? AN UNJUSTIFIED GRUDGE?
YOU! I'VE COMMITTED YOUR NAME TO MEMORY!!
I WILL CRUSH BOTH YOU AND AKI MIKAGE IN THIS MEET! PREPARE YOURSELF FOR DEFEAT!!
ERM...WHAT WAS IT......? SHICHIKEN?
BI (JAB)
YOU ALREADY FORGOT MY NAME!!? GEEZ, THIS GIRL IS STUPID!!

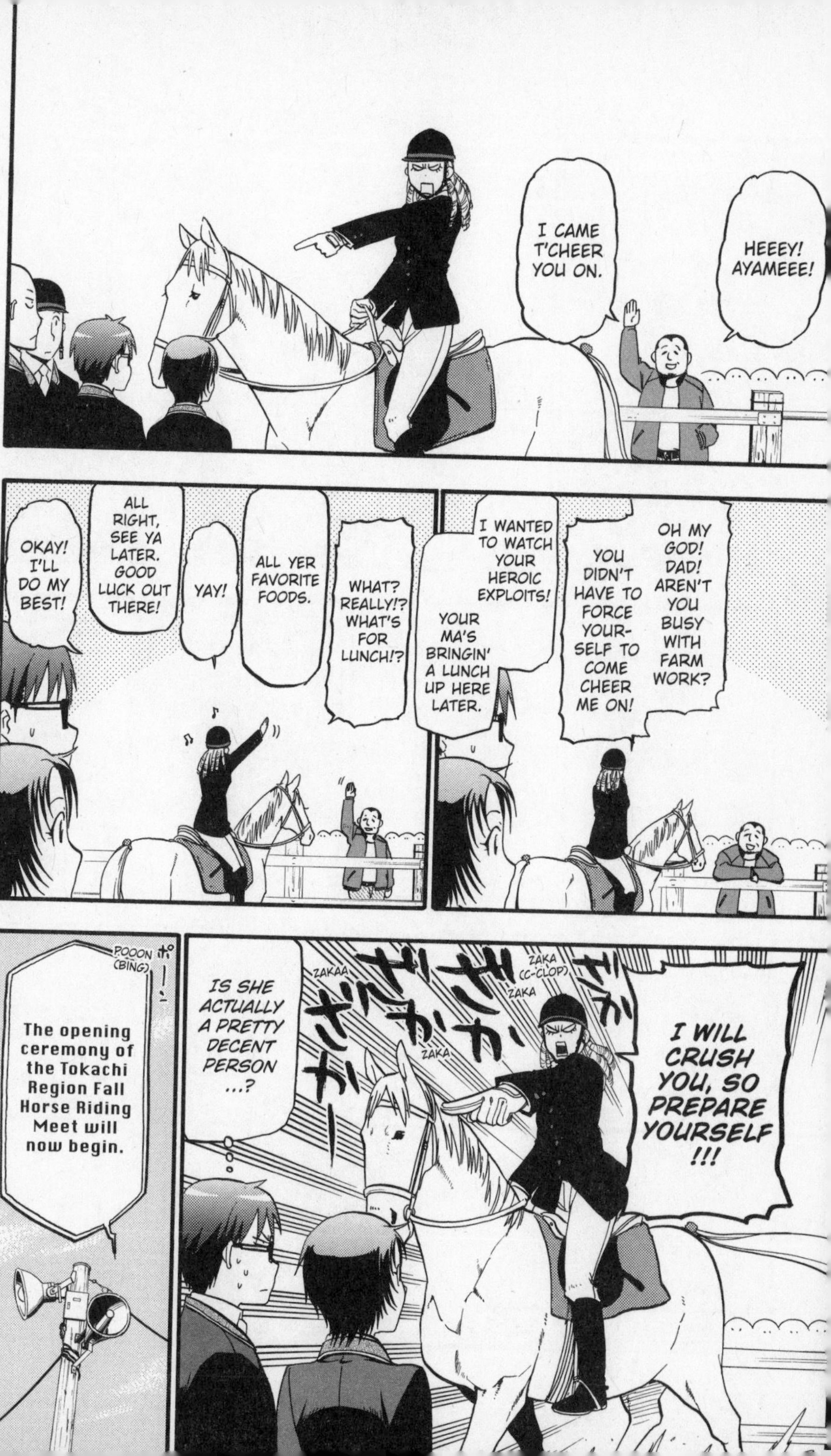
HEEEY! AYAMEEE!
I CAME T'CHEER YOU ON.
OH MY GOD! DAD! AREN'T YOU BUSY WITH FARM WORK?
YOU DIDN'T HAVE TO FORCE YOURSELF TO COME CHEER ME ON!
I WANTED TO WATCH YOUR HEROIC EXPLOITS!
YOUR MA'S BRINGIN' A LUNCH UP HERE LATER.
WHAT? REALLY!? WHAT'S FOR LUNCH!?
ALL YER FAVORITE FOODS.
YAY!
ALL RIGHT, SEE YA LATER. GOOD LUCK OUT THERE!
OKAY! I'LL DO MY BEST!
ZAKA (C-CLOP)
ZAKA
I WILL CRUSH YOU, SO PREPARE YOURSELF!!!
ZAKAA
ZAKA
IS SHE ACTUALLY A PRETTY DECENT PERSON...?
POOON (BING)
The opening ceremony of the Tokachi Region Fall Horse Riding Meet will now begin.

Silver Spoon

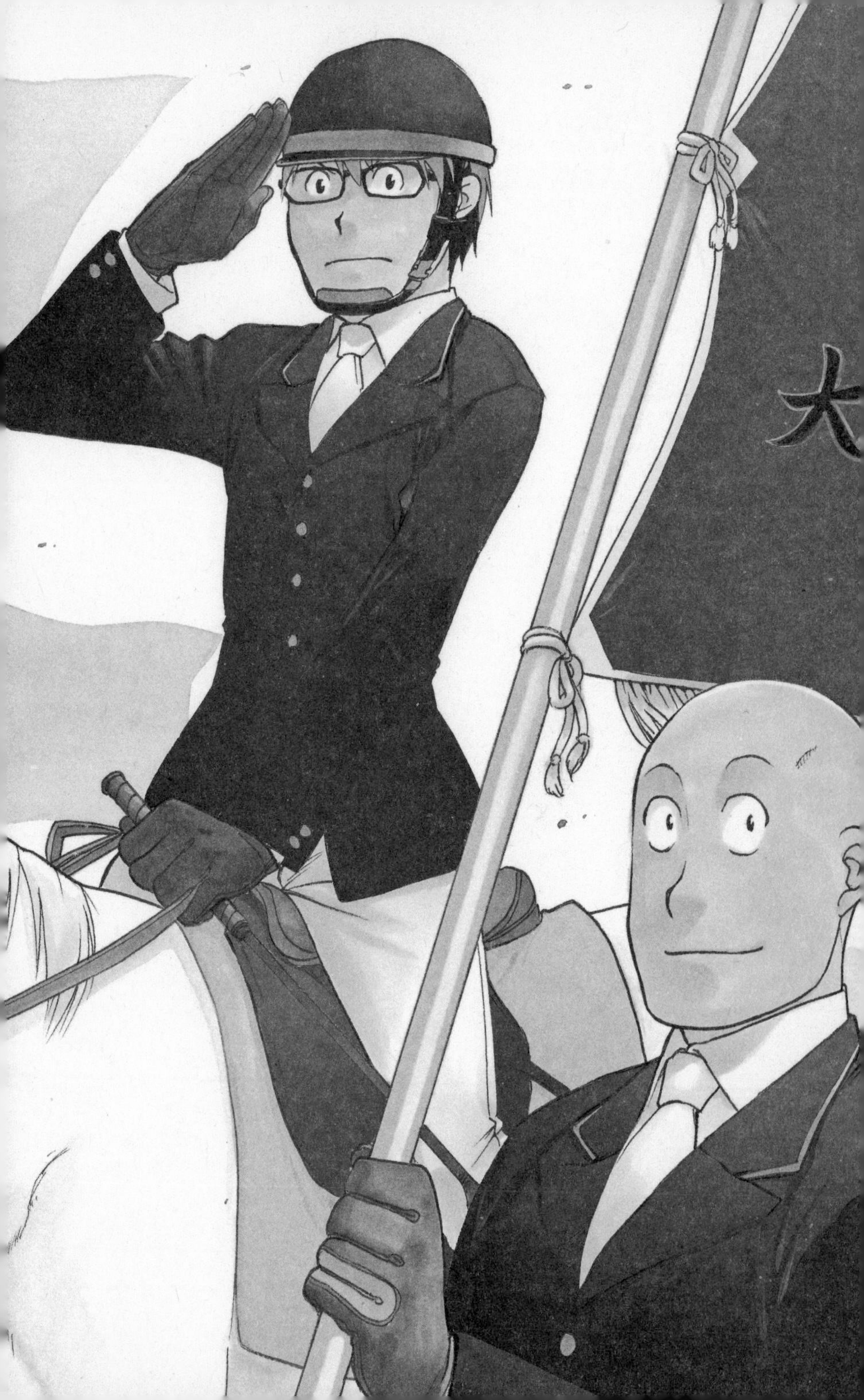
大

Chapter 46:
Tale of Autumn ⑮

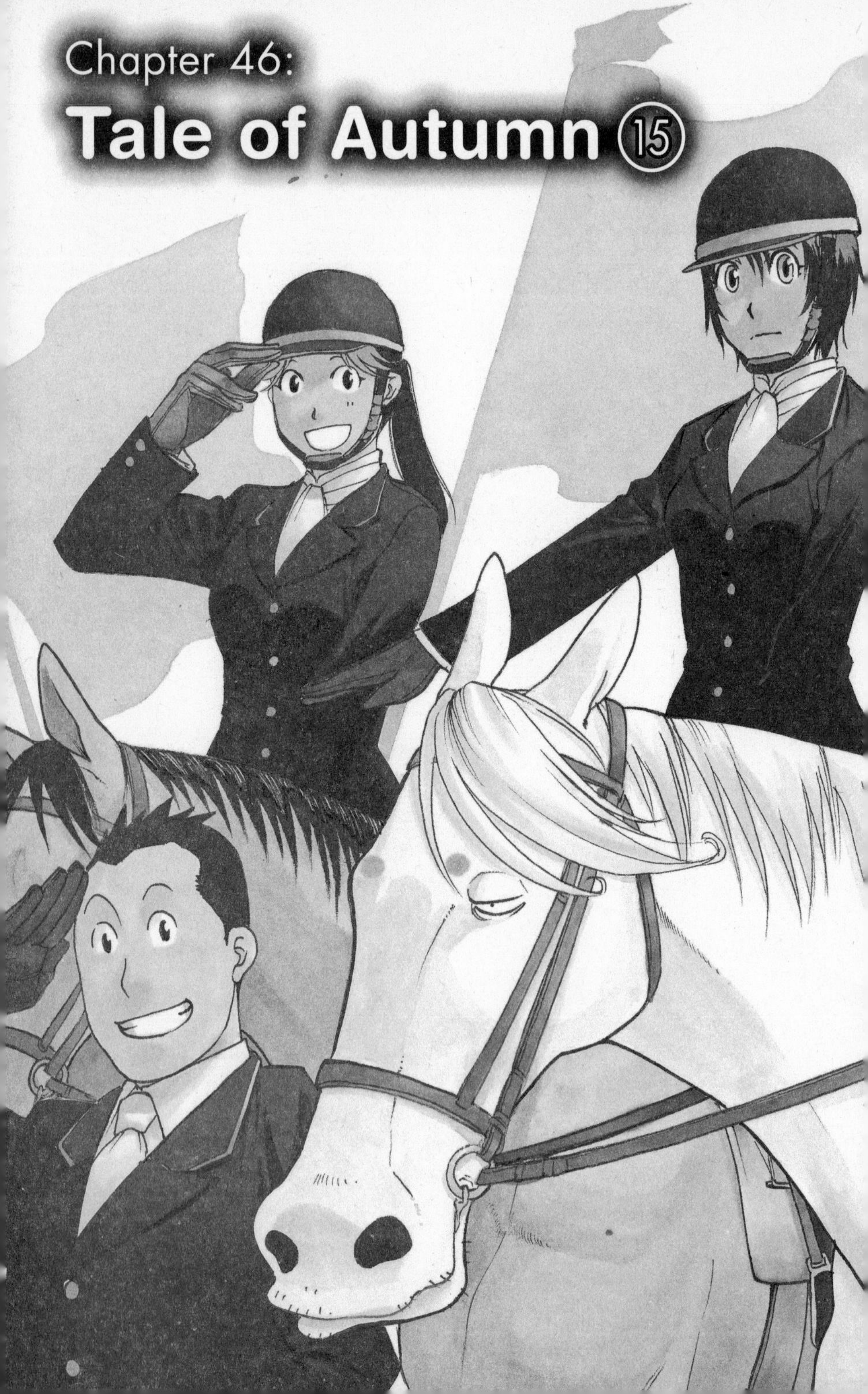

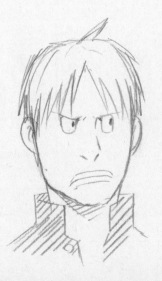

TAKEHIRO
KASHIWAGAOKA

NAKASHIKAOI
MIDDLE SCHOOL

KARATE CLUB

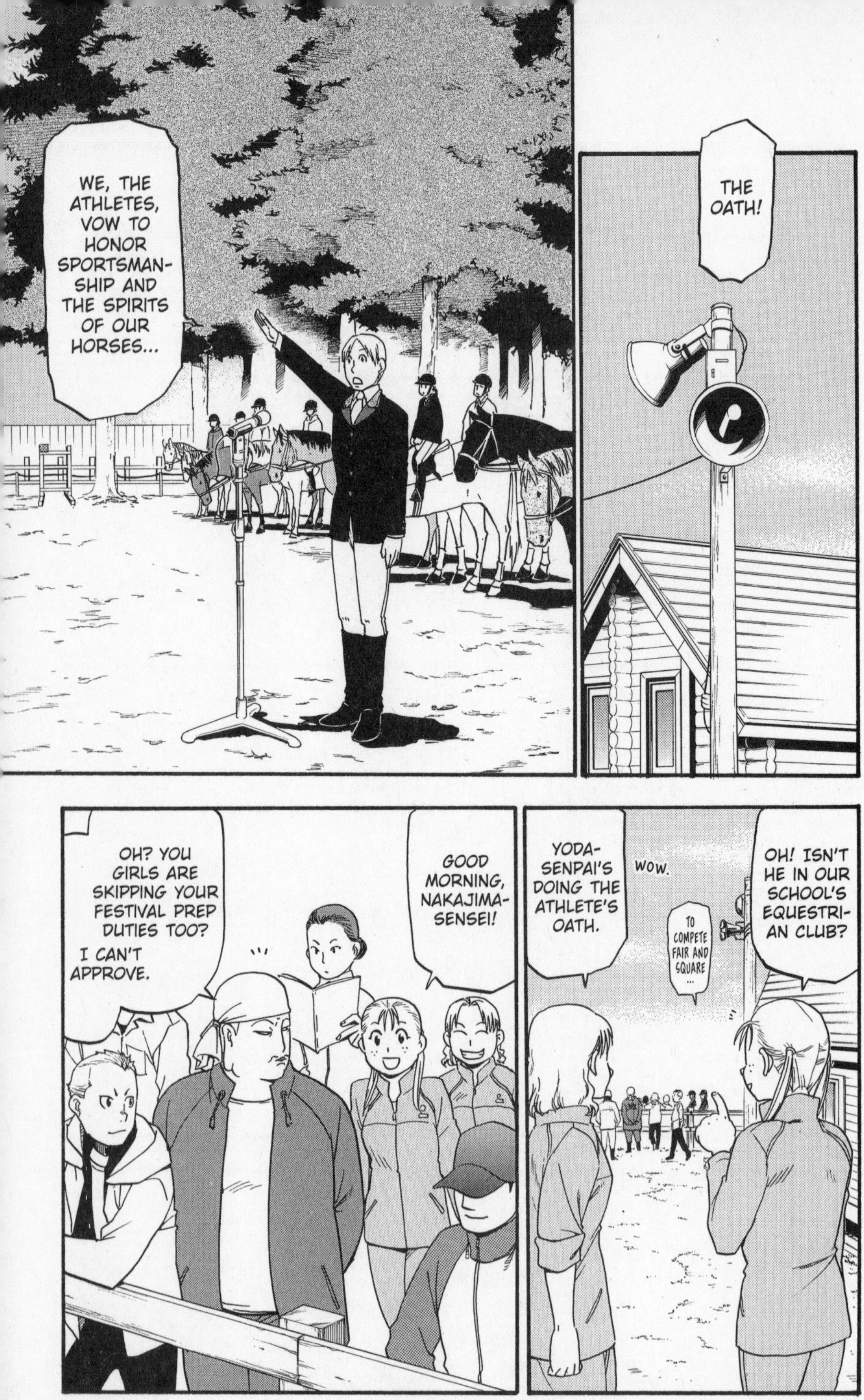
THE OATH!
WE, THE ATHLETES, VOW TO HONOR SPORTSMAN-SHIP AND THE SPIRITS OF OUR HORSES...
OH! ISN'T HE IN OUR SCHOOL'S EQUESTRI-AN CLUB?
YODA-SENPAI'S DOING THE ATHLETE'S OATH.
WOW.
TO COMPETE FAIR AND SQUARE ...
GOOD MORNING, NAKAJIMA-SENSEI!
OH? YOU GIRLS ARE SKIPPING YOUR FESTIVAL PREP DUTIES TOO?
I CAN'T APPROVE.

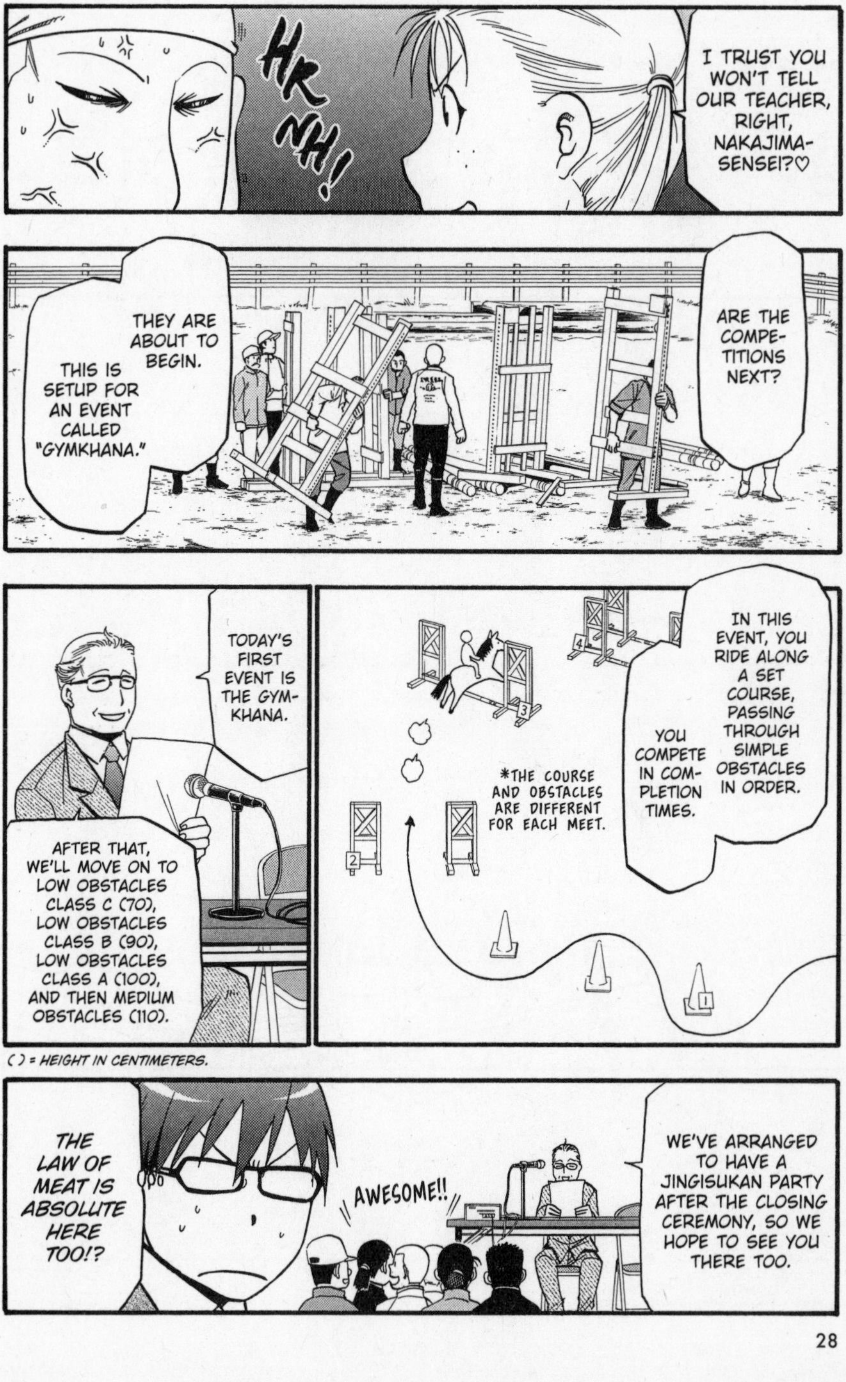
I TRUST YOU WON'T TELL OUR TEACHER, RIGHT, NAKAJIMA-SENSEI?♡
HKNH!
ARE THE COMPETITIONS NEXT?
THEY ARE ABOUT TO BEGIN.
THIS IS SETUP FOR AN EVENT CALLED "GYMKHANA."
IN THIS EVENT, YOU RIDE ALONG A SET COURSE, PASSING THROUGH SIMPLE OBSTACLES IN ORDER.
YOU COMPETE IN COMPLETION TIMES.
*THE COURSE AND OBSTACLES ARE DIFFERENT FOR EACH MEET.
TODAY'S FIRST EVENT IS THE GYMKHANA.
AFTER THAT, WE'LL MOVE ON TO LOW OBSTACLES CLASS C (70), LOW OBSTACLES CLASS B (90), LOW OBSTACLES CLASS A (100), AND THEN MEDIUM OBSTACLES (110).
( ) = HEIGHT IN CENTIMETERS.
WE'VE ARRANGED TO HAVE A JINGISUKAN PARTY AFTER THE CLOSING CEREMONY, SO WE HOPE TO SEE YOU THERE TOO.
AWESOME!!
THE LAW OF MEAT IS ABSOLUTE HERE TOO!?

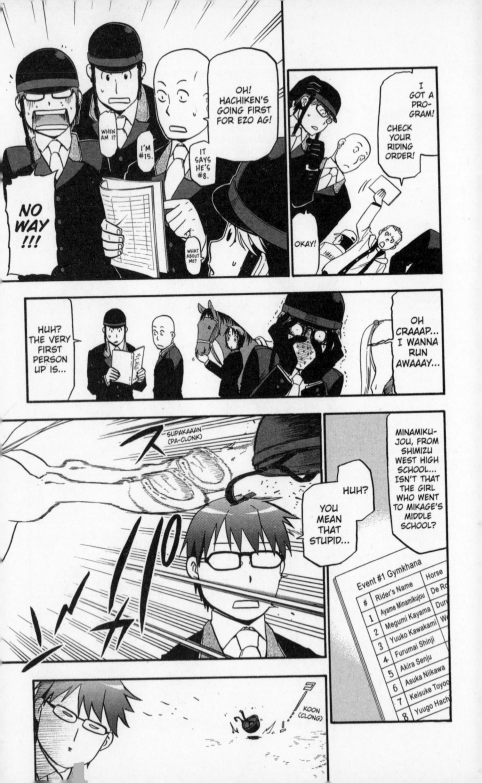

OH! HACHIKEN'S GOING FIRST FOR EZO AG!

IT SAYS HE'S #8.

WHEN AM I?

I'M #15.

NO WAY!!!

WHAT ABOUT ME?

I GOT A PRO-GRAM! CHECK YOUR RIDING ORDER!

OKAY!

HUH? THE VERY FIRST PERSON UP IS...

OH CRAAAP... I WANNA RUN AWAAAY...

—SUPAKAAAN (PA-CLONK)

HUH? YOU MEAN THAT STUPID...

MINAMIKU-JOU, FROM SHIMIZU WEST HIGH SCHOOL... ISN'T THAT THE GIRL WHO WENT TO MIKAGE'S MIDDLE SCHOOL?

KOON (CLONG)

Event #1 Gymkhana		
#	Rider's Name	Horse
1	Ayame Minamikujou	De Ro
2	Megumi Kayama	Dur
3	Yuuko Kawakami	W
4	Furumai Shinji	
5	Akira Senju	
6	Asuka Niikawa	
7	Keisuke Toyoo	
8	Yuugo Hach	

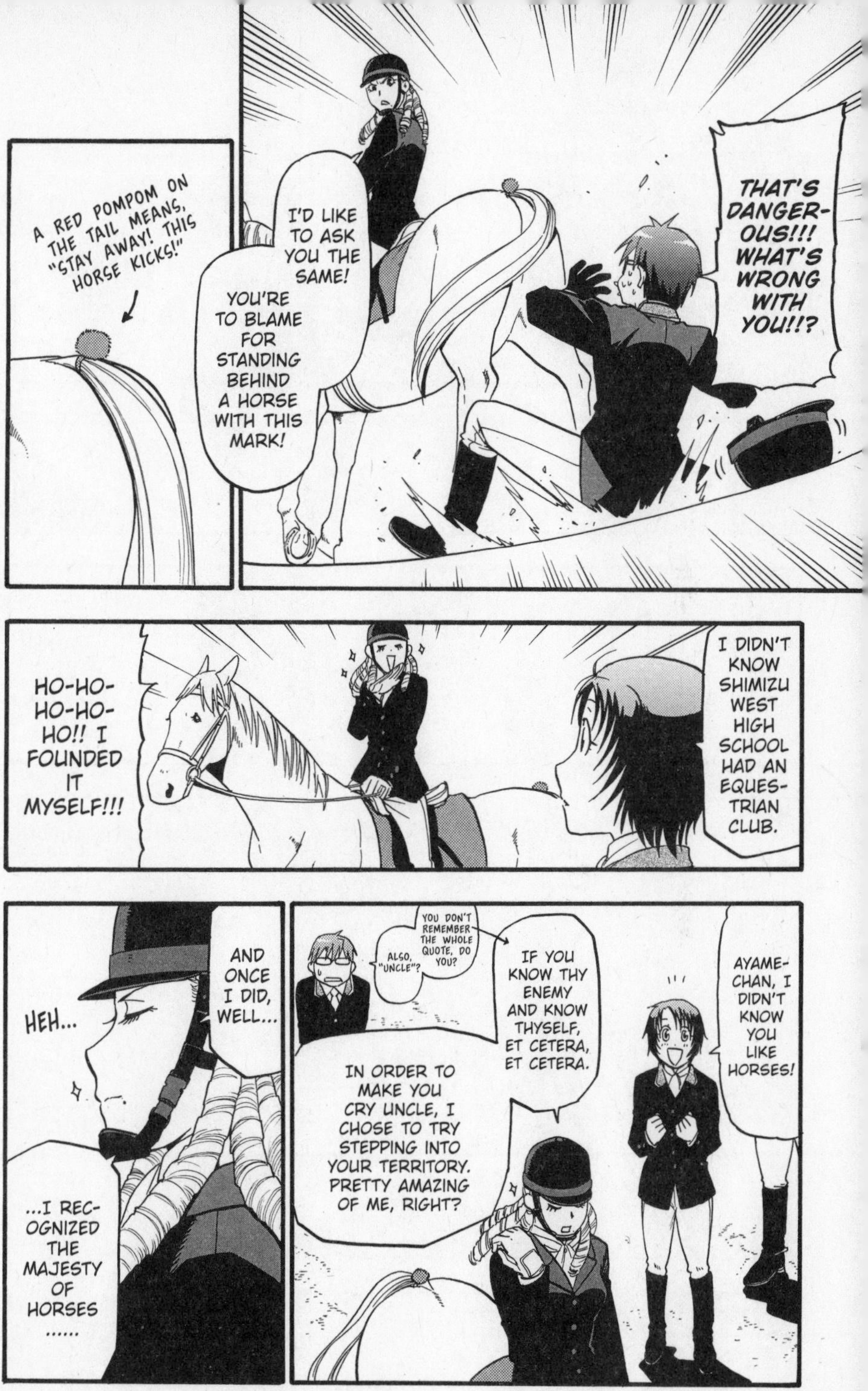
THAT'S DANGEROUS!!! WHAT'S WRONG WITH YOU!!?
I'D LIKE TO ASK YOU THE SAME!
YOU'RE TO BLAME FOR STANDING BEHIND A HORSE WITH THIS MARK!
A RED POMPOM ON THE TAIL MEANS, "STAY AWAY! THIS HORSE KICKS!"
I DIDN'T KNOW SHIMIZU WEST HIGH SCHOOL HAD AN EQUESTRIAN CLUB.
HO-HO-HO-HO-HO!! I FOUNDED IT MYSELF!!!
AYAME-CHAN, I DIDN'T KNOW YOU LIKE HORSES!
IN ORDER TO MAKE YOU CRY UNCLE, I CHOSE TO TRY STEPPING INTO YOUR TERRITORY. PRETTY AMAZING OF ME, RIGHT?
IF YOU KNOW THY ENEMY AND KNOW THYSELF, ET CETERA, ET CETERA.
YOU DON'T REMEMBER THE WHOLE QUOTE, DO YOU?
ALSO, "UNCLE"?
AND ONCE I DID, WELL...
HEH...
...I RECOGNIZED THE MAJESTY OF HORSES ......

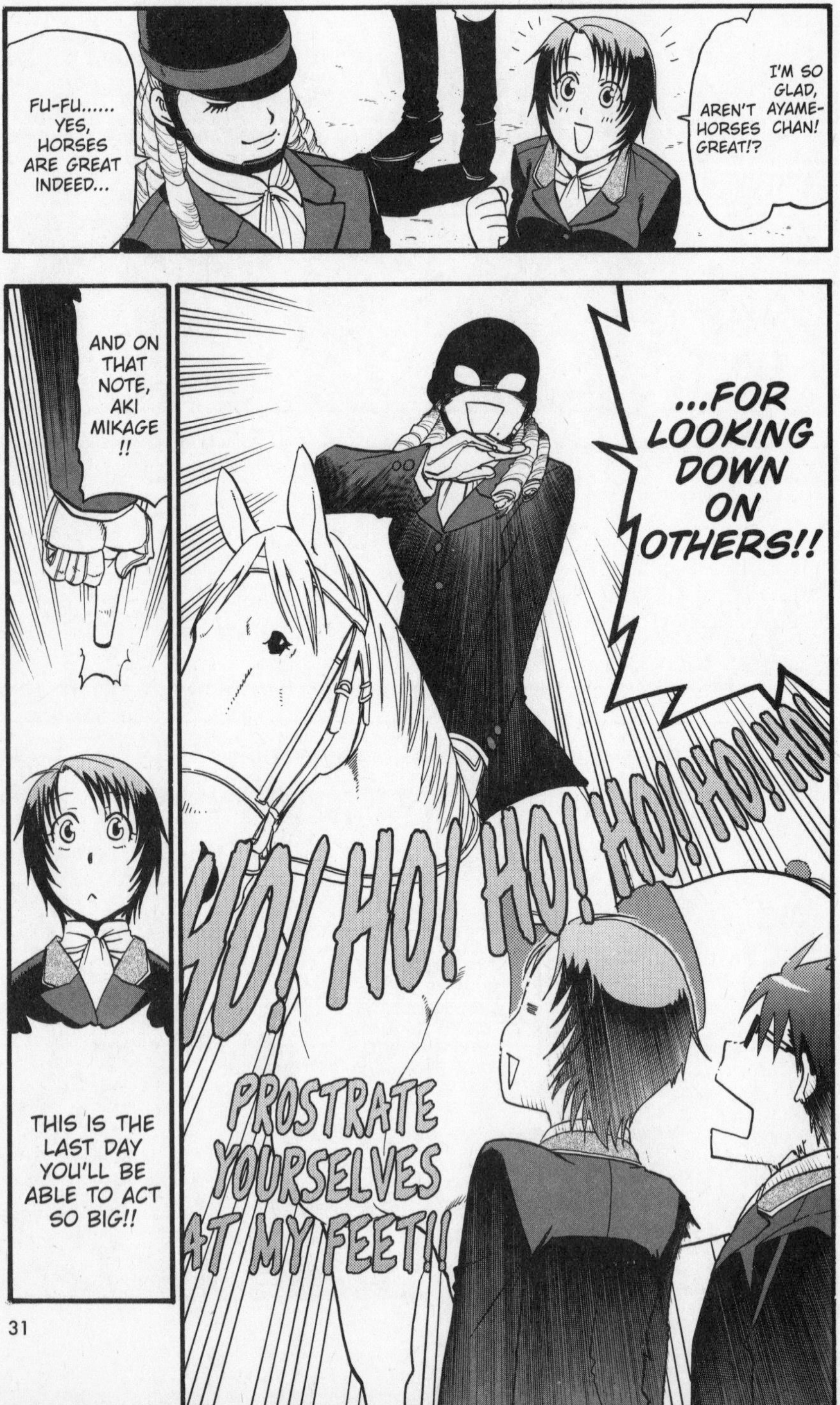
I'M SO GLAD, AYAME-CHAN! AREN'T HORSES GREAT!?
FU-FU...... YES, HORSES ARE GREAT INDEED...
AND ON THAT NOTE, AKI MIKAGE !!
THIS IS THE LAST DAY YOU'LL BE ABLE TO ACT SO BIG!!
...FOR LOOKING DOWN ON OTHERS!!
HO! HO! HO! HO! HO! HO! HO!
PROSTRATE YOURSELVES AT MY FEET!!

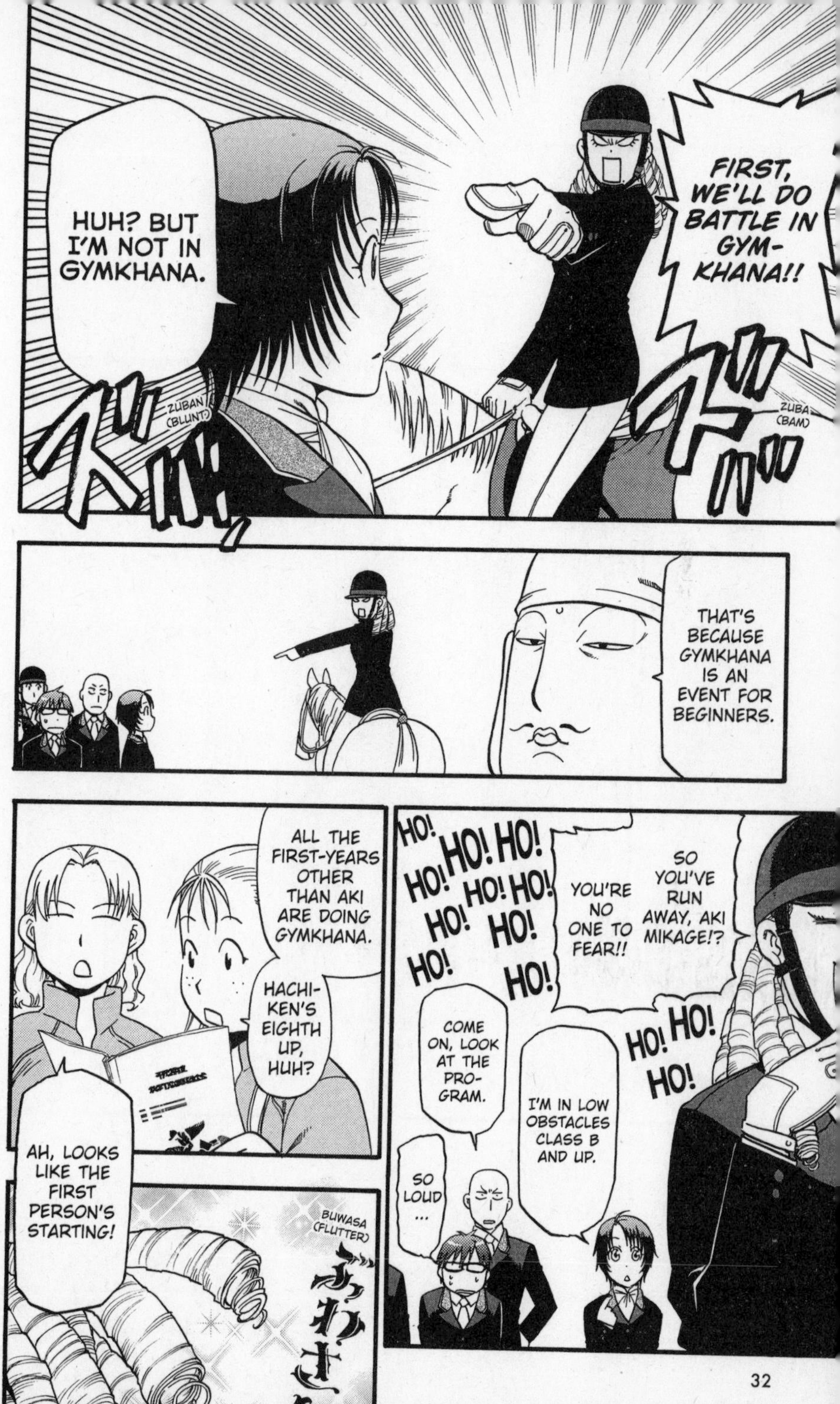
FIRST, WE'LL DO BATTLE IN GYM-KHANA!!
ZUBA (BAM)
HUH? BUT I'M NOT IN GYMKHANA.
ZUBAN (BLUNT)
THAT'S BECAUSE GYMKHANA IS AN EVENT FOR BEGINNERS.
SO YOU'VE RUN AWAY, AKI MIKAGE!?
YOU'RE NO ONE TO FEAR!!
HO! HO! HO! HO! HO! HO! HO! HO! HO! HO!
HO! HO! HO!
COME ON, LOOK AT THE PRO-GRAM.
I'M IN LOW OBSTACLES CLASS B AND UP.
SO LOUD...
ALL THE FIRST-YEARS OTHER THAN AKI ARE DOING GYMKHANA.
HACHI-KEN'S EIGHTH UP, HUH?
AH, LOOKS LIKE THE FIRST PERSON'S STARTING!
BUWASA (FLUTTER)

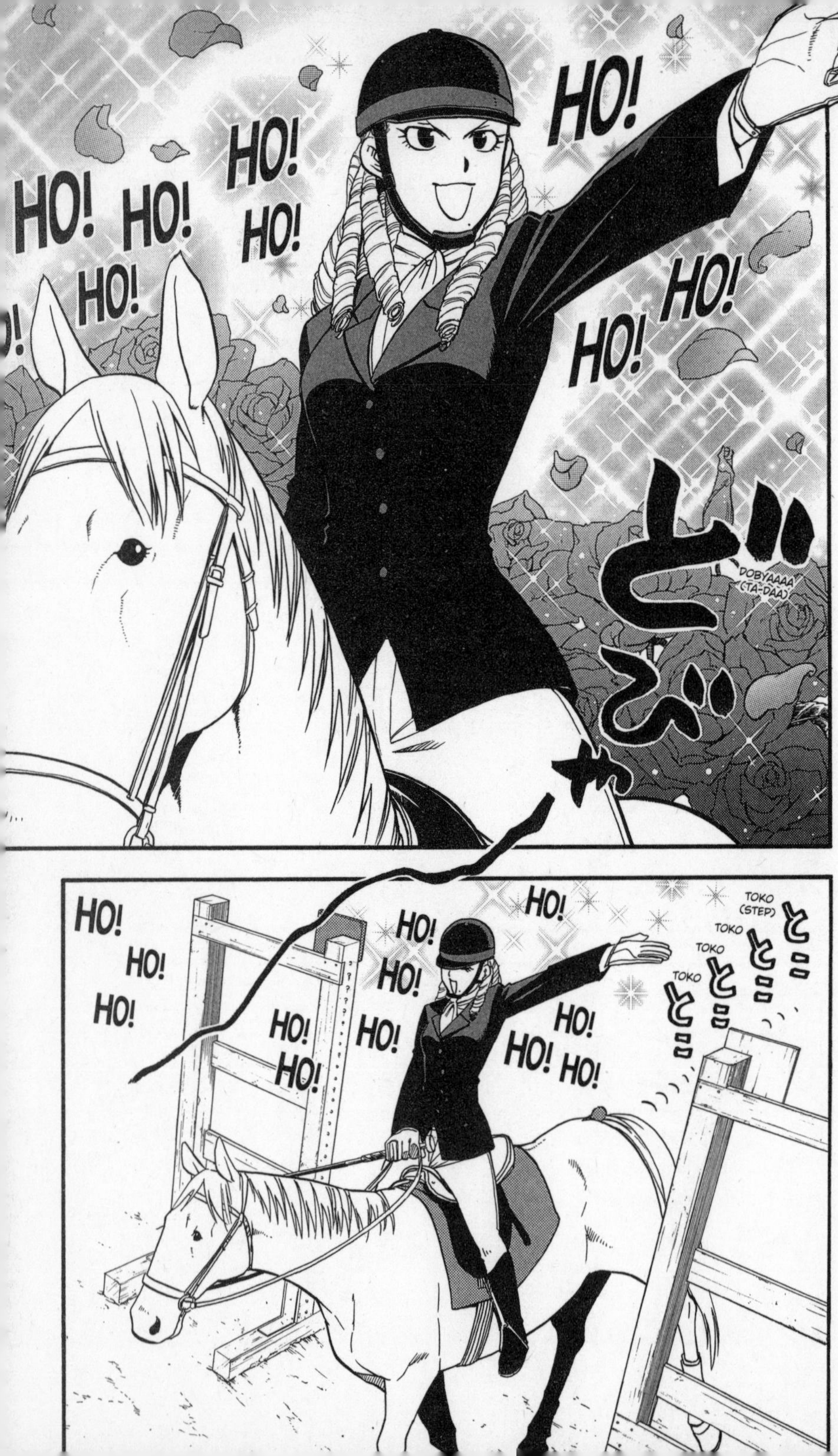
HO!
HO!
HO!
どびゃ
DOBYAAAA (TA-DAA)
HO!
HO!
HO!
HO!
HO!
HO!
!
と
TOKO (STEP)
と
TOKO
と
TOKO
と
TOKO
HO!
HO!
HO!
HO!
HO!
HO!
HO!
HO!
HO!
HO!
HO!
HO!

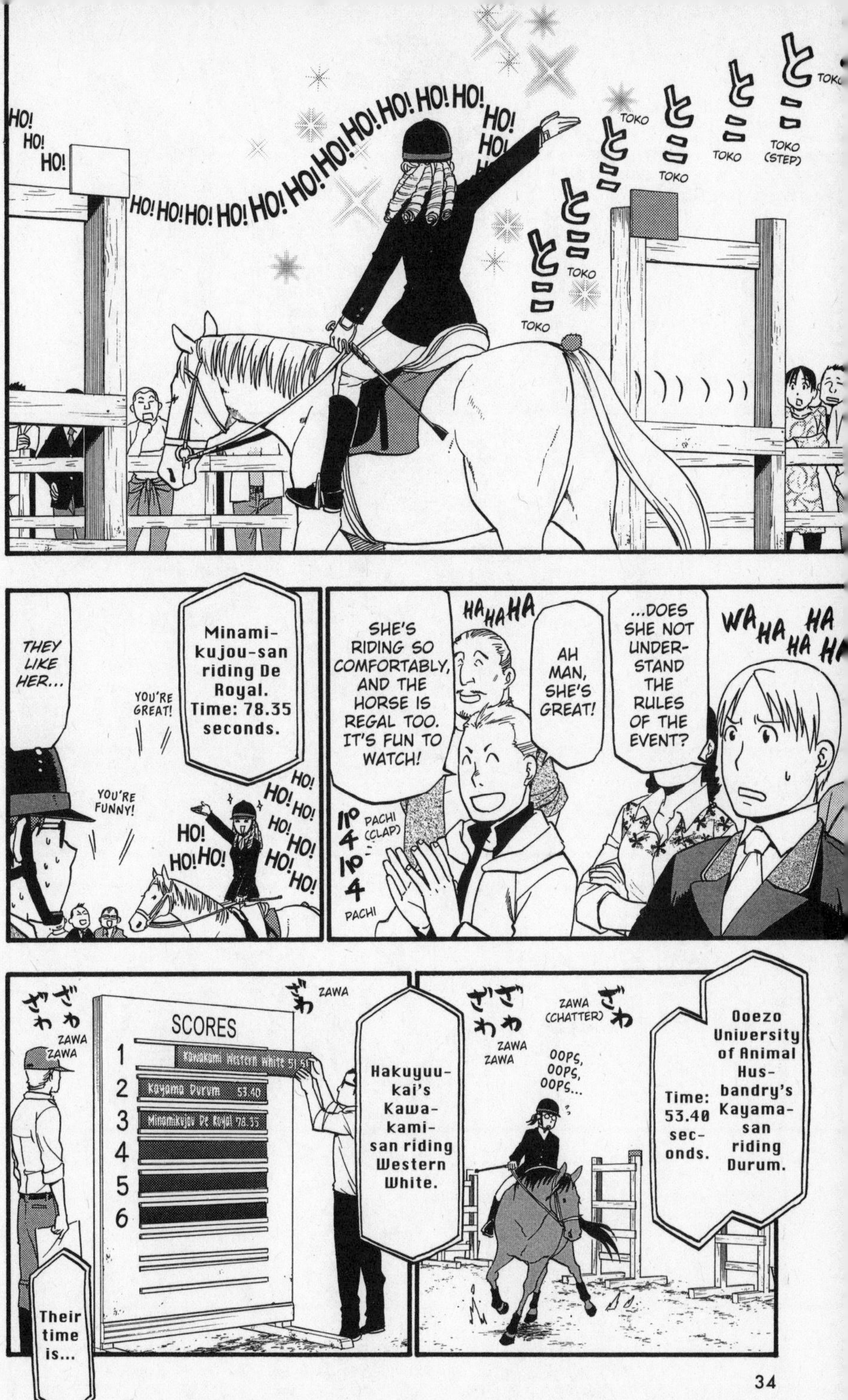
とっ TOKO
とっ TOKO (STEP)
とっ TOKO
とっ TOKO
とっ TOKO
とっ TOKO
とっ TOKO
HO! HO! HO! HO! HO! HO! HO! HO! HO! HO! HO! HO! HO! HO! HO! HO!
WA HA HA HA HA HA
...DOES SHE NOT UNDER-STAND THE RULES OF THE EVENT?
AH MAN, SHE'S GREAT!
HA HA HA
SHE'S RIDING SO COMFORTABLY, AND THE HORSE IS REGAL TOO. IT'S FUN TO WATCH!
パチ PACHI (CLAP)
パチ PACHI
Minami-kujou-san riding De Royal. Time: 78.35 seconds.
HO! HO! HO! HO! HO! HO! HO! HO! HO! HO!
YOU'RE GREAT!
YOU'RE FUNNY!
THEY LIKE HER...
Ooezo University of Animal Hus-bandry's Kayama-san riding Durum.
Time: 53.40 sec-onds.
ざわ ZAWA (CHATTER)
ざわざわ ZAWA ZAWA
OOPS, OOPS, OOPS...
Hakuyuu-kai's Kawa-kami-san riding Western White.
ざわ ZAWA
SCORES
1 Kawakami Western White 51.51
2 Kayama Durum 53.40
3 Minamikujou De Royal 78.35
4
5
6
ざわざわ ZAWA ZAWA
Their time is...

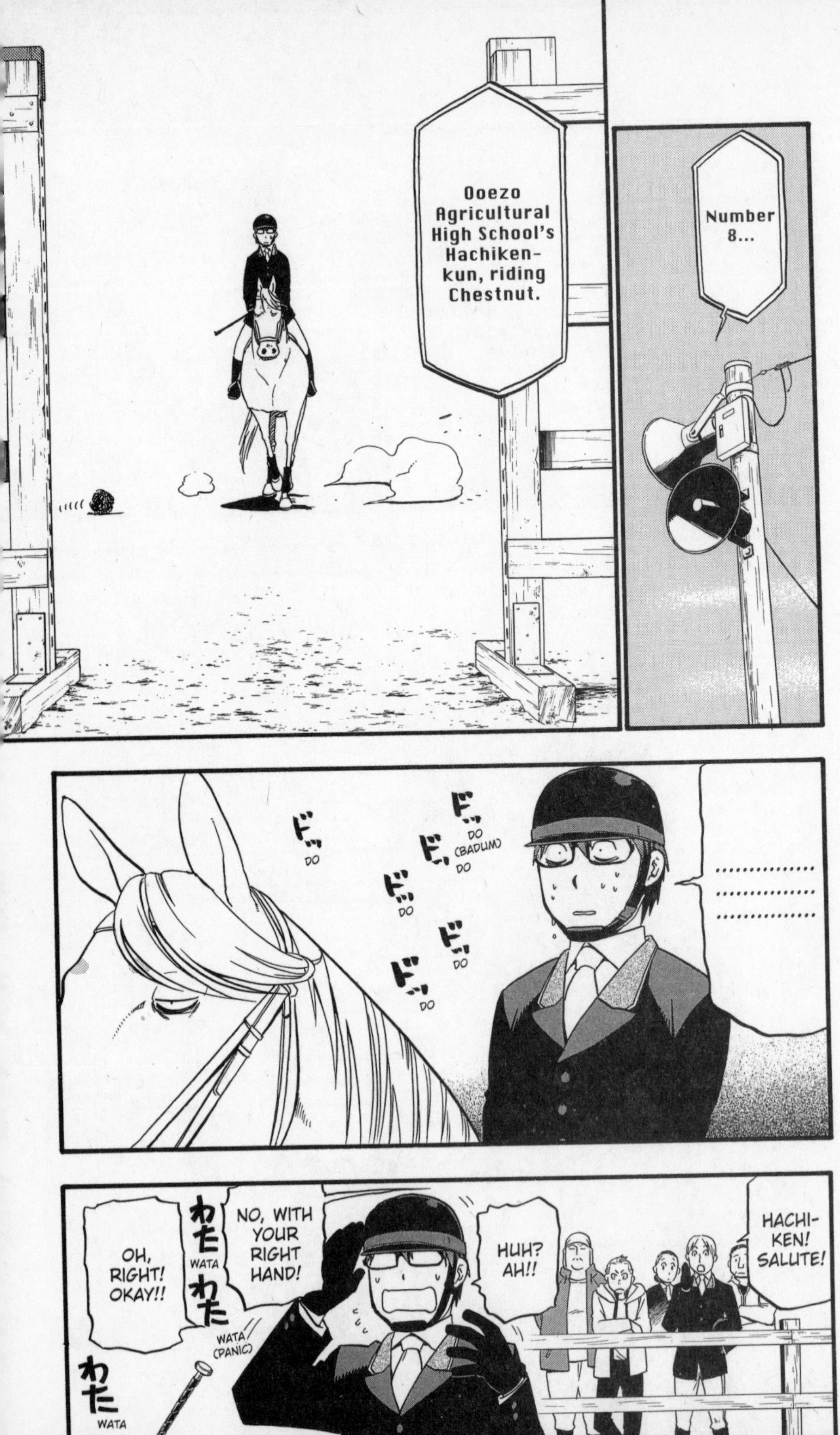
Number 8...
Ooezo Agricultural High School's Hachiken-kun, riding Chestnut.
....
....
....
ドッ DO
ド、 DO (BADUM) DO
ドッ DO
ドッ DO
ドッ DO
ドッ DO
HACHI-KEN! SALUTE!
HUH? AH!!
NO, WITH YOUR RIGHT HAND!
わた WATA
わた WATA (PANIC)
OH, RIGHT! OKAY!!
わた WATA

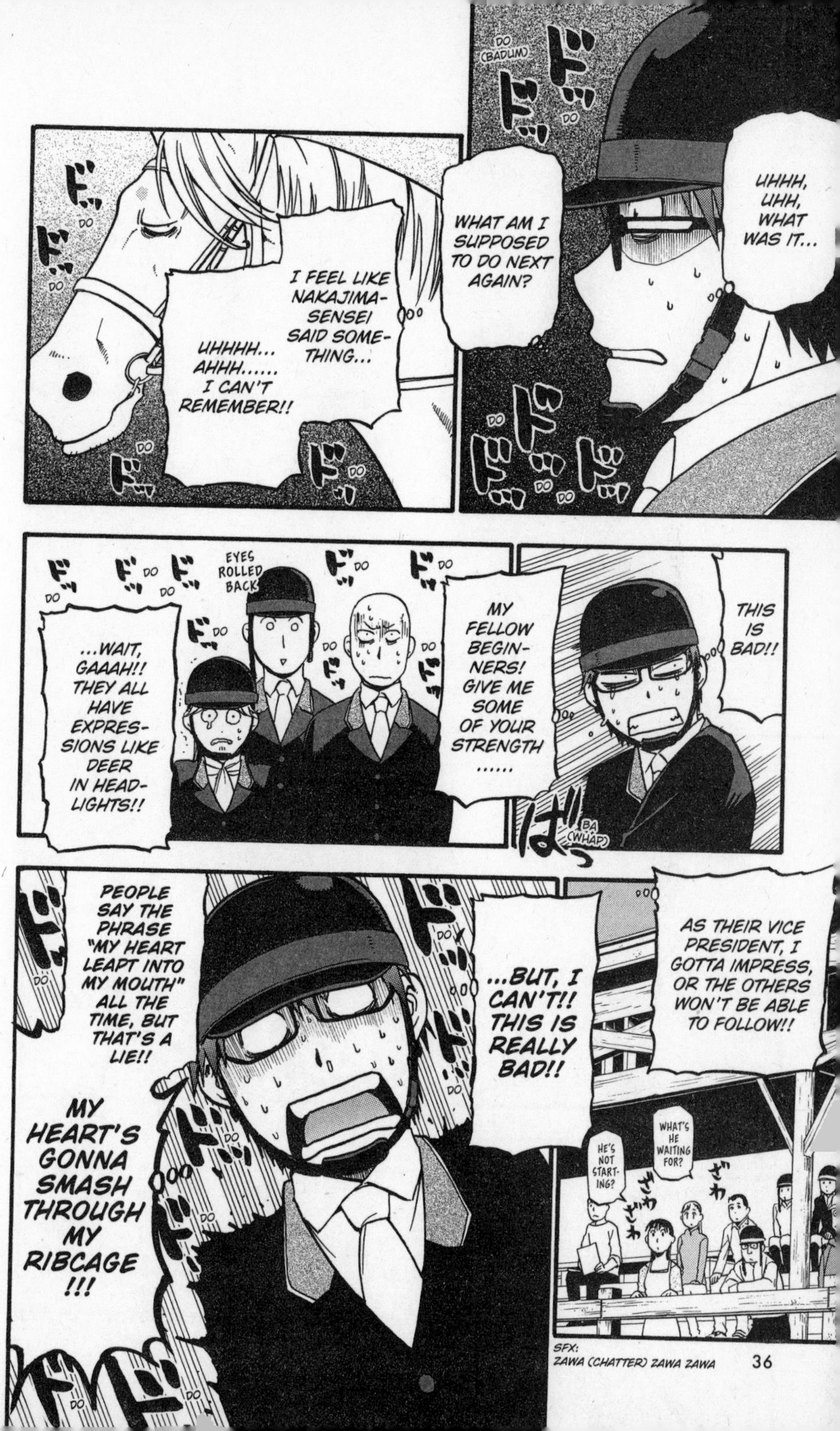
DO (BADUM)
DO
UHHH, UHH, WHAT WAS IT...
WHAT AM I SUPPOSED TO DO NEXT AGAIN?
DO DO DO DO
I FEEL LIKE NAKAJIMA-SENSEI SAID SOMETHING...
UHHHH... AHHH...... I CAN'T REMEMBER!!
DO DO DO DO
THIS IS BAD!!
MY FELLOW BEGINNERS! GIVE ME SOME OF YOUR STRENGTH ......
BA (WHAP)
DO DO DO DO DO DO DO
EYES ROLLED BACK
...WAIT, GAAAH!! THEY ALL HAVE EXPRESSIONS LIKE DEER IN HEADLIGHTS!!
AS THEIR VICE PRESIDENT, I GOTTA IMPRESS, OR THE OTHERS WON'T BE ABLE TO FOLLOW!!
WHAT'S HE WAITING FOR?
HE'S NOT STARTING?
...BUT, I CAN'T!! THIS IS REALLY BAD!!
DO DO DO
PEOPLE SAY THE PHRASE "MY HEART LEAPT INTO MY MOUTH" ALL THE TIME, BUT THAT'S A LIE!!
MY HEART'S GONNA SMASH THROUGH MY RIBCAGE!!!
DO DO DO DO DO

SFX: ZAWA (CHATTER) ZAWA ZAWA

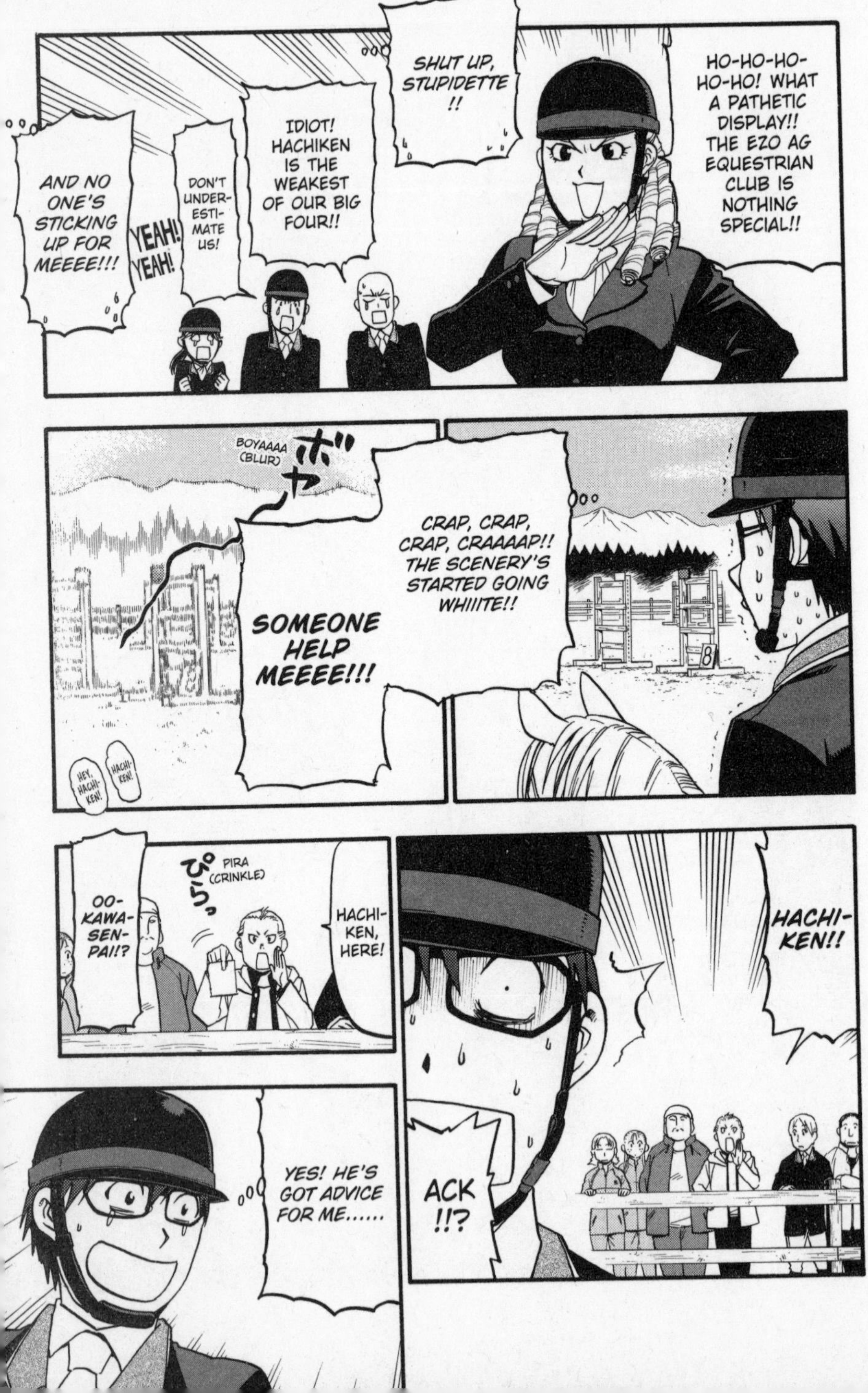
HO-HO-HO-HO-HO! WHAT A PATHETIC DISPLAY!! THE EZO AG EQUESTRIAN CLUB IS NOTHING SPECIAL!!
SHUT UP, STUPIDETTE !!
IDIOT! HACHIKEN IS THE WEAKEST OF OUR BIG FOUR!!
DON'T UNDER-ESTI-MATE US!
YEAH! YEAH!
AND NO ONE'S STICKING UP FOR MEEEE!!!
CRAP, CRAP, CRAP, CRAAAAP!! THE SCENERY'S STARTED GOING WHIIITE!!
ボヤ
BOYAAAA (BLUR)
SOMEONE HELP MEEEE!!!
HACHI-KEN!
HEY, HACHI-KEN!
HACHI-KEN!!
ACK !!?
HACHI-KEN, HERE!
ぴらっ
PIRA (CRINKLE)
OO-KAWA-SENPAI!?
YES! HE'S GOT ADVICE FOR ME......

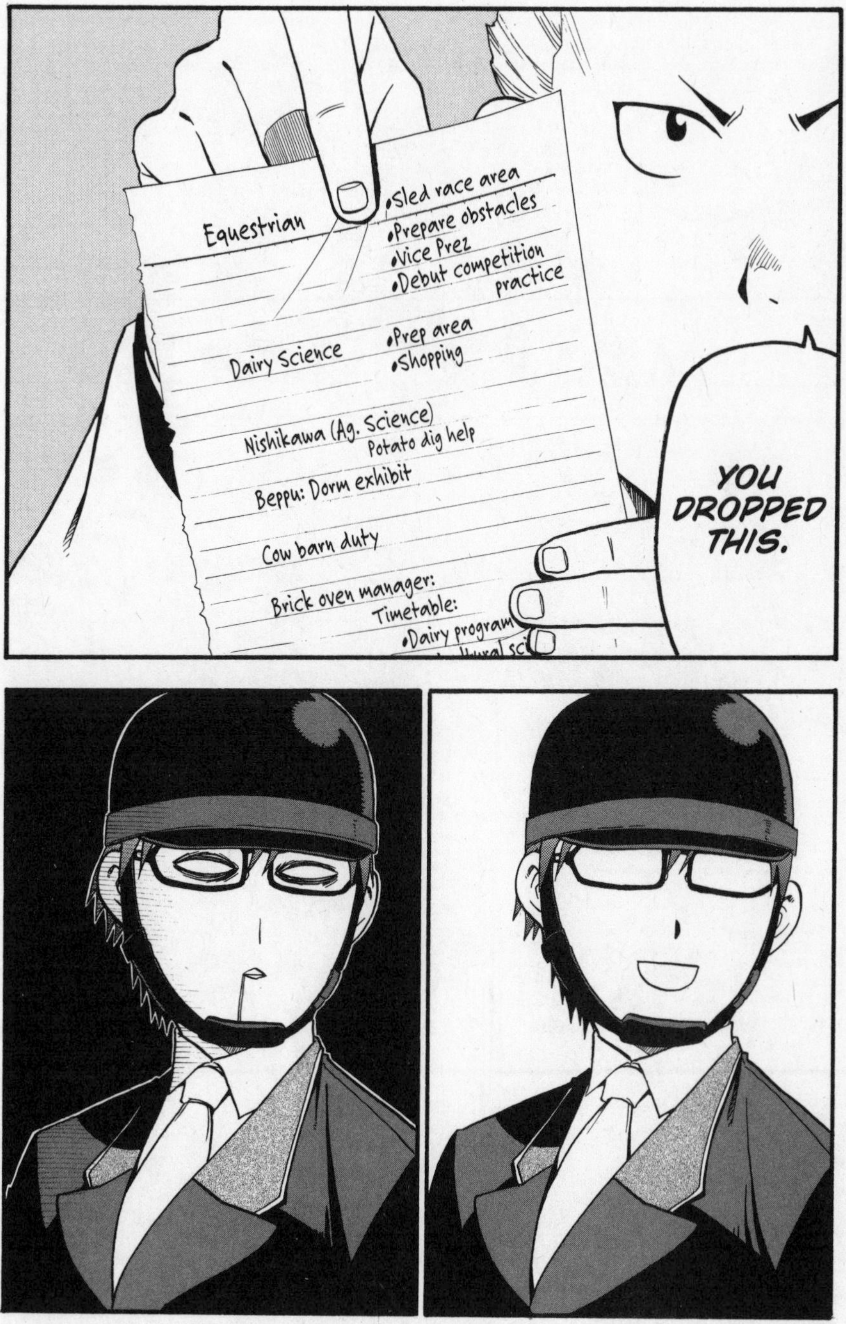
Equestrian
•Sled race area
•Prepare obstacles
•Vice Prez
•Debut competition practice
Dairy Science
•Prep area
•Shopping
Nishikawa (Ag. Science)
Potato dig help
Beppu: Dorm exhibit
Cow barn duty
Brick oven manager:
Timetable:
•Dairy program
YOU DROPPED THIS.

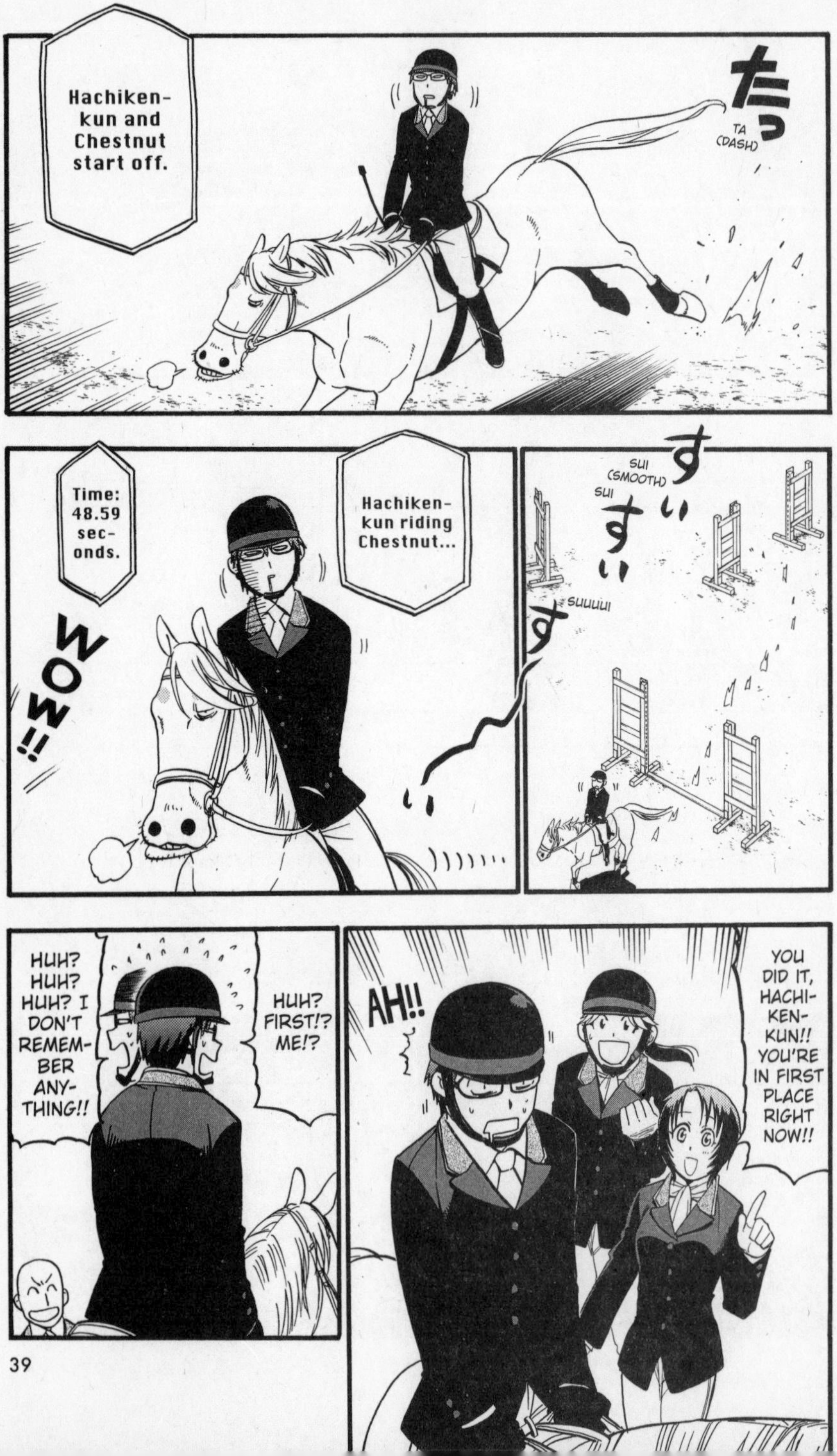
Hachiken-kun and Chestnut start off.
たっ
TA (DASH)
すい
SUI (SMOOTH)
すい
SUI
すー
SUUUUU
Hachiken-kun riding Chestnut...
Time: 48.59 seconds.
WOW!!
AH!!
YOU DID IT, HACHIKEN-KUN!! YOU'RE IN FIRST PLACE RIGHT NOW!!
HUH? FIRST!? ME!?
HUH? HUH? HUH? I DON'T REMEMBER ANYTHING!!

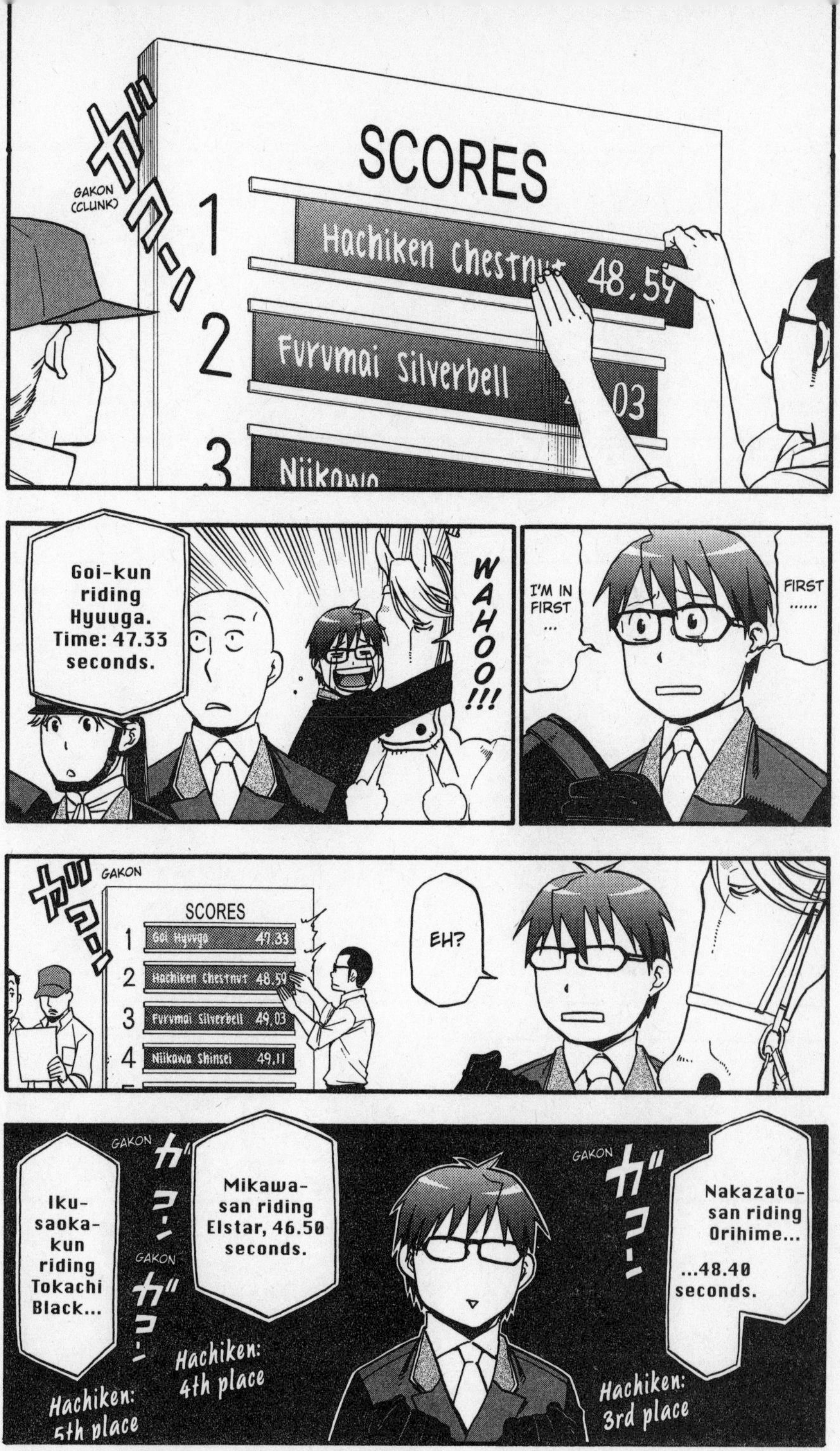
GAKON (CLUNK)
SCORES
1 Hachiken Chestnut 48.59
2 Furumai Silverbell
3
FIRST ......
I'M IN FIRST ...
WAHOO!!!
Goi-kun riding Hyuuga. Time: 47.33 seconds.
EH?
GAKON
SCORES
1 Goi Hyuuga 47.33
2 Hachiken Chestnut 48.59
3 Furumai Silverbell 49.03
4 Niikawa Shinsei 49.11
Nakazato-san riding Orihime... ...48.40 seconds.
GAKON
Hachiken: 3rd place
Mikawa-san riding Elstar, 46.50 seconds.
GAKON
Hachiken: 4th place
Iku-saoka-kun riding Tokachi Black...
GAKON
Hachiken: 5th place

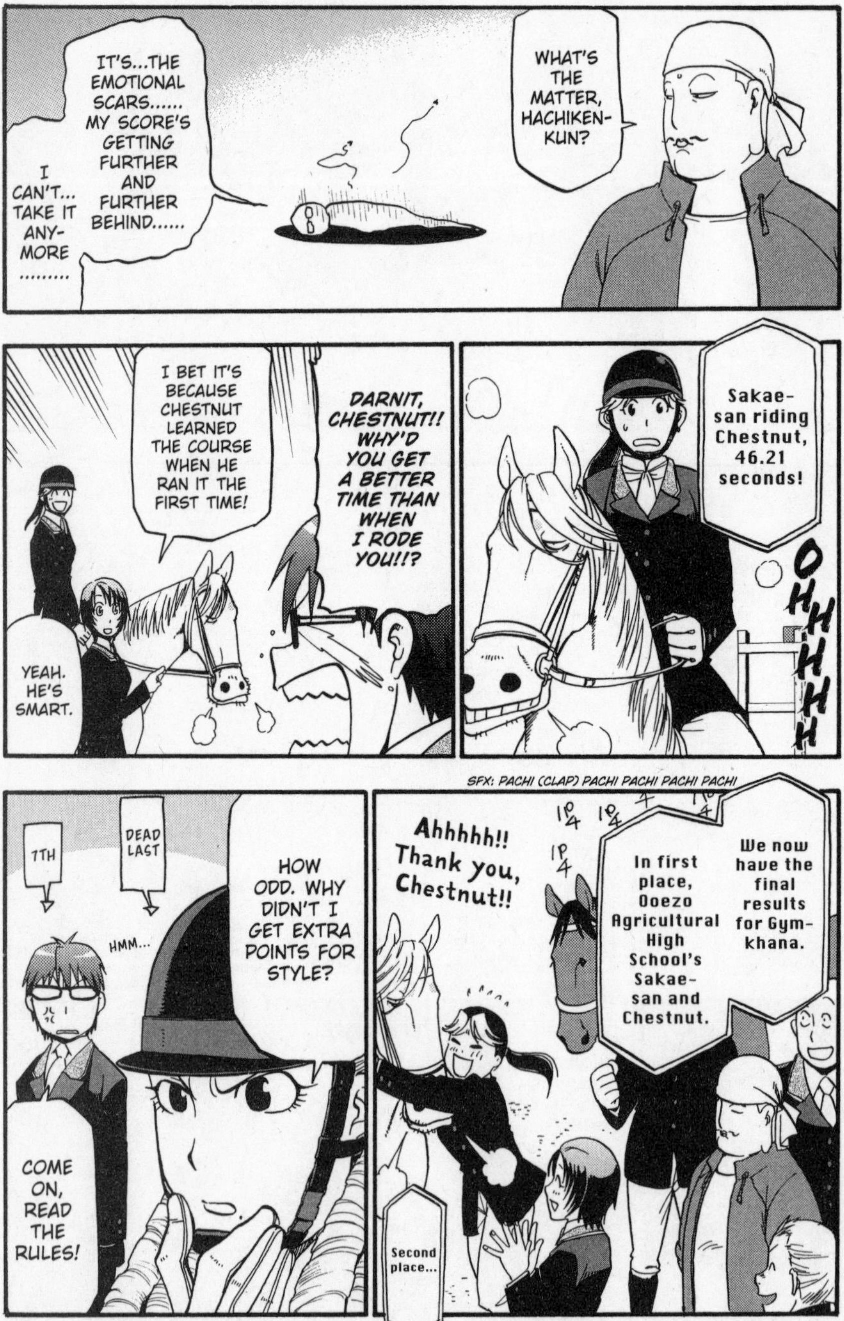
WHAT'S THE MATTER, HACHIKEN-KUN?
IT'S...THE EMOTIONAL SCARS...... MY SCORE'S GETTING FURTHER AND FURTHER BEHIND......
I CAN'T... TAKE IT ANYMORE.........
Sakae-san riding Chestnut, 46.21 seconds!
OHHHHHH
DARNIT, CHESTNUT!! WHY'D YOU GET A BETTER TIME THAN WHEN I RODE YOU!!?
I BET IT'S BECAUSE CHESTNUT LEARNED THE COURSE WHEN HE RAN IT THE FIRST TIME!
YEAH. HE'S SMART.
SFX: PACHI (CLAP) PACHI PACHI PACHI PACHI
We now have the final results for Gymkhana.
In first place, Ooezo Agricultural High School's Sakae-san and Chestnut.
Ahhhhh!! Thank you, Chestnut!!
Second place...
HOW ODD. WHY DIDN'T I GET EXTRA POINTS FOR STYLE?
DEAD LAST
7TH
HMM...
COME ON, READ THE RULES!

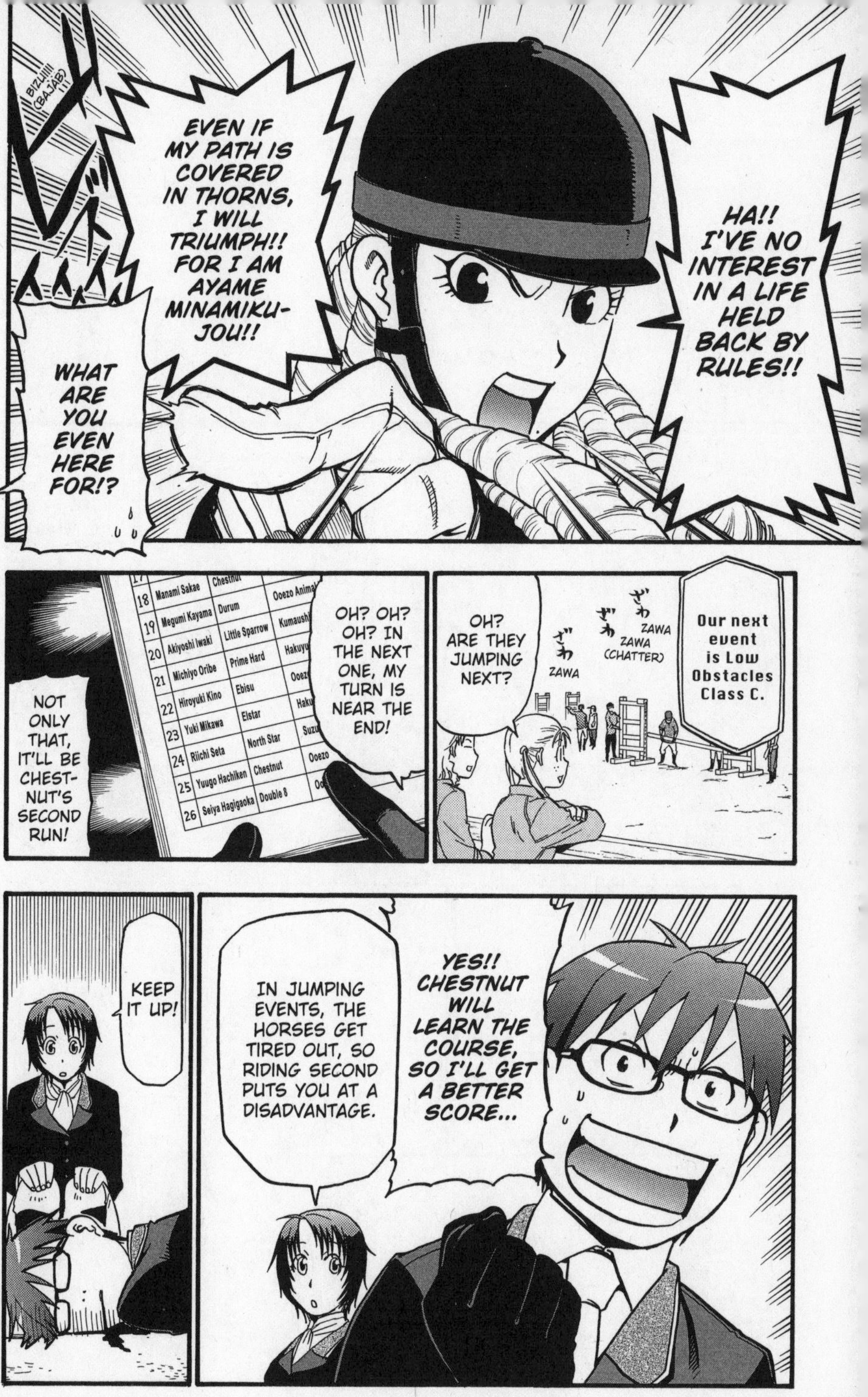
HA!! I'VE NO INTEREST IN A LIFE HELD BACK BY RULES!!
EVEN IF MY PATH IS COVERED IN THORNS, I WILL TRIUMPH!! FOR I AM AYAME MINAMIKUJOU!!
BIZU!!!! (BAJAB)
WHAT ARE YOU EVEN HERE FOR!?
Our next event is Low Obstacles Class C.
ざわ ZAWA
ざわ ZAWA (CHATTER)
ざわ ZAWA
OH? ARE THEY JUMPING NEXT?
OH? OH? OH? IN THE NEXT ONE, MY TURN IS NEAR THE END!
18 Manami Sakae Chestnut
19 Megumi Kayama Durum
20 Akiyoshi Iwaki Little Sparrow
21 Michiyo Oribe Prime Hard
22 Hiroyuki Kino Ebisu
23 Yuki Mikawa Elstar
24 Riichi Seta North Star
25 Yuugo Hachiken Chestnut
26 Seiya Hagigaoka Double 8
NOT ONLY THAT, IT'LL BE CHESTNUT'S SECOND RUN!
YES!! CHESTNUT WILL LEARN THE COURSE, SO I'LL GET A BETTER SCORE...
IN JUMPING EVENTS, THE HORSES GET TIRED OUT, SO RIDING SECOND PUTS YOU AT A DISADVANTAGE.
KEEP IT UP!

Silver Spoon

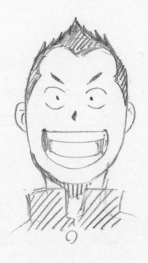

TAKASHI SHIRAITO

ASHORO RAWAN MIDDLE
SCHOOL

TAKES THIRTY MINUTES
TO SET HIS HAIR EVERY
MORNING

TRACK & FIELD

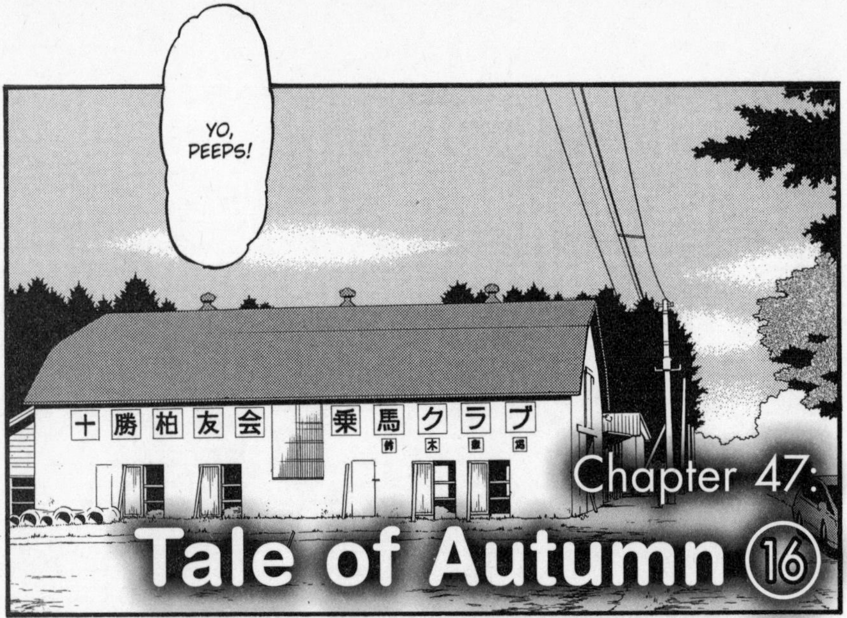
YO, PEEPS!
十勝柏友会 乗馬クラブ
Chapter 47:
Tale of Autumn ⑯
SIGN: TOKACHI HAKUYUUKAI RIDING CLUB

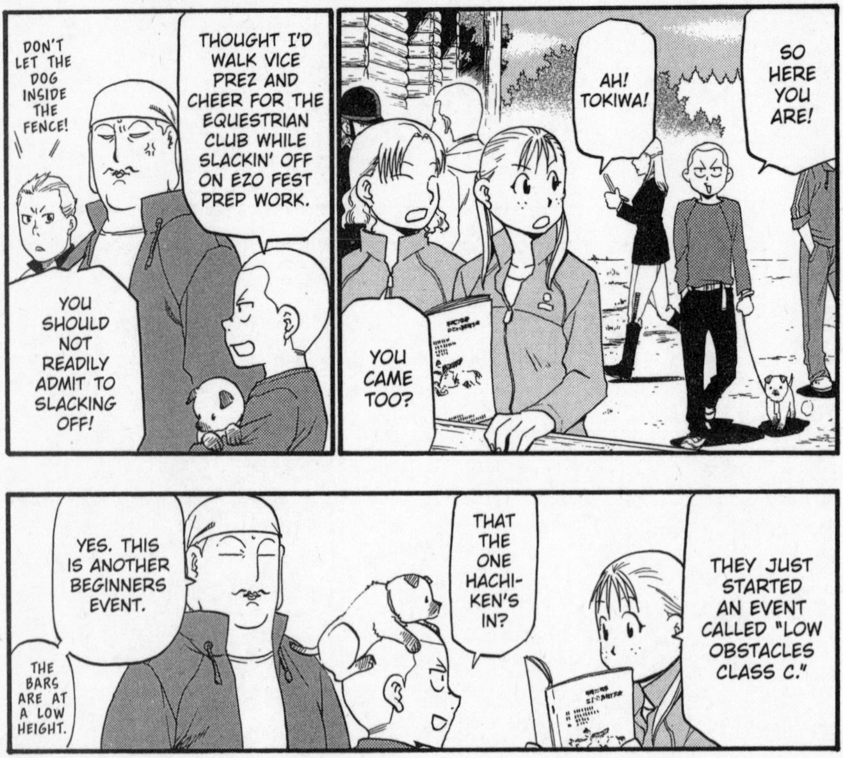
SO HERE YOU ARE!
AH! TOKIWA!
YOU CAME TOO?
THOUGHT I'D WALK VICE PREZ AND CHEER FOR THE EQUESTRIAN CLUB WHILE SLACKIN' OFF ON EZO FEST PREP WORK.
DON'T LET THE DOG INSIDE THE FENCE!
YOU SHOULD NOT READILY ADMIT TO SLACKING OFF!
THEY JUST STARTED AN EVENT CALLED "LOW OBSTACLES CLASS C."
THAT THE ONE HACHI-KEN'S IN?
YES. THIS IS ANOTHER BEGINNERS EVENT.
THE BARS ARE AT A LOW HEIGHT.

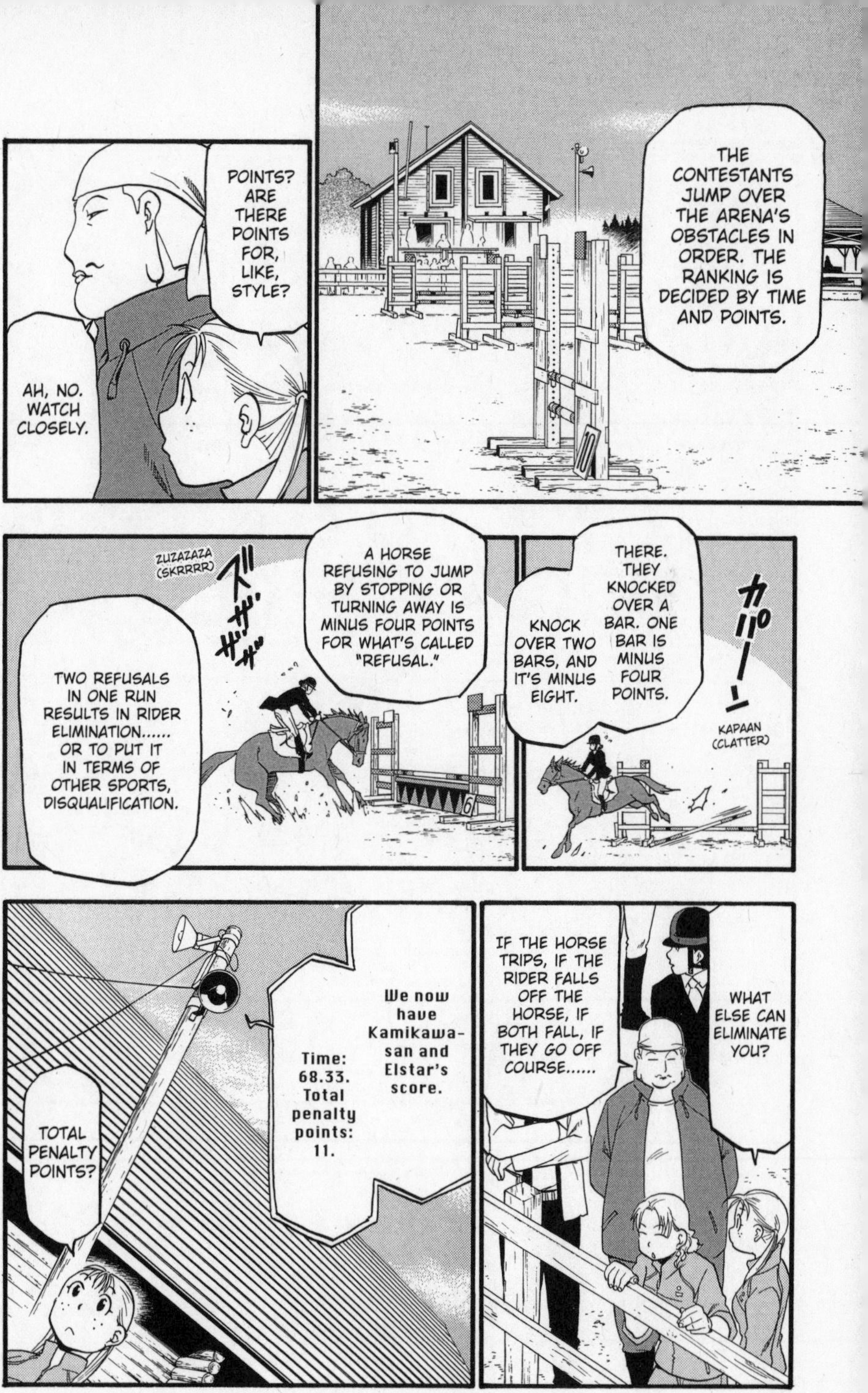
THE CONTESTANTS JUMP OVER THE ARENA'S OBSTACLES IN ORDER. THE RANKING IS DECIDED BY TIME AND POINTS.
POINTS? ARE THERE POINTS FOR, LIKE, STYLE?
AH, NO. WATCH CLOSELY.
THERE. THEY KNOCKED OVER A BAR. ONE BAR IS MINUS FOUR POINTS.
KNOCK OVER TWO BARS, AND IT'S MINUS EIGHT.
KAPAAN (CLATTER)
A HORSE REFUSING TO JUMP BY STOPPING OR TURNING AWAY IS MINUS FOUR POINTS FOR WHAT'S CALLED "REFUSAL."
ZUZAZAZA (SKRRRR)
TWO REFUSALS IN ONE RUN RESULTS IN RIDER ELIMINATION...... OR TO PUT IT IN TERMS OF OTHER SPORTS, DISQUALIFICATION.
WHAT ELSE CAN ELIMINATE YOU?
IF THE HORSE TRIPS, IF THE RIDER FALLS OFF THE HORSE, IF BOTH FALL, IF THEY GO OFF COURSE......
We now have Kamikawa-san and Elstar's score.
Time: 68.33. Total penalty points: 11.
TOTAL PENALTY POINTS?

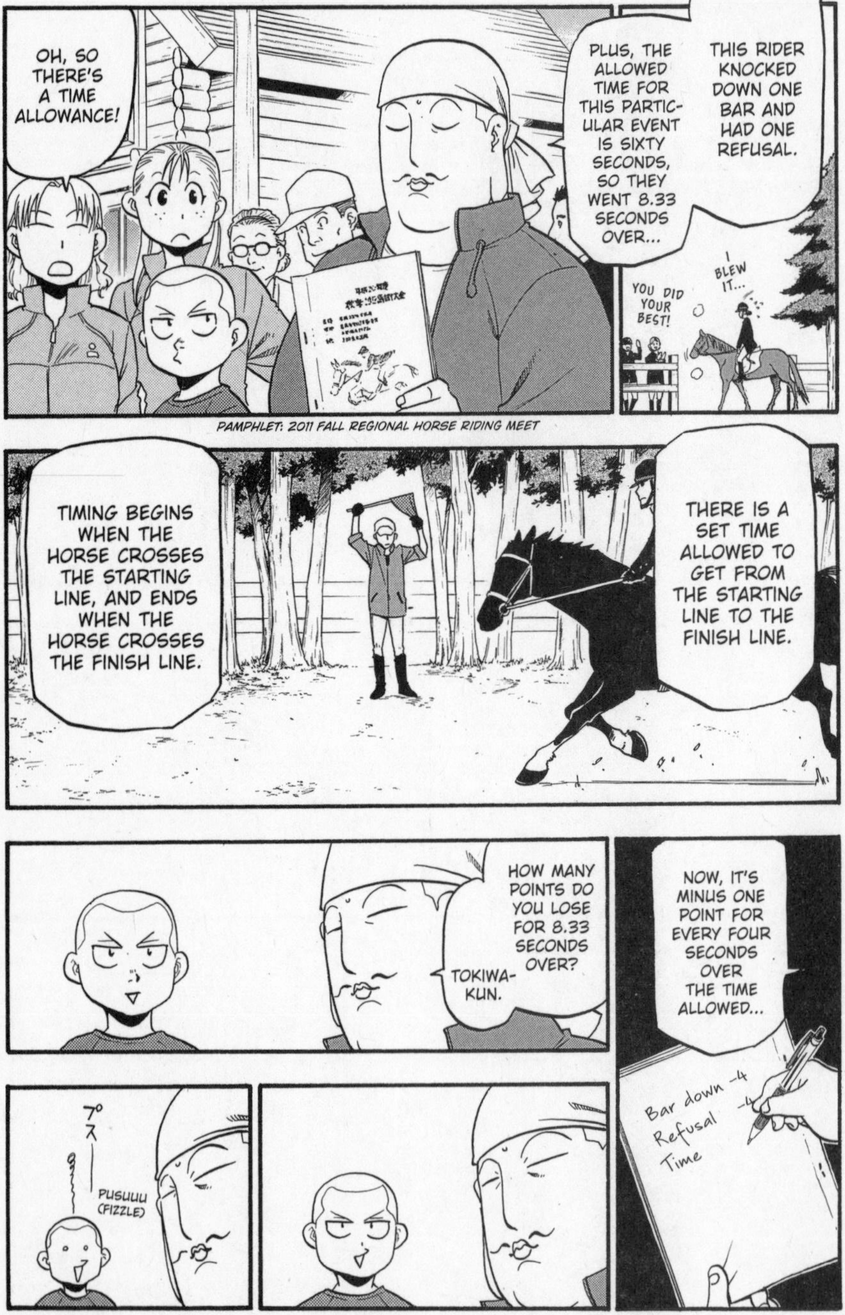

THIS RIDER KNOCKED DOWN ONE BAR AND HAD ONE REFUSAL.
I BLEW IT...
YOU DID YOUR BEST!
PLUS, THE ALLOWED TIME FOR THIS PARTICULAR EVENT IS SIXTY SECONDS, SO THEY WENT 8.33 SECONDS OVER...
OH, SO THERE'S A TIME ALLOWANCE!
PAMPHLET: 2011 FALL REGIONAL HORSE RIDING MEET
THERE IS A SET TIME ALLOWED TO GET FROM THE STARTING LINE TO THE FINISH LINE.
TIMING BEGINS WHEN THE HORSE CROSSES THE STARTING LINE, AND ENDS WHEN THE HORSE CROSSES THE FINISH LINE.
NOW, IT'S MINUS ONE POINT FOR EVERY FOUR SECONDS OVER THE TIME ALLOWED...
Bar down -4
Refusal -4
Time
HOW MANY POINTS DO YOU LOSE FOR 8.33 SECONDS OVER?
TOKIWA-KUN.
プスー
PUSUUU (FIZZLE)

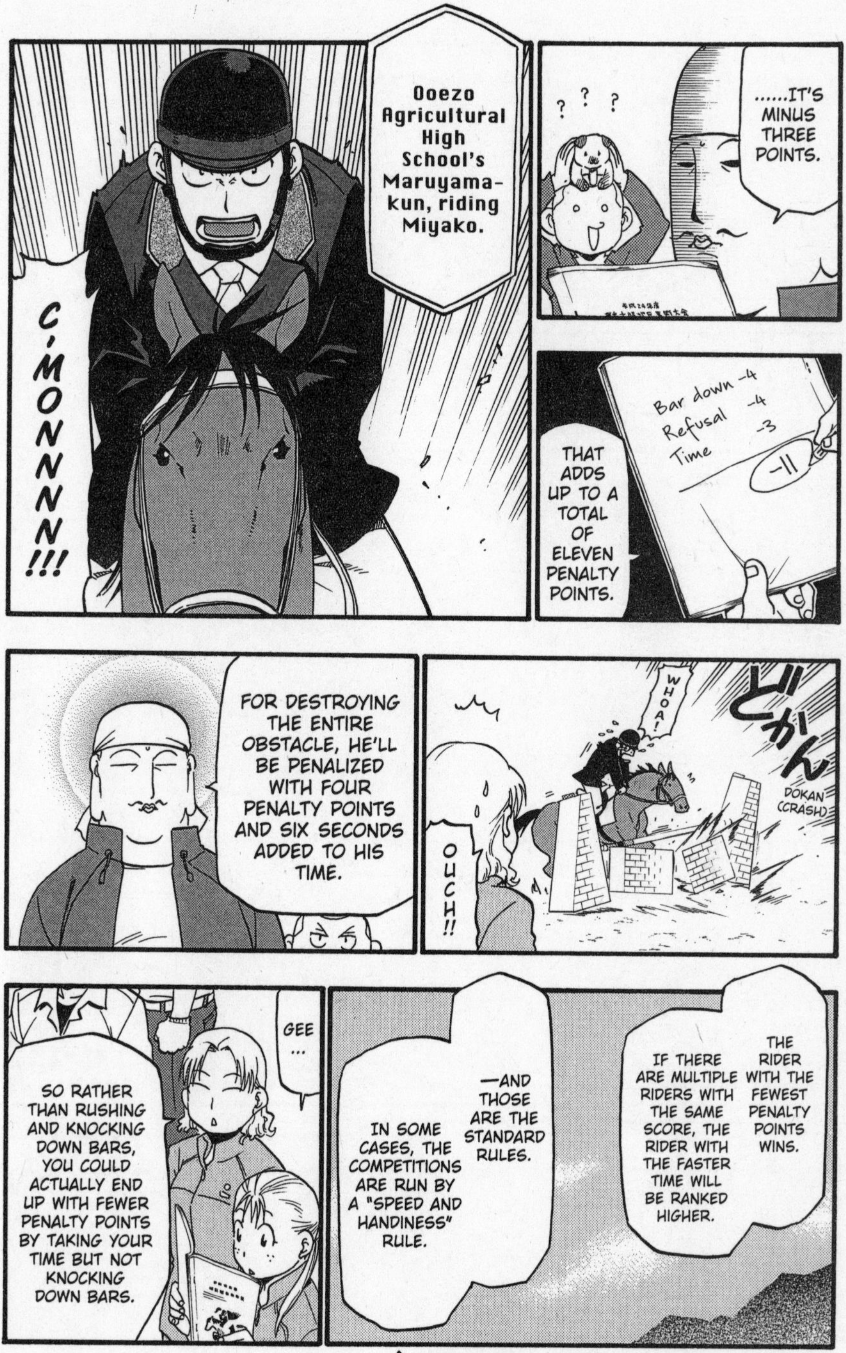
......IT'S MINUS THREE POINTS.
Bar down -4
Refusal -4
Time -3
-11
THAT ADDS UP TO A TOTAL OF ELEVEN PENALTY POINTS.
Ooezo Agricultural High School's Maruyama-kun, riding Miyako.
C'MONNNNN!!!
どかん
DOKAN (CRASH)
WHOA!
OUCH!!
FOR DESTROYING THE ENTIRE OBSTACLE, HE'LL BE PENALIZED WITH FOUR PENALTY POINTS AND SIX SECONDS ADDED TO HIS TIME.
THE RIDER WITH THE FEWEST PENALTY POINTS WINS.
IF THERE ARE MULTIPLE RIDERS WITH THE SAME SCORE, THE RIDER WITH THE FASTER TIME WILL BE RANKED HIGHER.
—AND THOSE ARE THE STANDARD RULES.
IN SOME CASES, THE COMPETITIONS ARE RUN BY A "SPEED AND HANDINESS" RULE.
GEE...
SO RATHER THAN RUSHING AND KNOCKING DOWN BARS, YOU COULD ACTUALLY END UP WITH FEWER PENALTY POINTS BY TAKING YOUR TIME BUT NOT KNOCKING DOWN BARS.

↑ A RULE WHERE THE PENALTY FOR MISTAKES IS EXTRA SECONDS ADDED TO YOUR TIME.

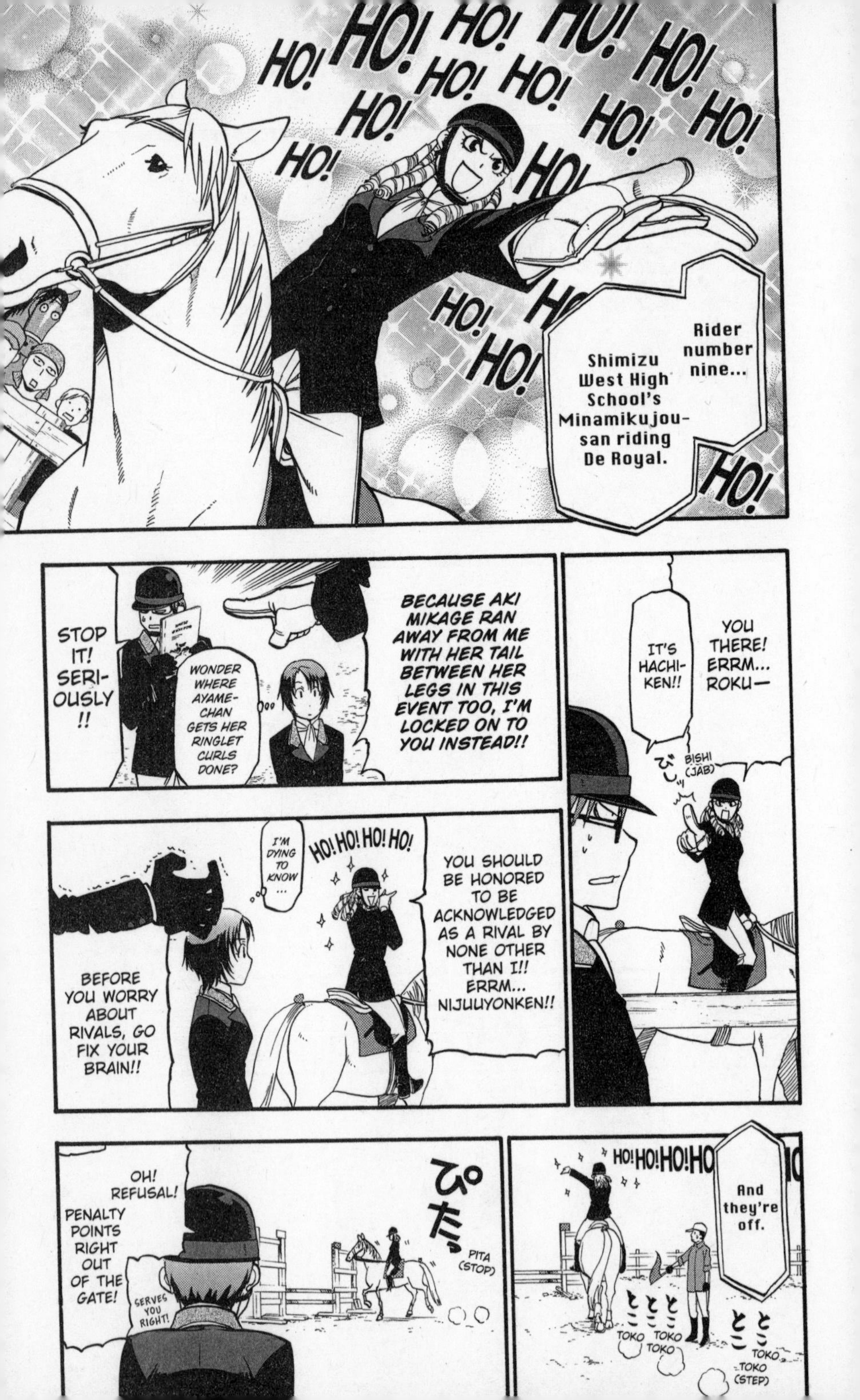
HO! HO! HO! HO! HO! HO! HO! HO! HO! HO! HO! HO! HO! HO! HO! HO!
Rider number nine... Shimizu West High School's Minamikujou-san riding De Royal.
YOU THERE! ERRM... ROKU—
IT'S HACHIKEN!!
BISHI (JAB)
BECAUSE AKI MIKAGE RAN AWAY FROM ME WITH HER TAIL BETWEEN HER LEGS IN THIS EVENT TOO, I'M LOCKED ON TO YOU INSTEAD!!
STOP IT! SERIOUSLY!!
WONDER WHERE AYAME-CHAN GETS HER RINGLET CURLS DONE?
YOU SHOULD BE HONORED TO BE ACKNOWLEDGED AS A RIVAL BY NONE OTHER THAN I!! ERRM... NIJUUYONKEN!!
HO! HO! HO! HO!
I'M DYING TO KNOW...
BEFORE YOU WORRY ABOUT RIVALS, GO FIX YOUR BRAIN!!
And they're off.
HO! HO! HO! HO
TOKO TOKO
TOKO TOKO
TOKO TOKO (STEP)
PITA (STOP)
OH! REFUSAL! PENALTY POINTS RIGHT OUT OF THE GATE!
SERVES YOU RIGHT!

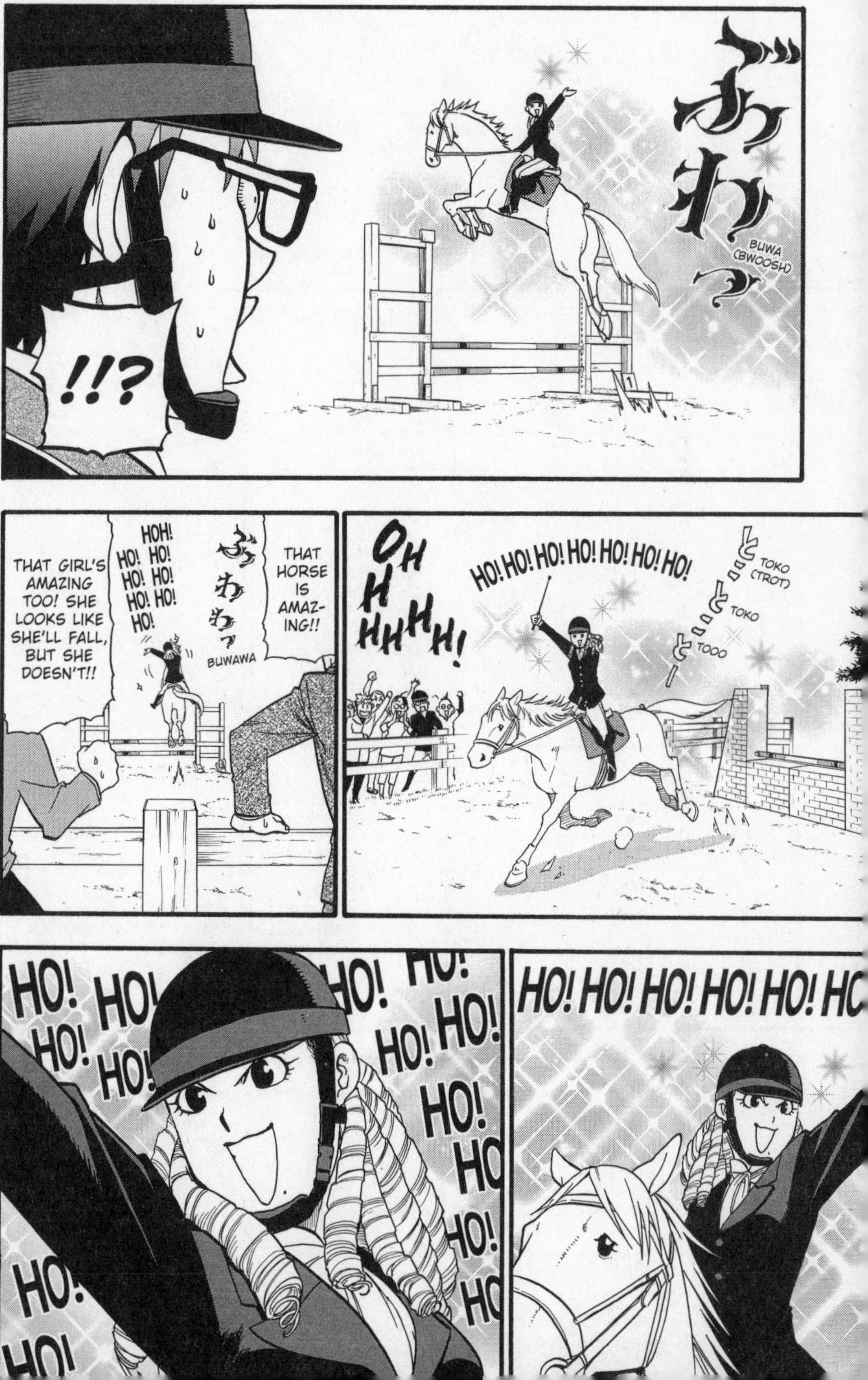
BUWA (BWOOSH)
!!?
TOKO (TROT)
TOKO
TOOO
HO! HO! HO! HO! HO! HO! HO!
OHHHHHH!
THAT HORSE IS AMAZ-ING!!
BUWAWA
HOH! HO! HO! HO! HO! HO! HO! HO!
THAT GIRL'S AMAZING TOO! SHE LOOKS LIKE SHE'LL FALL, BUT SHE DOESN'T!!
HO! HO! HO! HO! HO! HO
HO! HO! HO! HO! HO! HO! HO! HO! HO! HO! HO! HO!

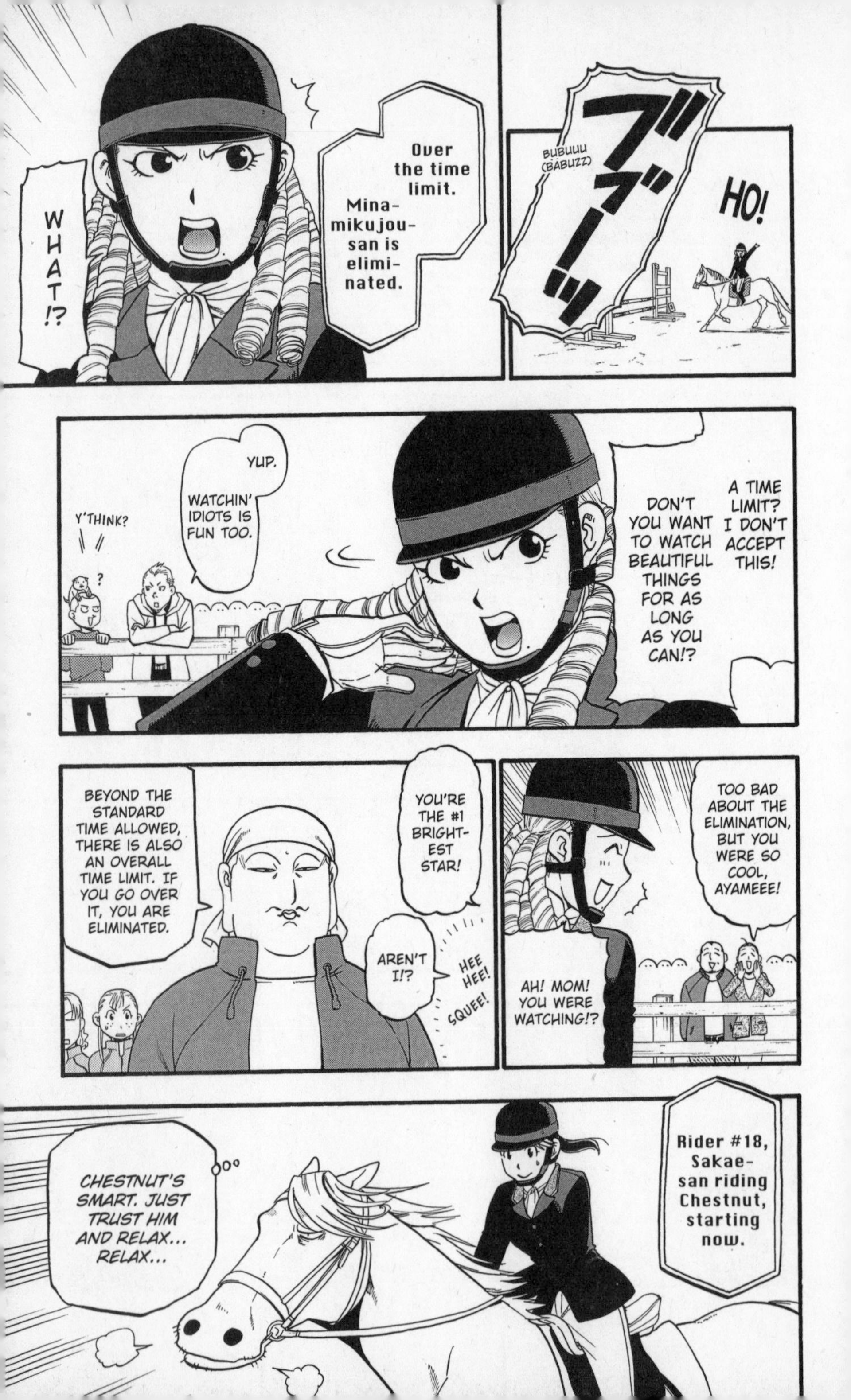
BUBUUU (BABUZZ)
HO!
Over the time limit.
Mina-mikujou-san is elimi-nated.
WHAT!?
A TIME LIMIT? I DON'T ACCEPT THIS!
DON'T YOU WANT TO WATCH BEAUTIFUL THINGS FOR AS LONG AS YOU CAN!?
YUP.
WATCHIN' IDIOTS IS FUN TOO.
Y'THINK?
?
TOO BAD ABOUT THE ELIMINATION, BUT YOU WERE SO COOL, AYAMEEE!
AH! MOM! YOU WERE WATCHING!?
YOU'RE THE #1 BRIGHT-EST STAR!
AREN'T I!?
HEE HEE!
SQUEE!
BEYOND THE STANDARD TIME ALLOWED, THERE IS ALSO AN OVERALL TIME LIMIT. IF YOU GO OVER IT, YOU ARE ELIMINATED.
Rider #18, Sakae-san riding Chestnut, starting now.
CHESTNUT'S SMART. JUST TRUST HIM AND RELAX... RELAX...

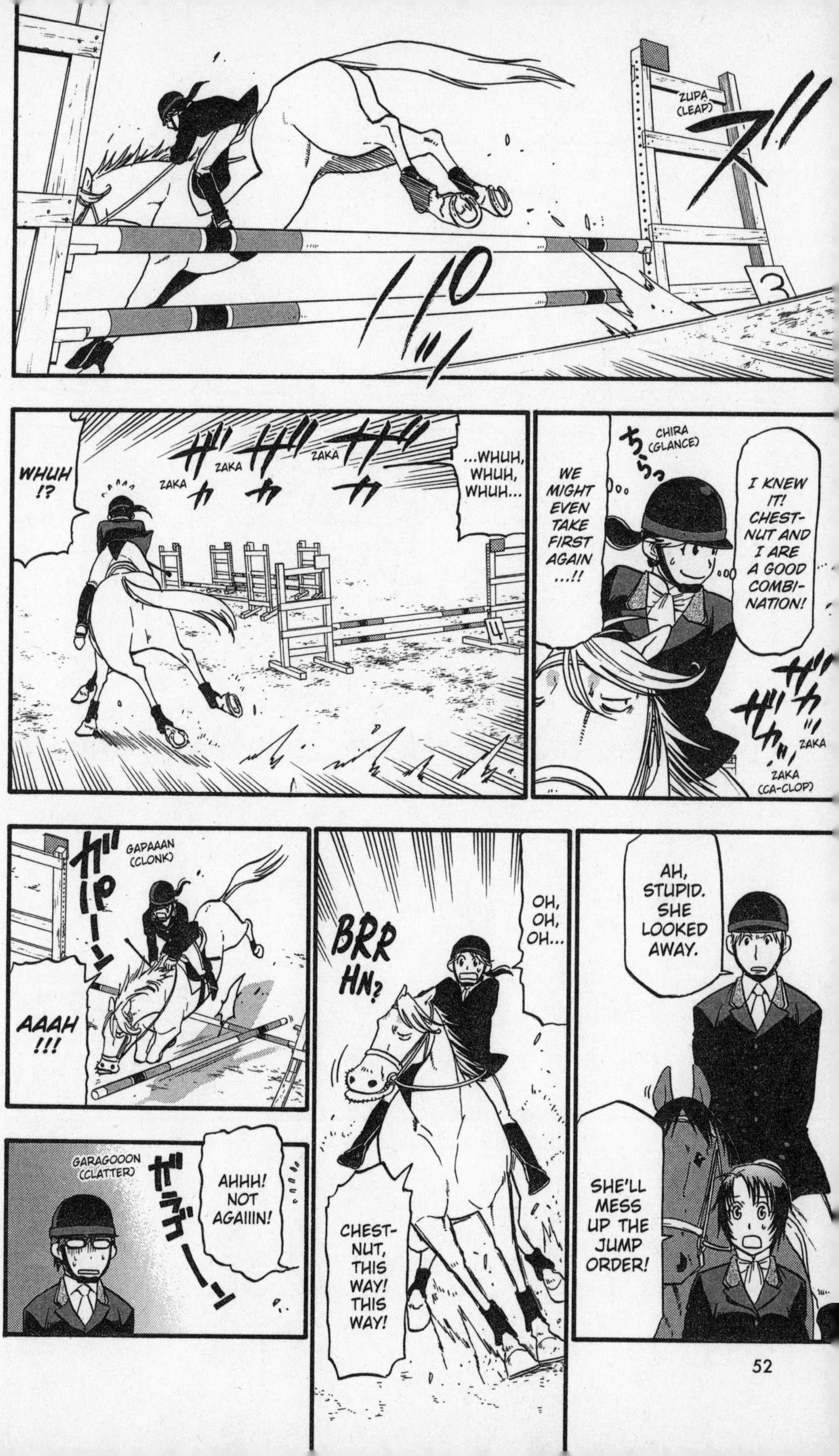
ZUPA (LEAP)
CHIRA (GLANCE)
I KNEW IT! CHEST-NUT AND I ARE A GOOD COMBI-NATION!
WE MIGHT EVEN TAKE FIRST AGAIN ...!!
ZAKA
ZAKA (CA-CLOP)
...WHUH, WHUH, WHUH...
ZAKA
ZAKA
ZAKA
WHUH !?
AH, STUPID. SHE LOOKED AWAY.
SHE'LL MESS UP THE JUMP ORDER!
OH, OH, OH...
BRR HN?
CHEST-NUT, THIS WAY! THIS WAY!
GAPAAAN (CLONK)
AAAH !!!
GARAGOOON (CLATTER)
AHHH! NOT AGAIIIN!

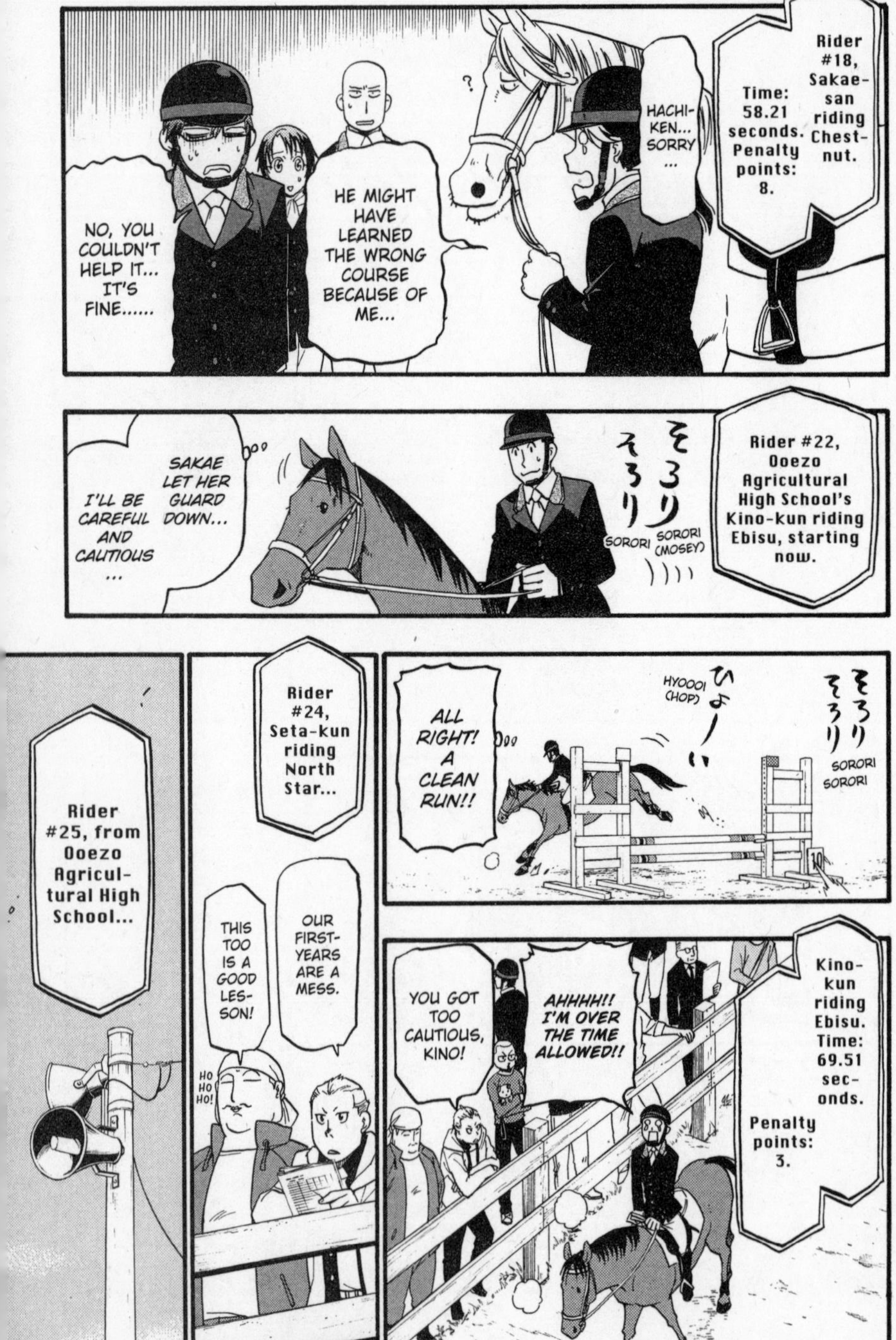
Rider #18, Sakae-san riding Chestnut.
Time: 58.21 seconds. Penalty points: 8.
HACHI-KEN... SORRY...
HE MIGHT HAVE LEARNED THE WRONG COURSE BECAUSE OF ME...
NO, YOU COULDN'T HELP IT... IT'S FINE......
Rider #22, Ooezo Agricultural High School's Kino-kun riding Ebisu, starting now.
そろり そろり
SORORI SORORI (MOSEY)
SAKAE LET HER GUARD DOWN...
I'LL BE CAREFUL AND CAUTIOUS...
そろり そろり
SORORI SORORI
ひょーい
HYOOOI (HOP)
ALL RIGHT! A CLEAN RUN!!
Kino-kun riding Ebisu. Time: 69.51 seconds.
Penalty points: 3.
AHHHH!! I'M OVER THE TIME ALLOWED!!
YOU GOT TOO CAUTIOUS, KINO!
Rider #24, Seta-kun riding North Star...
OUR FIRST-YEARS ARE A MESS.
THIS TOO IS A GOOD LESSON!
HO HO HO!
Rider #25, from Ooezo Agricultural High School...

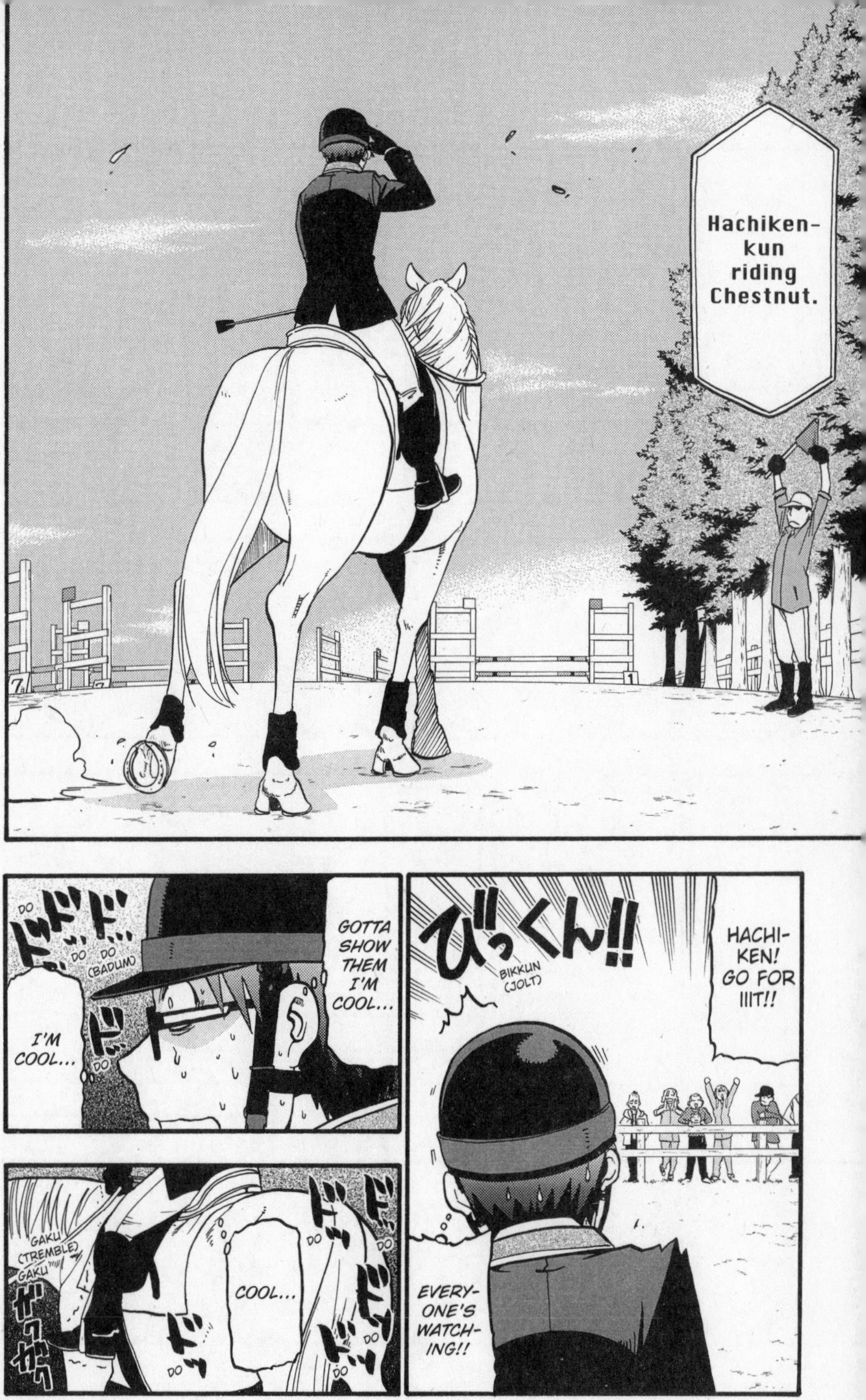
Hachiken-kun riding Chestnut.
HACHI-KEN! GO FOR IIIT!!
びっくん!!
BIKKUN (JOLT)
EVERY-ONE'S WATCHING!!
GOTTA SHOW THEM I'M COOL...
ドド ド
DO DO DO (BADUM)
I'M COOL...
ド
DO
ドド ド
DO DO DO
COOL...
ドド
DO DO
GAKU (TREMBLE) GAKU
ガクガク

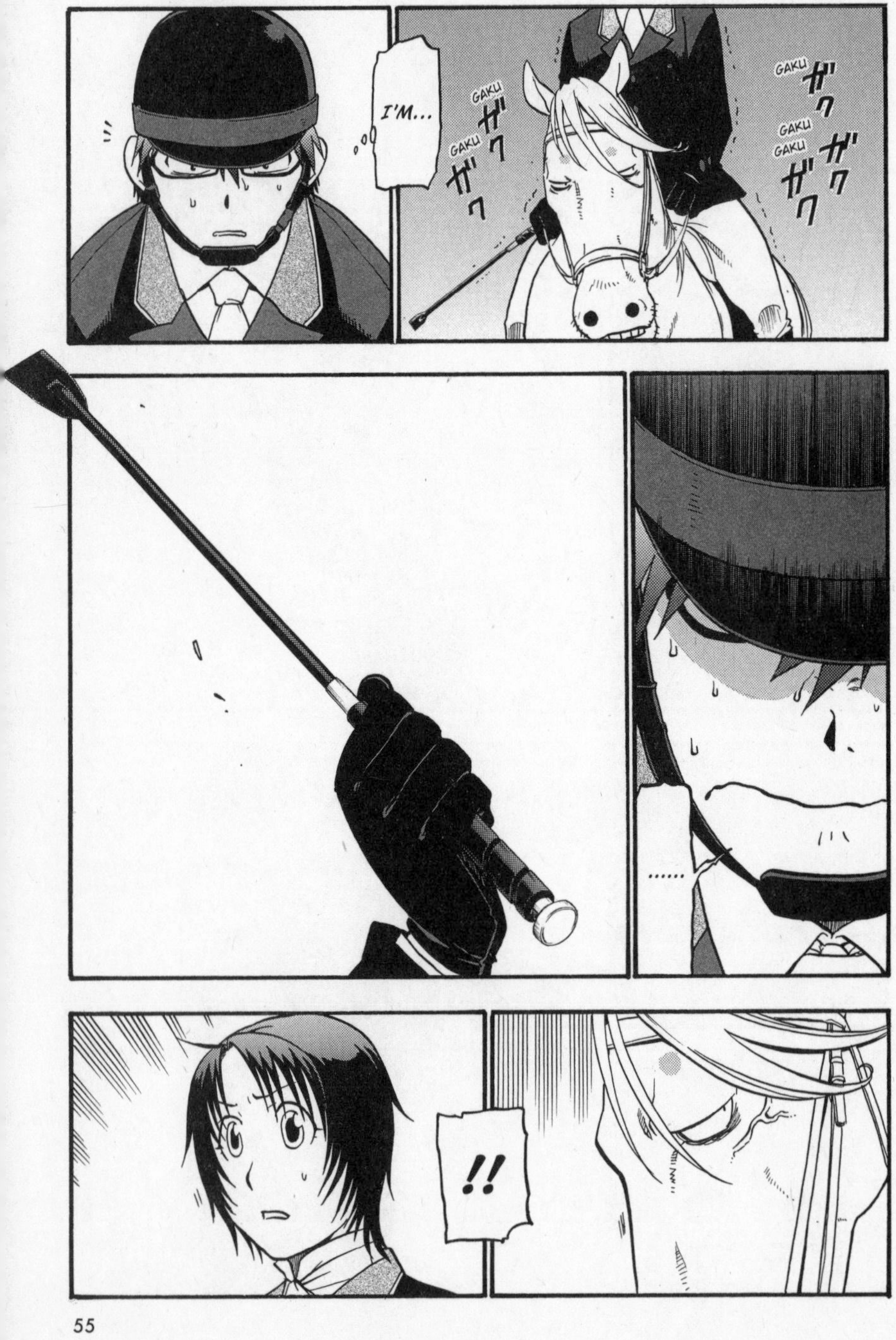
GAKU ガク
GAKU ガク
GAKU ガク
GAKU ガク
GAKU ガク
I'M...
......
!!

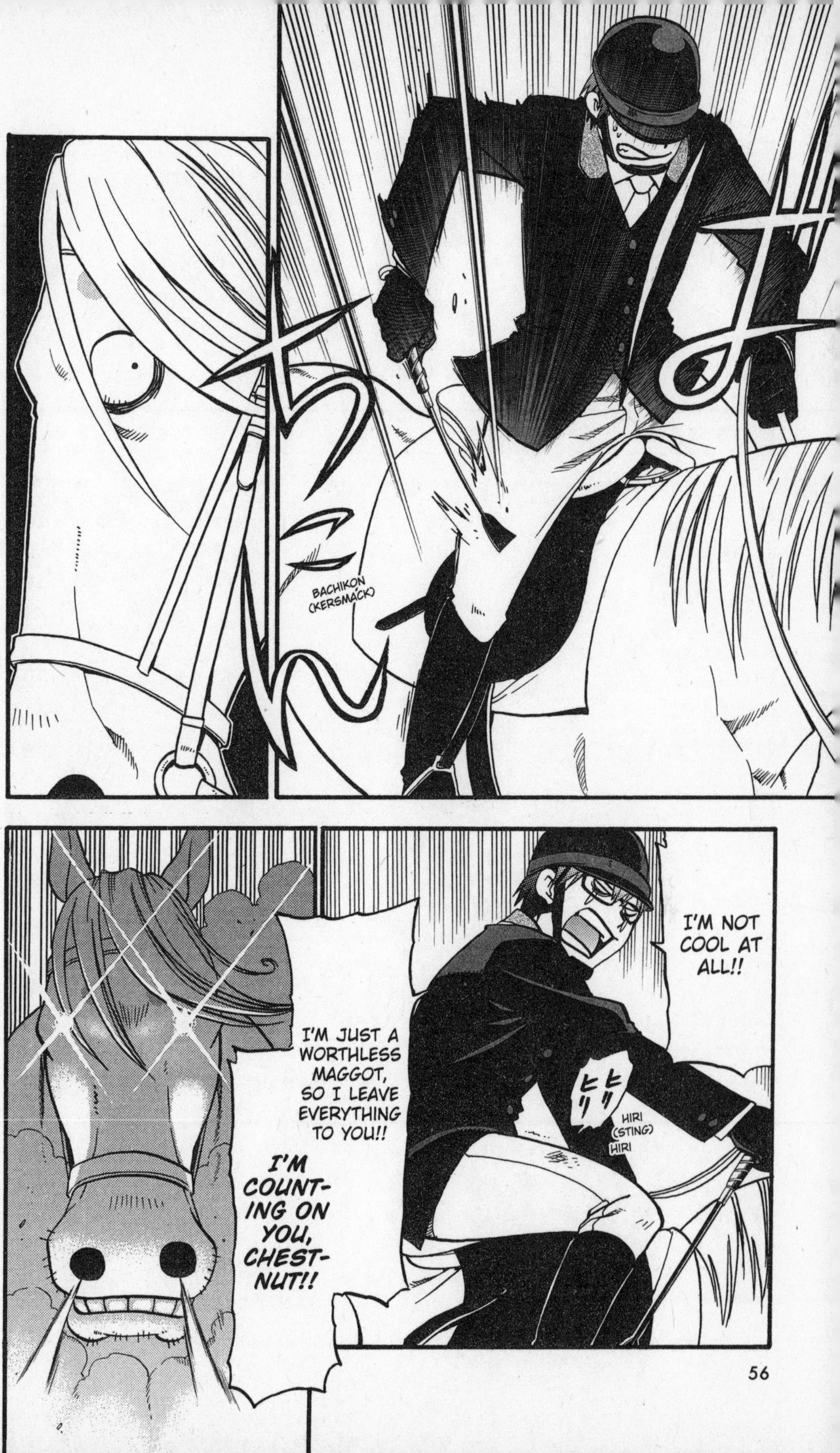
BACHIKON (KERSMACK)
I'M NOT COOL AT ALL!!
HIRI (STING) HIRI
I'M JUST A WORTHLESS MAGGOT, SO I LEAVE EVERYTHING TO YOU!!
I'M COUNTING ON YOU, CHESTNUT!!

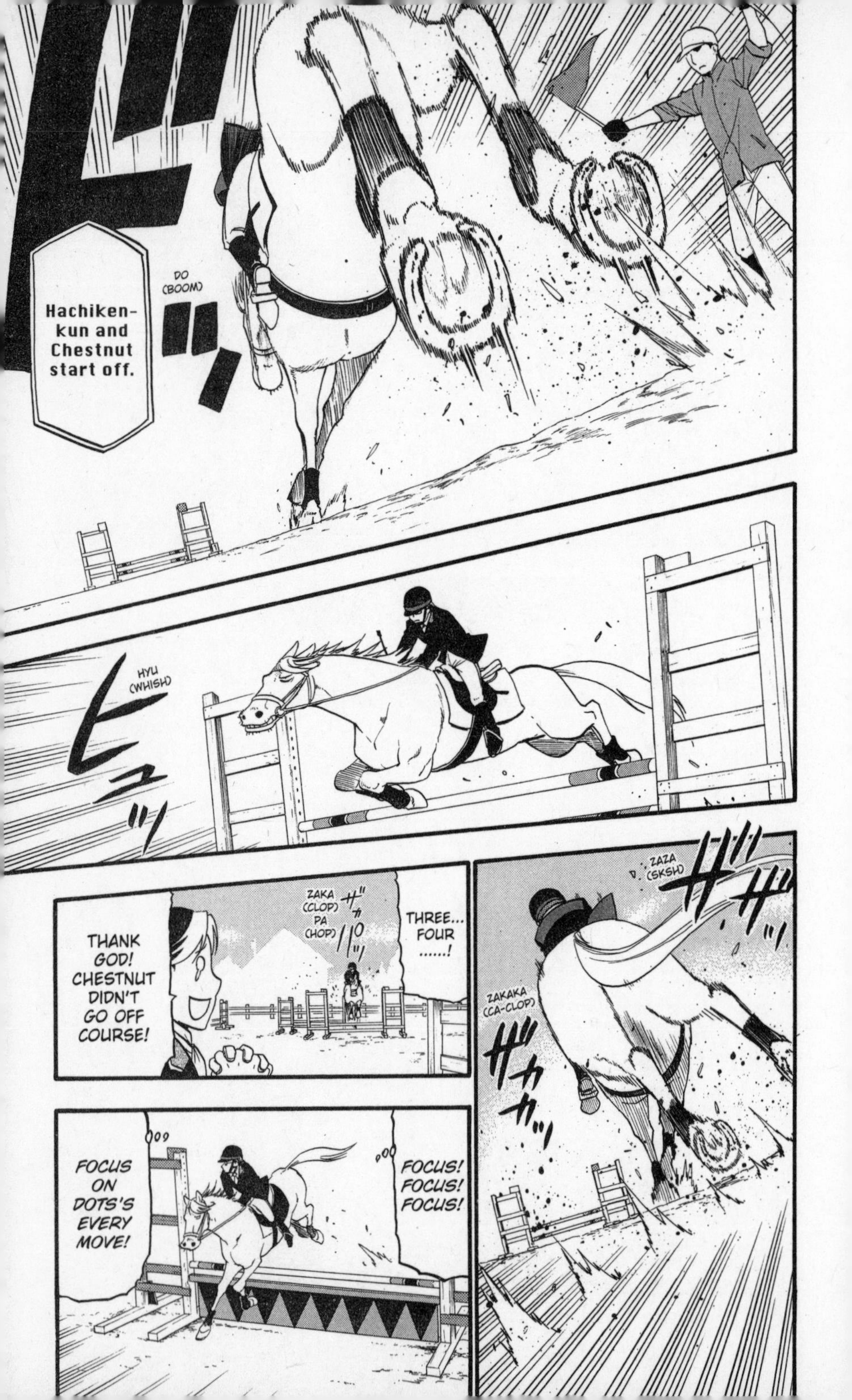
DO (BOOM)
Hachiken-kun and Chestnut start off.
HYU (WHISH)
ZAZA (SKSH)
ZAKAKA (CA-CLOP)
THREE... FOUR ......!
ZAKA (CLOP) PA (HOP)
THANK GOD! CHESTNUT DIDN'T GO OFF COURSE!
FOCUS! FOCUS! FOCUS!
FOCUS ON DOTS'S EVERY MOVE!

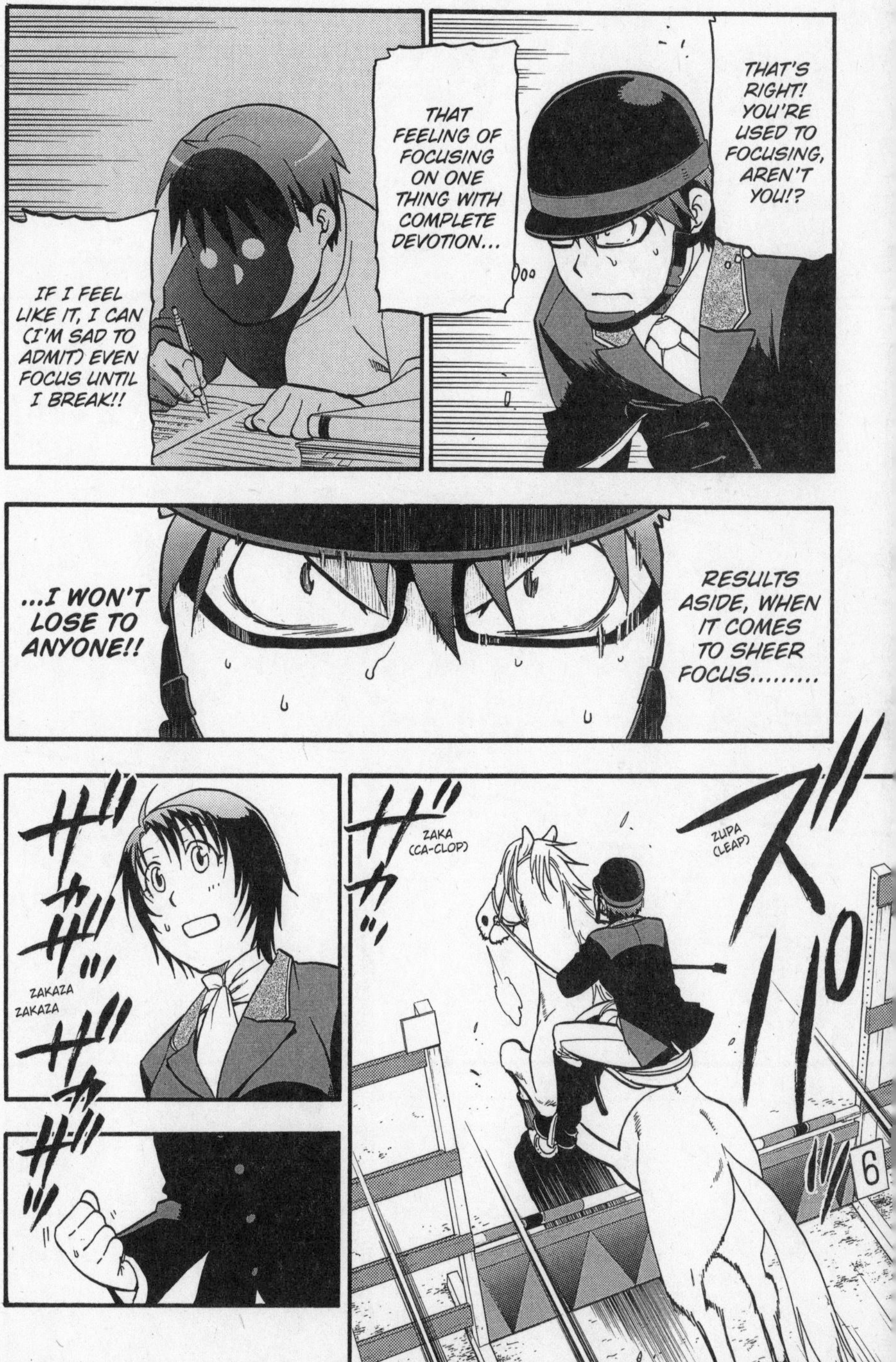
THAT'S RIGHT! YOU'RE USED TO FOCUSING, AREN'T YOU!?
THAT FEELING OF FOCUSING ON ONE THING WITH COMPLETE DEVOTION...
IF I FEEL LIKE IT, I CAN (I'M SAD TO ADMIT) EVEN FOCUS UNTIL I BREAK!!
RESULTS ASIDE, WHEN IT COMES TO SHEER FOCUS.........
...I WON'T LOSE TO ANYONE!!
ZUPA (LEAP)
ZAKA (CA-CLOP)
6
ZAKAZA ZAKAZA

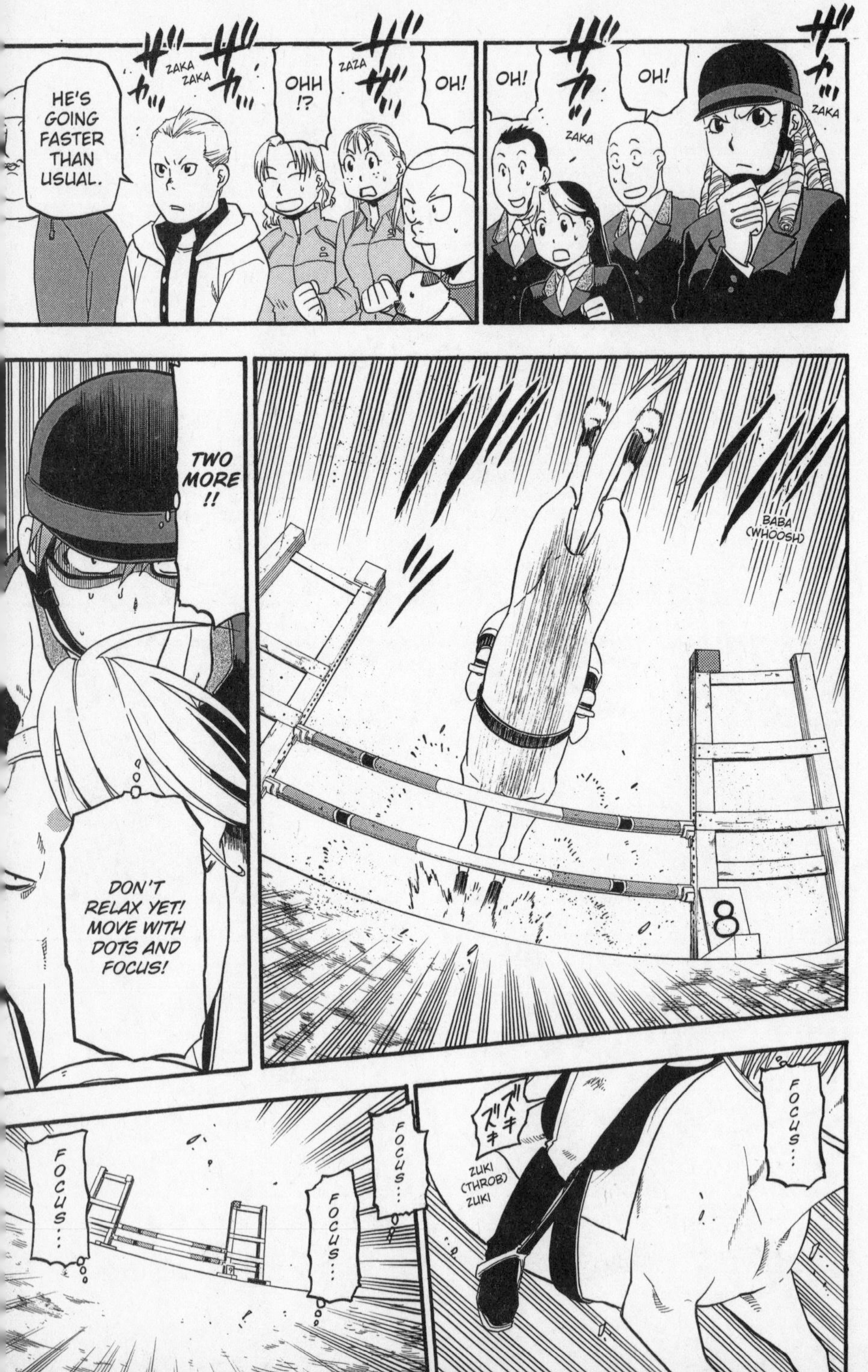
ZAKA
OH!
ZAKA
OH!
OH!
ZAZA
OHH !?
ZAKA ZAKA
HE'S GOING FASTER THAN USUAL.
BABA (WHOOSH)
TWO MORE !!
DON'T RELAX YET! MOVE WITH DOTS AND FOCUS!
FOCUS...
ZUKI (THROB) ZUKI
FOCUS...
FOCUS...
FOCUS...

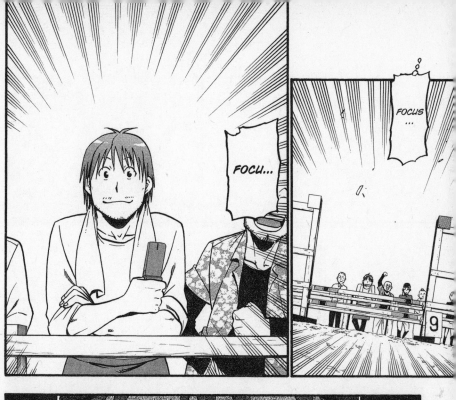

FOCU...

FOCUS
...

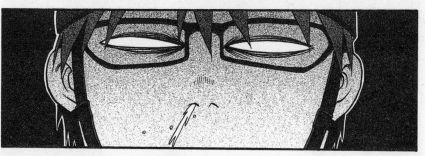

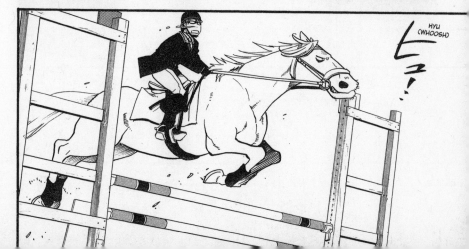

HYU
(WHOOSH)

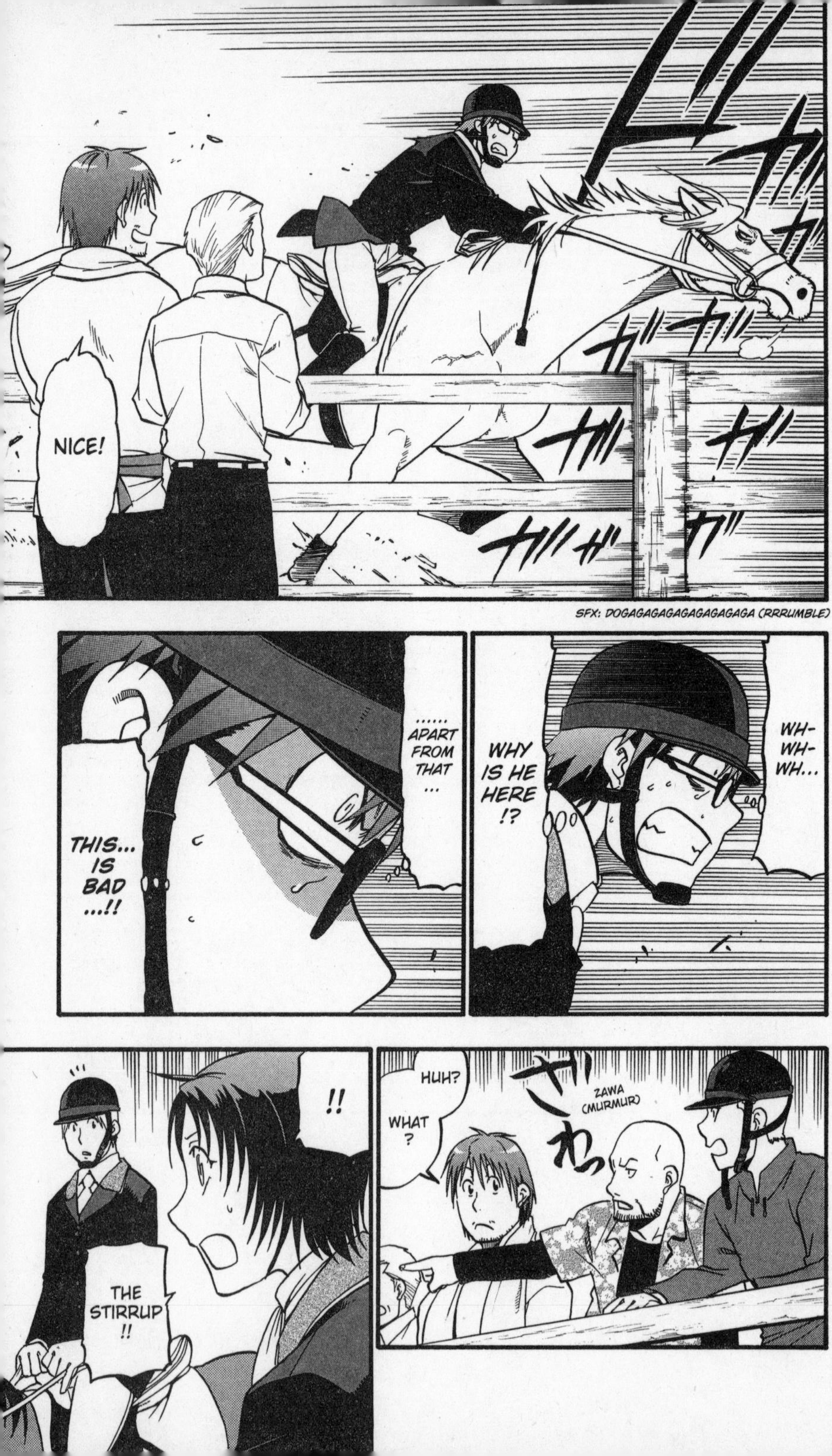
NICE!
SFX: DOGAGAGAGAGAGAGAGAGA (RRRUMBLE)
WH-WH-WH...
WHY IS HE HERE!?
......APART FROM THAT...
THIS... IS BAD ...!!
ZAWA (MURMUR)
HUH?
WHAT?
!!
THE STIRRUP !!

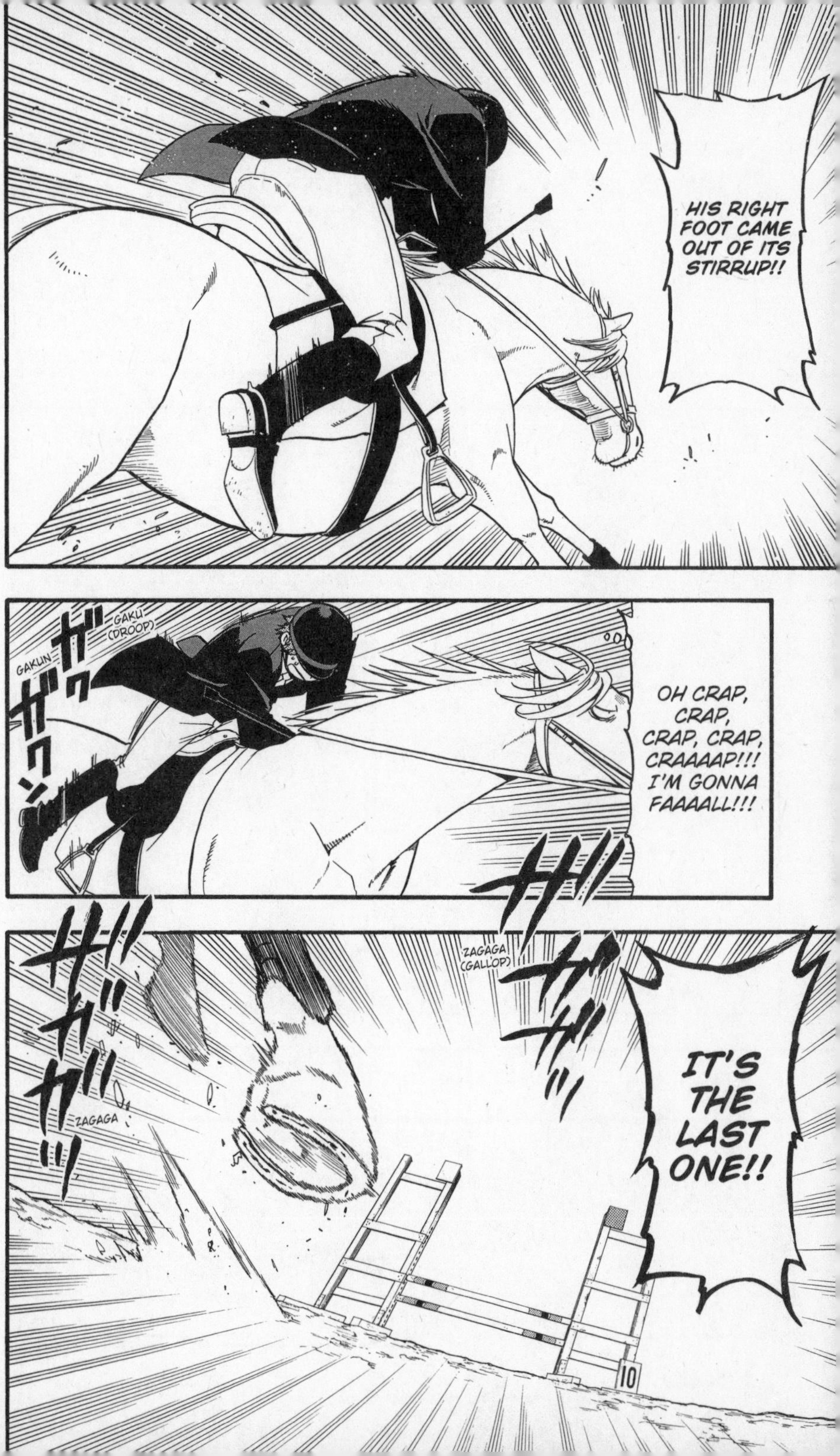
HIS RIGHT FOOT CAME OUT OF ITS STIRRUP!!
OH CRAP, CRAP, CRAP, CRAP, CRAAAAP!!! I'M GONNA FAAAALL!!!
GAKU (DROOP)
GAKUN
IT'S THE LAST ONE!!
ZAGAGA (GALLOP)
ZAGAGA
10

Silver Spoon

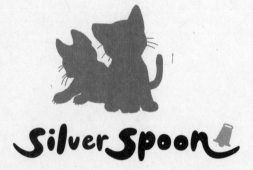

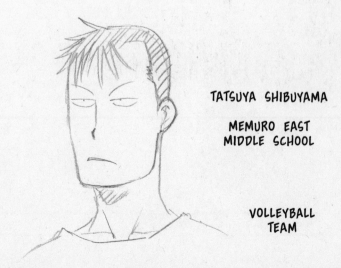

TATSUYA SHIBUYAMA

MEMURO EAST
MIDDLE SCHOOL

VOLLEYBALL
TEAM

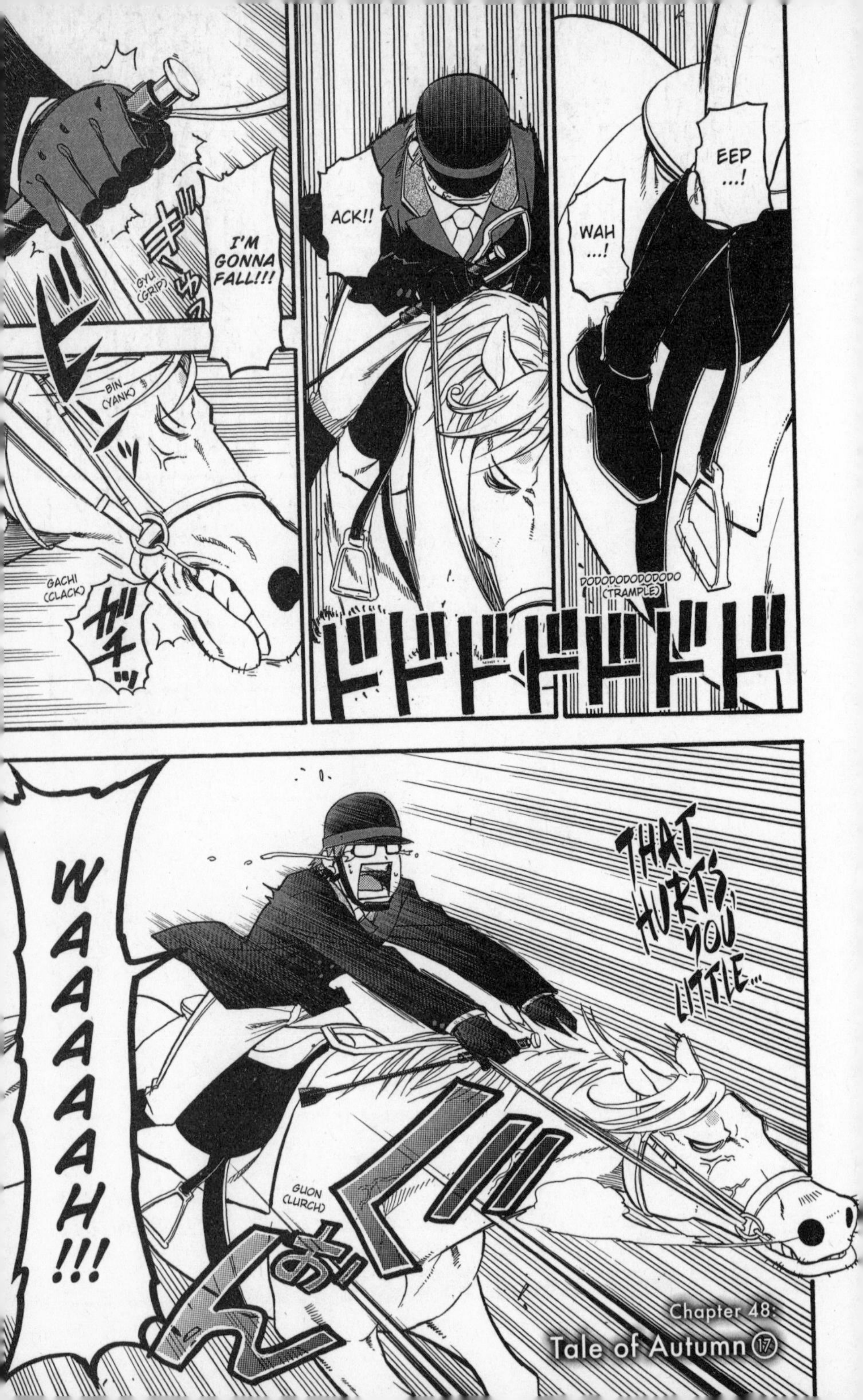
EEP ...!
WAH ...!
DODODODODODODO (TRAMPLE)
ACK!!
I'M GONNA FALL!!!
GYU (GRIP)
BIN (YANK)
GACHI (CLACK)
THAT HURTS, YOU LITTLE...
WAAAAAAAH!!!
GUON (LURCH)

Chapter 48: Tale of Autumn ⑰

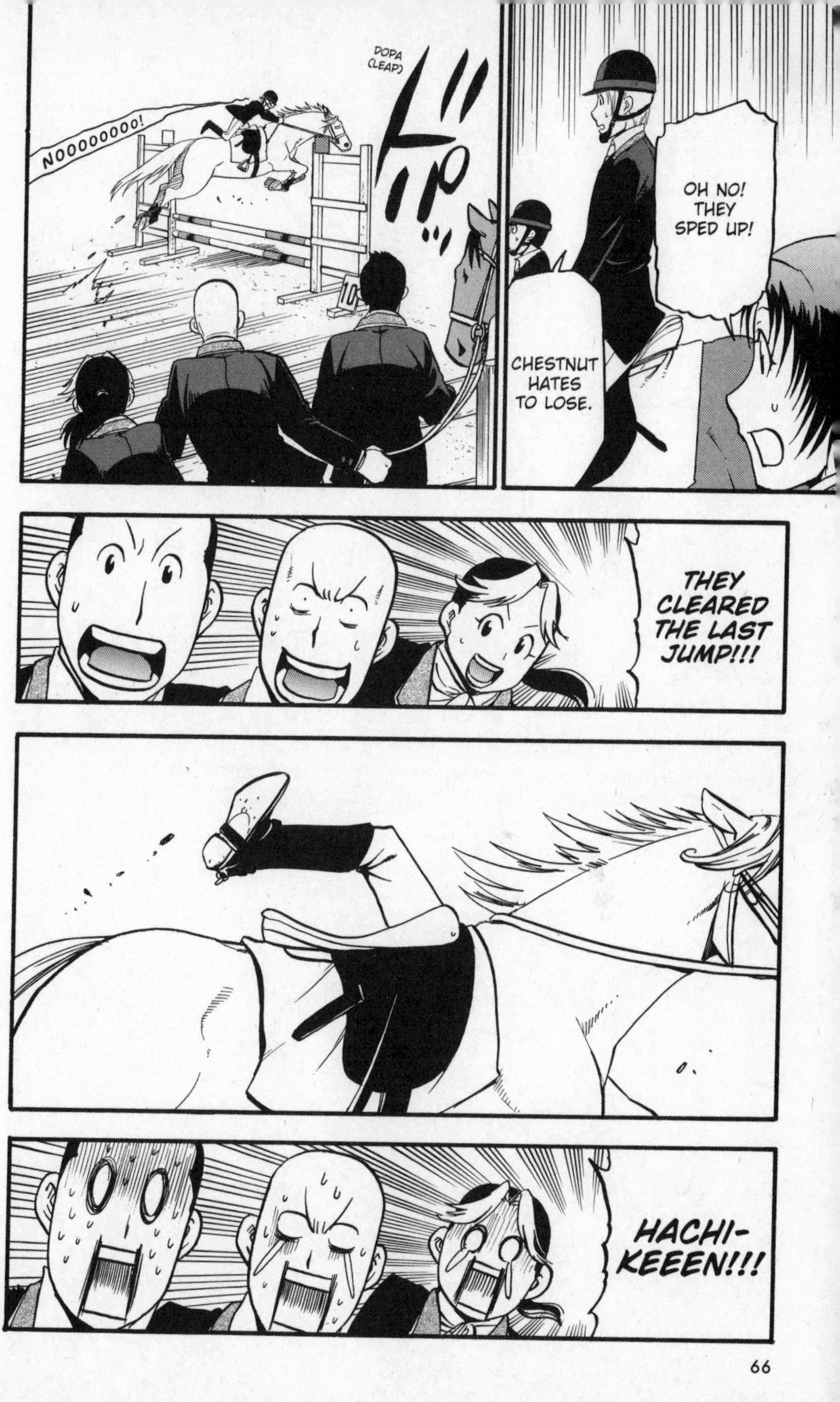
OH NO! THEY SPED UP!
CHESTNUT HATES TO LOSE.
DOPA (LEAP)
NOOOOOOOOO!
THEY CLEARED THE LAST JUMP!!!
HACHI-KEEEN!!!

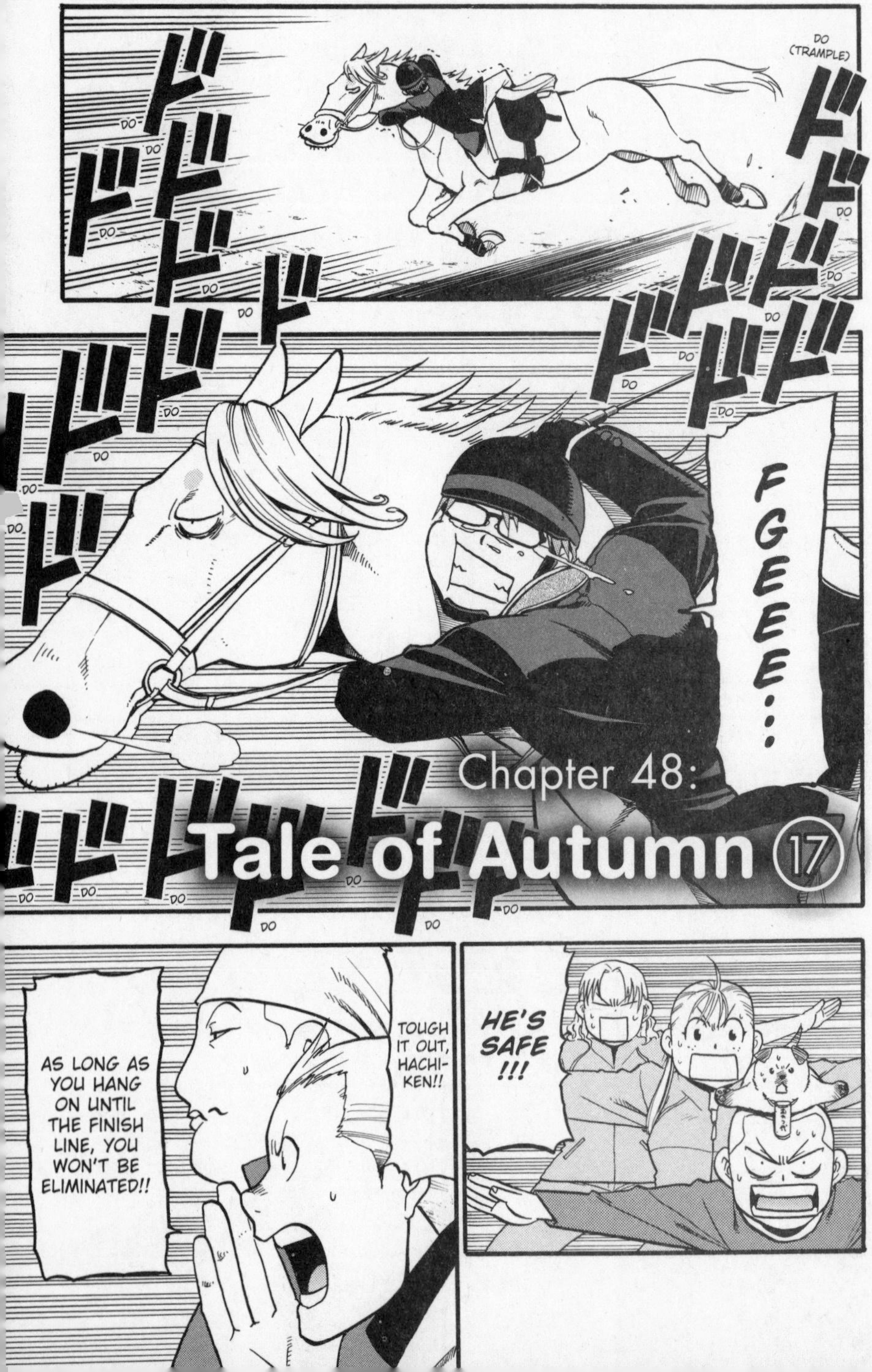
ドドドドド
DO (TRAMPLE)
ドドドドドドド
FGEEEE...
Chapter 48:
Tale of Autumn ⑰
HE'S SAFE!!!
TOUGH IT OUT, HACHI-KEN!!
AS LONG AS YOU HANG ON UNTIL THE FINISH LINE, YOU WON'T BE ELIMINATED!!

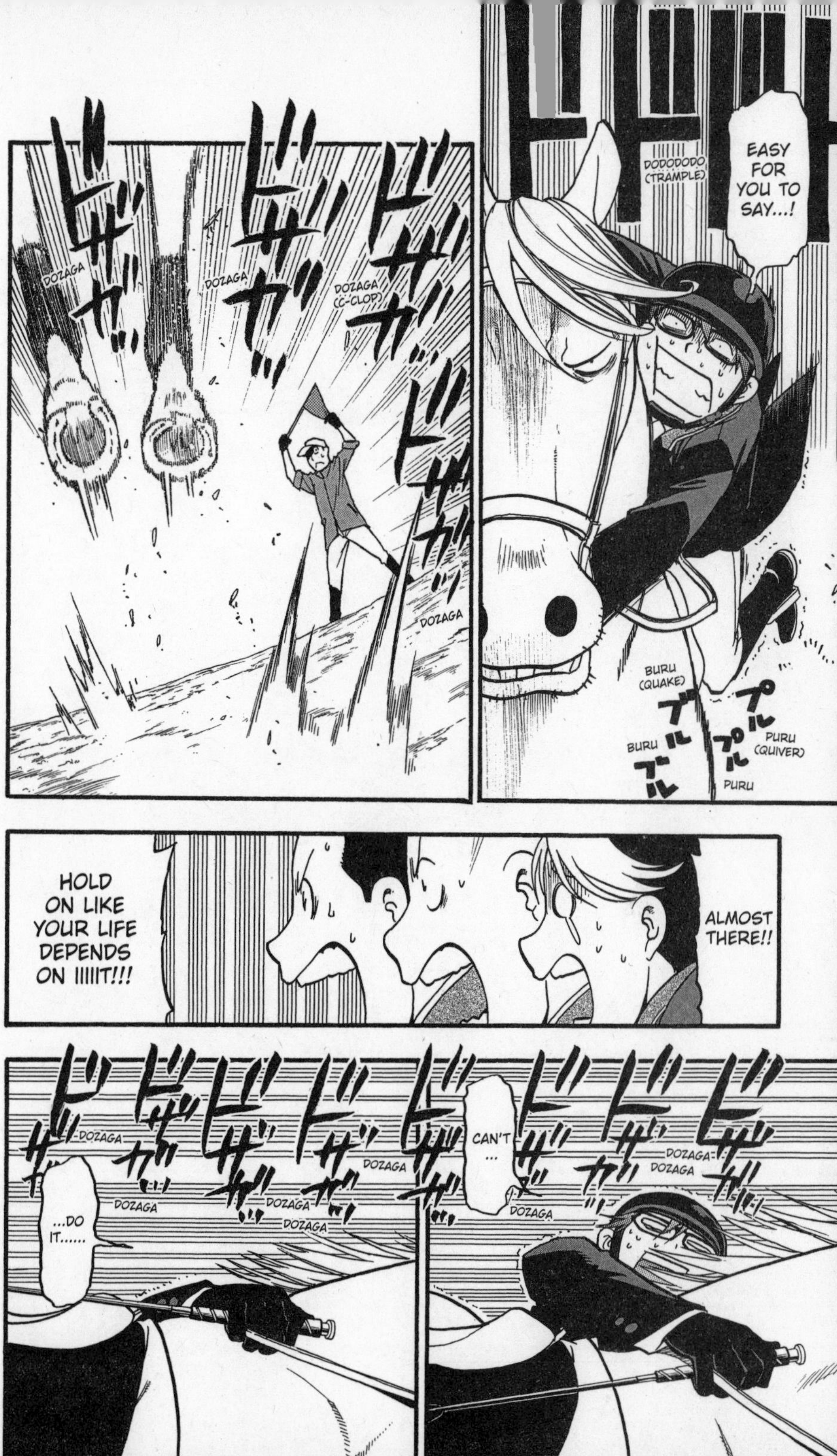

DODODODO (TRAMPLE)
EASY FOR YOU TO SAY...!
BURU (QUAKE)
BURU
PURU (QUIVER)
PURU
DOZAGA (C-CLOP)
DOZAGA
DOZAGA
DOZAGA
ALMOST THERE!!
HOLD ON LIKE YOUR LIFE DEPENDS ON IIIIIT!!!
DOZAGA DOZAGA
CAN'T ...
DOZAGA
DOZAGA
DOZAGA
DOZAGA
DOZAGA
DOZAGA
...DO IT......

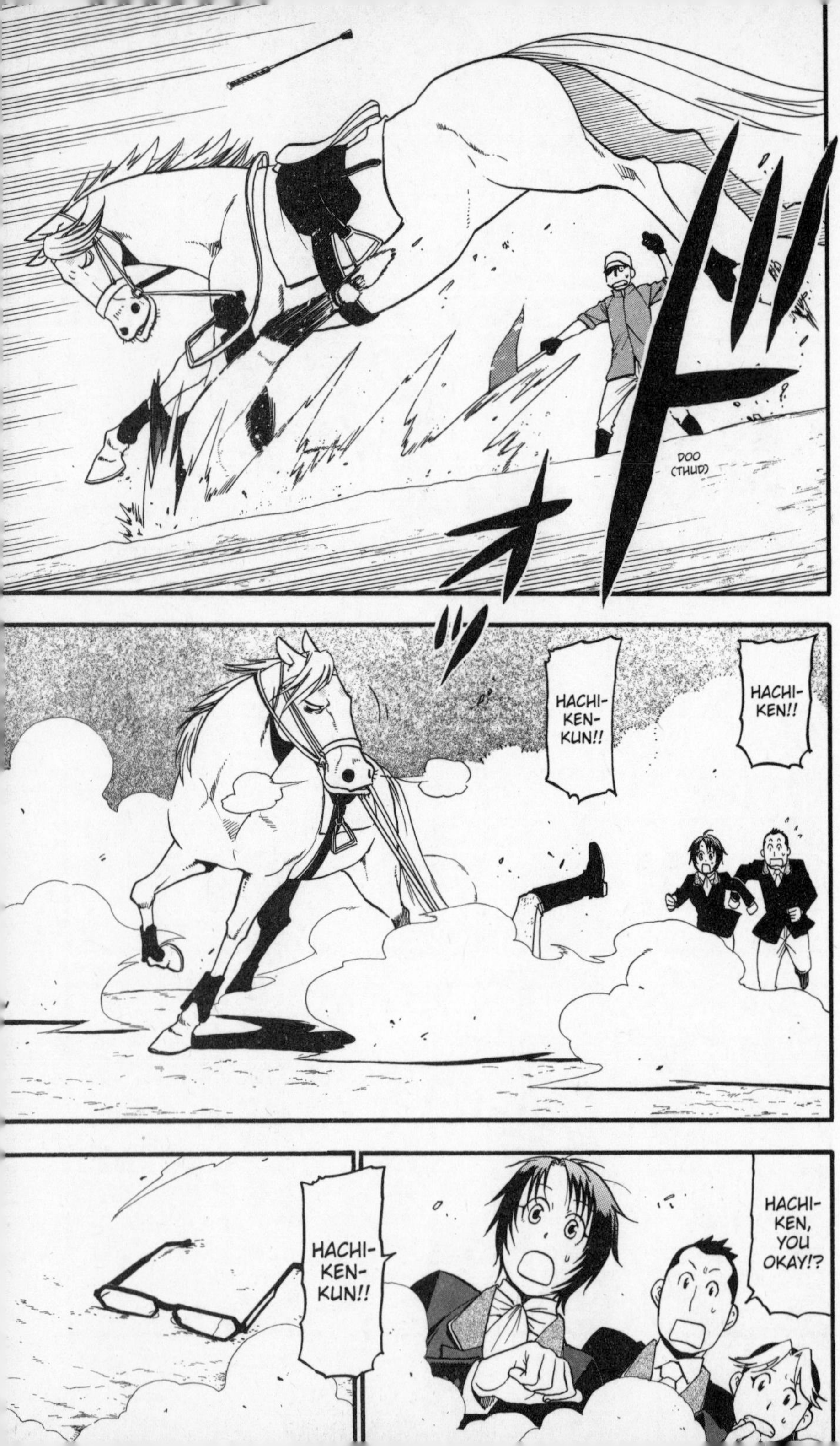
DOO
(THUD)
HACHI-KEN!!
HACHI-KEN-KUN!!
HACHI-KEN, YOU OKAY!?
HACHI-KEN-KUN!!

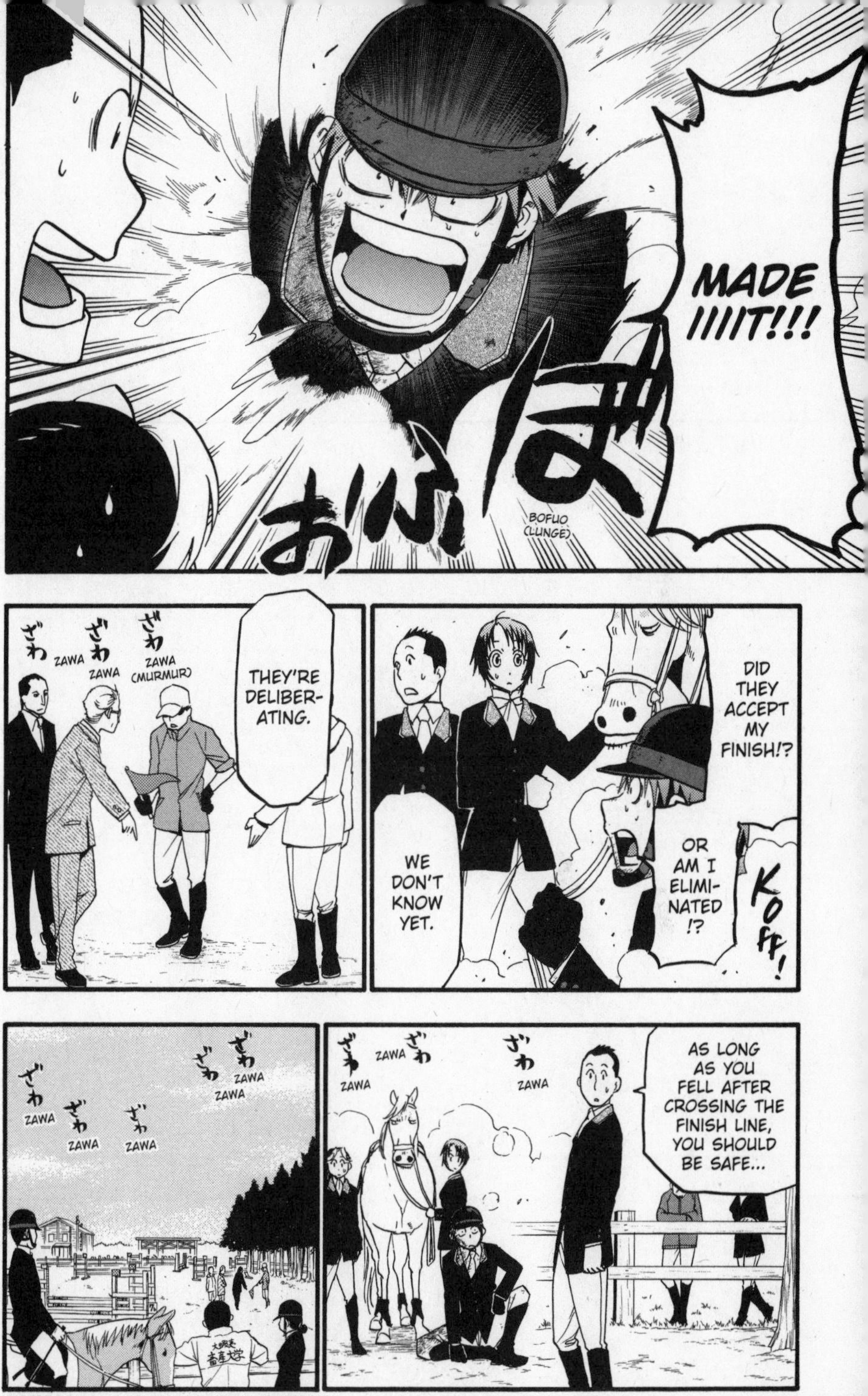
MADE IIIIIT!!!
ぼふお
BOFUO (LUNGE)
DID THEY ACCEPT MY FINISH!?
OR AM I ELIMINATED!?
KOFF!
WE DON'T KNOW YET.
THEY'RE DELIBERATING.
ざわ
ざわ ZAWA
ざわ ZAWA (MURMUR)
AS LONG AS YOU FELL AFTER CROSSING THE FINISH LINE, YOU SHOULD BE SAFE...
ざわ ZAWA
ざわ ZAWA
ざわ ZAWA
ざわ ZAWA
ざわ ZAWA
ざわ ZAWA
ざわ ZAWA
ざわ ZAWA

JACKET: OOEZO UNIVERSITY OF ANIMAL HUSBANDRY

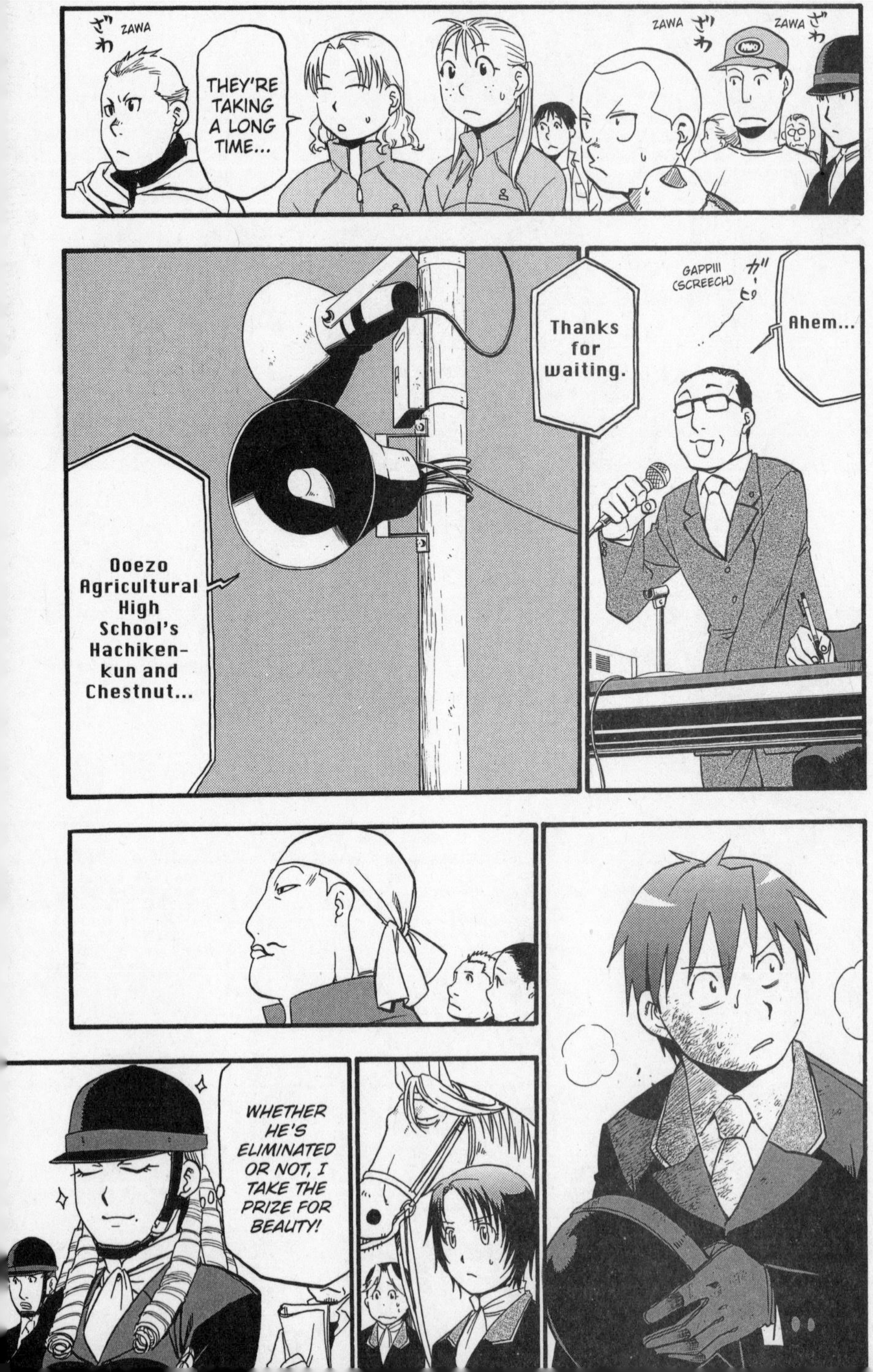
ZAWA ざわ
ZAWA ざわ
THEY'RE TAKING A LONG TIME...
ざわ ZAWA
Ahem...
GAPPIII (SCREECH) ガピ
Thanks for waiting.
Ooezo Agricultural High School's Hachiken-kun and Chestnut...
WHETHER HE'S ELIMINATED OR NOT, I TAKE THE PRIZE FOR BEAUTY!

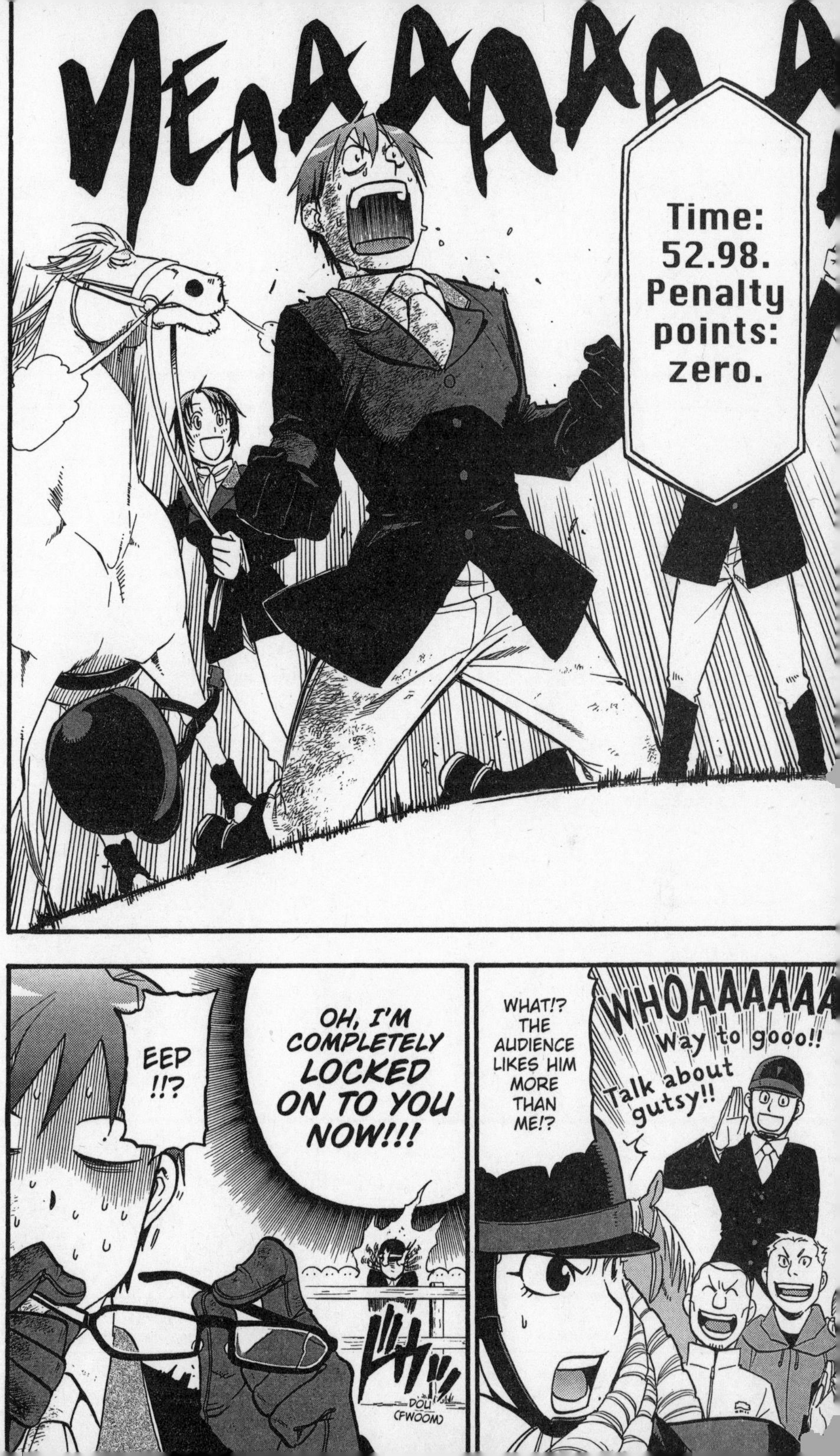
NEAAAAAA
Time: 52.98. Penalty points: zero.
WHOAAAAAA
Way to gooo!!
Talk about gutsy!!
WHAT!? THE AUDIENCE LIKES HIM MORE THAN ME!?
OH, I'M COMPLETELY LOCKED ON TO YOU NOW!!!
EEP !!?
DOU (FWOOM)

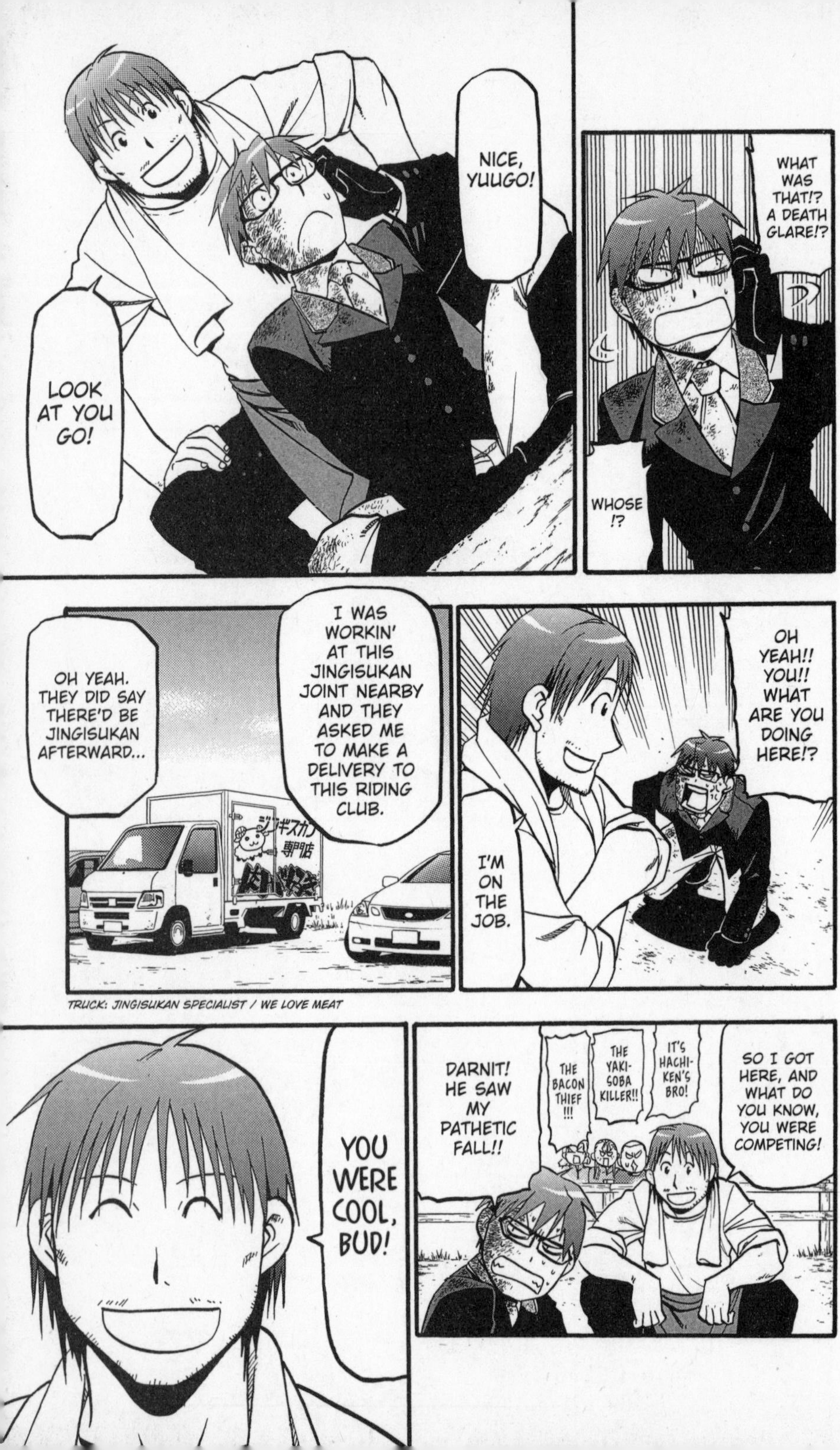
WHAT WAS THAT!? A DEATH GLARE!?
WHOSE!?
NICE, YUUGO!
LOOK AT YOU GO!
OH YEAH!! YOU!! WHAT ARE YOU DOING HERE!?
I'M ON THE JOB.
I WAS WORKIN' AT THIS JINGISUKAN JOINT NEARBY AND THEY ASKED ME TO MAKE A DELIVERY TO THIS RIDING CLUB.
OH YEAH. THEY DID SAY THERE'D BE JINGISUKAN AFTERWARD...
TRUCK: JINGISUKAN SPECIALIST / WE LOVE MEAT
SO I GOT HERE, AND WHAT DO YOU KNOW, YOU WERE COMPETING!
IT'S HACHIKEN'S BRO!
THE YAKI-SOBA KILLER!!
THE BACON THIEF!!!
DARNIT! HE SAW MY PATHETIC FALL!!
YOU WERE COOL, BUD!

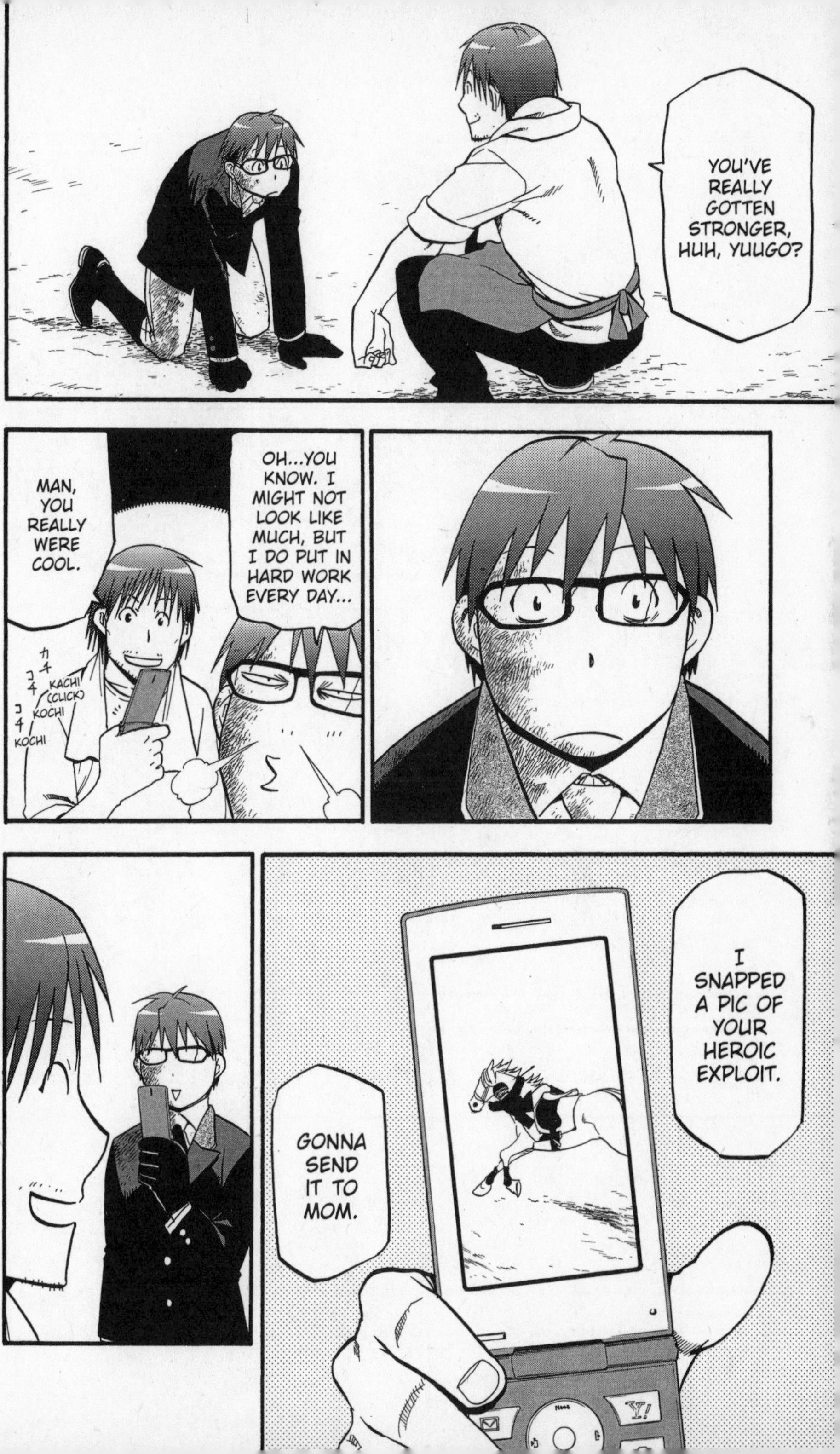
YOU'VE REALLY GOTTEN STRONGER, HUH, YUUGO?
OH...YOU KNOW. I MIGHT NOT LOOK LIKE MUCH, BUT I DO PUT IN HARD WORK EVERY DAY...
MAN, YOU REALLY WERE COOL.
カチ KACHI (CLICK)
コチ KOCHI
コチ KOCHI
I SNAPPED A PIC OF YOUR HEROIC EXPLOIT.
GONNA SEND IT TO MOM.

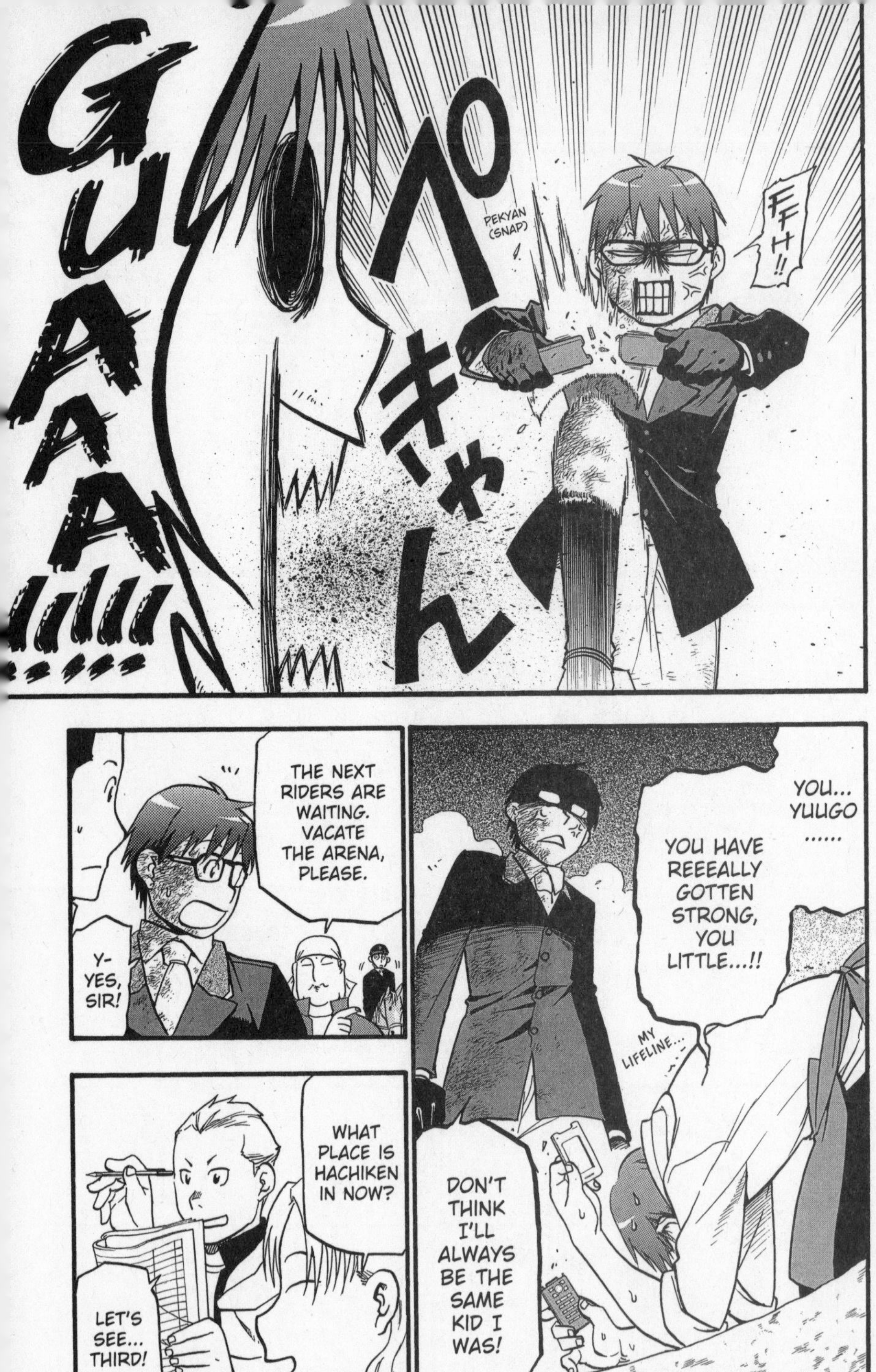
FFH!!
ぺきゃん
PEKYAN (SNAP)
GUAAA!!!!!
YOU... YUUGO ......
YOU HAVE REEEALLY GOTTEN STRONG, YOU LITTLE...!!
MY LIFELINE...
DON'T THINK I'LL ALWAYS BE THE SAME KID I WAS!
THE NEXT RIDERS ARE WAITING. VACATE THE ARENA, PLEASE.
Y-YES, SIR!
WHAT PLACE IS HACHIKEN IN NOW?
LET'S SEE... THIRD!

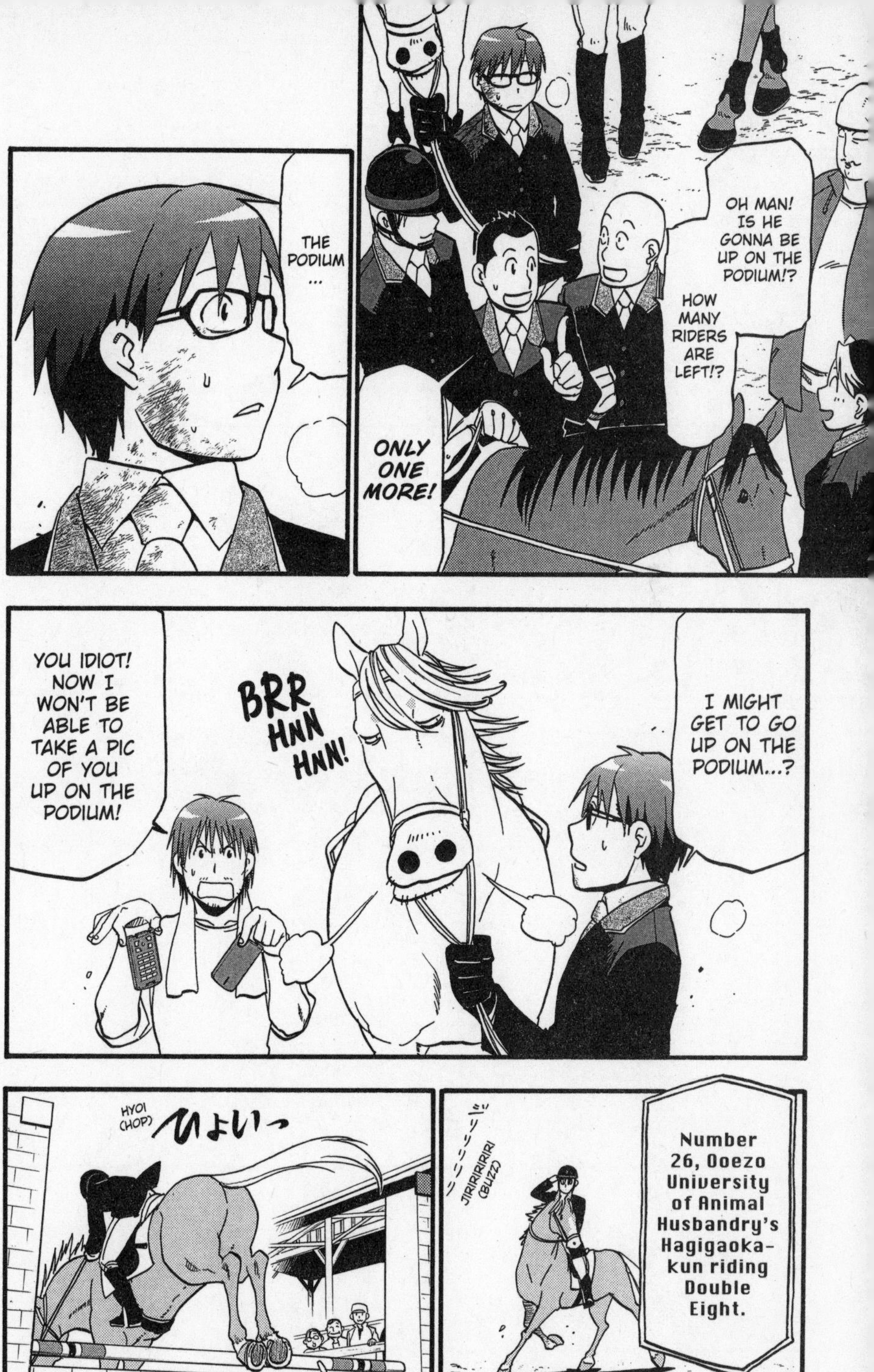
OH MAN! IS HE GONNA BE UP ON THE PODIUM!?
HOW MANY RIDERS ARE LEFT!?
ONLY ONE MORE!
THE PODIUM ...
I MIGHT GET TO GO UP ON THE PODIUM...?
BRR HNN HNN!
YOU IDIOT! NOW I WON'T BE ABLE TO TAKE A PIC OF YOU UP ON THE PODIUM!
Number 26, Ooezo University of Animal Husbandry's Hagigaoka-kun riding Double Eight.
ジリリリリ
JIRIRIRIRI (BUZZ)
HYOI (HOP)
ひよいっ

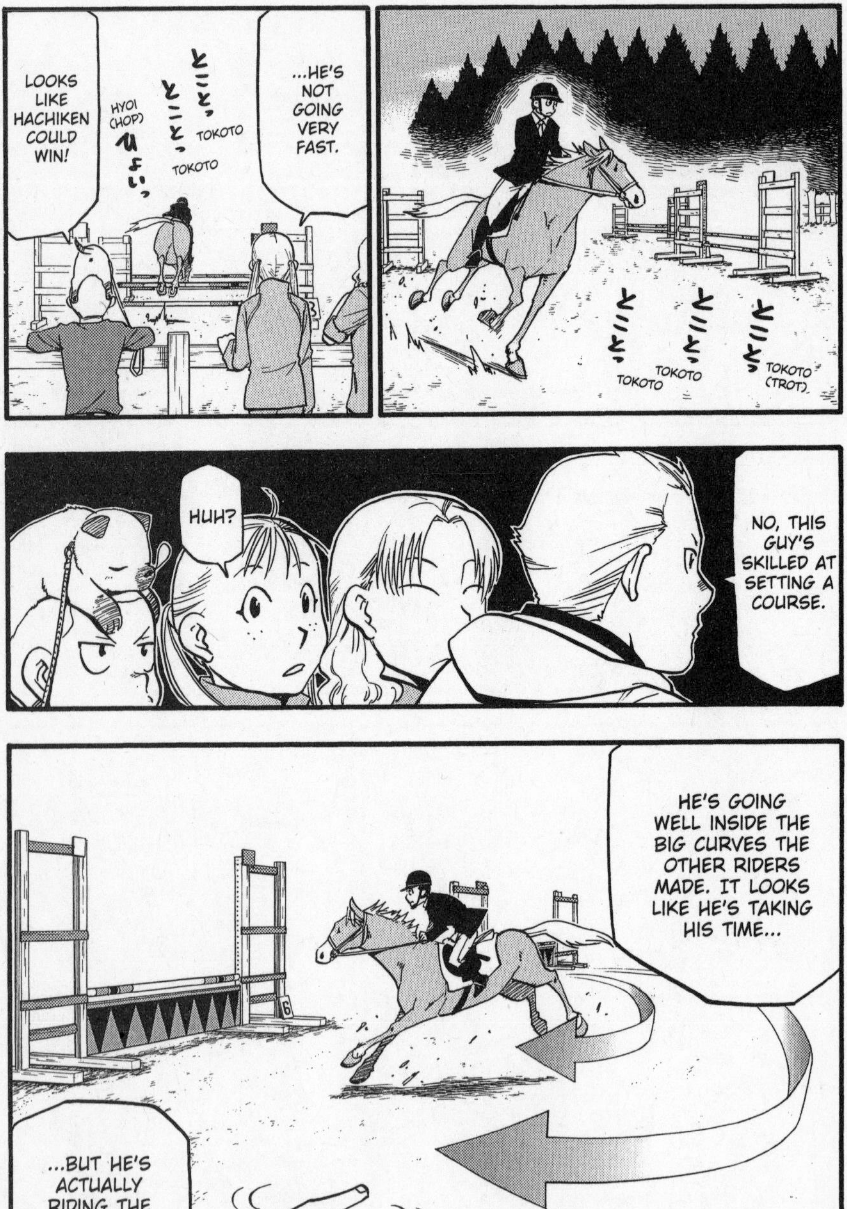
とことっ
とことっ
とことっ
TOKOTO (TROT)
TOKOTO
TOKOTO
...HE'S NOT GOING VERY FAST.
とことっ
とことっ
TOKOTO
TOKOTO
ひょいっ
HYOI (HOP)
LOOKS LIKE HACHIKEN COULD WIN!
NO, THIS GUY'S SKILLED AT SETTING A COURSE.
HUH?
HE'S GOING WELL INSIDE THE BIG CURVES THE OTHER RIDERS MADE. IT LOOKS LIKE HE'S TAKING HIS TIME...
...BUT HE'S ACTUALLY RIDING THE SHORTEST POSSIBLE DISTANCE.

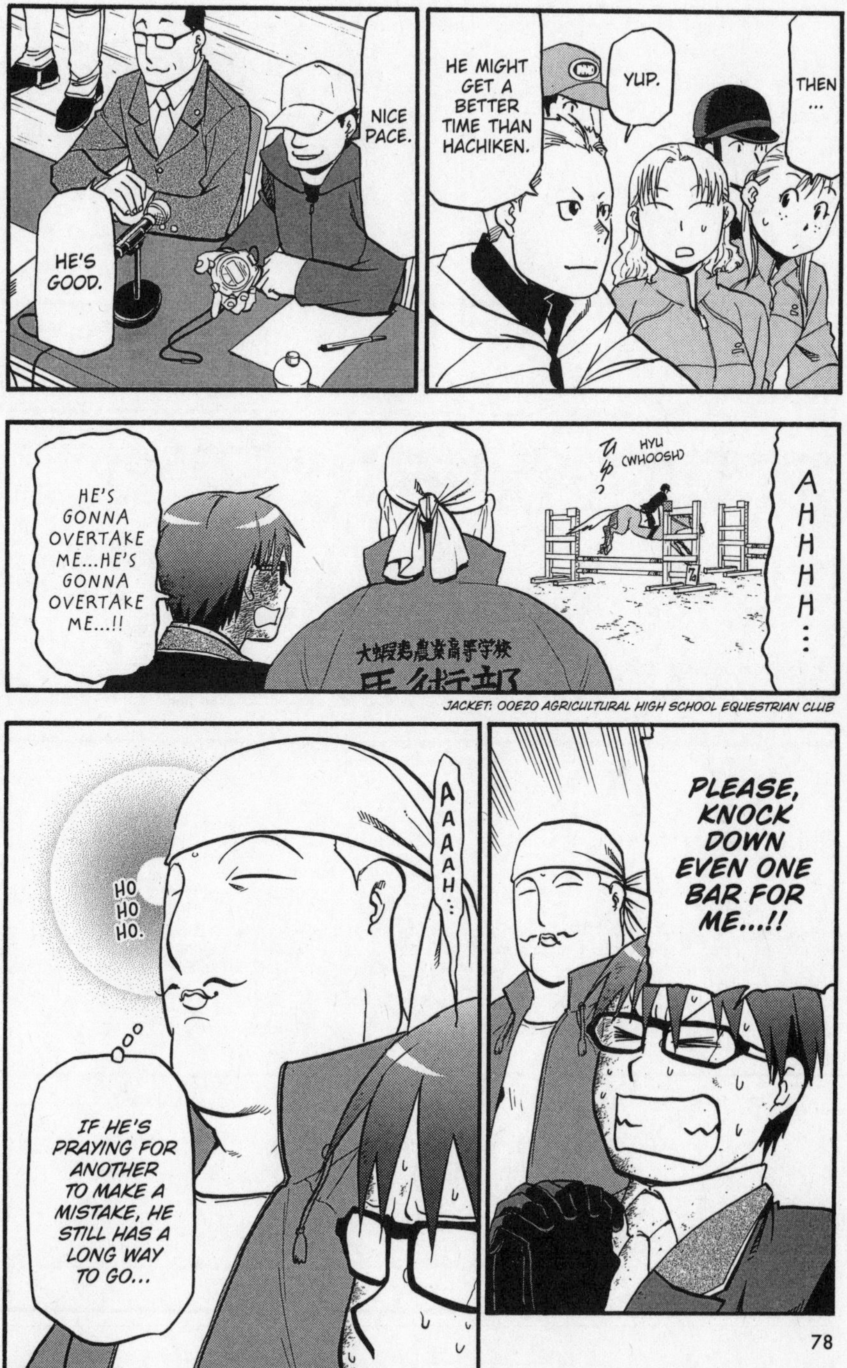
THEN...
YUP.
HE MIGHT GET A BETTER TIME THAN HACHIKEN.
NICE PACE.
HE'S GOOD.
AHHHH...
ひゅっ
HYU (WHOOSH)
HE'S GONNA OVERTAKE ME...HE'S GONNA OVERTAKE ME...!!
PLEASE, KNOCK DOWN EVEN ONE BAR FOR ME...!!
AAAAH...
HO HO HO.
IF HE'S PRAYING FOR ANOTHER TO MAKE A MISTAKE, HE STILL HAS A LONG WAY TO GO...

JACKET: OOEZO AGRICULTURAL HIGH SCHOOL EQUESTRIAN CLUB

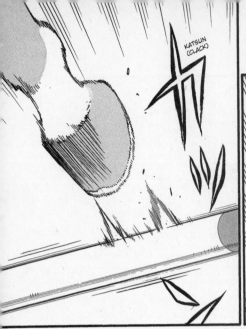

KATSUN
(CLACK)

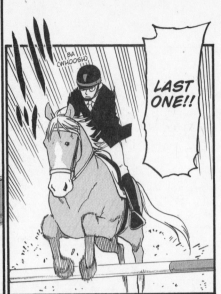

BA
(WHOOSH)

LAST
ONE!!

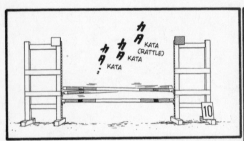

カタ
KATA

カタ
KATA

カタ
KATA
(RATTLE)

10

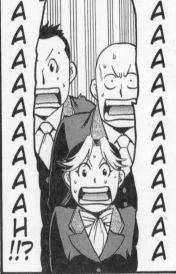

AAAAAAAAAH!!?

AAAAAAAAAAA

シン
SHIN
(SILENT)....

10

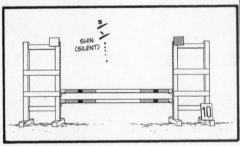

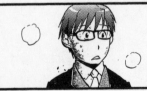

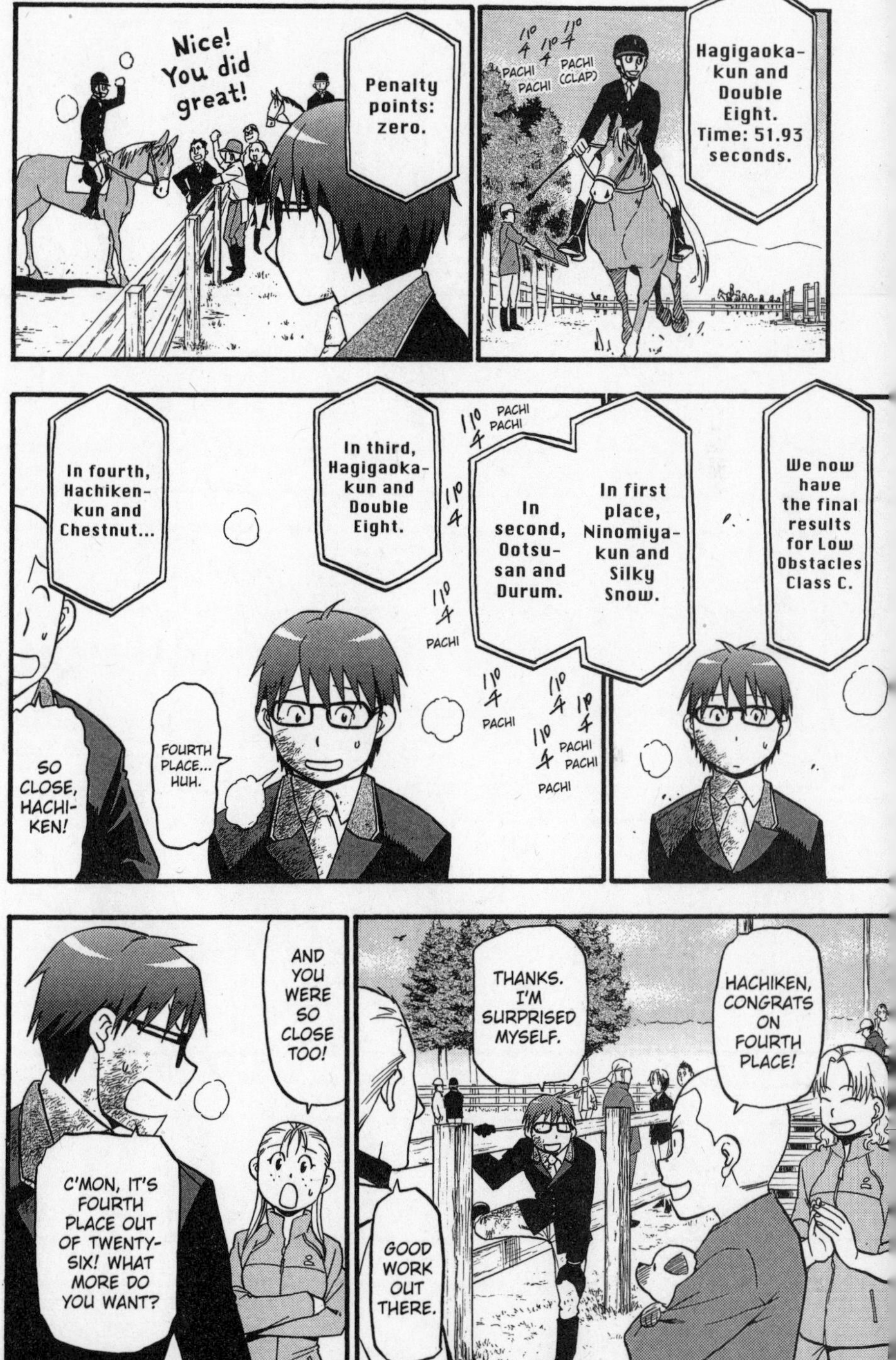
PACHI PACHI PACHI (CLAP)
Hagigaoka-kun and Double Eight. Time: 51.93 seconds.
Penalty points: zero.
Nice! You did great!
We now have the final results for Low Obstacles Class C.
PACHI PACHI
In first place, Ninomiya-kun and Silky Snow.
In second, Ootsu-san and Durum.
In third, Hagigaoka-kun and Double Eight.
In fourth, Hachiken-kun and Chestnut...
PACHI
PACHI
PACHI PACHI
PACHI
FOURTH PLACE... HUH.
SO CLOSE, HACHIKEN!
HACHIKEN, CONGRATS ON FOURTH PLACE!
THANKS. I'M SURPRISED MYSELF.
GOOD WORK OUT THERE.
AND YOU WERE SO CLOSE TOO!
C'MON, IT'S FOURTH PLACE OUT OF TWENTY-SIX! WHAT MORE DO YOU WANT?

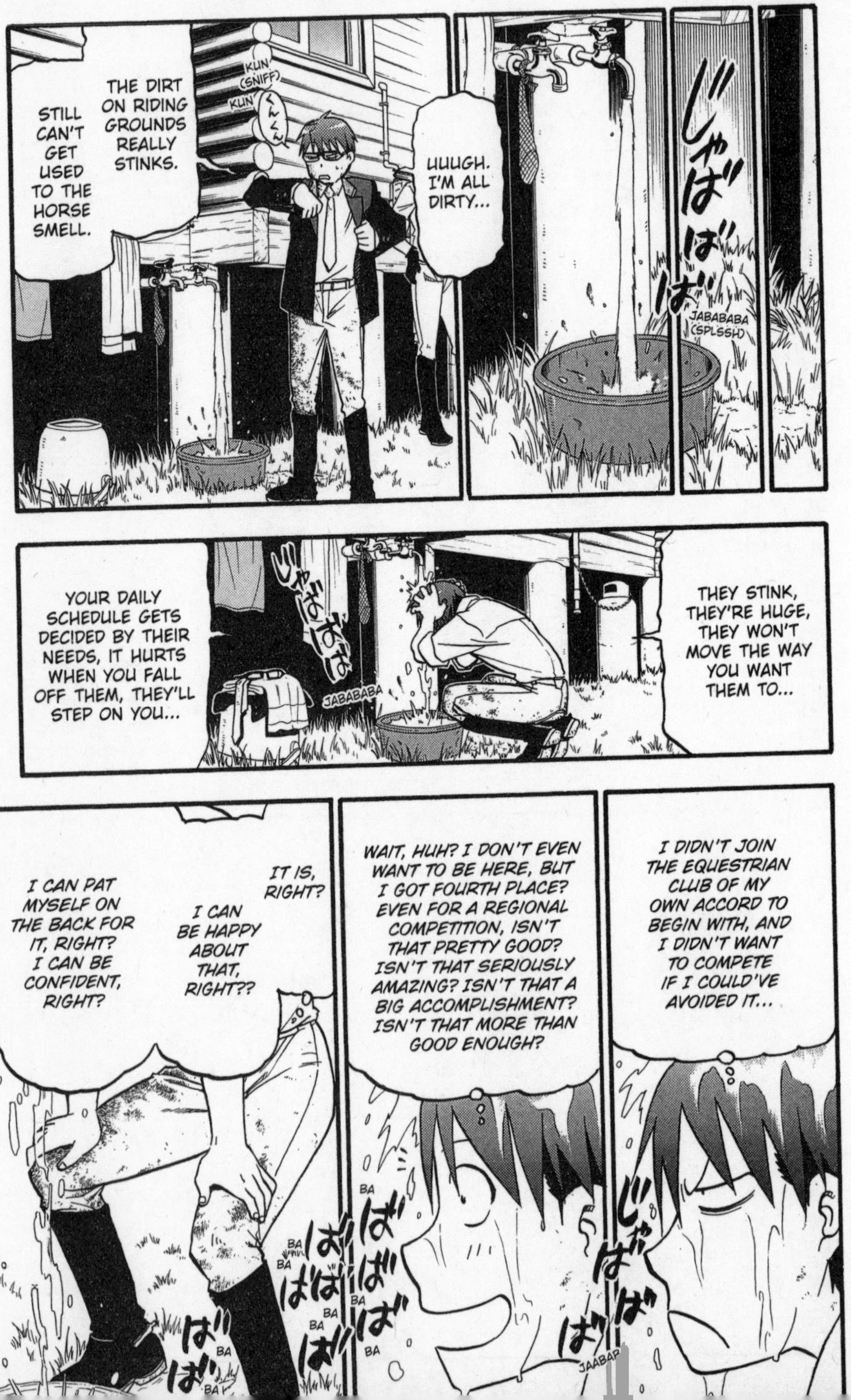

じゃばばば
JABABABA (SPLSSH)
UUUGH. I'M ALL DIRTY...
KUN (SNIFF) KUN
くんくん
THE DIRT ON RIDING GROUNDS REALLY STINKS.
STILL CAN'T GET USED TO THE HORSE SMELL.
THEY STINK, THEY'RE HUGE, THEY WON'T MOVE THE WAY YOU WANT THEM TO...
じゃばばば
JABABABA
YOUR DAILY SCHEDULE GETS DECIDED BY THEIR NEEDS, IT HURTS WHEN YOU FALL OFF THEM, THEY'LL STEP ON YOU...
I DIDN'T JOIN THE EQUESTRIAN CLUB OF MY OWN ACCORD TO BEGIN WITH, AND I DIDN'T WANT TO COMPETE IF I COULD'VE AVOIDED IT...
じゃばば
WAIT, HUH? I DON'T EVEN WANT TO BE HERE, BUT I GOT FOURTH PLACE? EVEN FOR A REGIONAL COMPETITION, ISN'T THAT PRETTY GOOD? ISN'T THAT SERIOUSLY AMAZING? ISN'T THAT A BIG ACCOMPLISHMENT? ISN'T THAT MORE THAN GOOD ENOUGH?
ばばば
BA BA BA
ばばば
BA BA BA
IT IS, RIGHT?
I CAN BE HAPPY ABOUT THAT, RIGHT??
I CAN PAT MYSELF ON THE BACK FOR IT, RIGHT? I CAN BE CONFIDENT, RIGHT?
ばば
BA BA

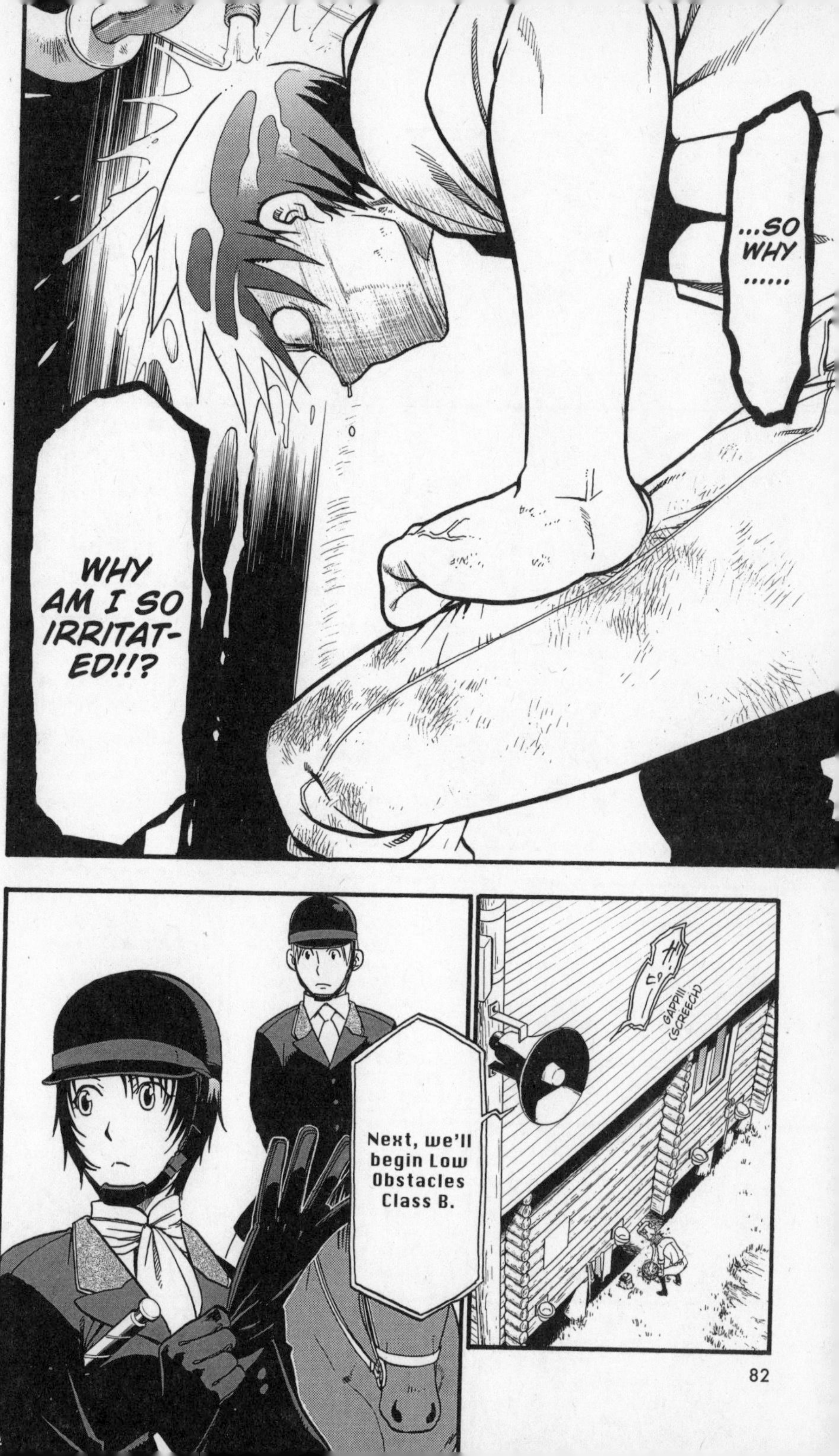
...SO WHY ......
WHY AM I SO IRRITAT-ED!!?
GAPP!! (SCREECH)
Next, we'll begin Low Obstacles Class B.

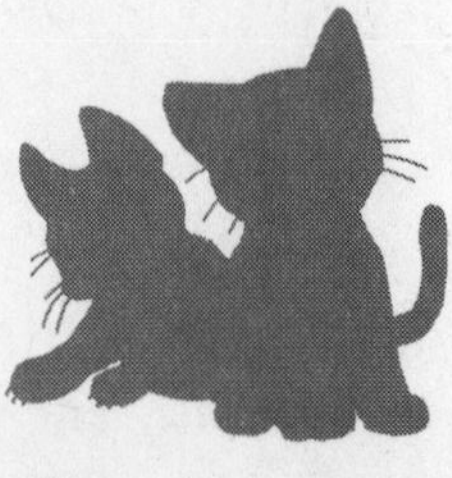

Silver Spoon

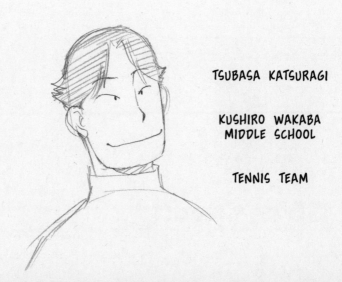

TSUBASA KATSURAGI

KUSHIRO WAKABA
MIDDLE SCHOOL

TENNIS TEAM

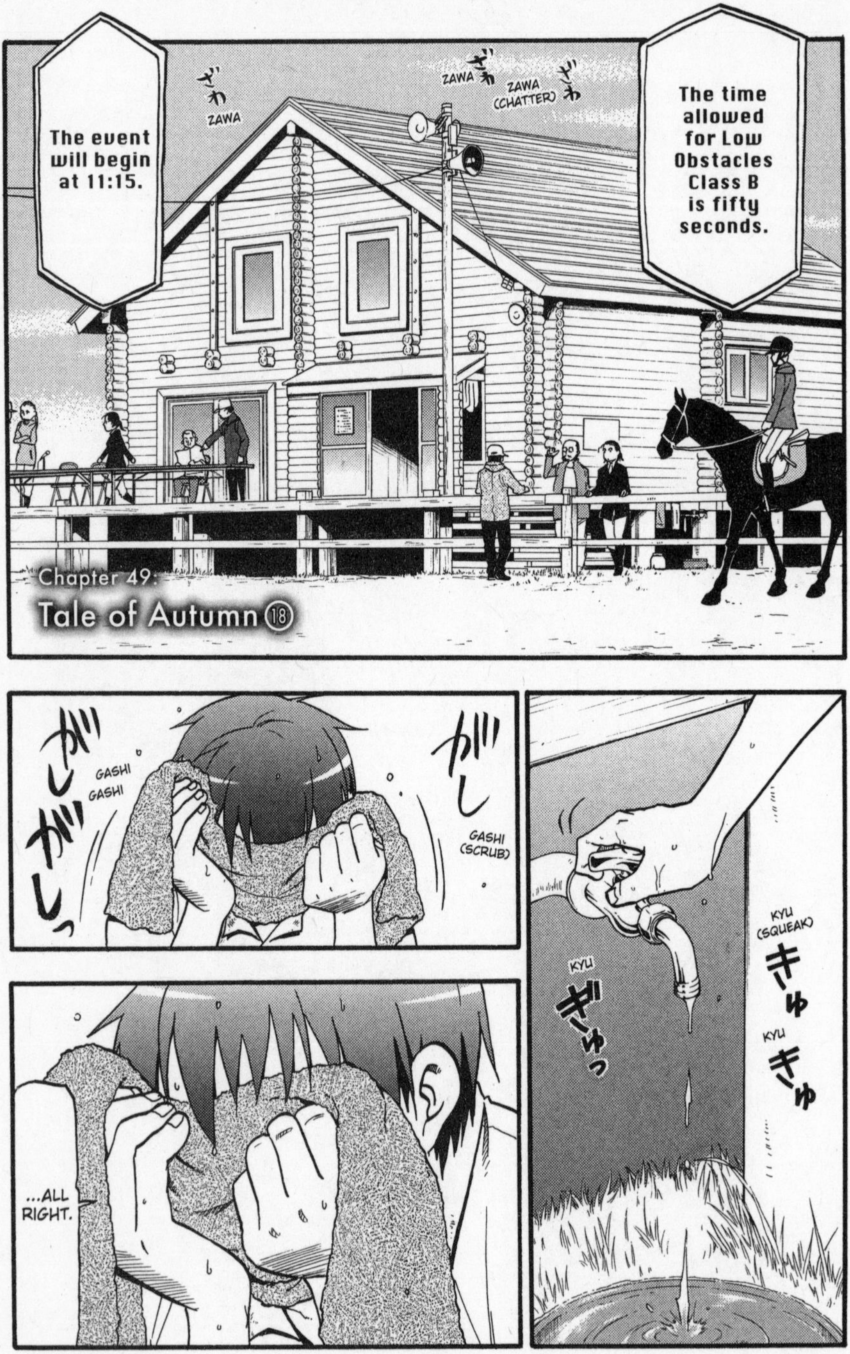
The time allowed for Low Obstacles Class B is fifty seconds.
ZAWA (CHATTER)
ZAWA
ZAWA
The event will begin at 11:15.
Chapter 49:
Tale of Autumn ⑱
KYU (SQUEAK)
KYU
KYU
GASHI (SCRUB)
GASHI GASHI
...ALL RIGHT.

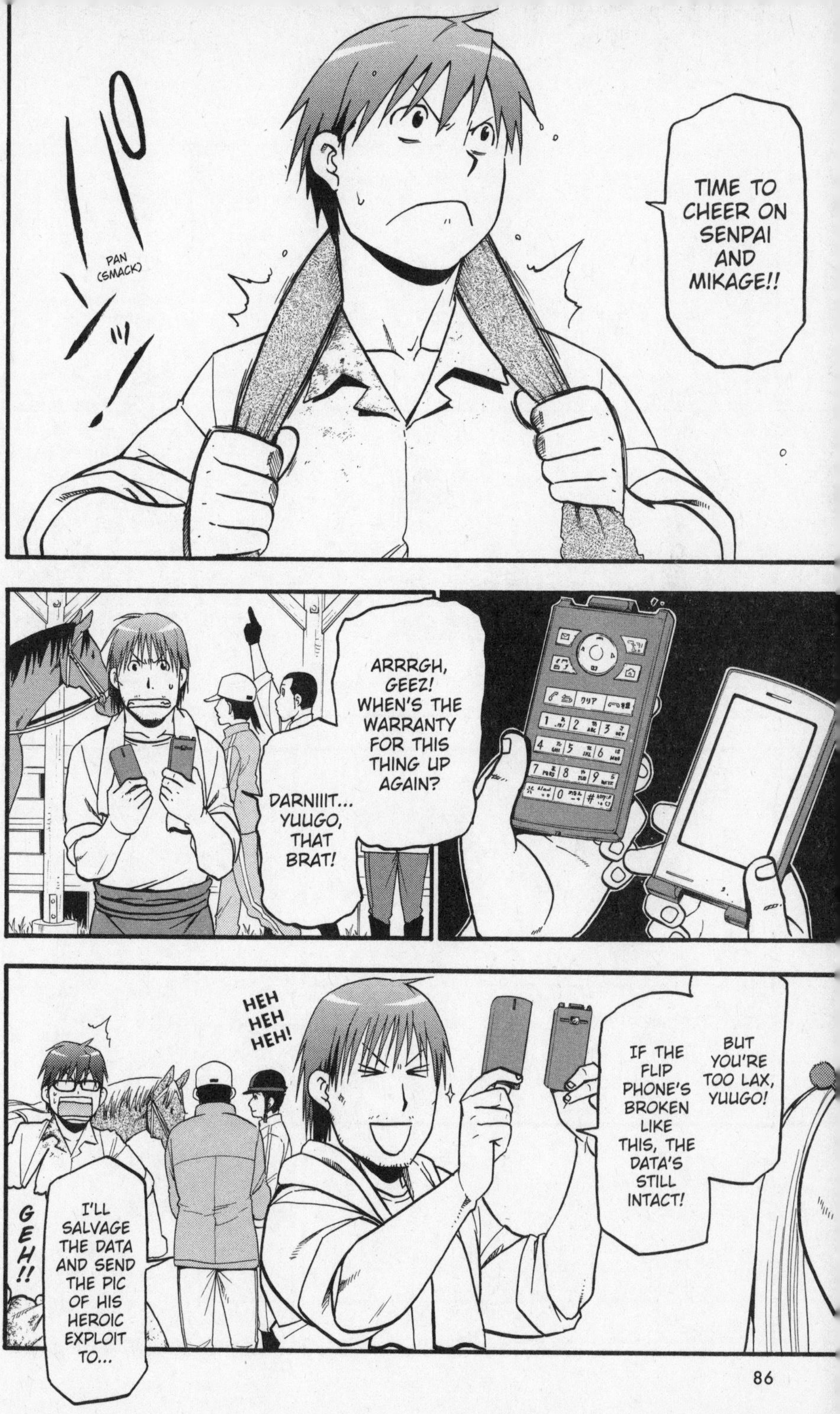
TIME TO CHEER ON SENPAI AND MIKAGE!!
PAN (SMACK)
ARRRGH, GEEZ! WHEN'S THE WARRANTY FOR THIS THING UP AGAIN?
DARNIIIT... YUUGO, THAT BRAT!
BUT YOU'RE TOO LAX, YUUGO!
IF THE FLIP PHONE'S BROKEN LIKE THIS, THE DATA'S STILL INTACT!
HEH HEH HEH!
I'LL SALVAGE THE DATA AND SEND THE PIC OF HIS HEROIC EXPLOIT TO...
GEH!!

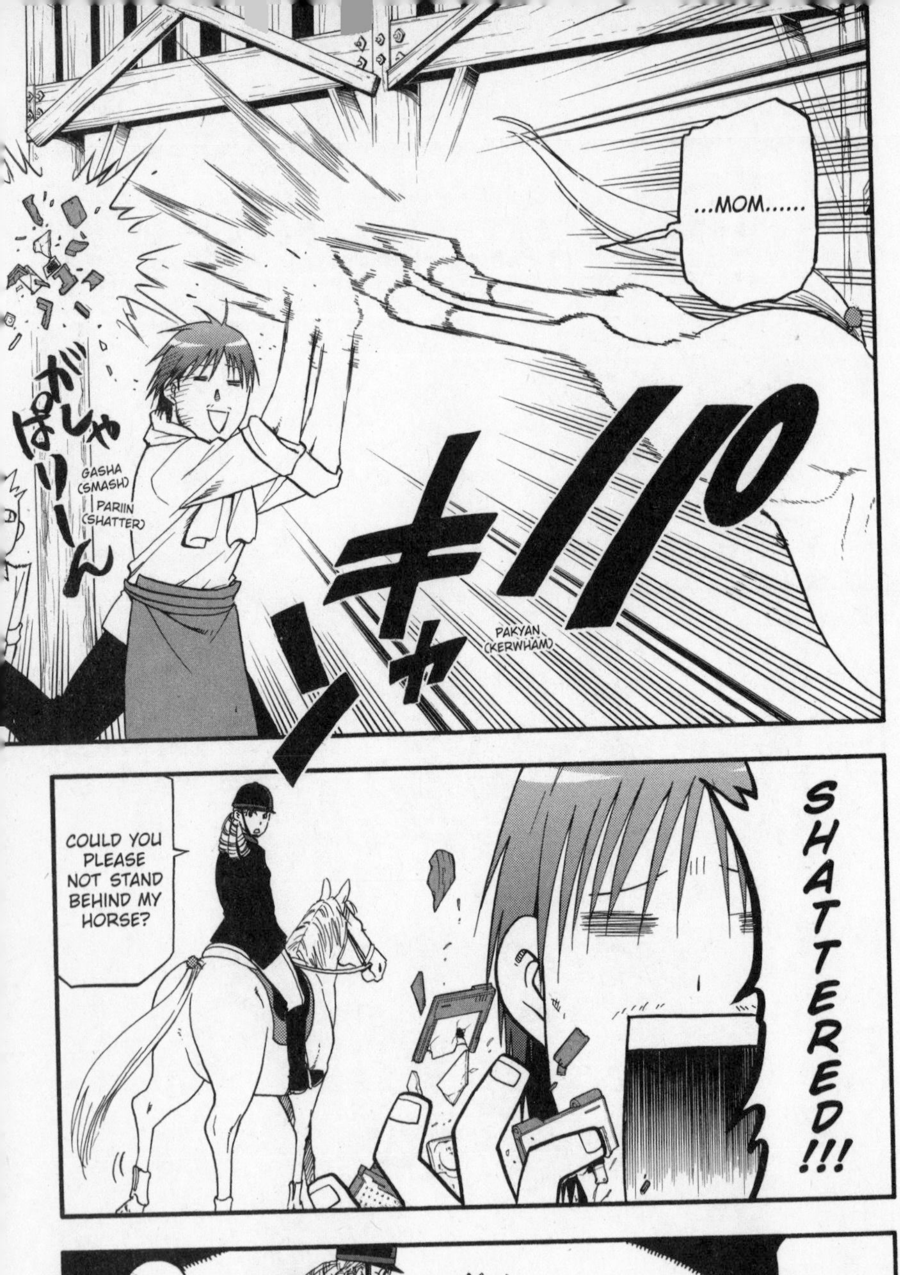
...MOM......
パキャーン
PAKYAN (KERWHAM)
がしゃ ぱりーん
GASHA (SMASH)
PARIIN (SHATTER)
SHATTERED!!!
COULD YOU PLEASE NOT STAND BEHIND MY HORSE?
CAN I GIVE DE ROYAL A CARROT LATER?
?
VERY WELL!

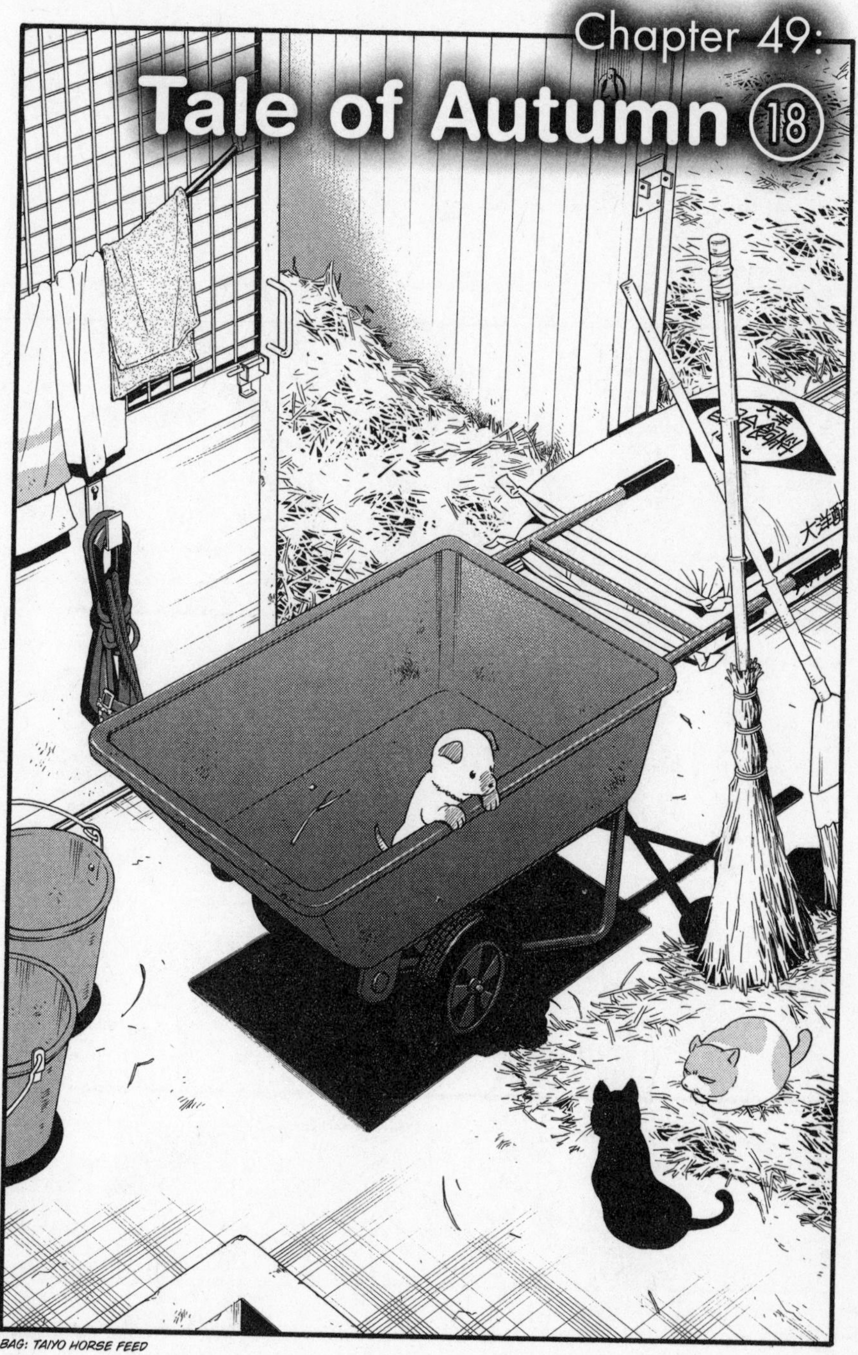
Chapter 49:
Tale of Autumn ⑱
BAG: TAIYO HORSE FEED

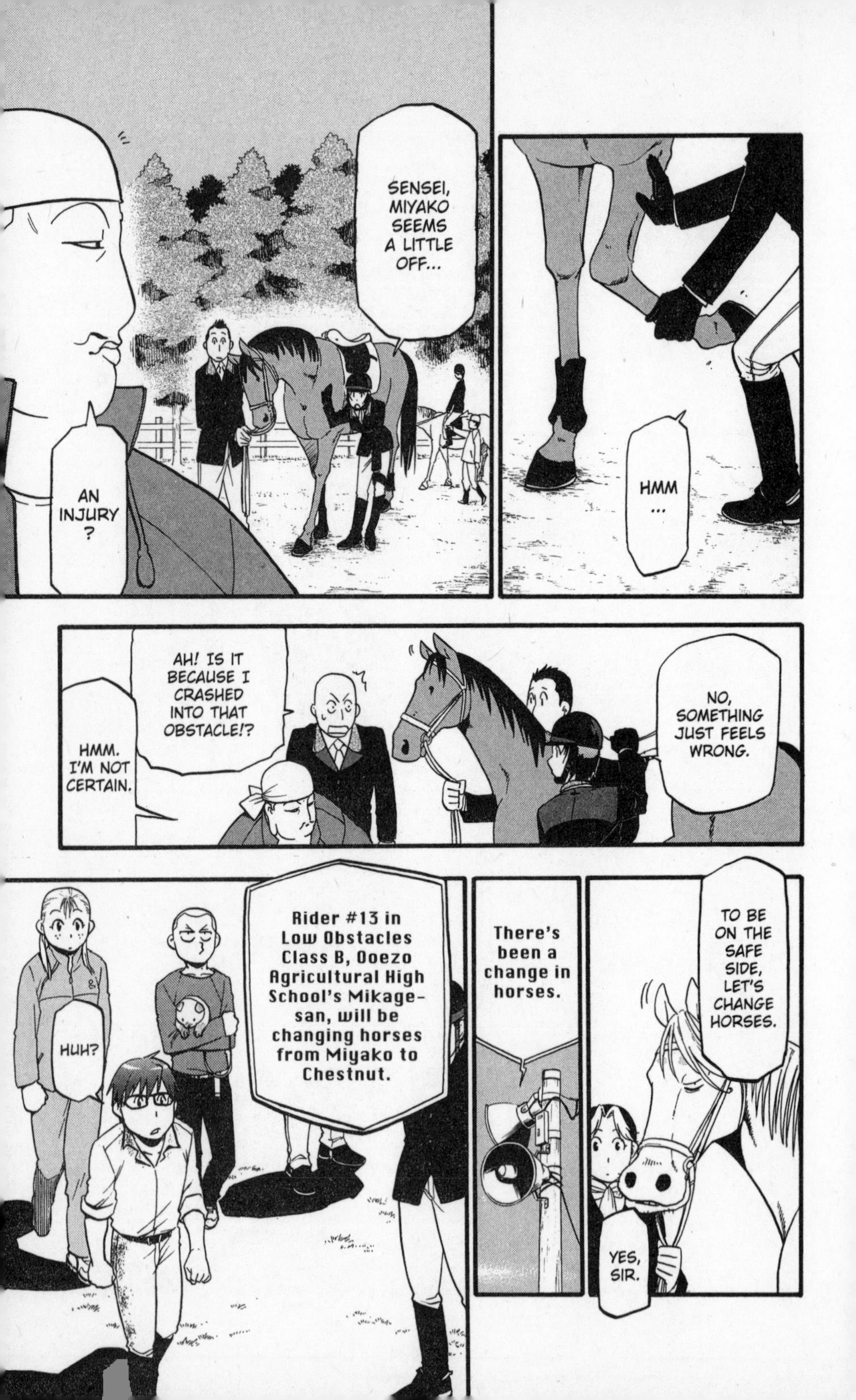
HMM...
SENSEI, MIYAKO SEEMS A LITTLE OFF...
AN INJURY?
NO, SOMETHING JUST FEELS WRONG.
AH! IS IT BECAUSE I CRASHED INTO THAT OBSTACLE!?
HMM. I'M NOT CERTAIN.
TO BE ON THE SAFE SIDE, LET'S CHANGE HORSES.
YES, SIR.
There's been a change in horses.
Rider #13 in Low Obstacles Class B, Ooezo Agricultural High School's Mikage-san, will be changing horses from Miyako to Chestnut.
HUH?

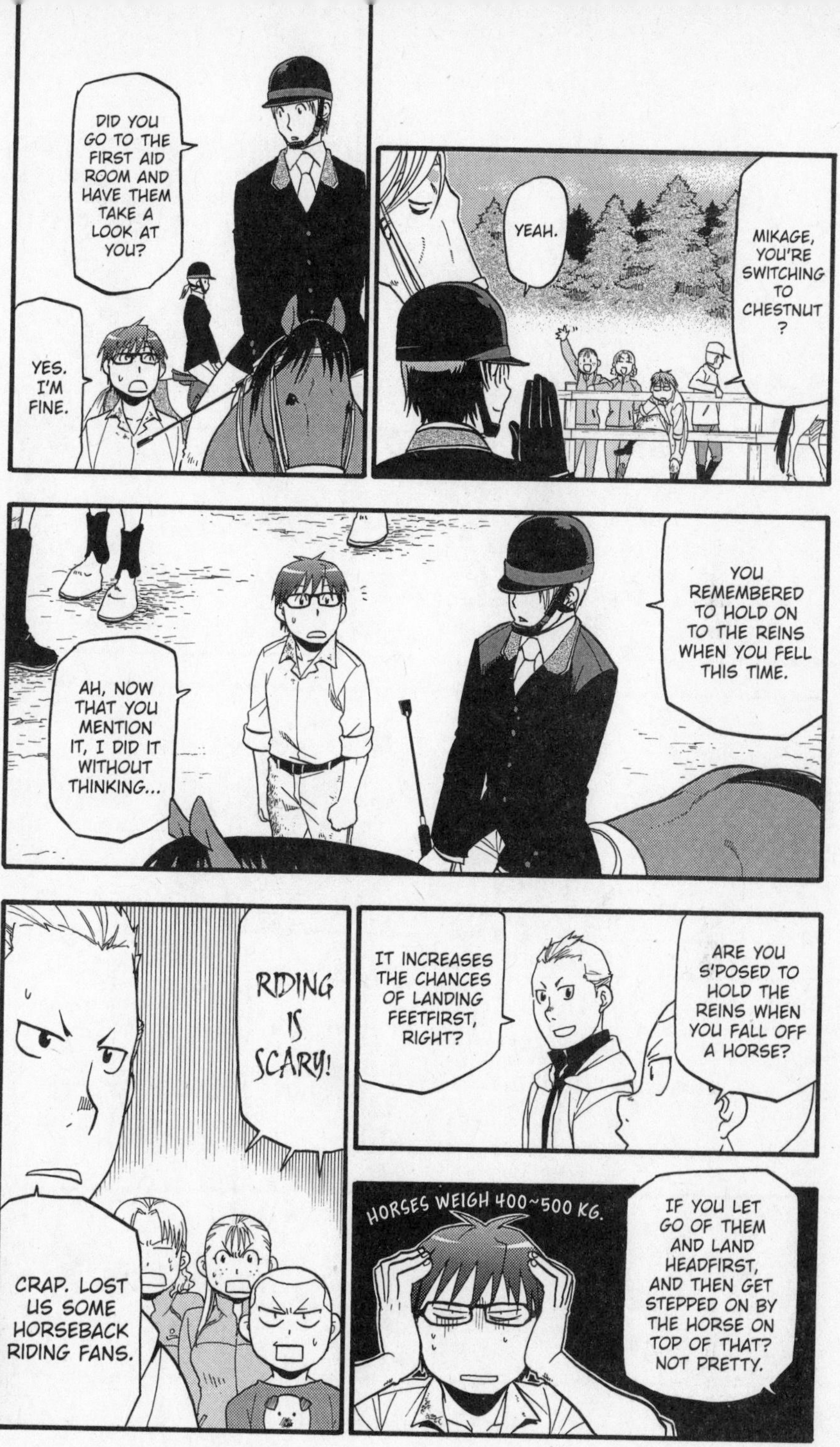
MIKAGE, YOU'RE SWITCHING TO CHESTNUT?
YEAH.
DID YOU GO TO THE FIRST AID ROOM AND HAVE THEM TAKE A LOOK AT YOU?
YES. I'M FINE.
YOU REMEMBERED TO HOLD ON TO THE REINS WHEN YOU FELL THIS TIME.
AH, NOW THAT YOU MENTION IT, I DID IT WITHOUT THINKING...
ARE YOU S'POSED TO HOLD THE REINS WHEN YOU FALL OFF A HORSE?
IT INCREASES THE CHANCES OF LANDING FEETFIRST, RIGHT?
IF YOU LET GO OF THEM AND LAND HEADFIRST, AND THEN GET STEPPED ON BY THE HORSE ON TOP OF THAT? NOT PRETTY.
HORSES WEIGH 400~500 KG.
RIDING IS SCARY!
CRAP. LOST US SOME HORSEBACK RIDING FANS.

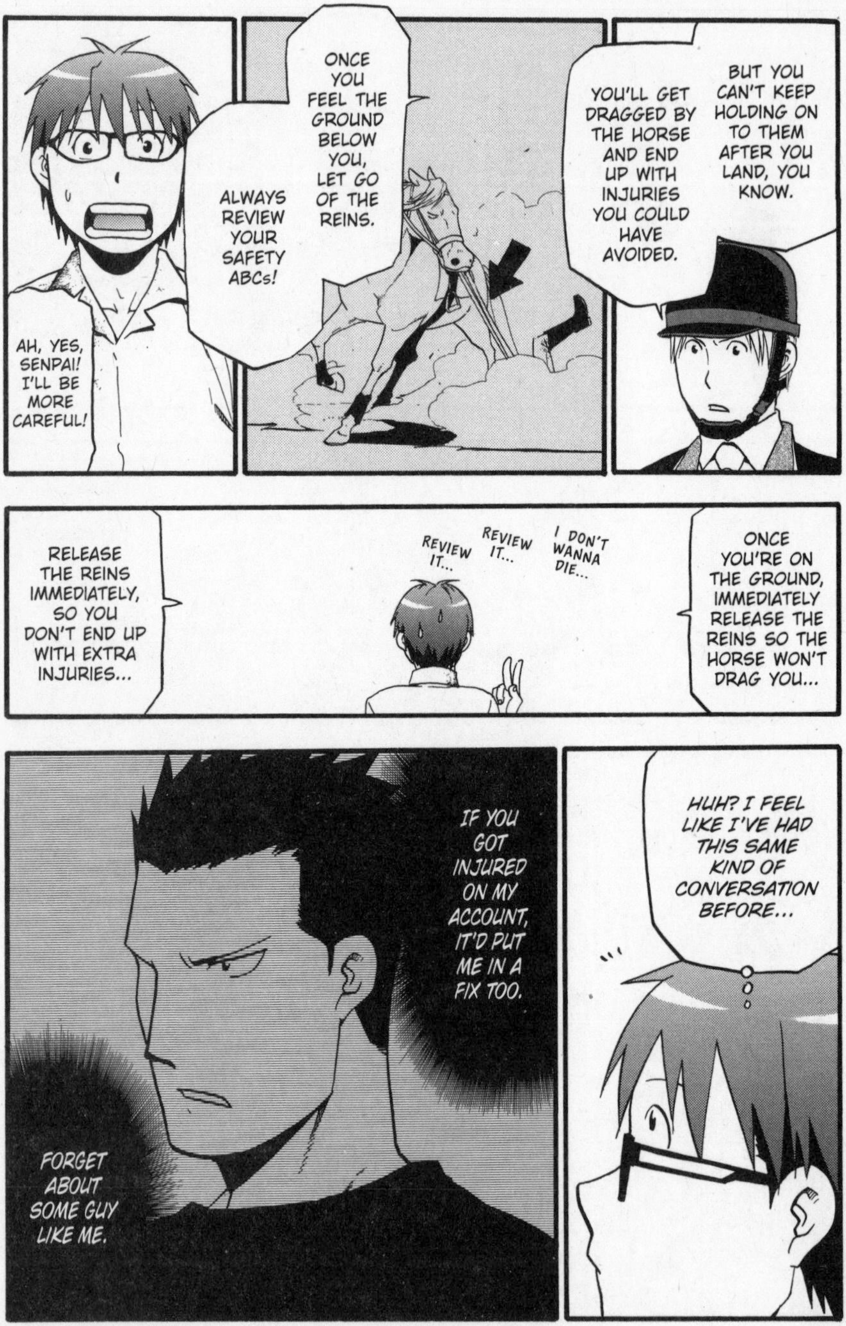
BUT YOU CAN'T KEEP HOLDING ON TO THEM AFTER YOU LAND, YOU KNOW.
YOU'LL GET DRAGGED BY THE HORSE AND END UP WITH INJURIES YOU COULD HAVE AVOIDED.
ONCE YOU FEEL THE GROUND BELOW YOU, LET GO OF THE REINS.
ALWAYS REVIEW YOUR SAFETY ABCs!
AH, YES, SENPAI! I'LL BE MORE CAREFUL!
ONCE YOU'RE ON THE GROUND, IMMEDIATELY RELEASE THE REINS SO THE HORSE WON'T DRAG YOU...
I DON'T WANNA DIE...
REVIEW IT...
REVIEW IT...
RELEASE THE REINS IMMEDIATELY, SO YOU DON'T END UP WITH EXTRA INJURIES...
HUH? I FEEL LIKE I'VE HAD THIS SAME KIND OF CONVERSATION BEFORE...
...
IF YOU GOT INJURED ON MY ACCOUNT, IT'D PUT ME IN A FIX TOO.
FORGET ABOUT SOME GUY LIKE ME.

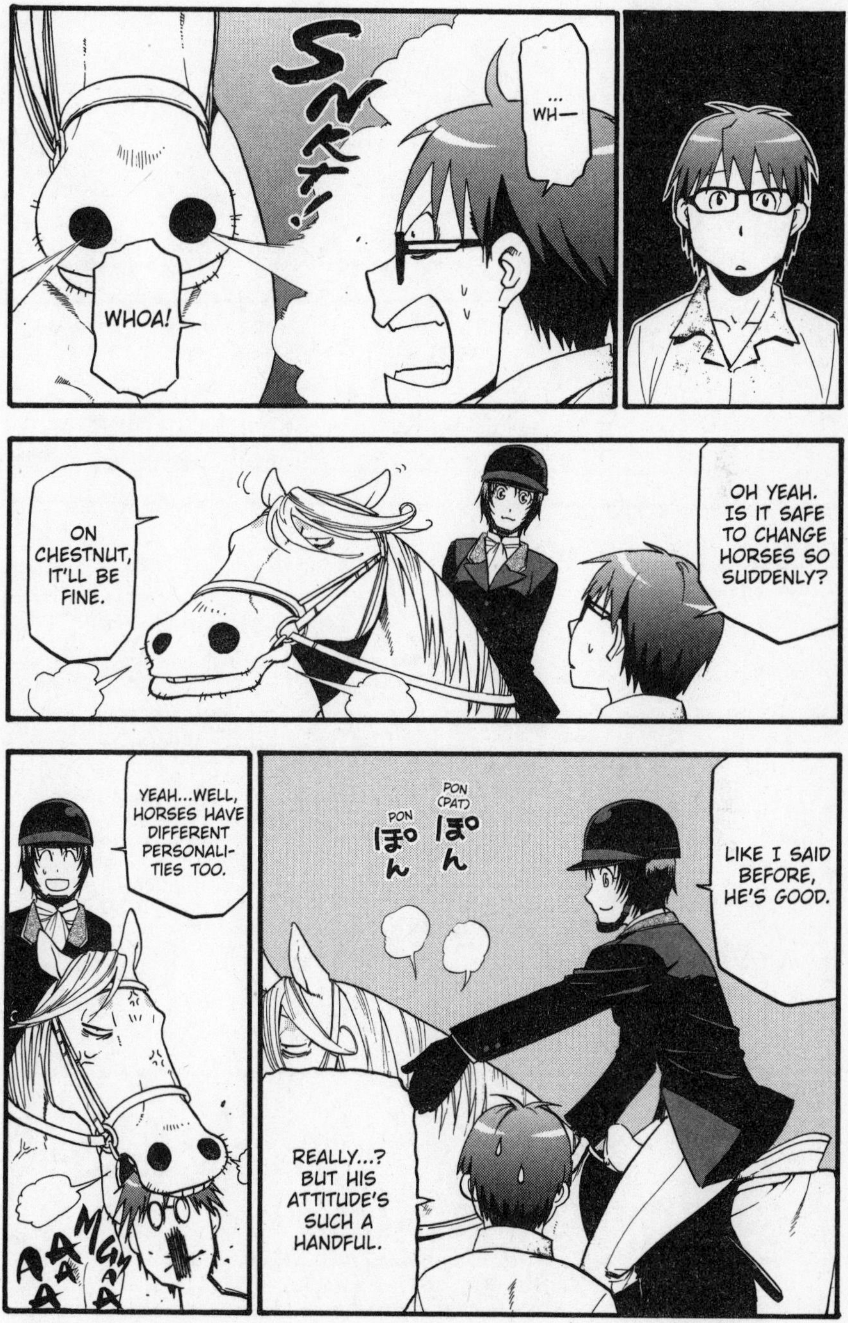
...WH—
SNRT!
WHOA!
OH YEAH. IS IT SAFE TO CHANGE HORSES SO SUDDENLY?
ON CHESTNUT, IT'LL BE FINE.
LIKE I SAID BEFORE, HE'S GOOD.
PON (PAT) ぽん
PON ぽん
REALLY...? BUT HIS ATTITUDE'S SUCH A HANDFUL.
YEAH...WELL, HORSES HAVE DIFFERENT PERSONALITIES TOO.

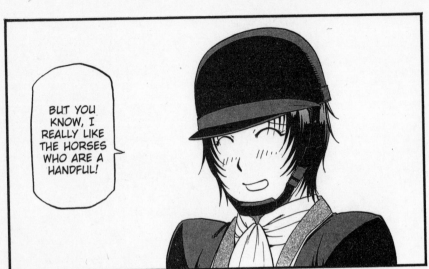

BUT YOU KNOW, I REALLY LIKE THE HORSES WHO ARE A HANDFUL!
AHHHH... HE REALLY IS GOOD...I JUST HOPE I CAN BRING OUT ENOUGH OF HIS POTENTIAL...
I'M NERVOUS!
GO GET 'EM, AKI!
WE KNOW YOU'LL DO GREAT!
WE KNOW YOU'LL DO SUPER-GREAT!
DON'T PUT PRESSURE ON ME!!
SO YOU CAN RIDE AS WELL AS MIKAGE AND STILL GET ALL ANXIOUS...
AS VICE PRESIDENT, I GOTTA CALM HER DOWN...!
UHHH, UHHH...
MIKA—
OH YEAH. HACHIKEN!
HERE'S THAT PAPER YOU DROPPED.
Equestrian
•Sled race area
•Prepare obstacles
•Vice Prez
•Debut competition practice
Dairy Science
•Prep area
•Shopping
Nishikawa (Ag. Science)
Potato dig help
Beppu: Dorm exhibit
Cow barn duty

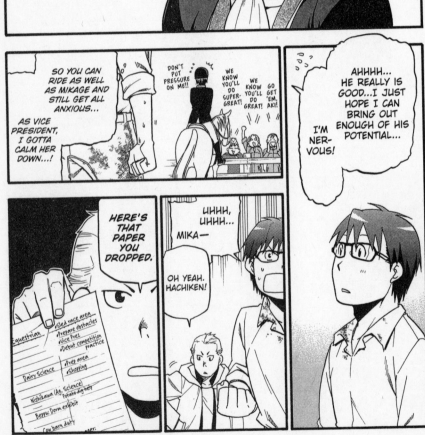

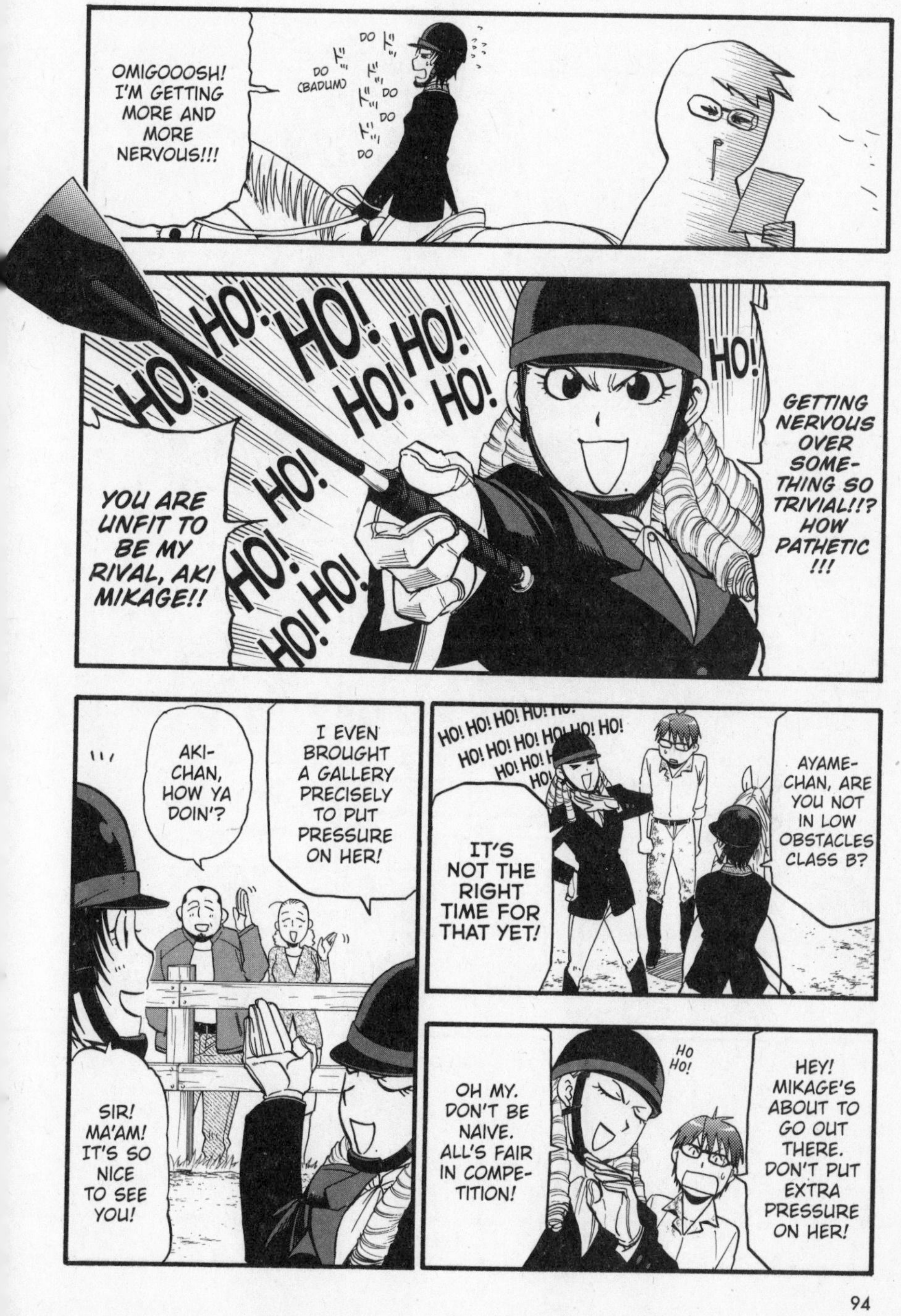
DO ド DO ド DO (BADUM) ド DO ド DO
OMIGOOOSH! I'M GETTING MORE AND MORE NERVOUS!!!
HO! HO! HO! HO! HO! HO! HO! HO! HO! HO! HO! HO!
GETTING NERVOUS OVER SOME-THING SO TRIVIAL!!? HOW PATHETIC!!!
YOU ARE UNFIT TO BE MY RIVAL, AKI MIKAGE!!
HO! HO! HO! HO! HO! HO! HO! HO! HO! HO!
AYAME-CHAN, ARE YOU NOT IN LOW OBSTACLES CLASS B?
IT'S NOT THE RIGHT TIME FOR THAT YET!
HEY! MIKAGE'S ABOUT TO GO OUT THERE. DON'T PUT EXTRA PRESSURE ON HER!
HO HO!
OH MY. DON'T BE NAIVE. ALL'S FAIR IN COMPE-TITION!
I EVEN BROUGHT A GALLERY PRECISELY TO PUT PRESSURE ON HER!
AKI-CHAN, HOW YA DOIN'?
SIR! MA'AM! IT'S SO NICE TO SEE YOU!

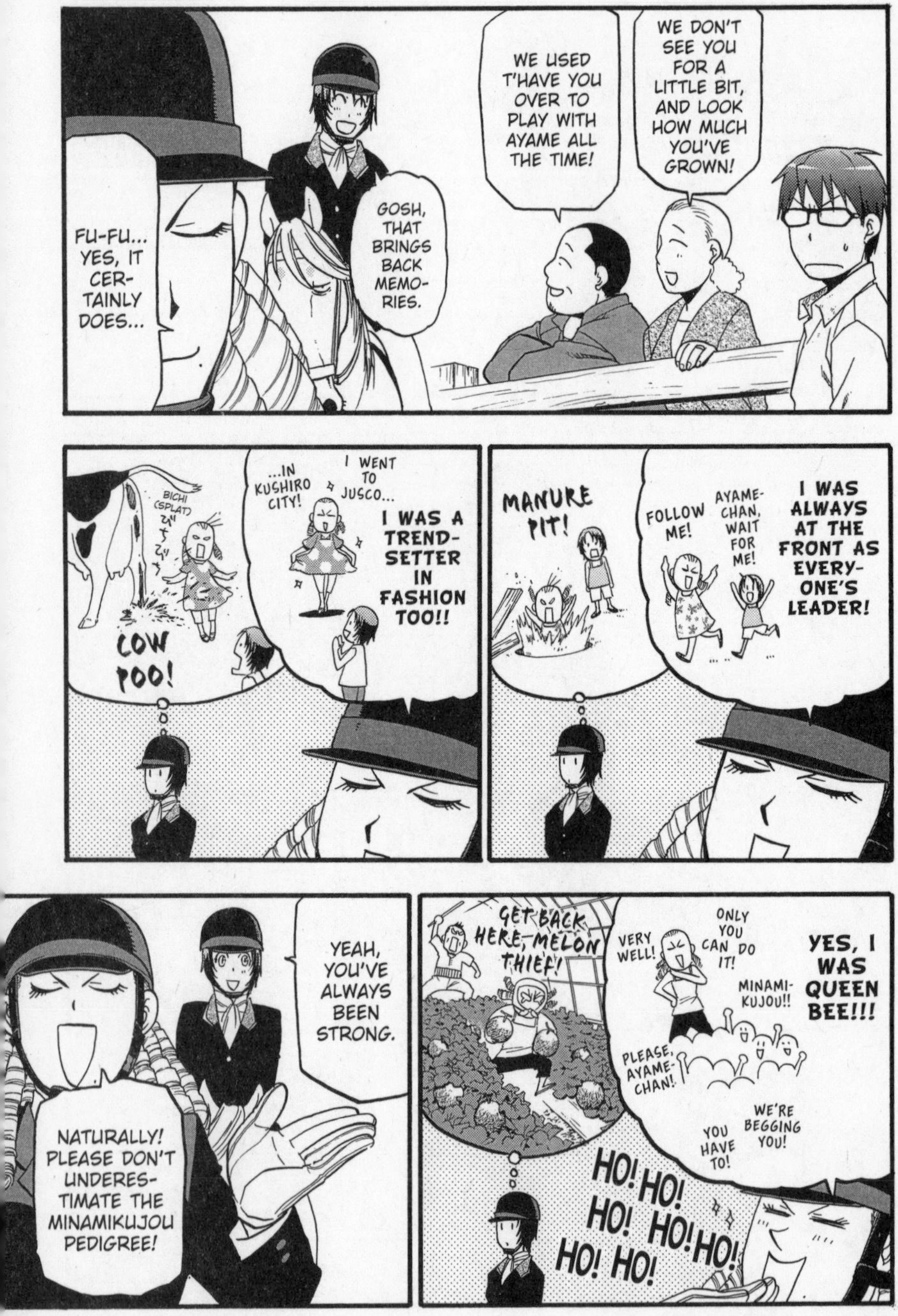
WE DON'T SEE YOU FOR A LITTLE BIT, AND LOOK HOW MUCH YOU'VE GROWN!
WE USED T'HAVE YOU OVER TO PLAY WITH AYAME ALL THE TIME!
GOSH, THAT BRINGS BACK MEMORIES.
FU-FU... YES, IT CERTAINLY DOES...
I WAS ALWAYS AT THE FRONT AS EVERYONE'S LEADER!
AYAME-CHAN, WAIT FOR ME!
FOLLOW ME!
MANURE PIT!
I WAS A TRENDSETTER IN FASHION TOO!!
I WENT TO JUSCO...
...IN KUSHIRO CITY!
BICHI (SPLAT)
COW POO!
YES, I WAS QUEEN BEE!!!
ONLY YOU CAN DO IT!
MINAMI-KUJOU!!
VERY WELL!
PLEASE, AYAME-CHAN!
WE'RE BEGGING YOU!
YOU HAVE TO!
GET BACK HERE, MELON THIEF!
HO! HO! HO! HO! HO! HO! HO!
YEAH, YOU'VE ALWAYS BEEN STRONG.
NATURALLY! PLEASE DON'T UNDERESTIMATE THE MINAMIKUJOU PEDIGREE!

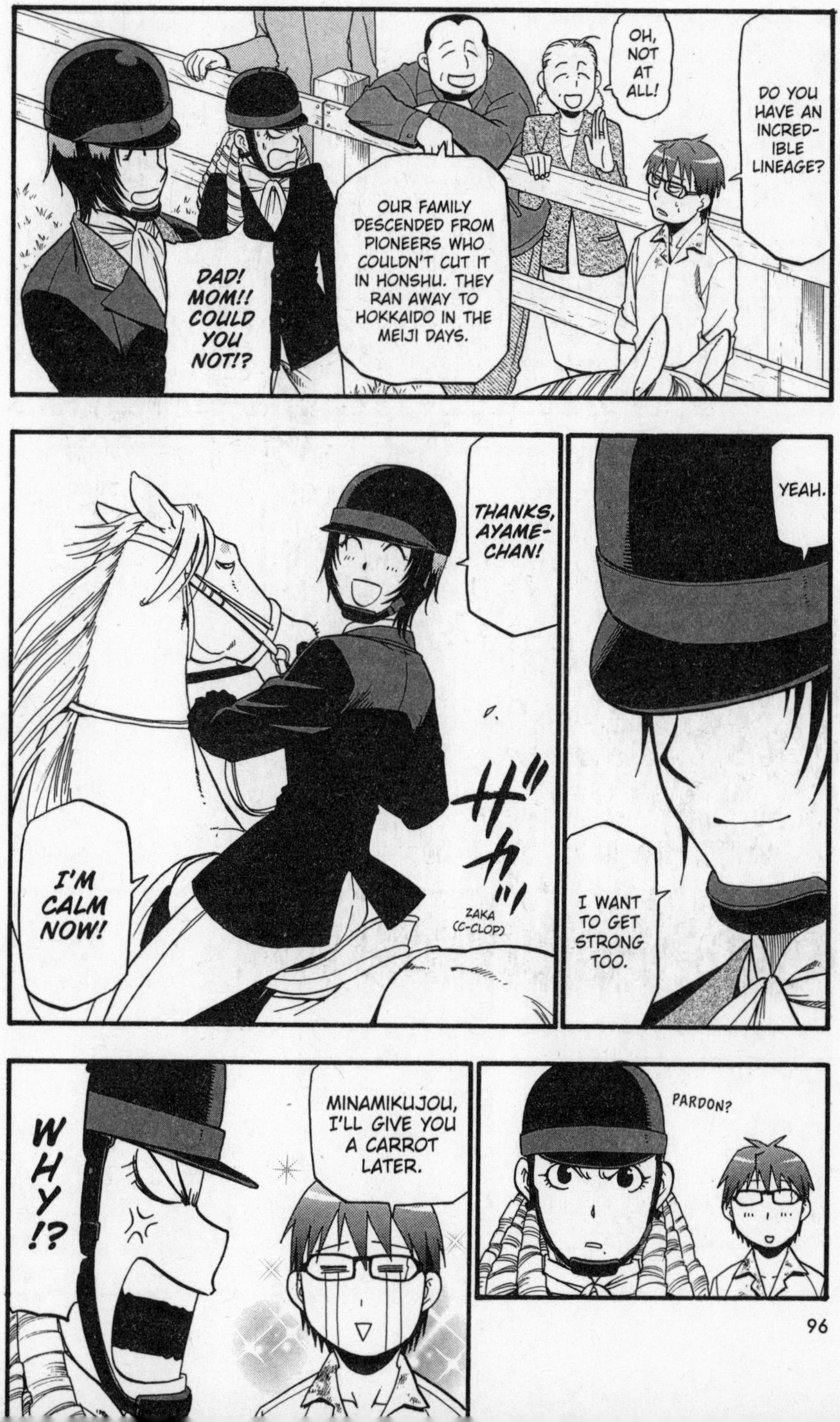
DO YOU HAVE AN INCRED-IBLE LINEAGE?
OH, NOT AT ALL!
OUR FAMILY DESCENDED FROM PIONEERS WHO COULDN'T CUT IT IN HONSHU. THEY RAN AWAY TO HOKKAIDO IN THE MEIJI DAYS.
DAD! MOM!! COULD YOU NOT!?
YEAH.
I WANT TO GET STRONG TOO.
THANKS, AYAME-CHAN!
ZAKA (C-CLOP)
I'M CALM NOW!
PARDON?
MINAMIKUJOU, I'LL GIVE YOU A CARROT LATER.
WHY!?

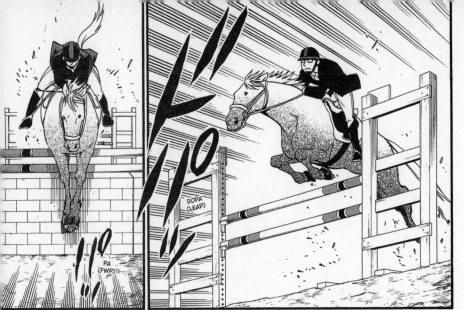

PA
(FWP)

DOPA
(LEAP)

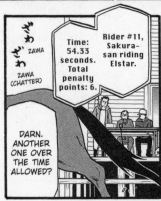

ZAWA

ZAWA
(CHATTER)

Time: 54.33 seconds. Total penalty points: 6.

Rider #11, Sakura-san riding Elstar.

DARN. ANOTHER ONE OVER THE TIME ALLOWED?

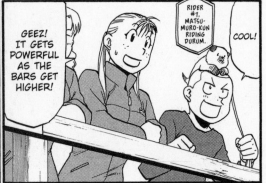

GEEZ! IT GETS POWERFUL AS THE BARS GET HIGHER!

RIDER #1, MATSU-MURO-KUN RIDING DURUM.

COOL!

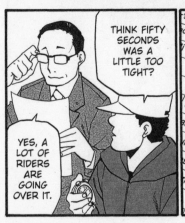

THINK FIFTY SECONDS WAS A LITTLE TOO TIGHT?

YES, A LOT OF RIDERS ARE GOING OVER IT.

HMM ...

's Na...	...rse	Affiliation	Time	Penalty Pt...
...ozo	...tar	Suzuki Ranch	55.32	
	...u	Taiki Nakajima H.S.		6
...We...	...hite	Ooezo Animal Hus. U	51.71	1
Silverbell		Hakuyuukai	49.07	0
...asahi		Hakuyuukai	48.20	0
...um		Taiki Nakajima H.S.	53.50	5
...shi		Ooezo Animal Hus. U	56.10	6
		Club Tokachi	50.69	
		Suzuki Ranch	60.98	1
		Nisei A...		

...tacles Class B (90)

97

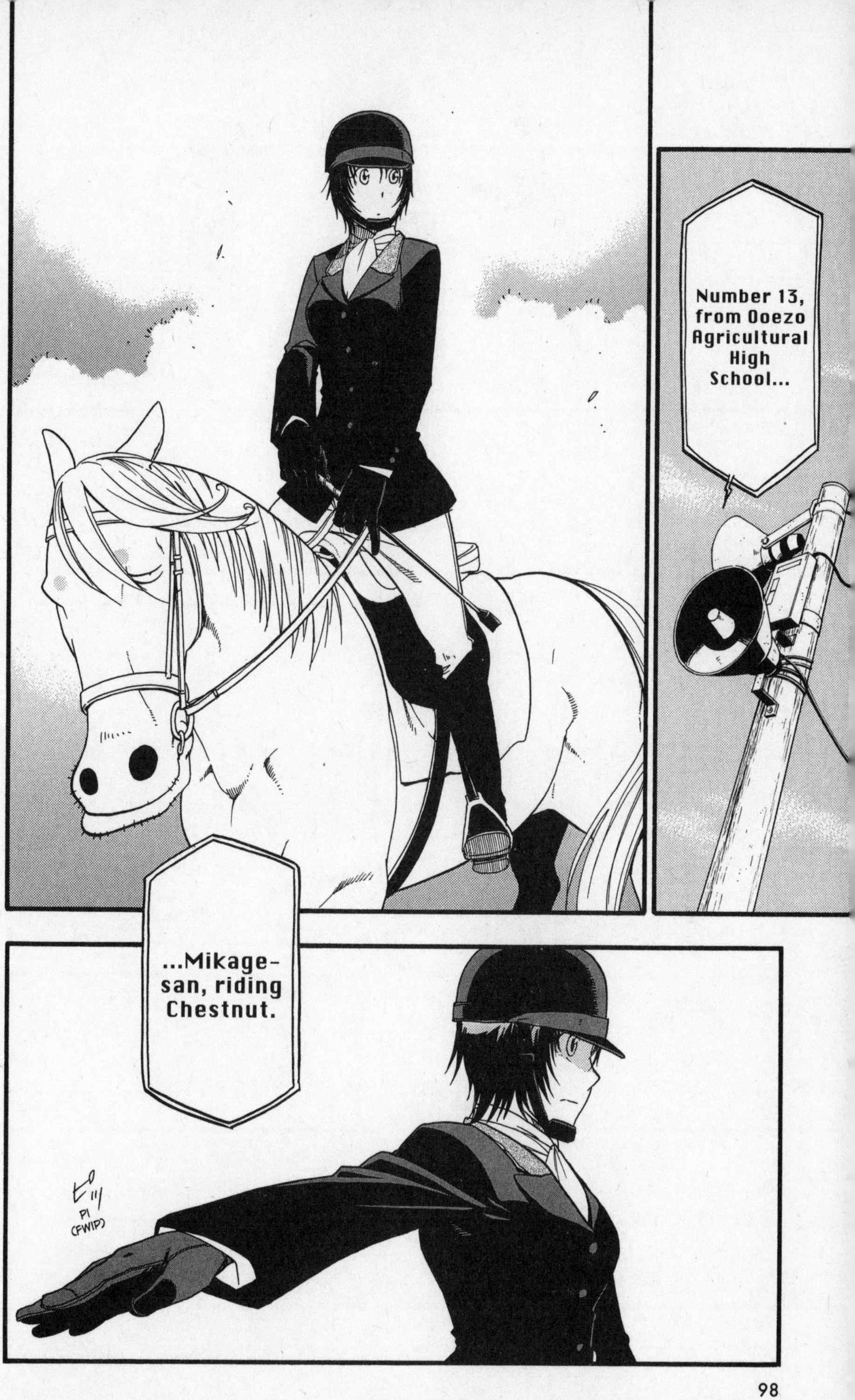
Number 13, from Ooezo Agricultural High School...
...Mikage-san, riding Chestnut.
PI (FWIP)

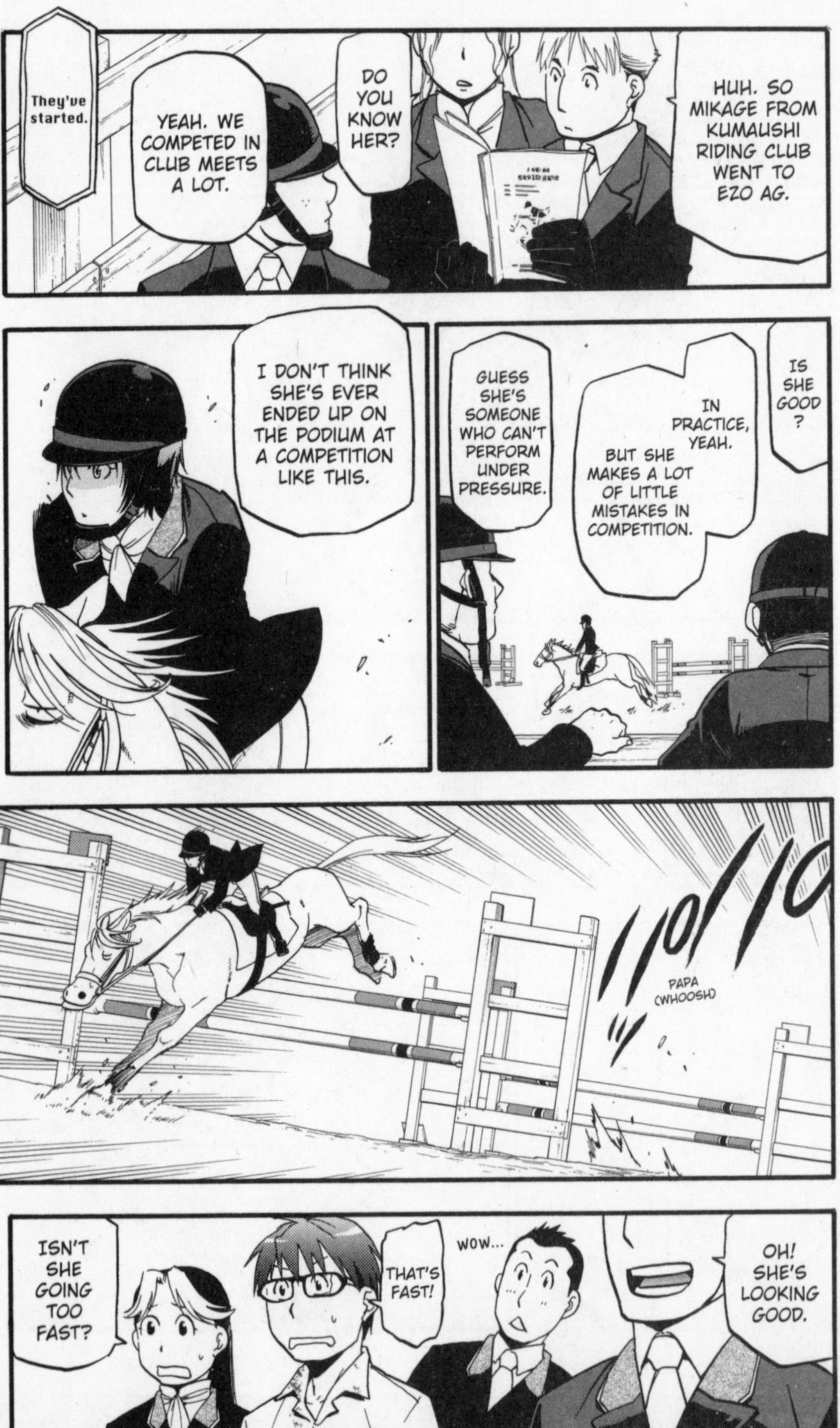
HUH. SO MIKAGE FROM KUMAUSHI RIDING CLUB WENT TO EZO AG.
DO YOU KNOW HER?
YEAH. WE COMPETED IN CLUB MEETS A LOT.
They've started.
IS SHE GOOD?
IN PRACTICE, YEAH.
BUT SHE MAKES A LOT OF LITTLE MISTAKES IN COMPETITION.
GUESS SHE'S SOMEONE WHO CAN'T PERFORM UNDER PRESSURE.
I DON'T THINK SHE'S EVER ENDED UP ON THE PODIUM AT A COMPETITION LIKE THIS.
PAPA (WHOOSH)
OH! SHE'S LOOKING GOOD.
WOW...
THAT'S FAST!
ISN'T SHE GOING TOO FAST?

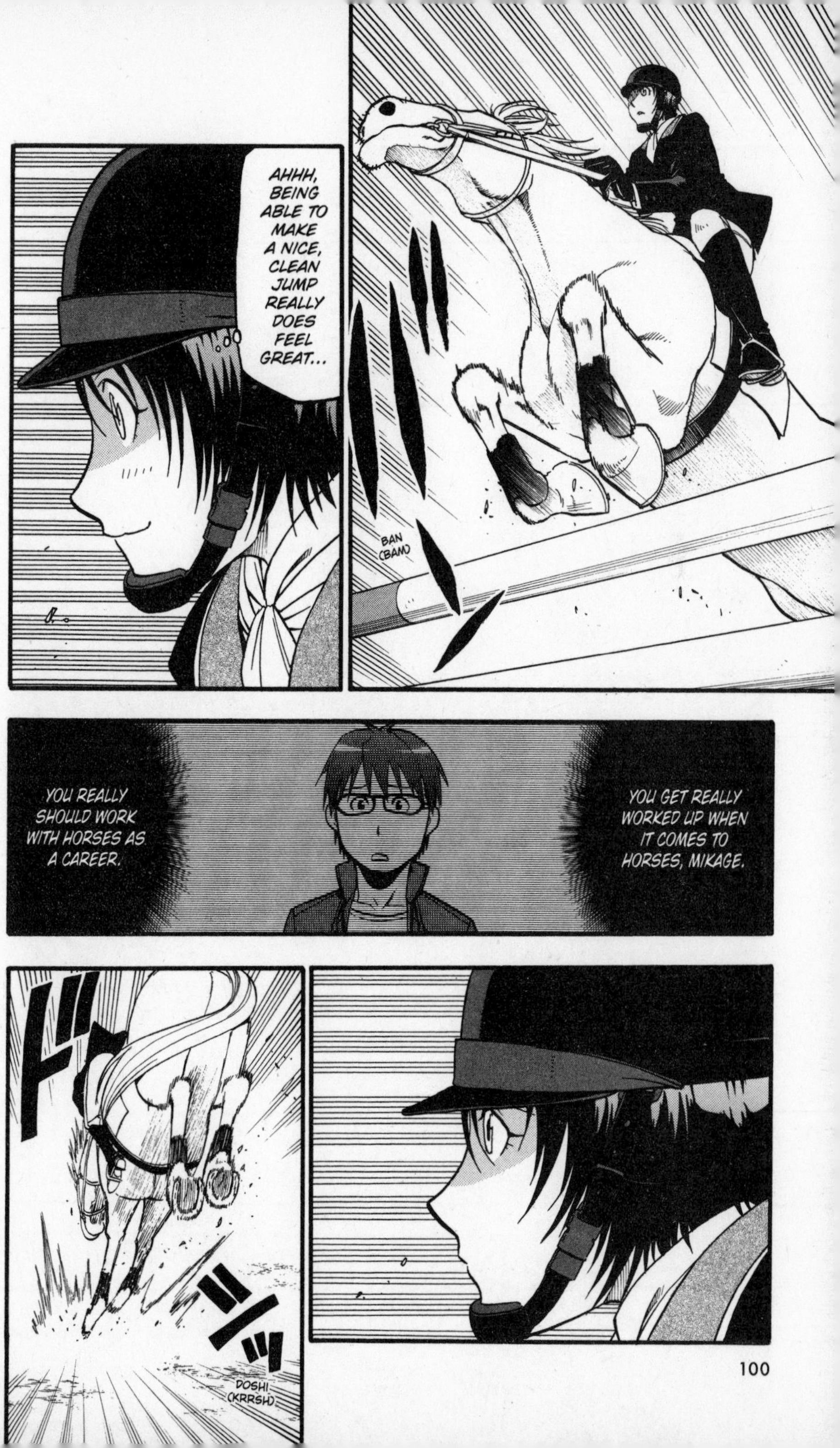
BAN (BAM)
AHHH, BEING ABLE TO MAKE A NICE, CLEAN JUMP REALLY DOES FEEL GREAT...
YOU GET REALLY WORKED UP WHEN IT COMES TO HORSES, MIKAGE.
YOU REALLY SHOULD WORK WITH HORSES AS A CAREER.
DOSHI (KRRSH)

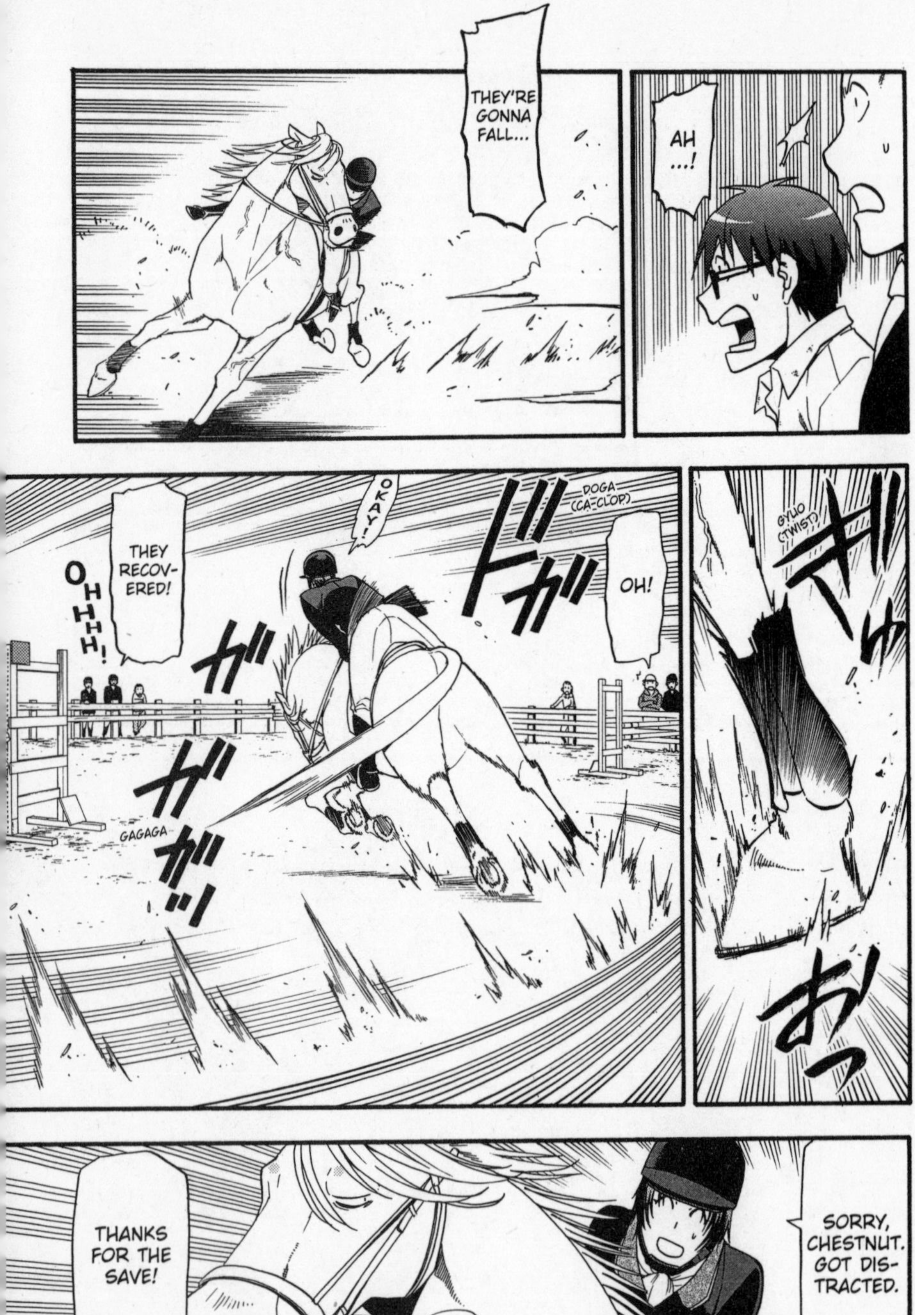
AH ...!
THEY'RE GONNA FALL...
GYUO (TWIST)
OH!
DOGA (CA-CLOP)
OKAY!
THEY RECOVERED!
OHHHH!
GAGAGA
SORRY, CHESTNUT. GOT DISTRACTED.
THANKS FOR THE SAVE!

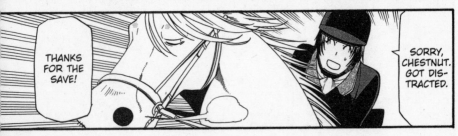

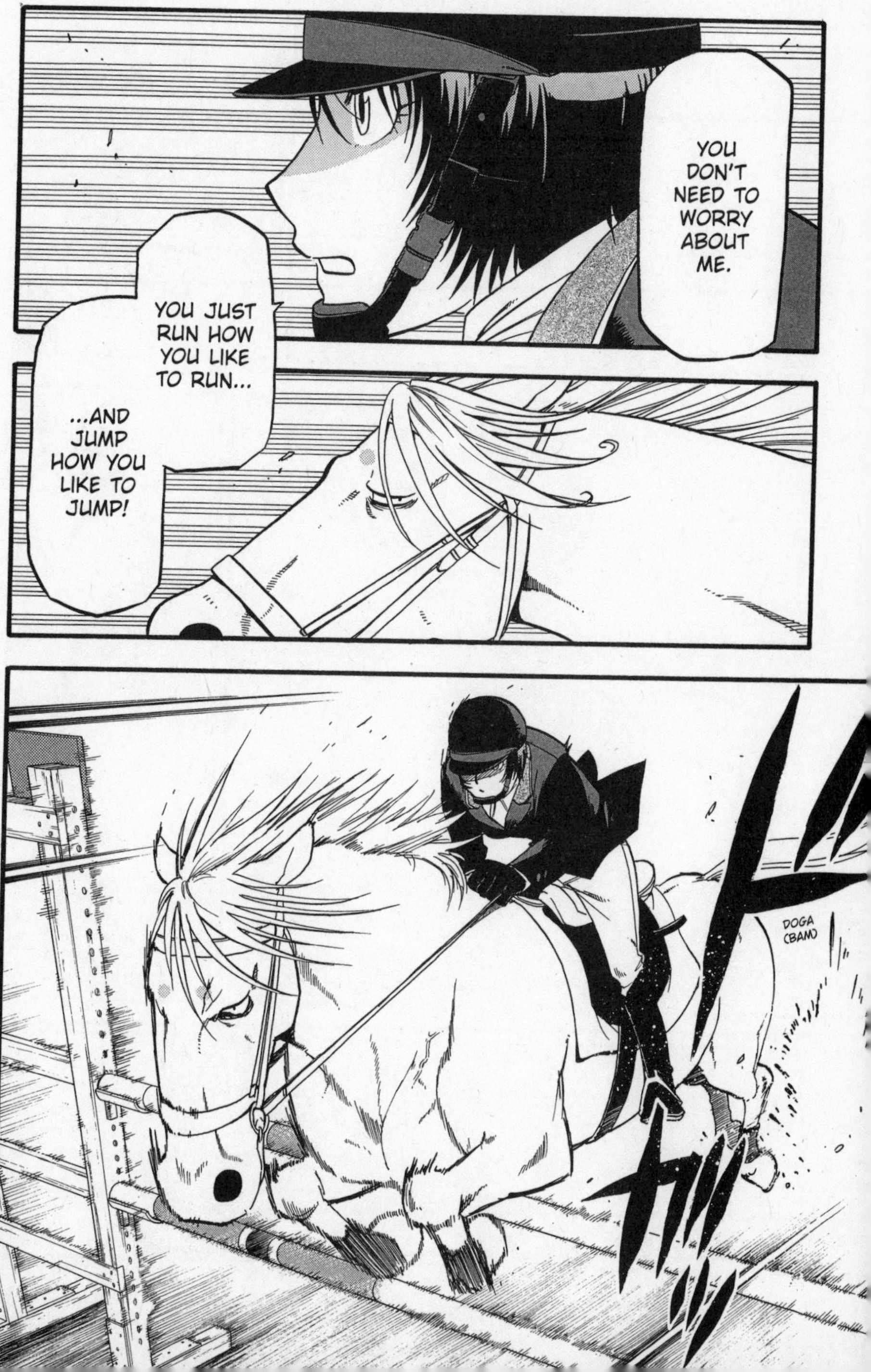
YOU DON'T NEED TO WORRY ABOUT ME.
YOU JUST RUN HOW YOU LIKE TO RUN...
...AND JUMP HOW YOU LIKE TO JUMP!
DOGA (BAM)

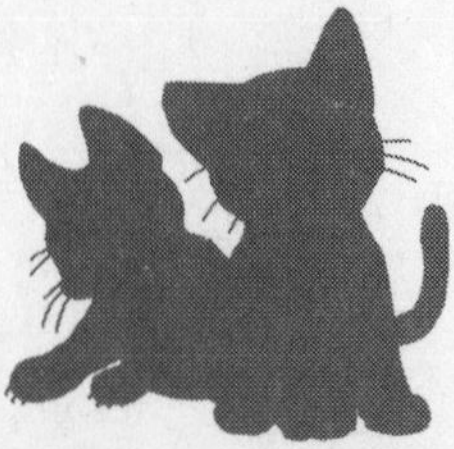

Silver Spoon

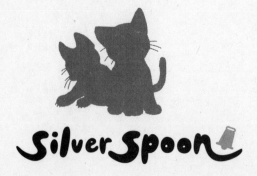

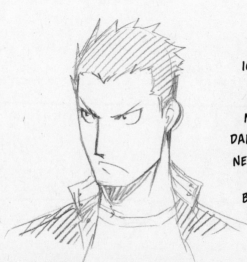

ICHIROU KOMABA

SHIMIZU FIRST
MIDDLE SCHOOL

DAIRY FARM FAMILY

NEIGHBORS OF THE
MIKAGES

BASEBALL TEAM

Chapter 50:
Tale of Autumn ⑲

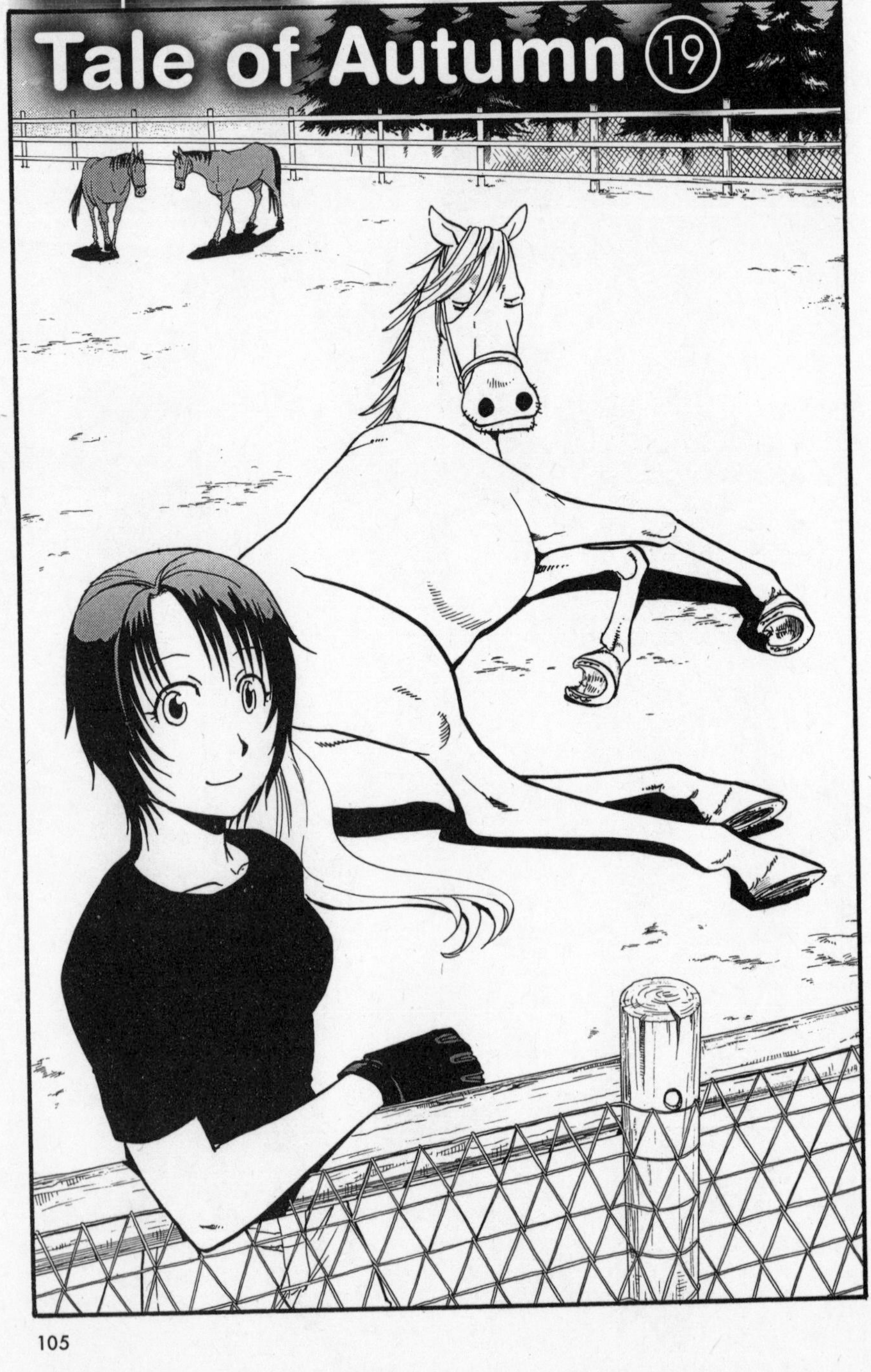

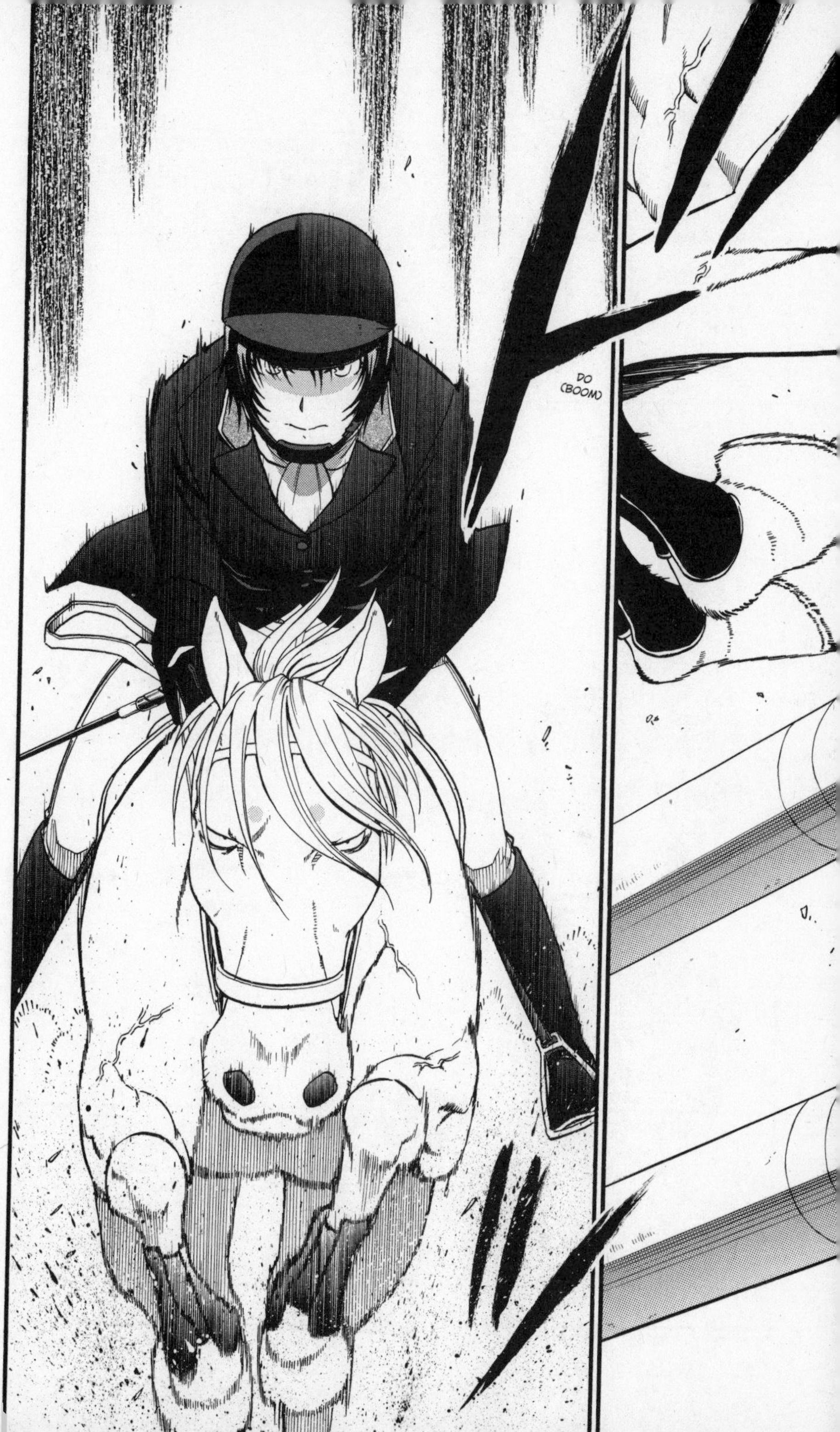
DO
(BOOM)

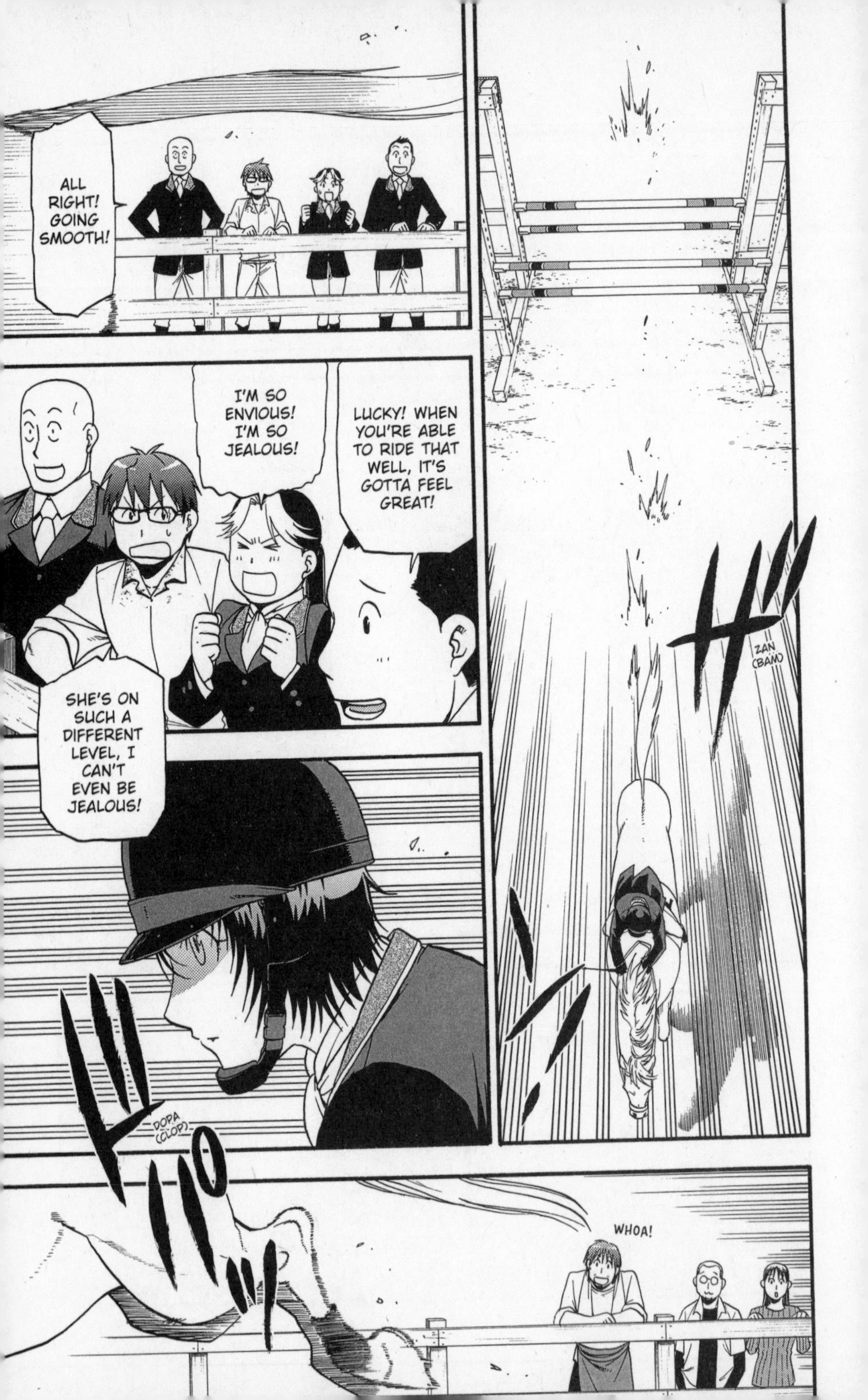
ZAN (BAM)
ALL RIGHT! GOING SMOOTH!
LUCKY! WHEN YOU'RE ABLE TO RIDE THAT WELL, IT'S GOTTA FEEL GREAT!
I'M SO ENVIOUS! I'M SO JEALOUS!
SHE'S ON SUCH A DIFFERENT LEVEL, I CAN'T EVEN BE JEALOUS!
DOPA (CLOP)
WHOA!

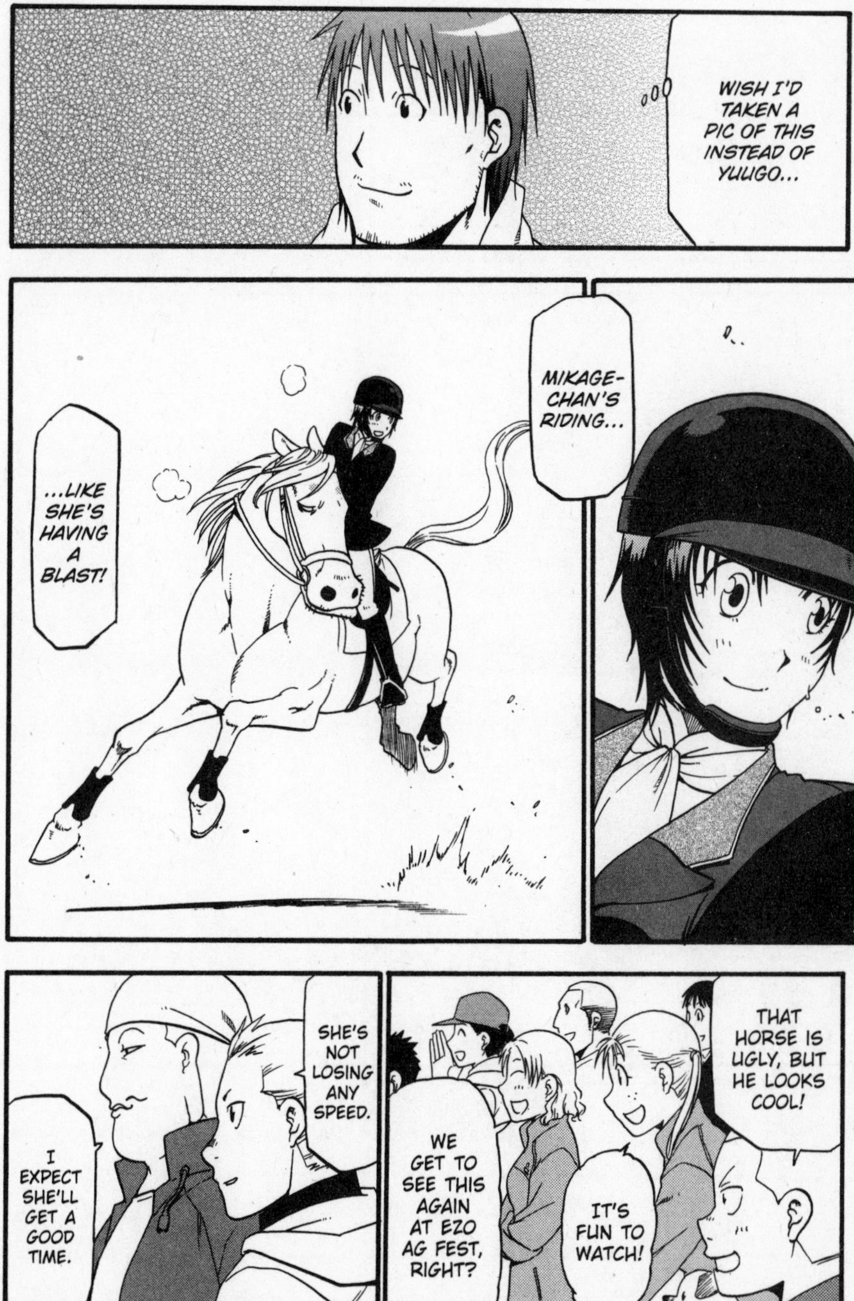
WISH I'D TAKEN A PIC OF THIS INSTEAD OF YUUGO...
MIKAGE-CHAN'S RIDING...
...LIKE SHE'S HAVING A BLAST!
THAT HORSE IS UGLY, BUT HE LOOKS COOL!
IT'S FUN TO WATCH!
WE GET TO SEE THIS AGAIN AT EZO AG FEST, RIGHT?
SHE'S NOT LOSING ANY SPEED.
I EXPECT SHE'LL GET A GOOD TIME.

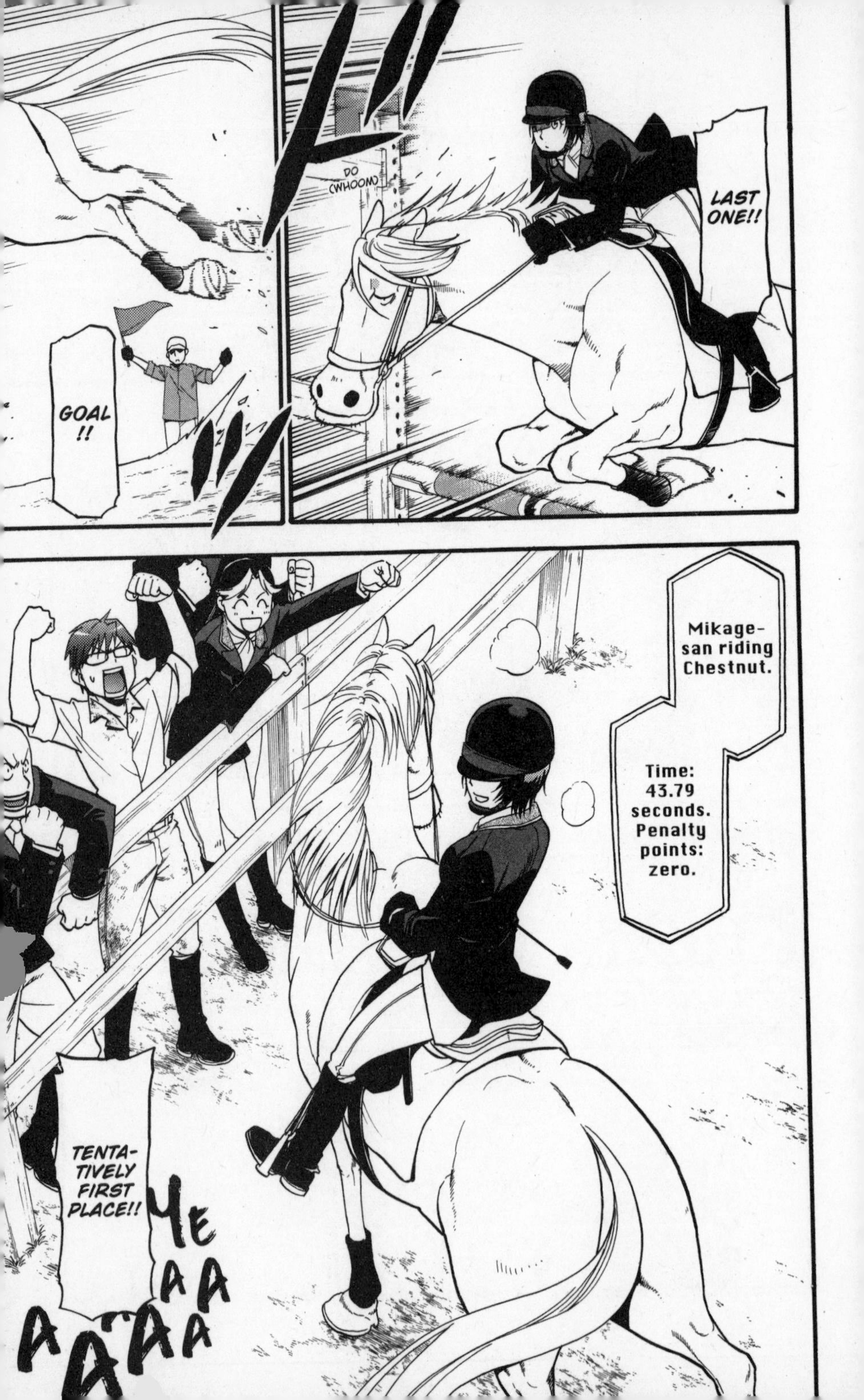
LAST ONE!!
DO (WHOOM)
GOAL !!
Mikage-san riding Chestnut.
Time: 43.79 seconds. Penalty points: zero.
TENTATIVELY FIRST PLACE!!
YEAAAAAAAA

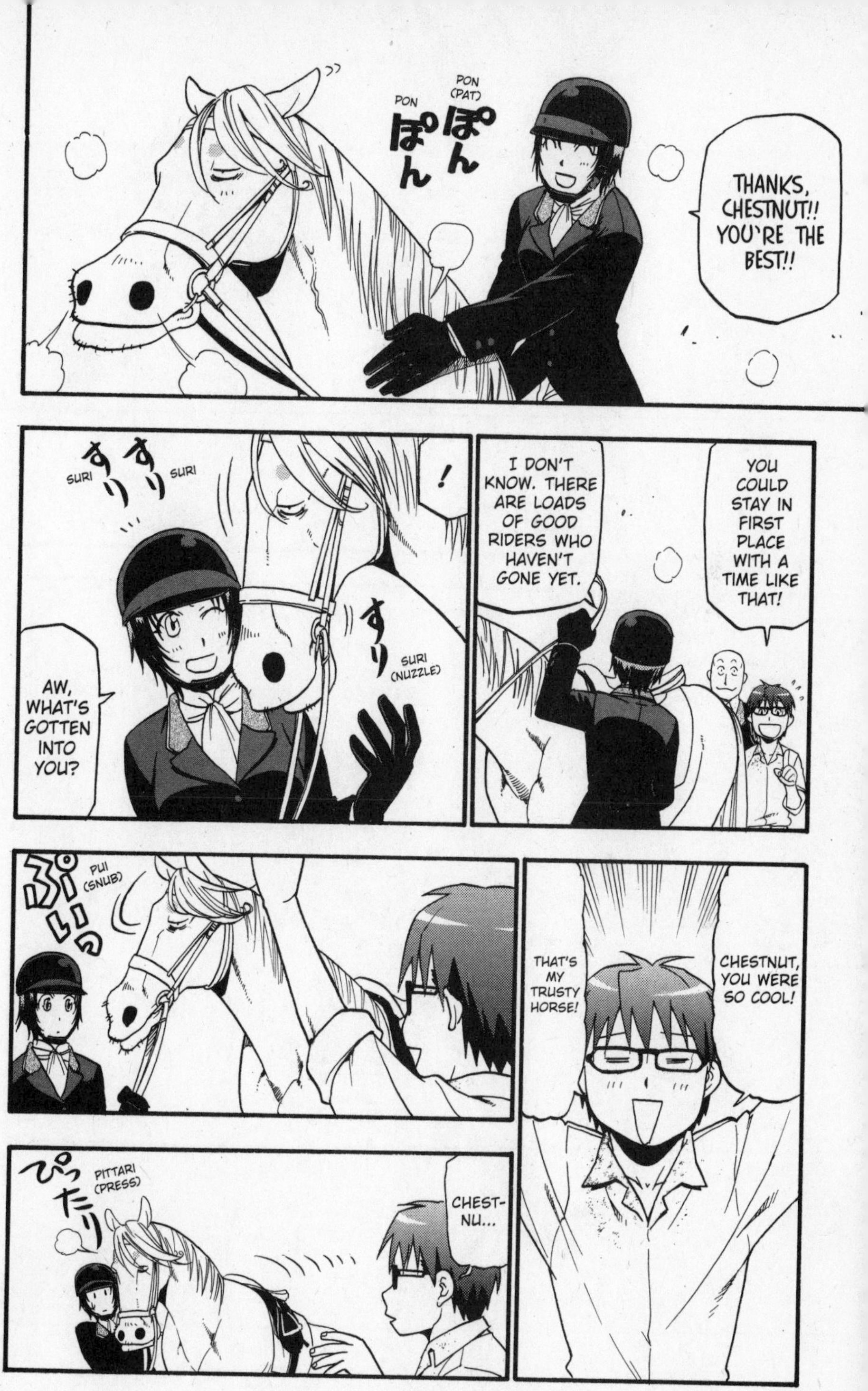
THANKS, CHESTNUT!! YOU'RE THE BEST!!
ぽん
PON (PAT)
ぽん
PON
YOU COULD STAY IN FIRST PLACE WITH A TIME LIKE THAT!
I DON'T KNOW. THERE ARE LOADS OF GOOD RIDERS WHO HAVEN'T GONE YET.
!
すり
SURI
すり
SURI
すり
SURI (NUZZLE)
AW, WHAT'S GOTTEN INTO YOU?
CHESTNUT, YOU WERE SO COOL!
THAT'S MY TRUSTY HORSE!
ぷいっ
PUI (SNUB)
CHEST-NU...
ぴったり
PITTARI (PRESS)

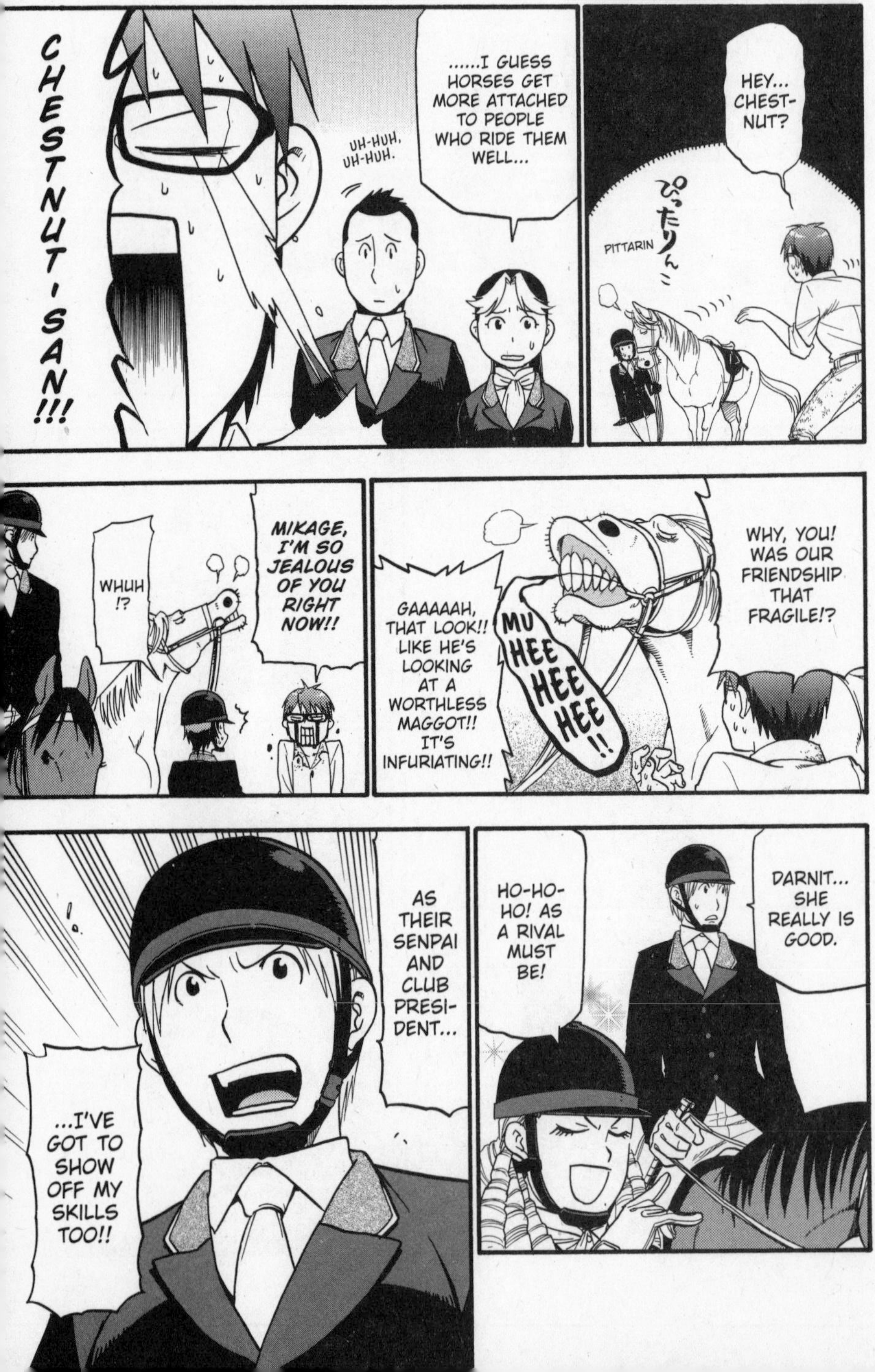
HEY... CHEST-NUT?
ぴったりんこ
PITTARIN
......I GUESS HORSES GET MORE ATTACHED TO PEOPLE WHO RIDE THEM WELL...
UH-HUH, UH-HUH.
CHESTNUT-SAN!!!
WHY, YOU! WAS OUR FRIENDSHIP THAT FRAGILE!?
MU HEE HEE HEE!!
GAAAAAH, THAT LOOK!! LIKE HE'S LOOKING AT A WORTHLESS MAGGOT!! IT'S INFURIATING!!
MIKAGE, I'M SO JEALOUS OF YOU RIGHT NOW!!
WHUH!?
DARNIT... SHE REALLY IS GOOD.
HO-HO-HO! AS A RIVAL MUST BE!
AS THEIR SENPAI AND CLUB PRESIDENT...
...I'VE GOT TO SHOW OFF MY SKILLS TOO!!

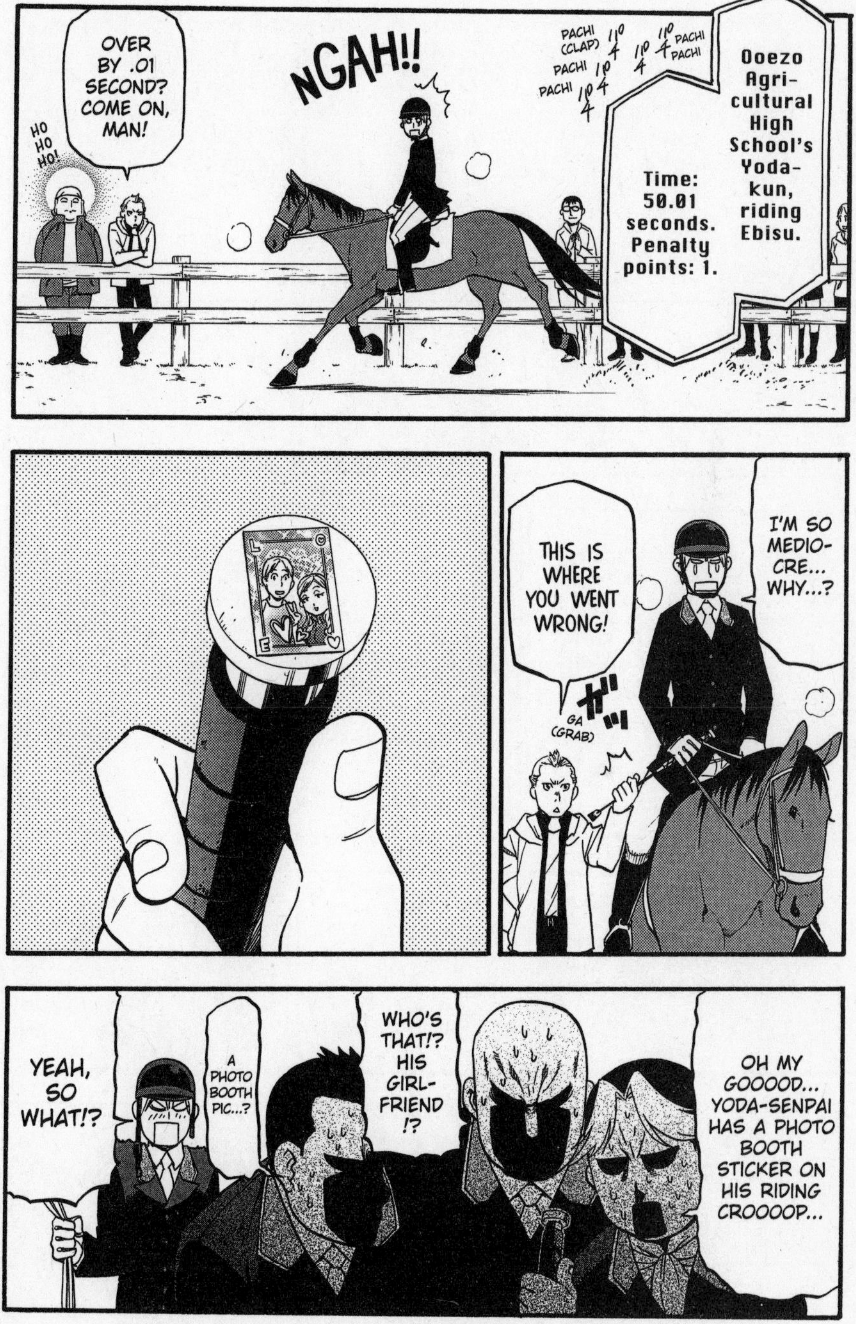
Ooezo Agri-cultural High School's Yoda-kun, riding Ebisu.
Time: 50.01 seconds. Penalty points: 1.
PACHI PACHI
PACHI (CLAP)
PACHI
PACHI
nGAH!!
OVER BY .01 SECOND? COME ON, MAN!
HO HO HO!
I'M SO MEDIO-CRE... WHY...?
THIS IS WHERE YOU WENT WRONG!
GA (GRAB)
OH MY GOOOOD... YODA-SENPAI HAS A PHOTO BOOTH STICKER ON HIS RIDING CROOOOP...
WHO'S THAT!? HIS GIRL-FRIEND !?
A PHOTO BOOTH PIC...?
YEAH, SO WHAT!?

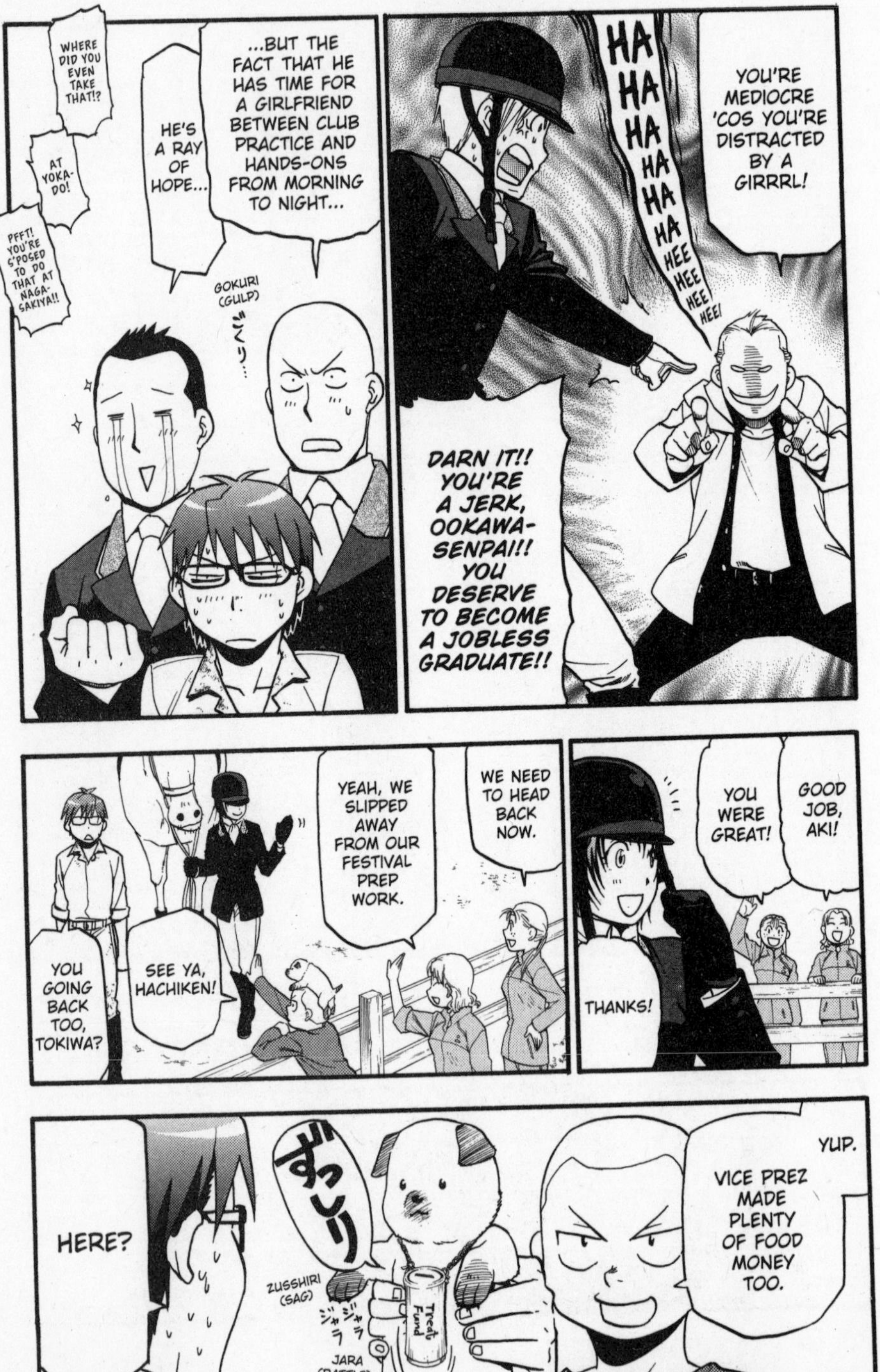
YOU'RE MEDIOCRE 'COS YOU'RE DISTRACTED BY A GIRRRL!
HA HA HA HA HA HA HEE HEE HEE HEE!
DARN IT!! YOU'RE A JERK, OOKAWA-SENPAI!! YOU DESERVE TO BECOME A JOBLESS GRADUATE!!
...BUT THE FACT THAT HE HAS TIME FOR A GIRLFRIEND BETWEEN CLUB PRACTICE AND HANDS-ONS FROM MORNING TO NIGHT...
HE'S A RAY OF HOPE...
WHERE DID YOU EVEN TAKE THAT!?
AT YOKA-DO!
PFFT! YOU'RE S'POSED TO DO THAT AT NAGA-SAKIYA!!
GOKURI (GULP)
ごくり…
GOOD JOB, AKI!
YOU WERE GREAT!
THANKS!
WE NEED TO HEAD BACK NOW.
YEAH, WE SLIPPED AWAY FROM OUR FESTIVAL PREP WORK.
SEE YA, HACHIKEN!
YOU GOING BACK TOO, TOKIWA?
YUP.
VICE PREZ MADE PLENTY OF FOOD MONEY TOO.
ずっしり
ZUSSHIRI (SAG)
Treat Fund
ジャラジャラ
JARA (RATTLE) JARA
HERE?

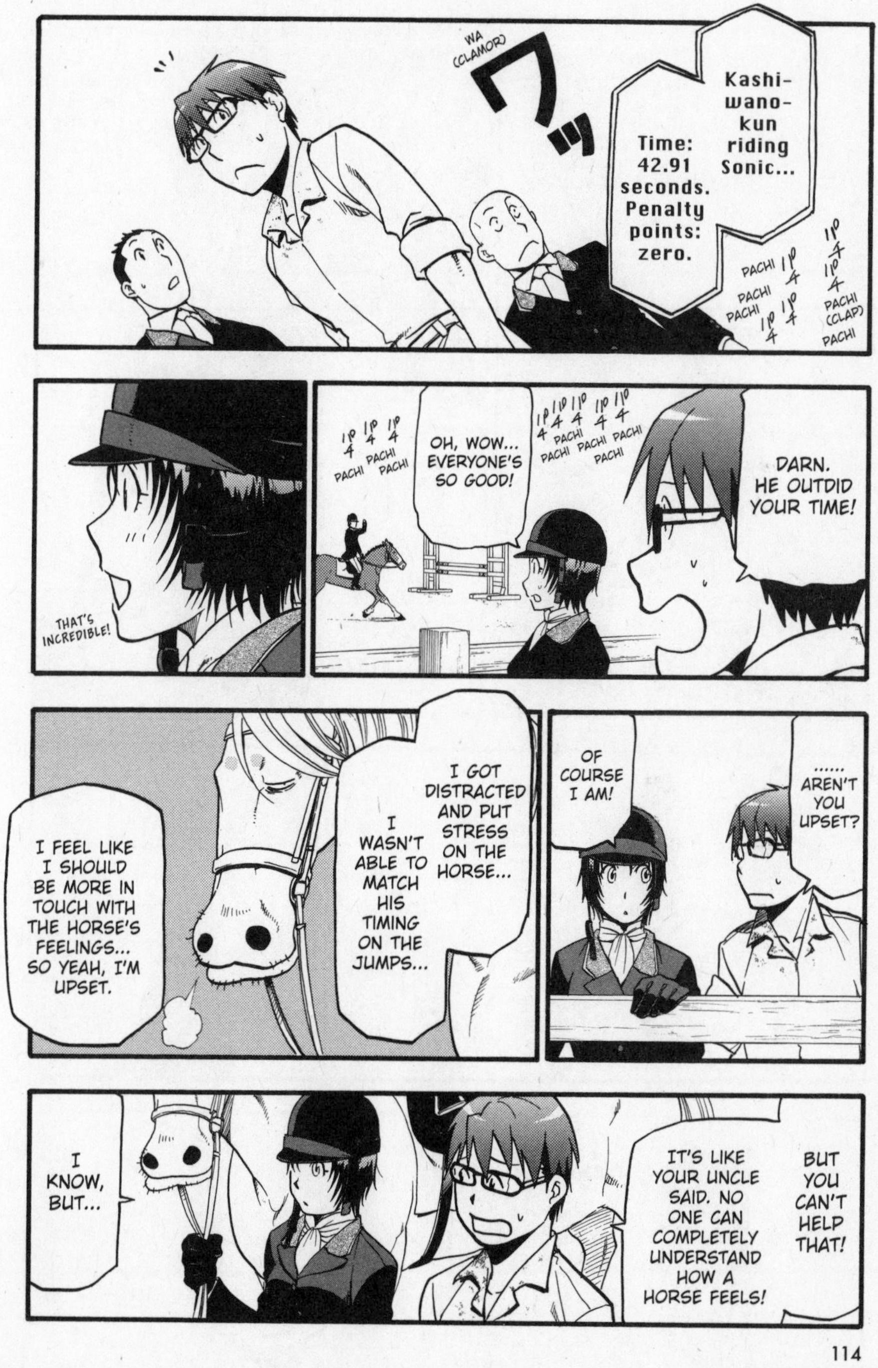
Kashi-wano-kun riding Sonic...
Time: 42.91 seconds. Penalty points: zero.
WA (CLAMOR)
PACHI (CLAP) PACHI PACHI PACHI PACHI
DARN. HE OUTDID YOUR TIME!
PACHI PACHI PACHI PACHI PACHI
OH, WOW... EVERYONE'S SO GOOD!
PACHI PACHI PACHI
THAT'S INCREDIBLE!
......AREN'T YOU UPSET?
OF COURSE I AM!
I GOT DISTRACTED AND PUT STRESS ON THE HORSE...
I WASN'T ABLE TO MATCH HIS TIMING ON THE JUMPS...
I FEEL LIKE I SHOULD BE MORE IN TOUCH WITH THE HORSE'S FEELINGS... SO YEAH, I'M UPSET.
BUT YOU CAN'T HELP THAT!
IT'S LIKE YOUR UNCLE SAID. NO ONE CAN COMPLETELY UNDERSTAND HOW A HORSE FEELS!
I KNOW, BUT...

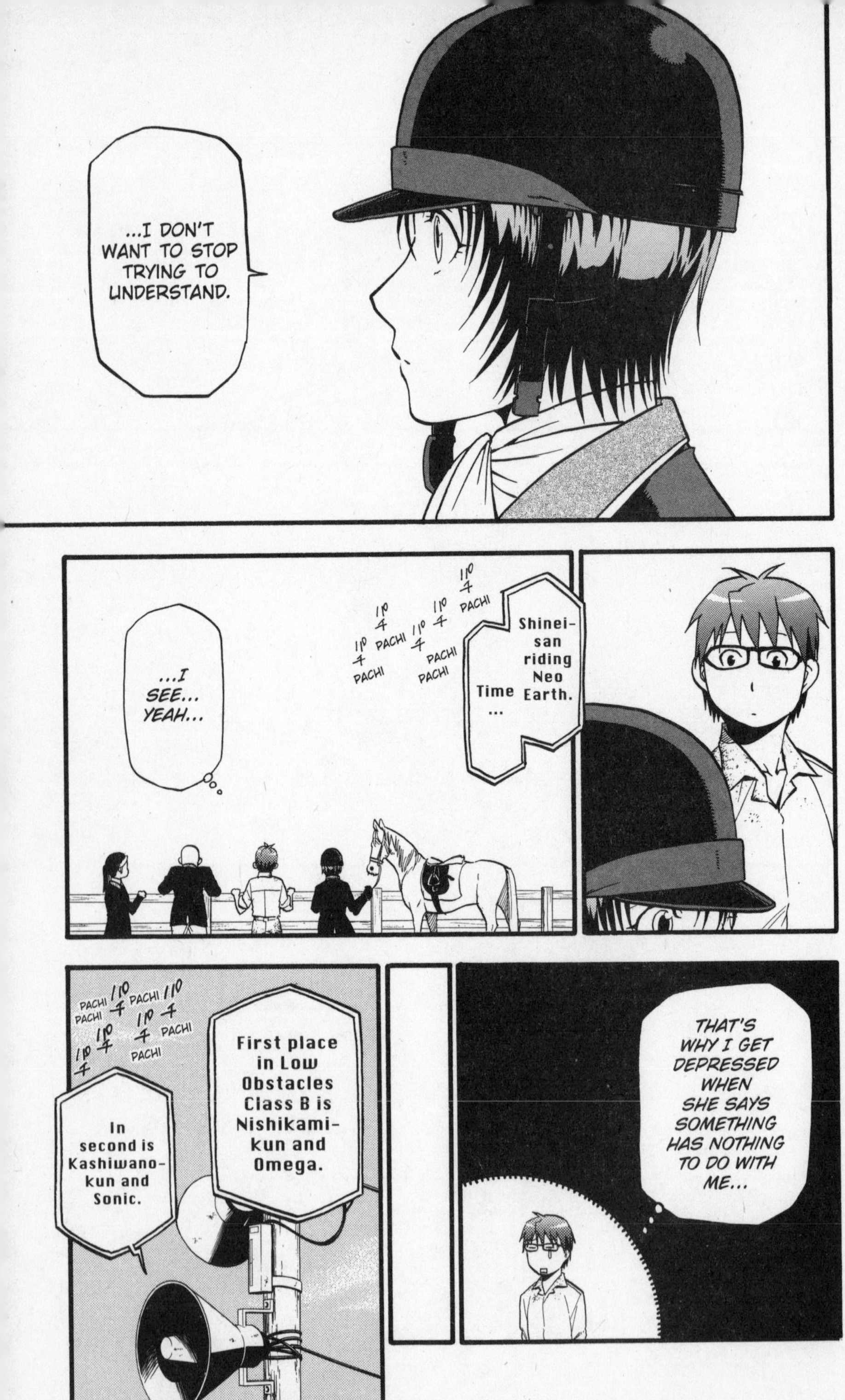
...I DON'T WANT TO STOP TRYING TO UNDERSTAND.
Shinei-san riding Neo Earth.
Time...
PACHI PACHI PACHI PACHI PACHI
...I SEE... YEAH...
THAT'S WHY I GET DEPRESSED WHEN SHE SAYS SOMETHING HAS NOTHING TO DO WITH ME...
PACHI PACHI PACHI PACHI PACHI
First place in Low Obstacles Class B is Nishikami-kun and Omega.
In second is Kashiwano-kun and Sonic.

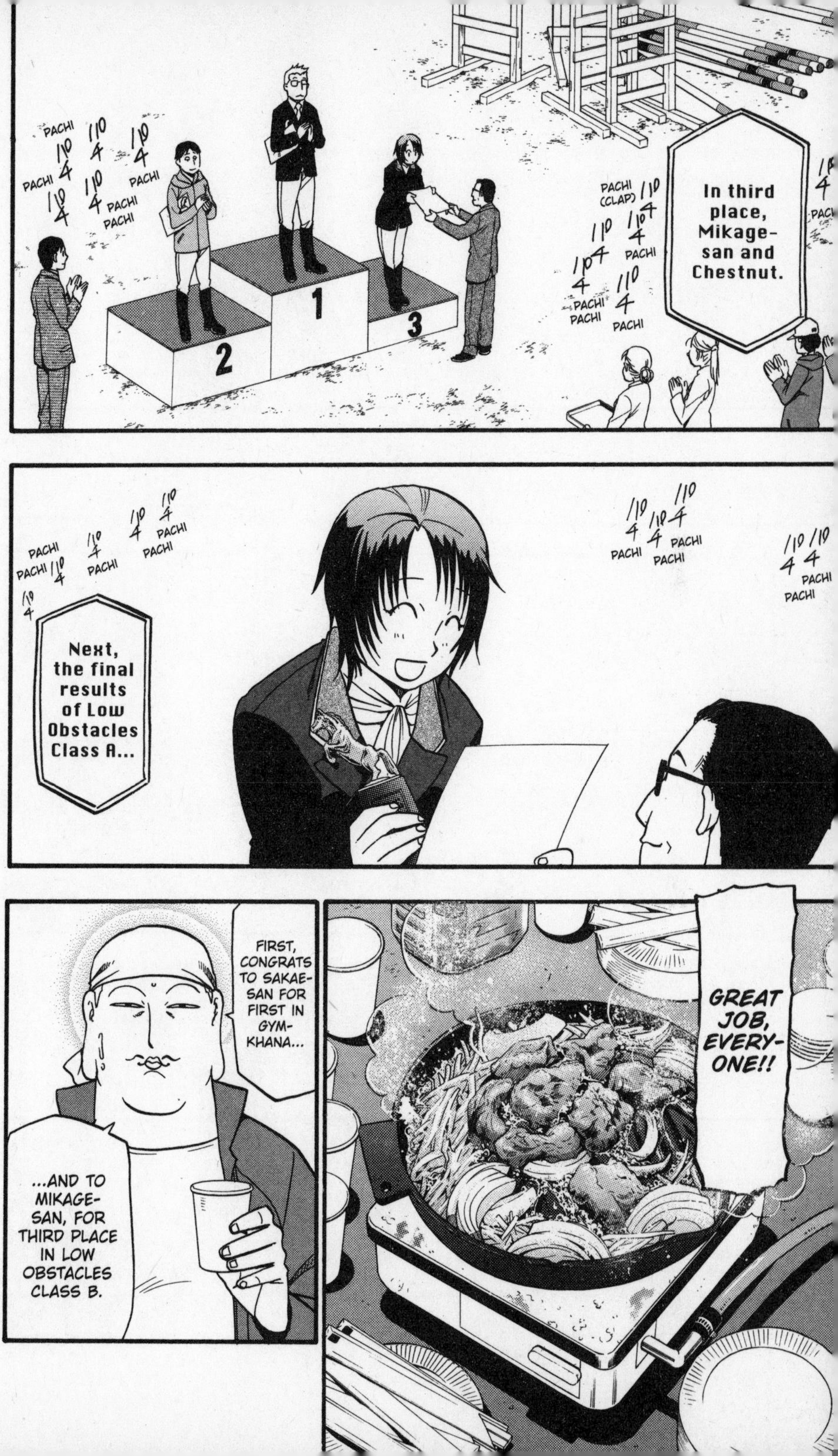
In third place, Mikage-san and Chestnut.
PACHI (CLAP)
PACHI
PACHI PACHI
PACHI
PACHI PACHI
PACHI
PACHI PACHI
Next, the final results of Low Obstacles Class A...
PACHI PACHI
PACHI PACHI
PACHI PACHI
PACHI PACHI
GREAT JOB, EVERYONE!!
FIRST, CONGRATS TO SAKAE-SAN FOR FIRST IN GYMKHANA...
...AND TO MIKAGE-SAN, FOR THIRD PLACE IN LOW OBSTACLES CLASS B.

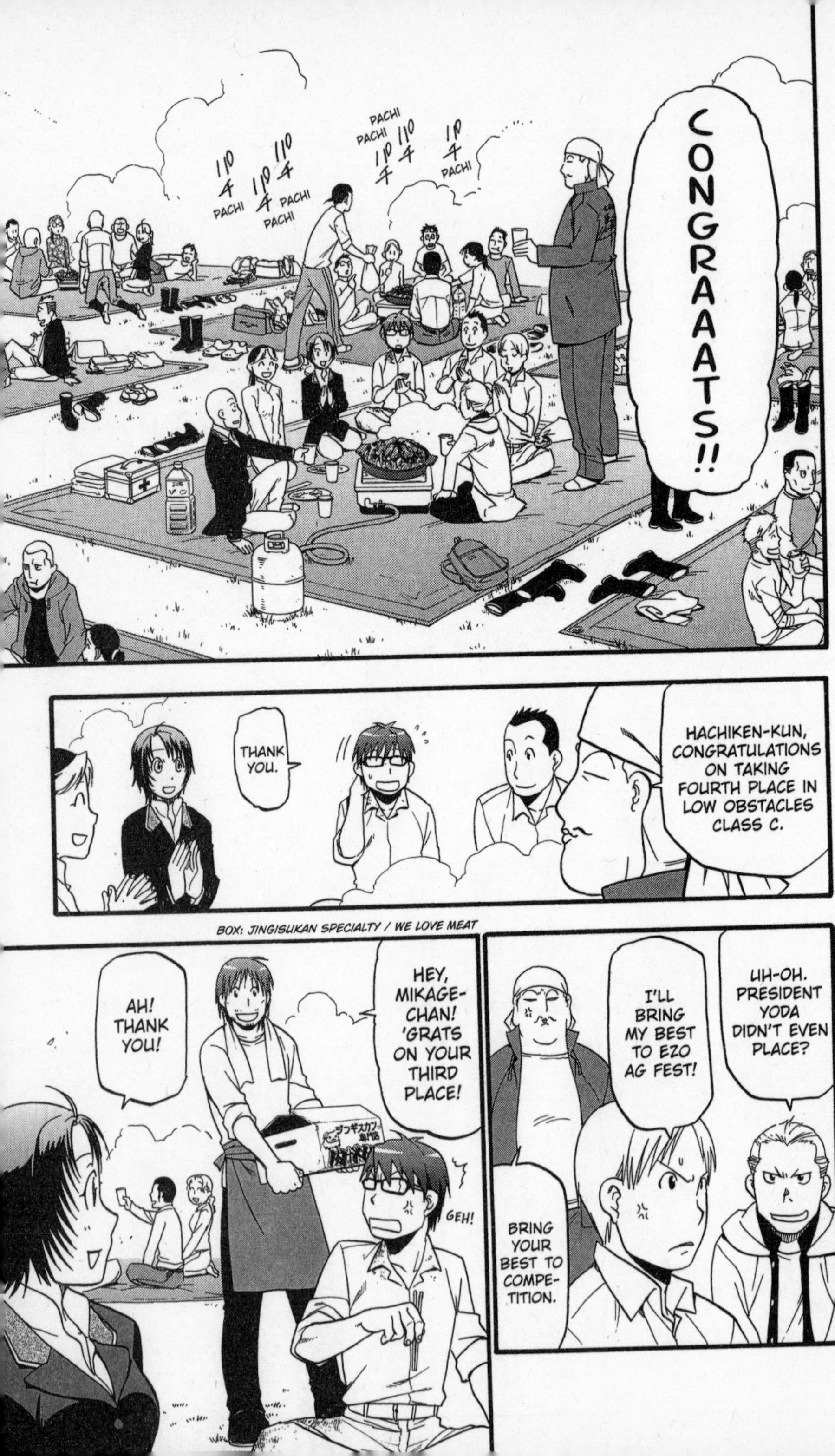
CONGRAAATS!!
PACHI PACHI
PACHI
PACHI
PACHI
PACHI
HACHIKEN-KUN, CONGRATULATIONS ON TAKING FOURTH PLACE IN LOW OBSTACLES CLASS C.
THANK YOU.
UH-OH. PRESIDENT YODA DIDN'T EVEN PLACE?
I'LL BRING MY BEST TO EZO AG FEST!
BRING YOUR BEST TO COMPETITION.
BOX: JINGISUKAN SPECIALTY / WE LOVE MEAT
HEY, MIKAGE-CHAN! 'GRATS ON YOUR THIRD PLACE!
AH! THANK YOU!
GEH!

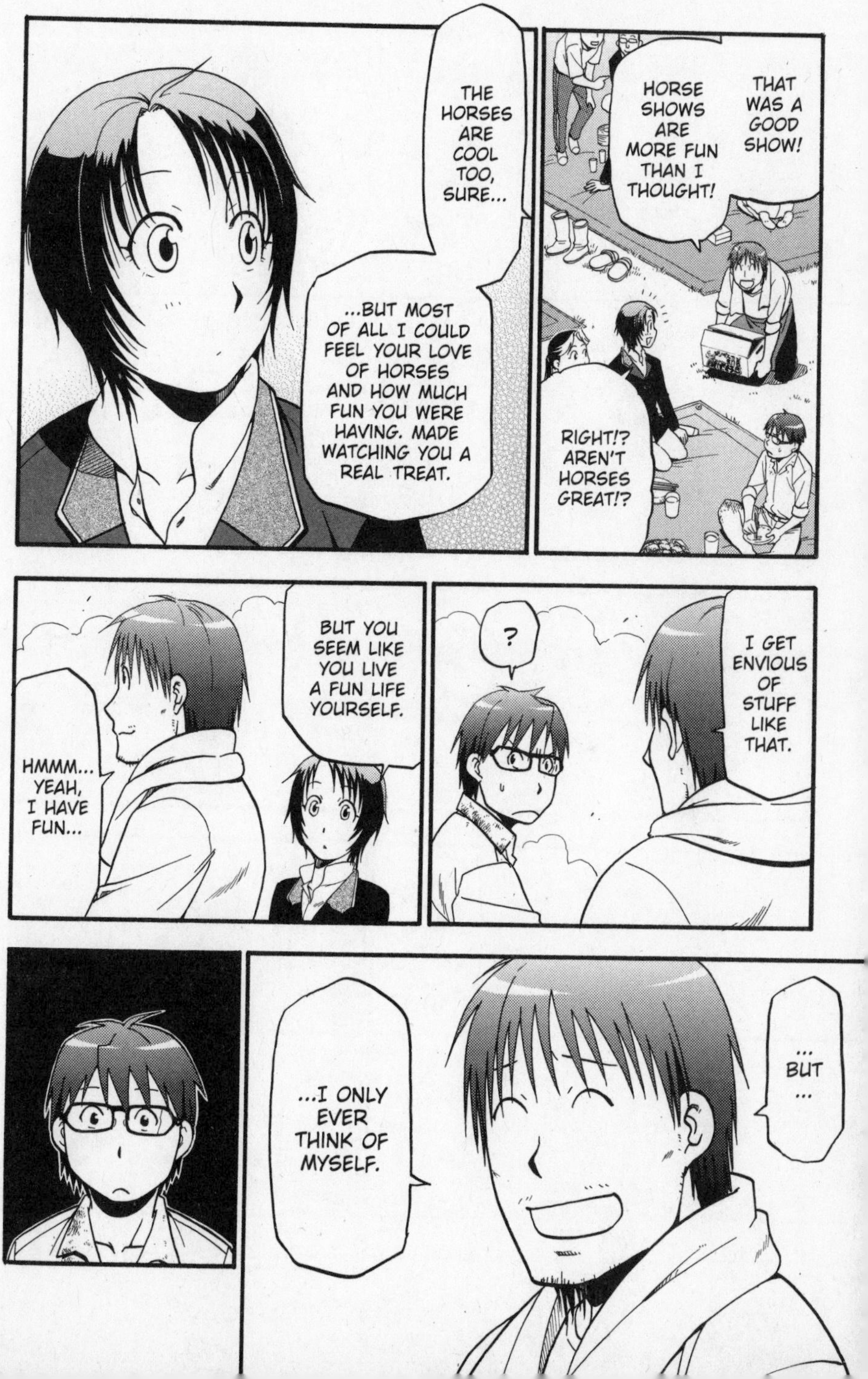
THAT WAS A GOOD SHOW!
HORSE SHOWS ARE MORE FUN THAN I THOUGHT!
RIGHT!? AREN'T HORSES GREAT!?
THE HORSES ARE COOL TOO, SURE...
...BUT MOST OF ALL I COULD FEEL YOUR LOVE OF HORSES AND HOW MUCH FUN YOU WERE HAVING. MADE WATCHING YOU A REAL TREAT.
I GET ENVIOUS OF STUFF LIKE THAT.
?
BUT YOU SEEM LIKE YOU LIVE A FUN LIFE YOURSELF.
HMMM... YEAH, I HAVE FUN...
...BUT...
...I ONLY EVER THINK OF MYSELF.

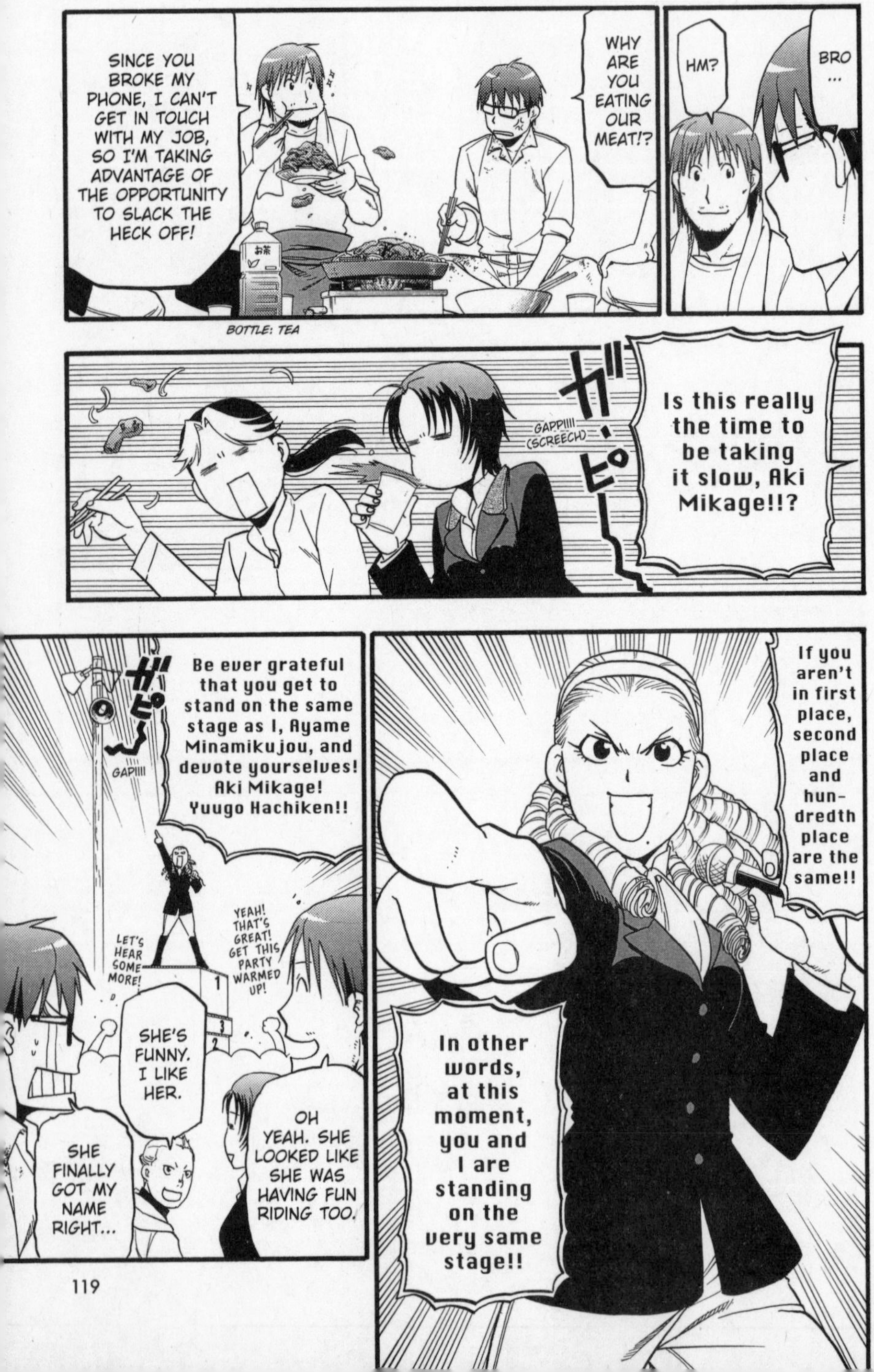
BRO ...
HM?
WHY ARE YOU EATING OUR MEAT!?
SINCE YOU BROKE MY PHONE, I CAN'T GET IN TOUCH WITH MY JOB, SO I'M TAKING ADVANTAGE OF THE OPPORTUNITY TO SLACK THE HECK OFF!
お茶
BOTTLE: TEA
Is this really the time to be taking it slow, Aki Mikage!!?
GAPP!!!! (SCREECH)
If you aren't in first place, second place and hun-dredth place are the same!!
In other words, at this moment, you and I are standing on the very same stage!!
Be ever grateful that you get to stand on the same stage as I, Ayame Minamikujou, and devote yourselves! Aki Mikage! Yuugo Hachiken!!
GAP!!!!
YEAH! THAT'S GREAT! GET THIS PARTY WARMED UP!
LET'S HEAR SOME MORE!
SHE'S FUNNY. I LIKE HER.
OH YEAH. SHE LOOKED LIKE SHE WAS HAVING FUN RIDING TOO.
SHE FINALLY GOT MY NAME RIGHT...

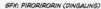

SFX: PIRORIRORIN (DINGALING)

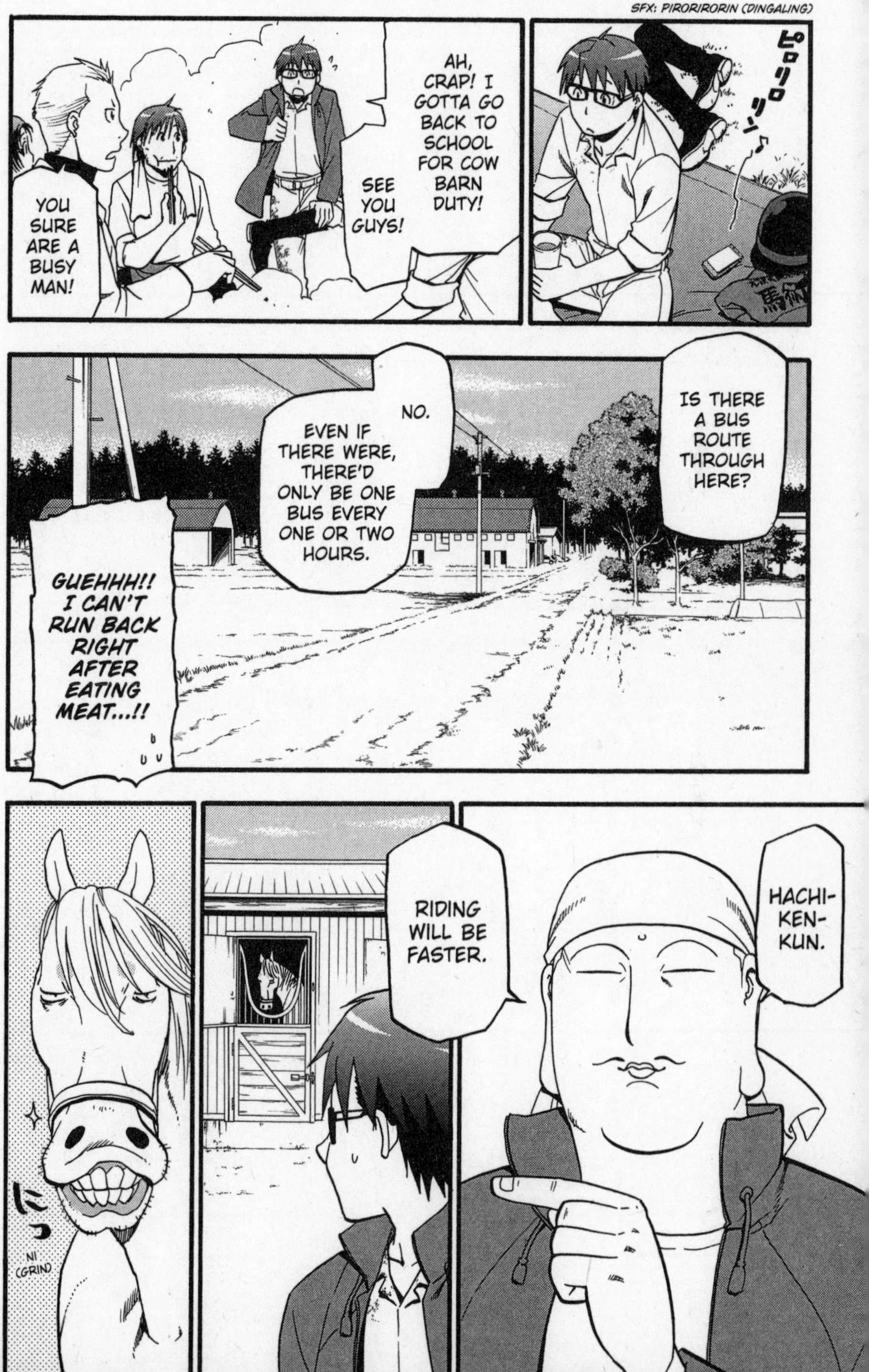
ピロリロリン♪
AH, CRAP! I GOTTA GO BACK TO SCHOOL FOR COW BARN DUTY!
SEE YOU GUYS!
YOU SURE ARE A BUSY MAN!
IS THERE A BUS ROUTE THROUGH HERE?
NO.
EVEN IF THERE WERE, THERE'D ONLY BE ONE BUS EVERY ONE OR TWO HOURS.
GUEHHH!! I CAN'T RUN BACK RIGHT AFTER EATING MEAT...!!
HACHI-KEN-KUN.
RIDING WILL BE FASTER.
にっ
NI (GRIND)

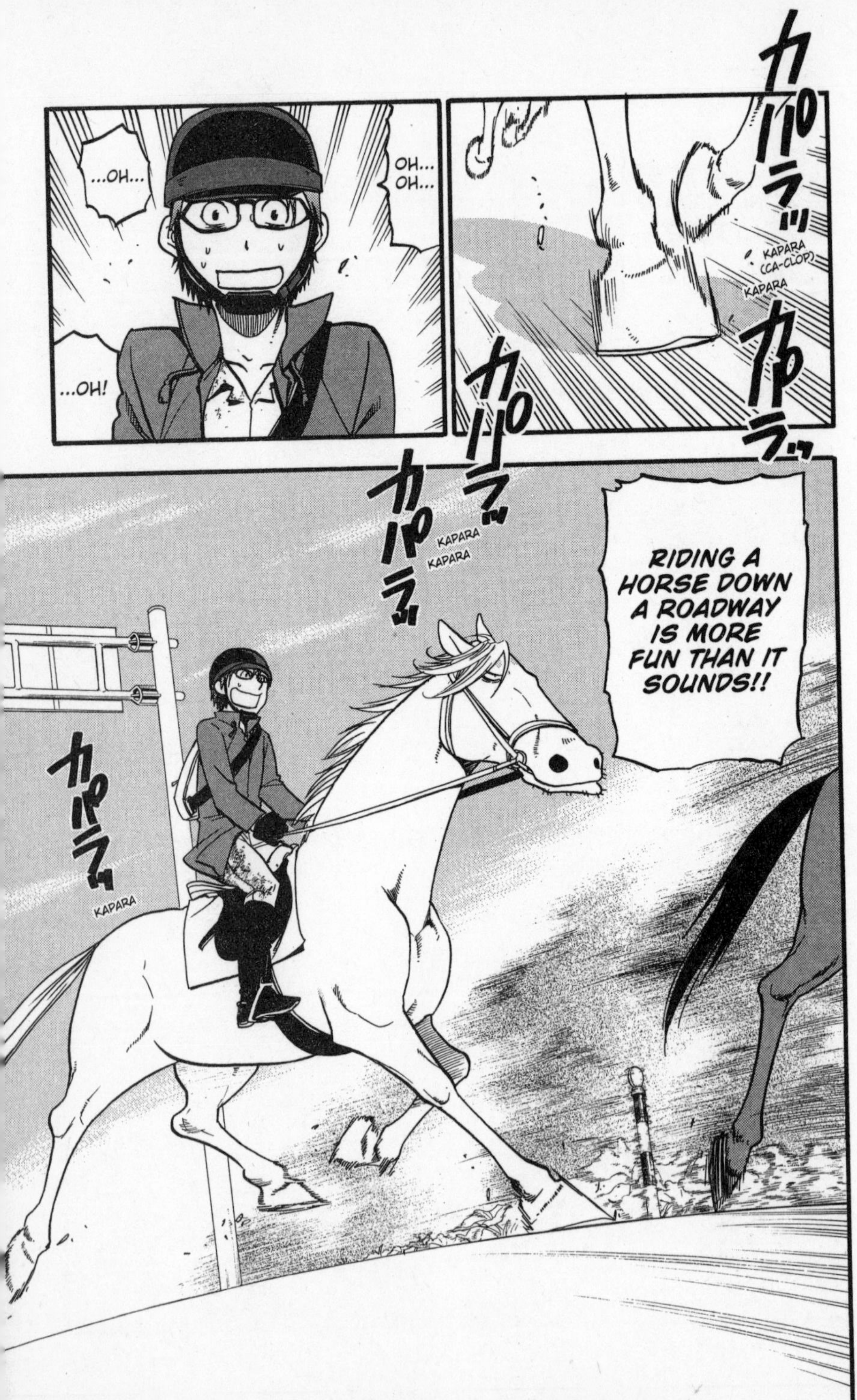
KAPARA (CA-CLOP)
KAPARA
OH... OH...
...OH...
...OH!
RIDING A HORSE DOWN A ROADWAY IS MORE FUN THAN IT SOUNDS!!
KAPARA KAPARA
KAPARA

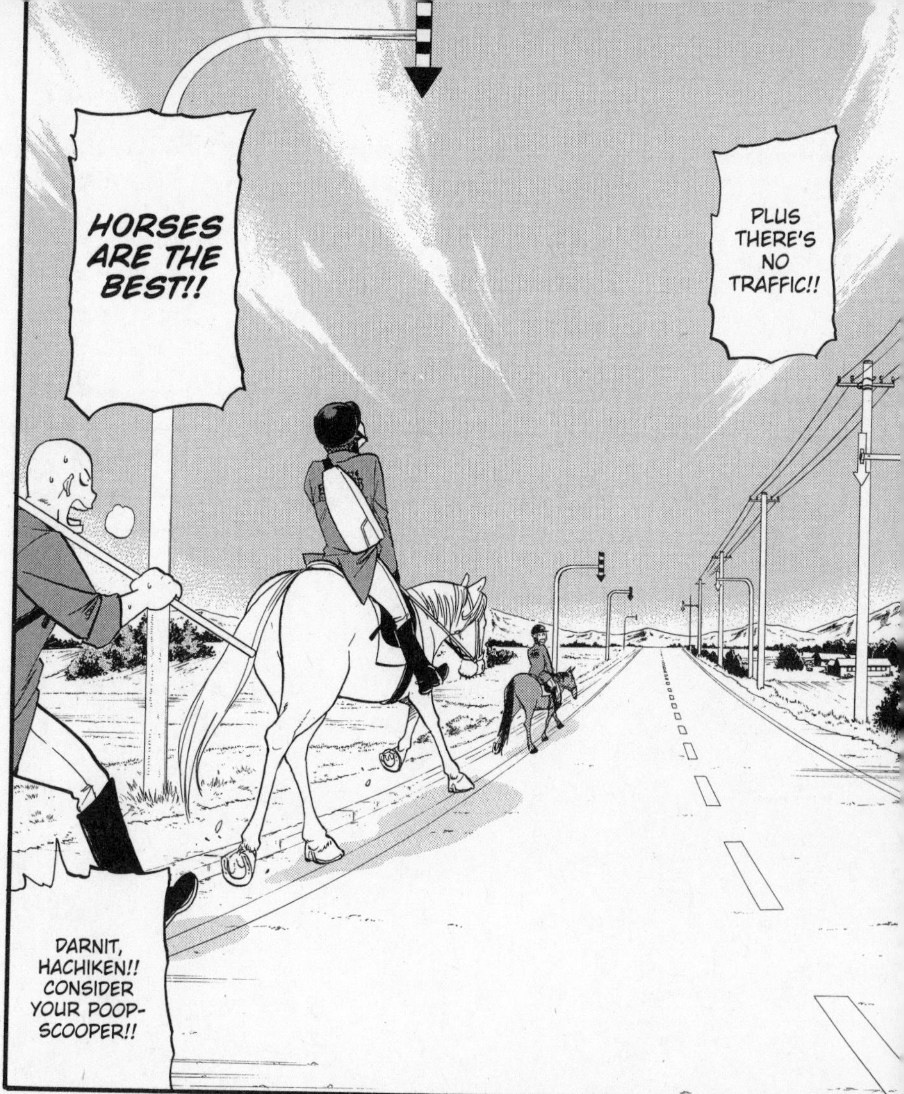
PLUS THERE'S NO TRAFFIC!!
HORSES ARE THE BEST!!
DARNIT, HACHIKEN!! CONSIDER YOUR POOP-SCOOPER!!

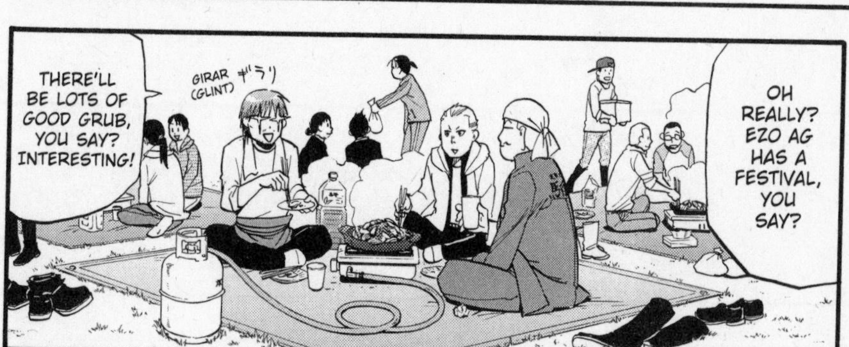
OH REALLY? EZO AG HAS A FESTIVAL, YOU SAY?
GIRAR (GLINT) ギラリ
THERE'LL BE LOTS OF GOOD GRUB, YOU SAY? INTERESTING!

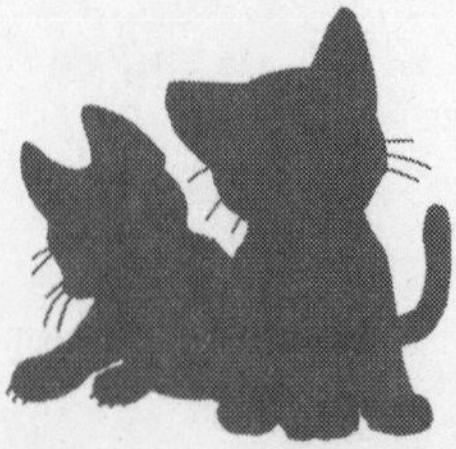

Silver Spoon

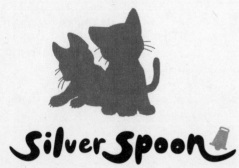

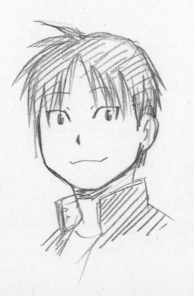

HARUHIKO MIYAMAI

OKUBETSUKAI MIDDLE
SCHOOL

BADMINTON TEAM

Chapter 51:
Tale of Autumn ⑳

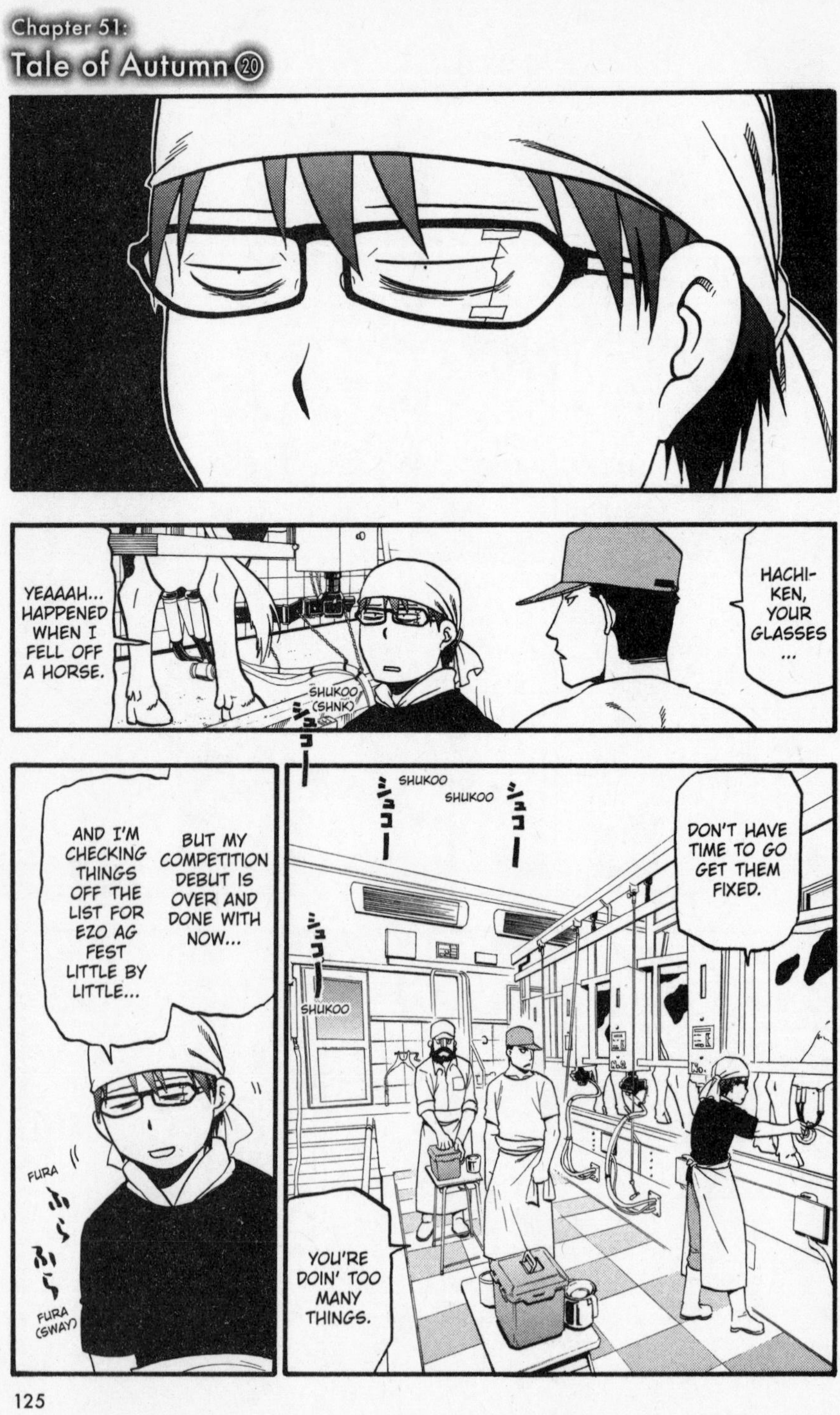
HACHIKEN, YOUR GLASSES...
YEAAAH... HAPPENED WHEN I FELL OFF A HORSE.
SHUKOO (SHNK)
SHUKOO
SHUKOO
DON'T HAVE TIME TO GO GET THEM FIXED.
SHUKOO
YOU'RE DOIN' TOO MANY THINGS.
BUT MY COMPETITION DEBUT IS OVER AND DONE WITH NOW...
AND I'M CHECKING THINGS OFF THE LIST FOR EZO AG FEST LITTLE BY LITTLE...
FURA
FURA (SWAY)

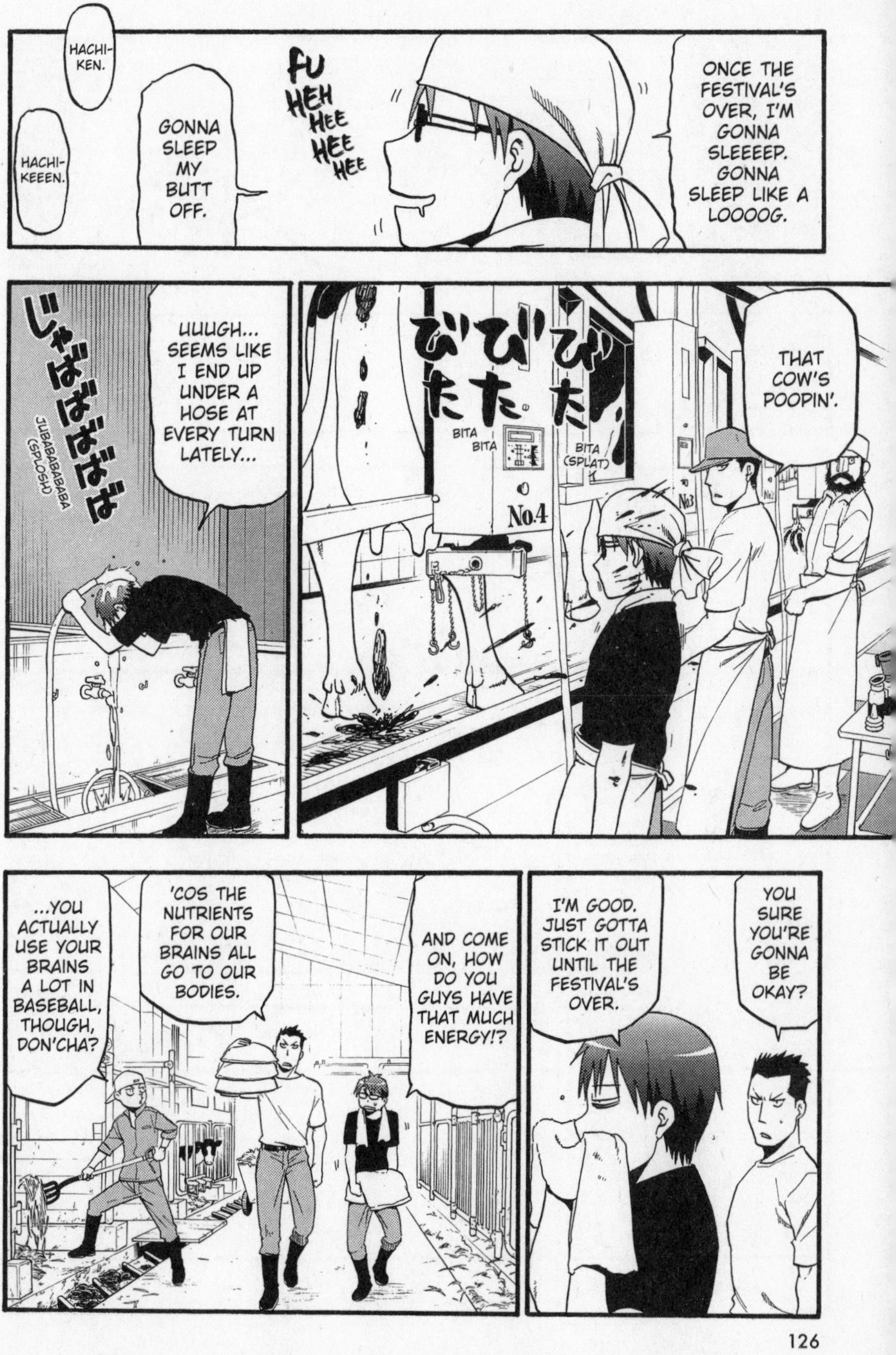
ONCE THE FESTIVAL'S OVER, I'M GONNA SLEEEEP. GONNA SLEEP LIKE A LOOOOG.
FU HEH HEE HEE HEE
GONNA SLEEP MY BUTT OFF.
HACHI-KEN.
HACHI-KEEEN.
THAT COW'S POOPIN'.
びたびたびた
BITA BITA
BITA (SPLAT)
No.4
UUUGH... SEEMS LIKE I END UP UNDER A HOSE AT EVERY TURN LATELY...
じゃばばばばば
JUBABABABA (SPLOSH)
YOU SURE YOU'RE GONNA BE OKAY?
I'M GOOD. JUST GOTTA STICK IT OUT UNTIL THE FESTIVAL'S OVER.
AND COME ON, HOW DO YOU GUYS HAVE THAT MUCH ENERGY!?
'COS THE NUTRIENTS FOR OUR BRAINS ALL GO TO OUR BODIES.
...YOU ACTUALLY USE YOUR BRAINS A LOT IN BASEBALL, THOUGH, DON'CHA?

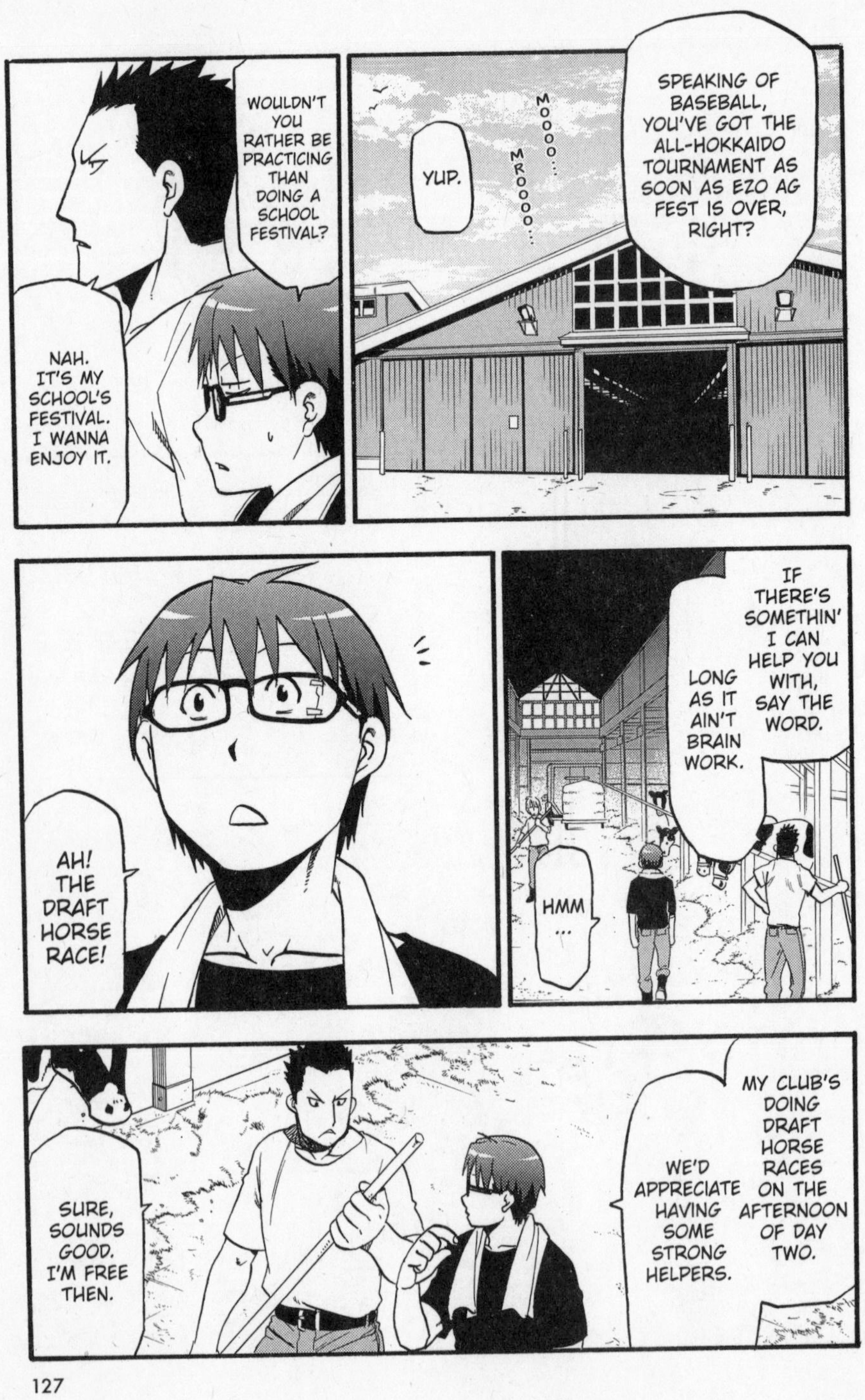
SPEAKING OF BASEBALL, YOU'VE GOT THE ALL-HOKKAIDO TOURNAMENT AS SOON AS EZO AG FEST IS OVER, RIGHT?
MOOOO...
MROOOOO...
YUP.
WOULDN'T YOU RATHER BE PRACTICING THAN DOING A SCHOOL FESTIVAL?
NAH. IT'S MY SCHOOL'S FESTIVAL. I WANNA ENJOY IT.
IF THERE'S SOMETHIN' I CAN HELP YOU WITH, SAY THE WORD.
LONG AS IT AIN'T BRAIN WORK.
HMM...
AH! THE DRAFT HORSE RACE!
MY CLUB'S DOING DRAFT HORSE RACES ON THE AFTERNOON OF DAY TWO.
WE'D APPRECIATE HAVING SOME STRONG HELPERS.
SURE, SOUNDS GOOD. I'M FREE THEN.

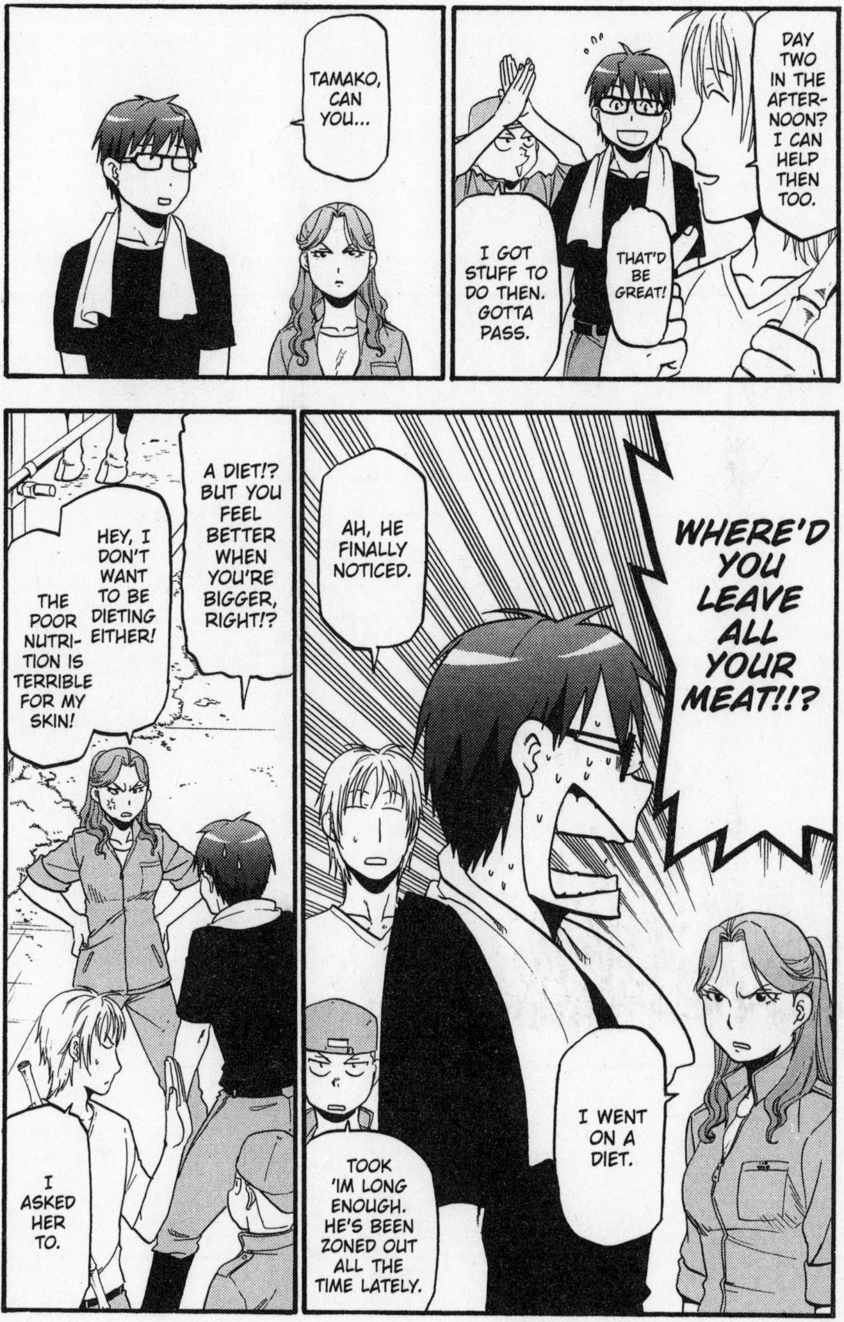
DAY TWO IN THE AFTERNOON? I CAN HELP THEN TOO.
THAT'D BE GREAT!
I GOT STUFF TO DO THEN. GOTTA PASS.
TAMAKO, CAN YOU...
WHERE'D YOU LEAVE ALL YOUR MEAT!!?
AH, HE FINALLY NOTICED.
I WENT ON A DIET.
TOOK 'IM LONG ENOUGH. HE'S BEEN ZONED OUT ALL THE TIME LATELY.
A DIET!? BUT YOU FEEL BETTER WHEN YOU'RE BIGGER, RIGHT!?
HEY, I DON'T WANT TO BE DIETING EITHER!
THE POOR NUTRITION IS TERRIBLE FOR MY SKIN!
I ASKED HER TO.

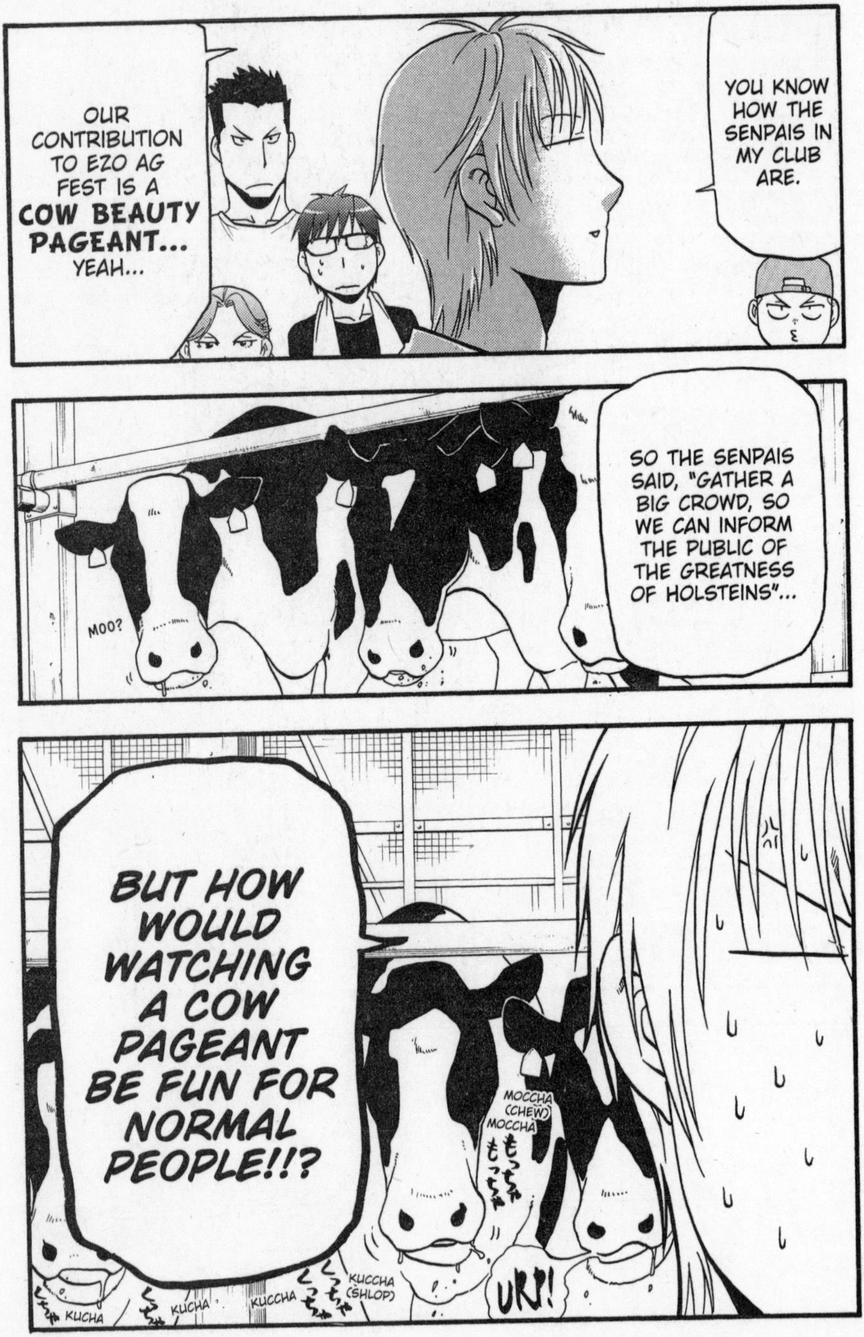
YOU KNOW HOW THE SENPAIS IN MY CLUB ARE.
OUR CONTRIBUTION TO EZO AG FEST IS A COW BEAUTY PAGEANT... YEAH...
SO THE SENPAIS SAID, "GATHER A BIG CROWD, SO WE CAN INFORM THE PUBLIC OF THE GREATNESS OF HOLSTEINS"...
MOO?
BUT HOW WOULD WATCHING A COW PAGEANT BE FUN FOR NORMAL PEOPLE!!?
URP!
MOCCHA (CHEW) MOCCHA
もっちゃ もっちゃ
KUCCHA (SHLOP)
くっちゃ くっちゃ
KUCCHA
KUCHA
KUCHA

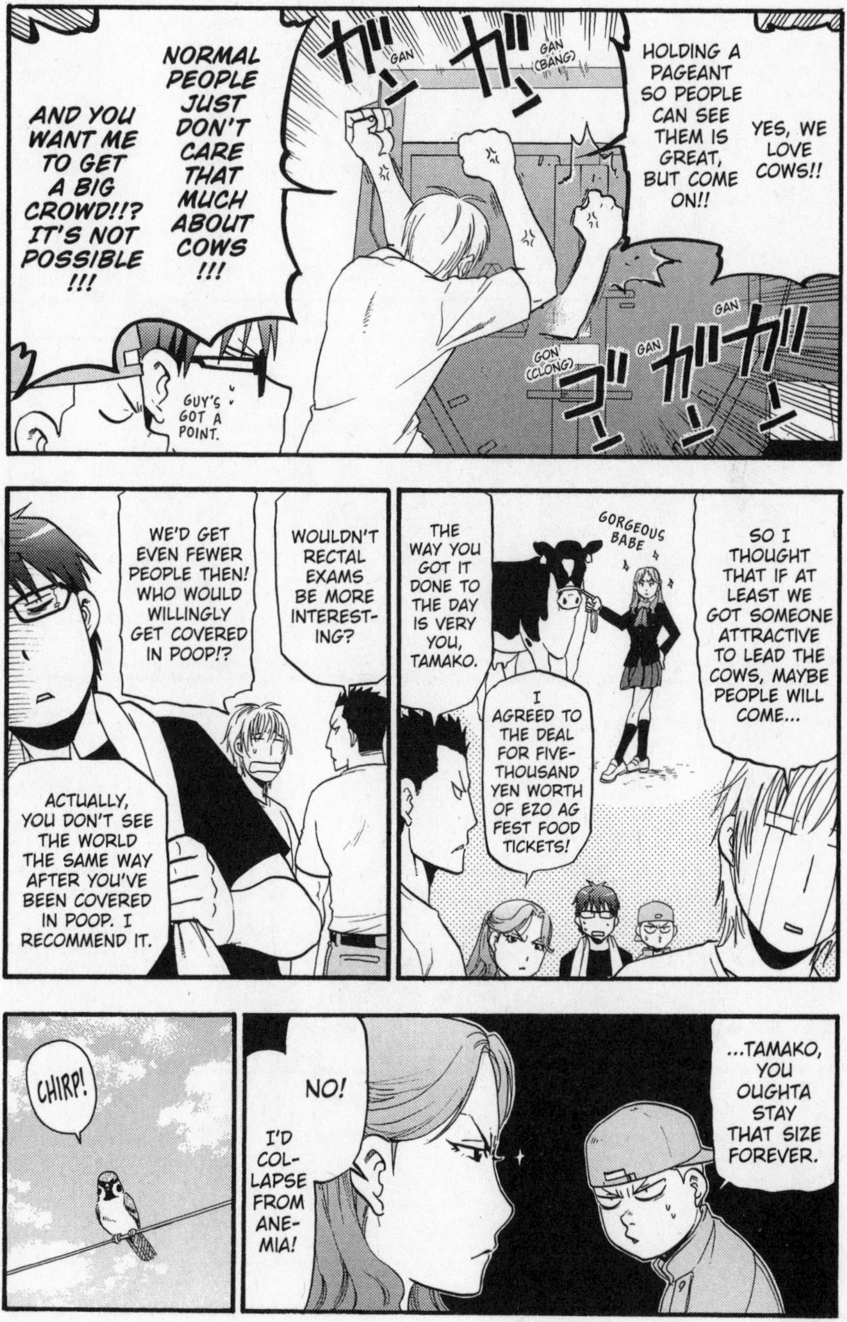
YES, WE LOVE COWS!!
HOLDING A PAGEANT SO PEOPLE CAN SEE THEM IS GREAT, BUT COME ON!!
GAN (BANG)
GAN
NORMAL PEOPLE JUST DON'T CARE THAT MUCH ABOUT COWS!!!
AND YOU WANT ME TO GET A BIG CROWD!!? IT'S NOT POSSIBLE!!!
GAN
GAN
GON (CLONG)
GUY'S GOT A POINT.
SO I THOUGHT THAT IF AT LEAST WE GOT SOMEONE ATTRACTIVE TO LEAD THE COWS, MAYBE PEOPLE WILL COME...
GORGEOUS BABE
THE WAY YOU GOT IT DONE TO THE DAY IS VERY YOU, TAMAKO.
I AGREED TO THE DEAL FOR FIVE-THOUSAND YEN WORTH OF EZO AG FEST FOOD TICKETS!
WOULDN'T RECTAL EXAMS BE MORE INTEREST-ING?
WE'D GET EVEN FEWER PEOPLE THEN! WHO WOULD WILLINGLY GET COVERED IN POOP!?
ACTUALLY, YOU DON'T SEE THE WORLD THE SAME WAY AFTER YOU'VE BEEN COVERED IN POOP. I RECOMMEND IT.
...TAMAKO, YOU OUGHTA STAY THAT SIZE FOREVER.
NO!
I'D COL-LAPSE FROM ANE-MIA!
CHIRP!

Chapter 51: Tale of Autumn 20

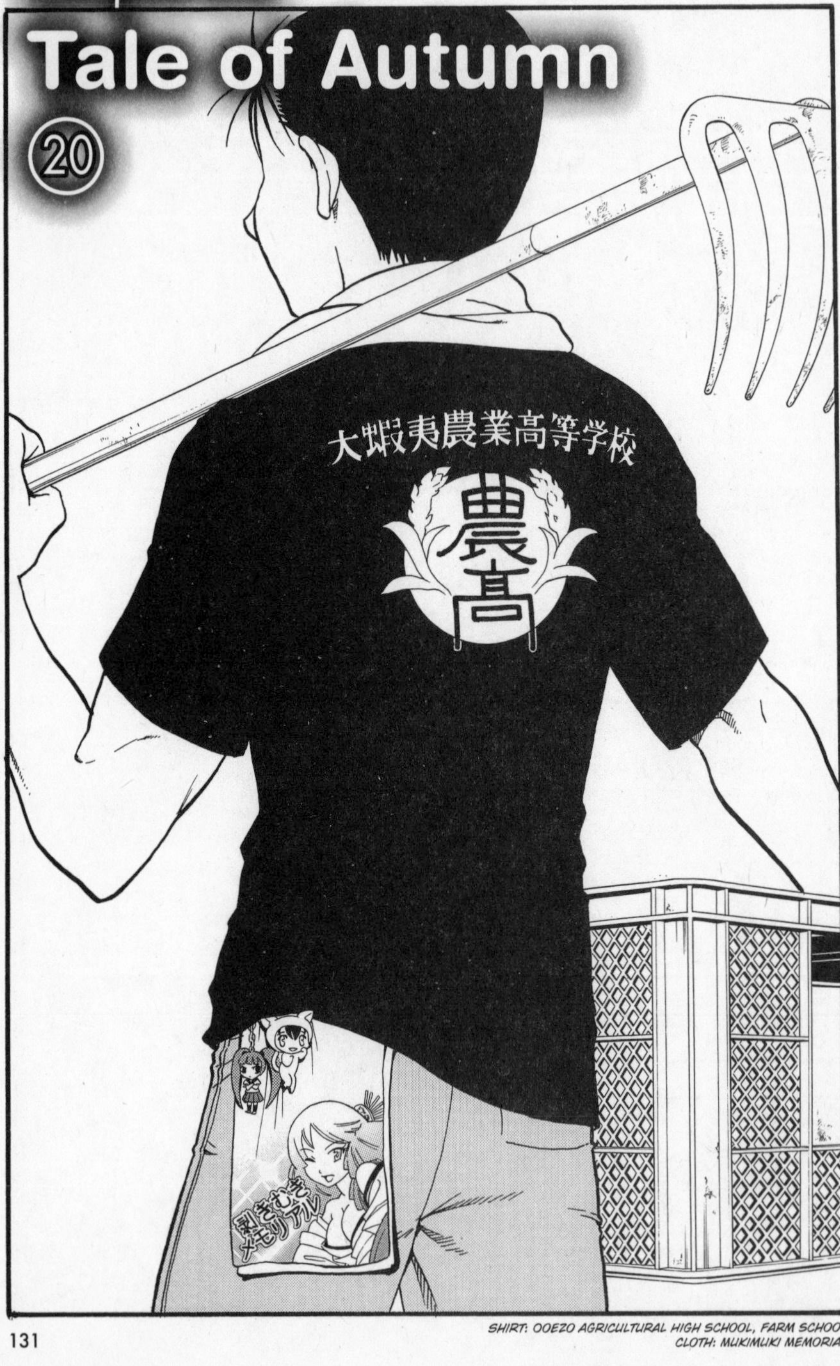
大蝦夷農業高等学校
農高

SHIRT: OOEZO AGRICULTURAL HIGH SCHOOL, FARM SCHOOL
CLOTH: MUKIMUKI MEMORIAL

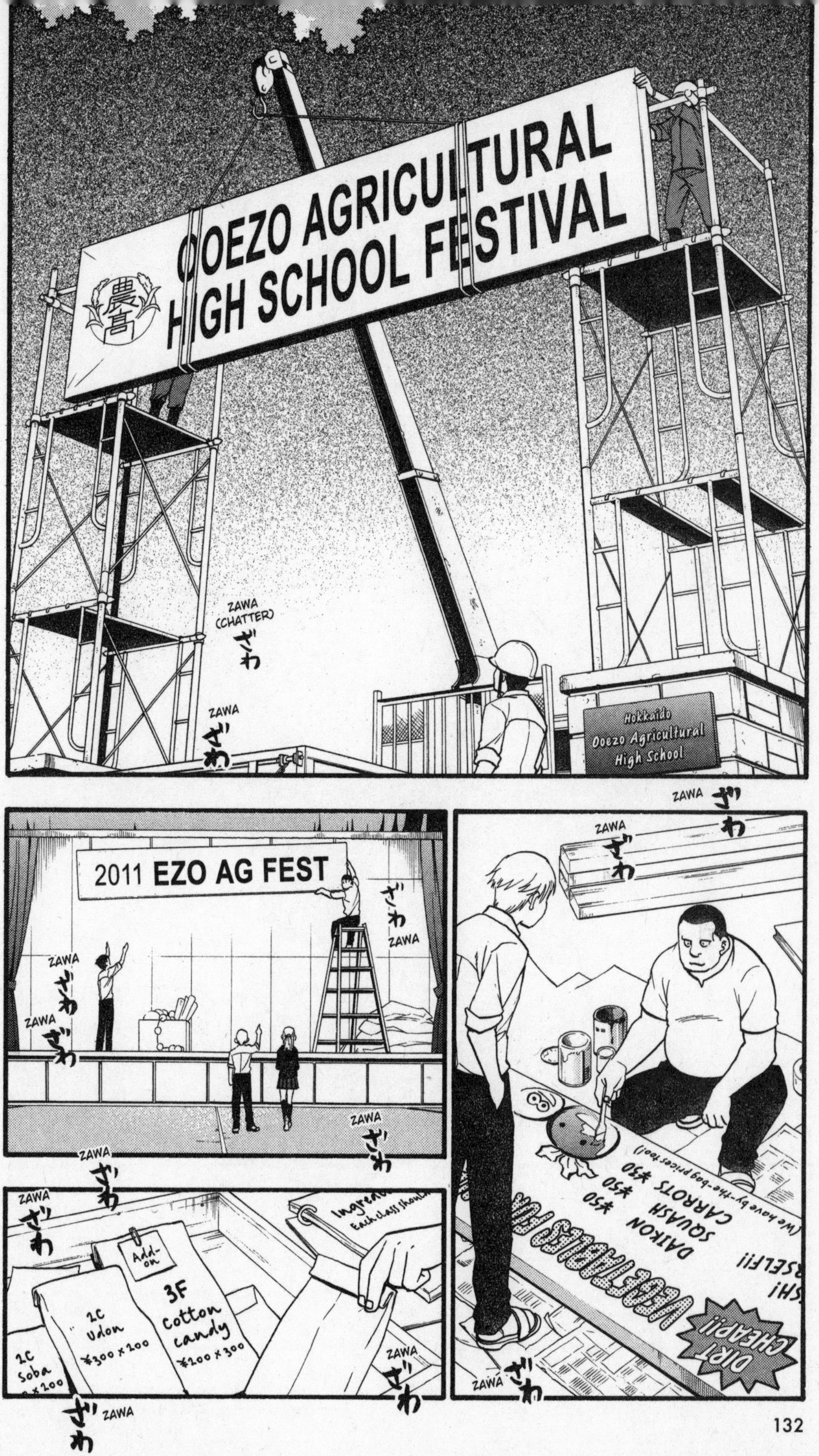
OOEZO AGRICULTURAL HIGH SCHOOL FESTIVAL
ZAWA (CHATTER) ざわ
ZAWA ざわ
Hokkaido Ooezo Agricultural High School
ZAWA ざわ
ZAWA ざわ
DAIKON ¥50
SQUASH ¥50
CARROTS ¥30
(We have by-the-bag prices too!)
DIRT CHEAP!!
ZAWA ざわ
2011 EZO AG FEST
ざわ ZAWA
ZAWA ざわ
ZAWA ざわ
ZAWA ざわ
ZAWA ざわ
ZAWA ざわ
Add-on
3F Cotton candy ¥200 x 300
2C Udon ¥300 x 200
2C Soba
ZAWA ざわ
ZAWA ざわ

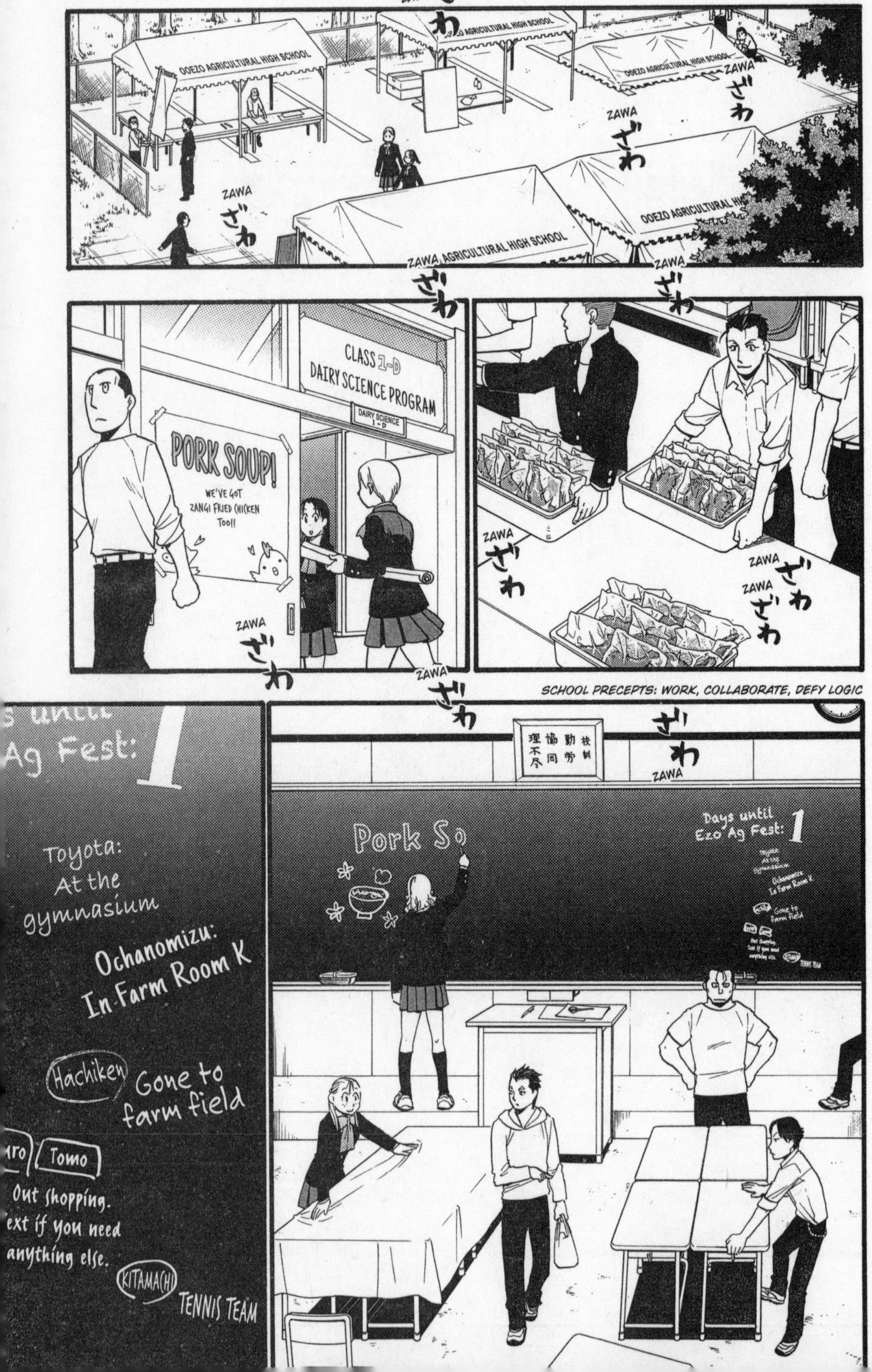
ZAWA ざわ
OOEZO AGRICULTURAL HIGH SCHOOL
ZAWA ざわ
ZAWA ざわ
OOEZO AGRICULTURAL HIGH SCHOOL
OOEZO AGRICULTURAL HIGH SCHOOL
ZAWA ざわ
OOEZO AGRICULTURAL HIGH SCHOOL
ZAWA AGRICULTURAL HIGH SCHOOL
ZAWA ざわ
ZAWA ざわ
ZAWA ざわ
ZAWA ざわ
ZAWA ざわ
CLASS 1-D
DAIRY SCIENCE PROGRAM
DAIRY SCIENCE 1-D
PORK SOUP!
WE'VE GOT ZANGI FRIED CHICKEN TOO!!
ZAWA ざわ
ZAWA ざわ
SCHOOL PRECEPTS: WORK, COLLABORATE, DEFY LOGIC
校訓 勤労 協同 理不尽
ざわ ZAWA
Pork So
Days until Ezo Ag Fest: 1
Toyota: At the gymnasium
Ochanomizu: In Farm Room K
Hachiken Gone to farm field
Out shopping. Text if you need anything else.
KITAMACHI TENNIS TEAM
Ag Fest: 1
Toyota: At the gymnasium
Ochanomizu: In Farm Room K
Hachiken Gone to farm field
Tomo
Out shopping.
anything else.
KITAMACHI TENNIS TEAM

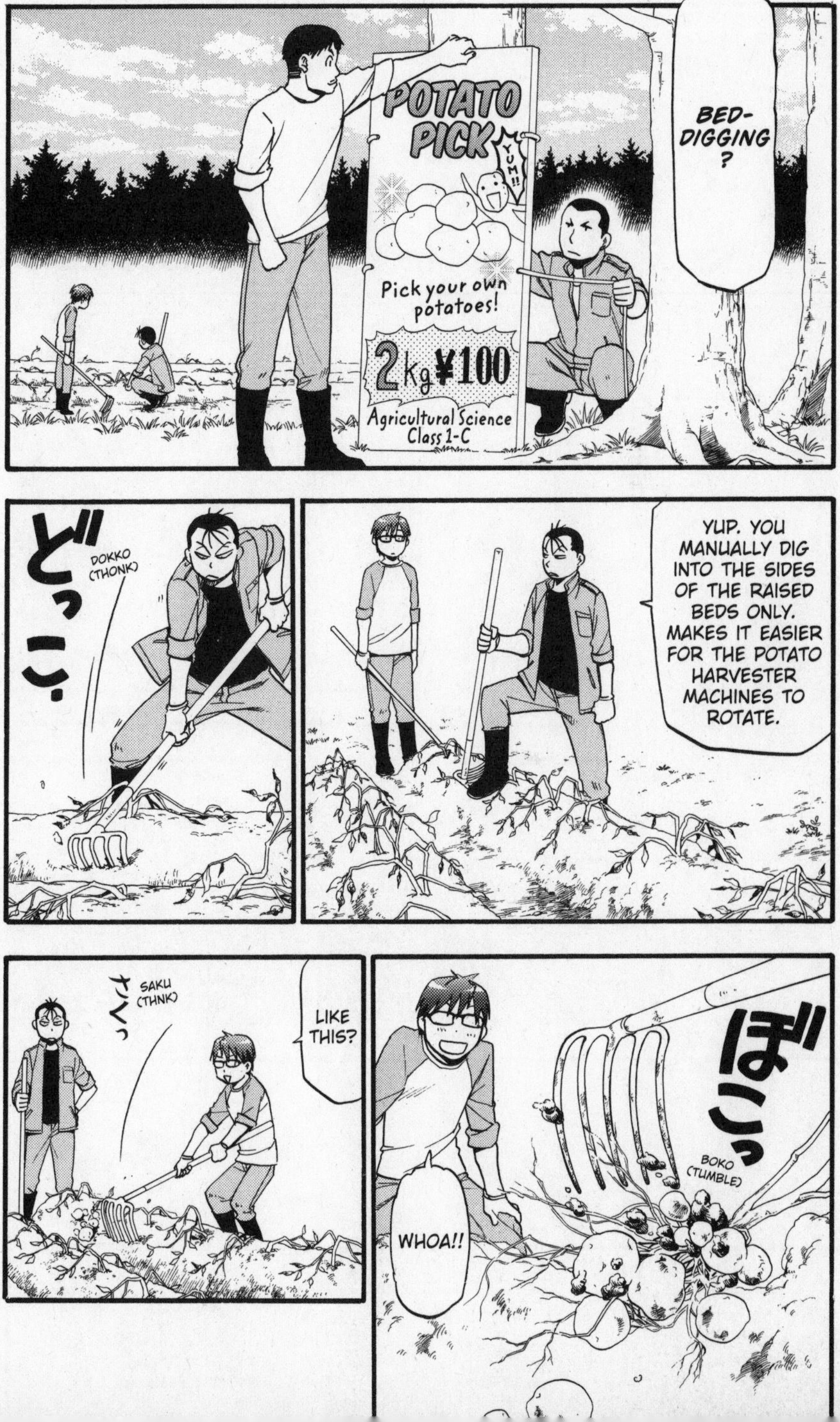
BED-DIGGING?
POTATO PICK
YUM!!
Pick your own potatoes!
2kg ¥100
Agricultural Science Class 1-C
YUP. YOU MANUALLY DIG INTO THE SIDES OF THE RAISED BEDS ONLY. MAKES IT EASIER FOR THE POTATO HARVESTER MACHINES TO ROTATE.
どっこ
DOKKO (THONK)
ぼこっ
BOKO (TUMBLE)
WHOA!!
LIKE THIS?
ざくっ
SAKU (THNK)

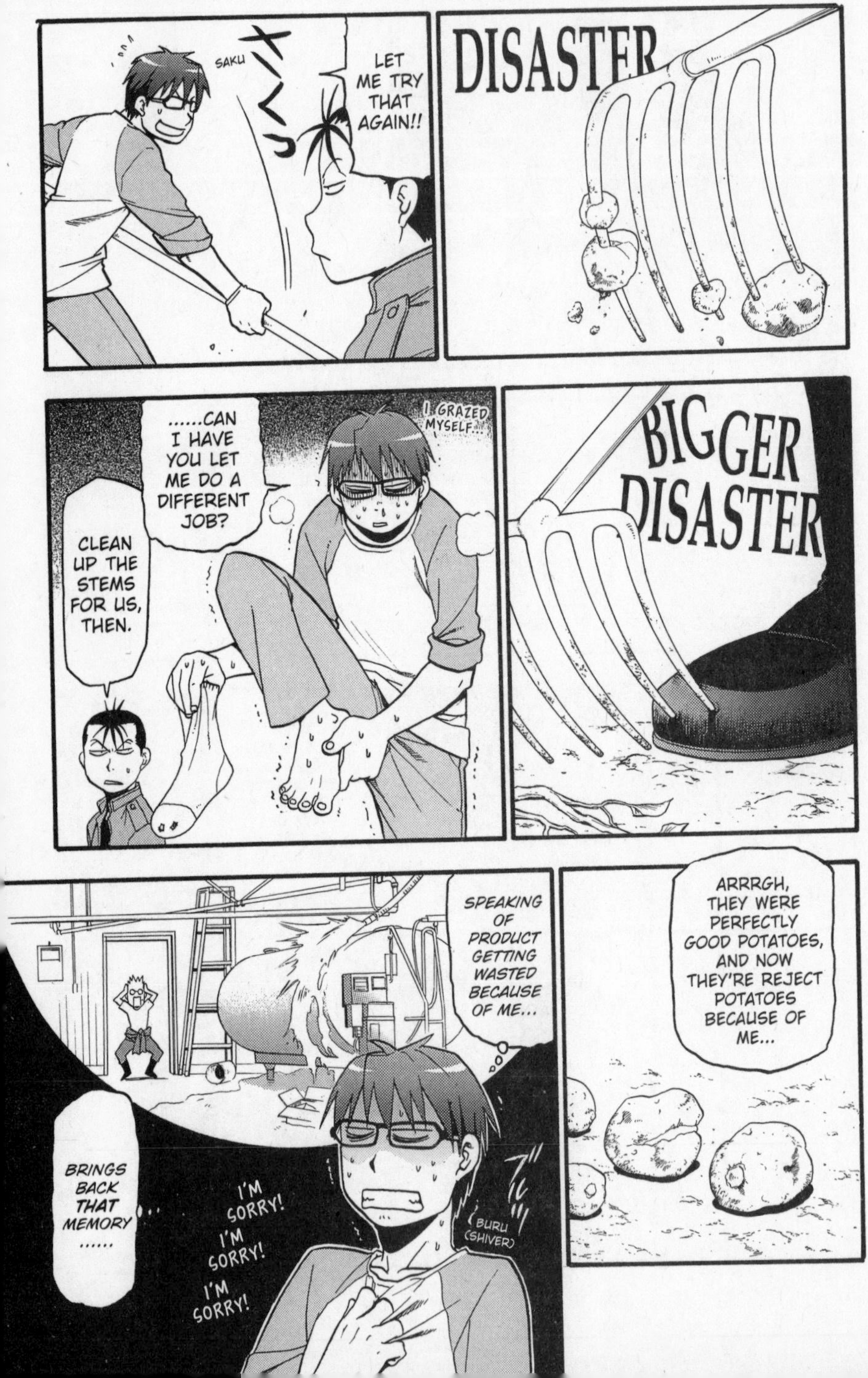
DISASTER
さくっ
SAKU
LET ME TRY THAT AGAIN!!
BIGGER DISASTER
I GRAZED MYSELF...
......CAN I HAVE YOU LET ME DO A DIFFERENT JOB?
CLEAN UP THE STEMS FOR US, THEN.
ARRRGH, THEY WERE PERFECTLY GOOD POTATOES, AND NOW THEY'RE REJECT POTATOES BECAUSE OF ME...
SPEAKING OF PRODUCT GETTING WASTED BECAUSE OF ME...
BURU (SHIVER)
I'M SORRY!
I'M SORRY!
I'M SORRY!
BRINGS BACK THAT MEMORY......

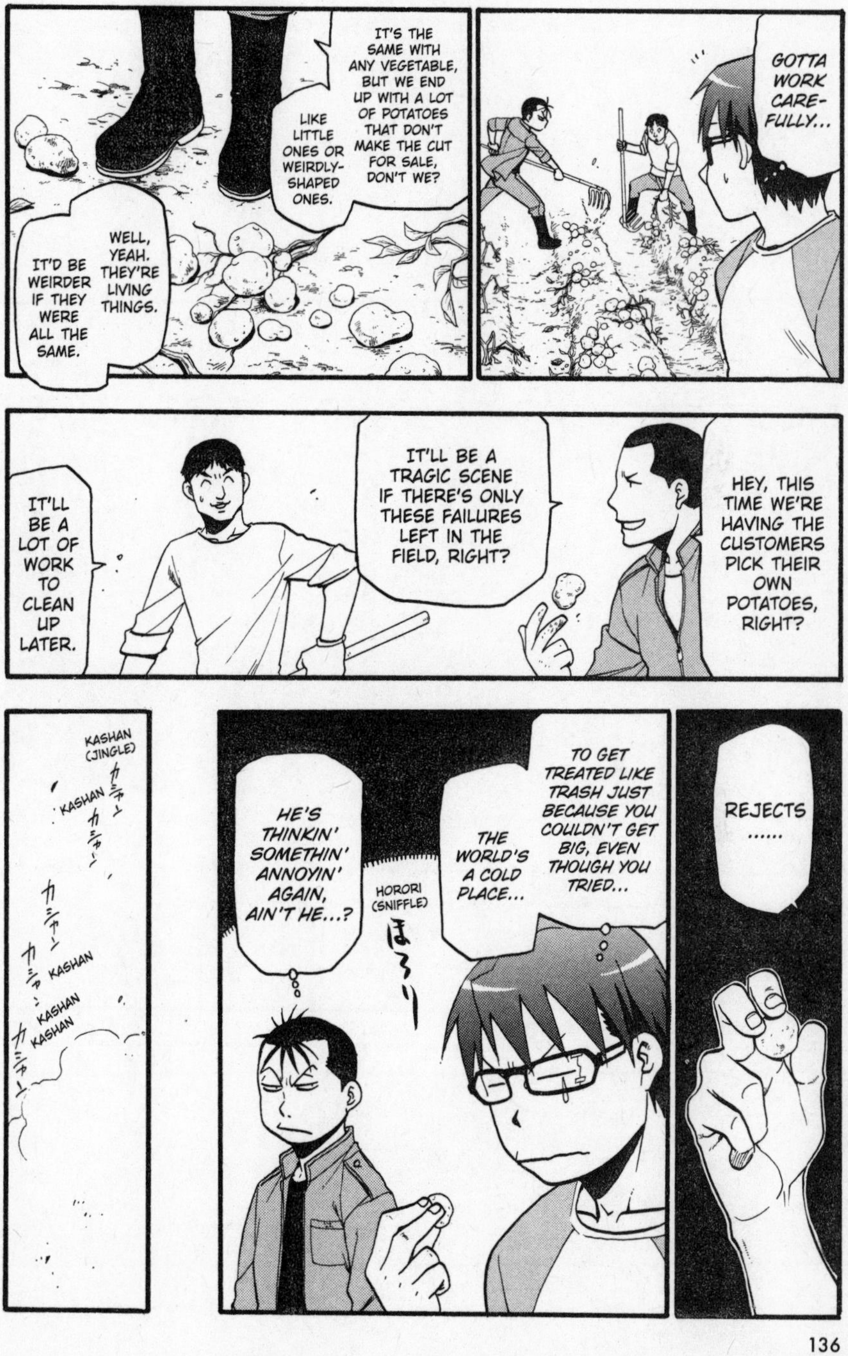
GOTTA WORK CAREFULLY...
IT'S THE SAME WITH ANY VEGETABLE, BUT WE END UP WITH A LOT OF POTATOES THAT DON'T MAKE THE CUT FOR SALE, DON'T WE?
LIKE LITTLE ONES OR WEIRDLY-SHAPED ONES.
WELL, YEAH. THEY'RE LIVING THINGS.
IT'D BE WEIRDER IF THEY WERE ALL THE SAME.
HEY, THIS TIME WE'RE HAVING THE CUSTOMERS PICK THEIR OWN POTATOES, RIGHT?
IT'LL BE A TRAGIC SCENE IF THERE'S ONLY THESE FAILURES LEFT IN THE FIELD, RIGHT?
IT'LL BE A LOT OF WORK TO CLEAN UP LATER.
REJECTS ......
TO GET TREATED LIKE TRASH JUST BECAUSE YOU COULDN'T GET BIG, EVEN THOUGH YOU TRIED...
THE WORLD'S A COLD PLACE...
HORORI (SNIFFLE)
HE'S THINKIN' SOMETHIN' ANNOYIN' AGAIN, AIN'T HE...?
KASHAN (JINGLE)
KASHAN
KASHAN
KASHAN
KASHAN

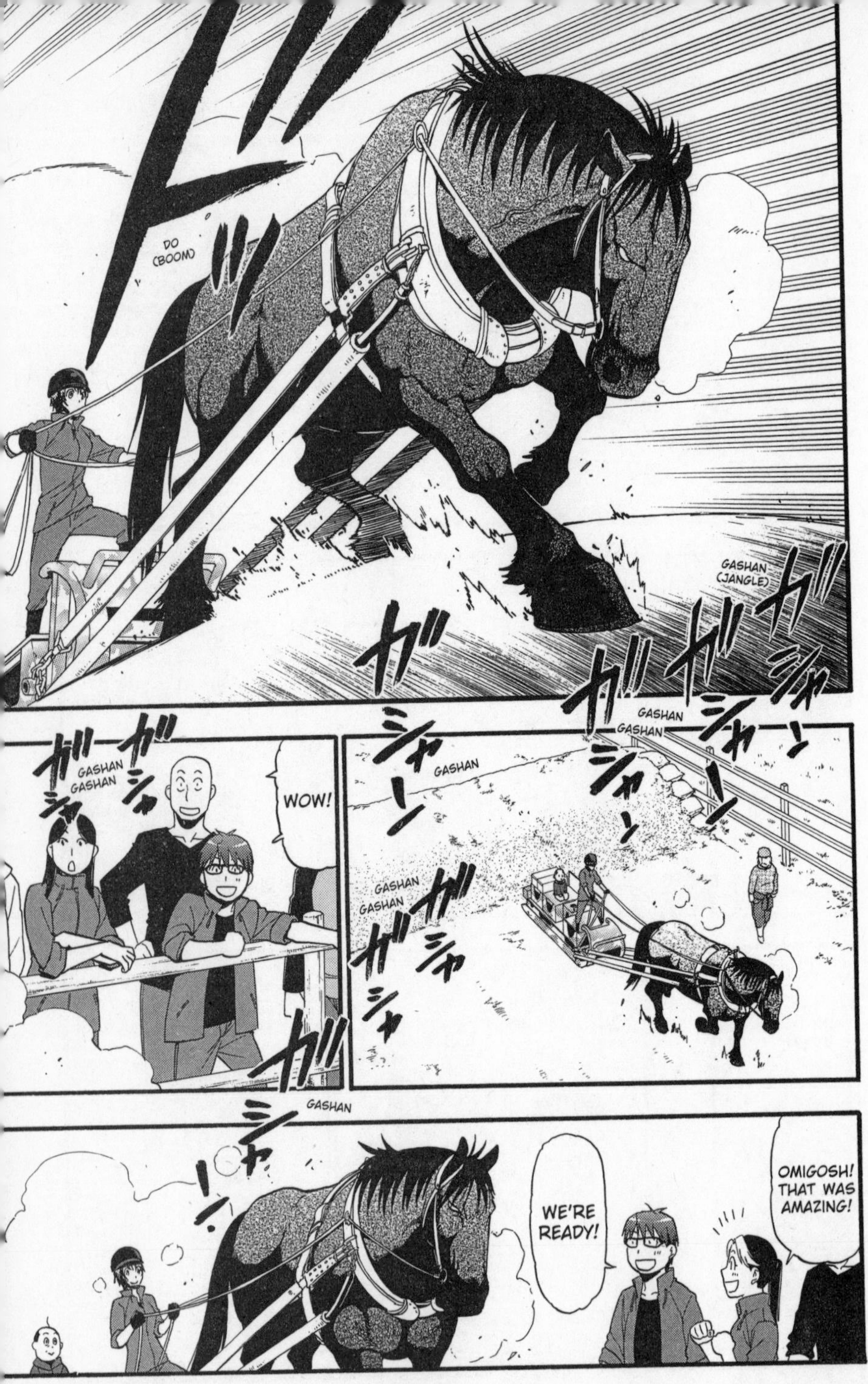
DO (BOOM)
GASHAN (JANGLE)
GASHAN
GASHAN
GASHAN
GASHAN
GASHAN
GASHAN
GASHAN
WOW!
OMIGOSH! THAT WAS AMAZING!
WE'RE READY!
GASHAN

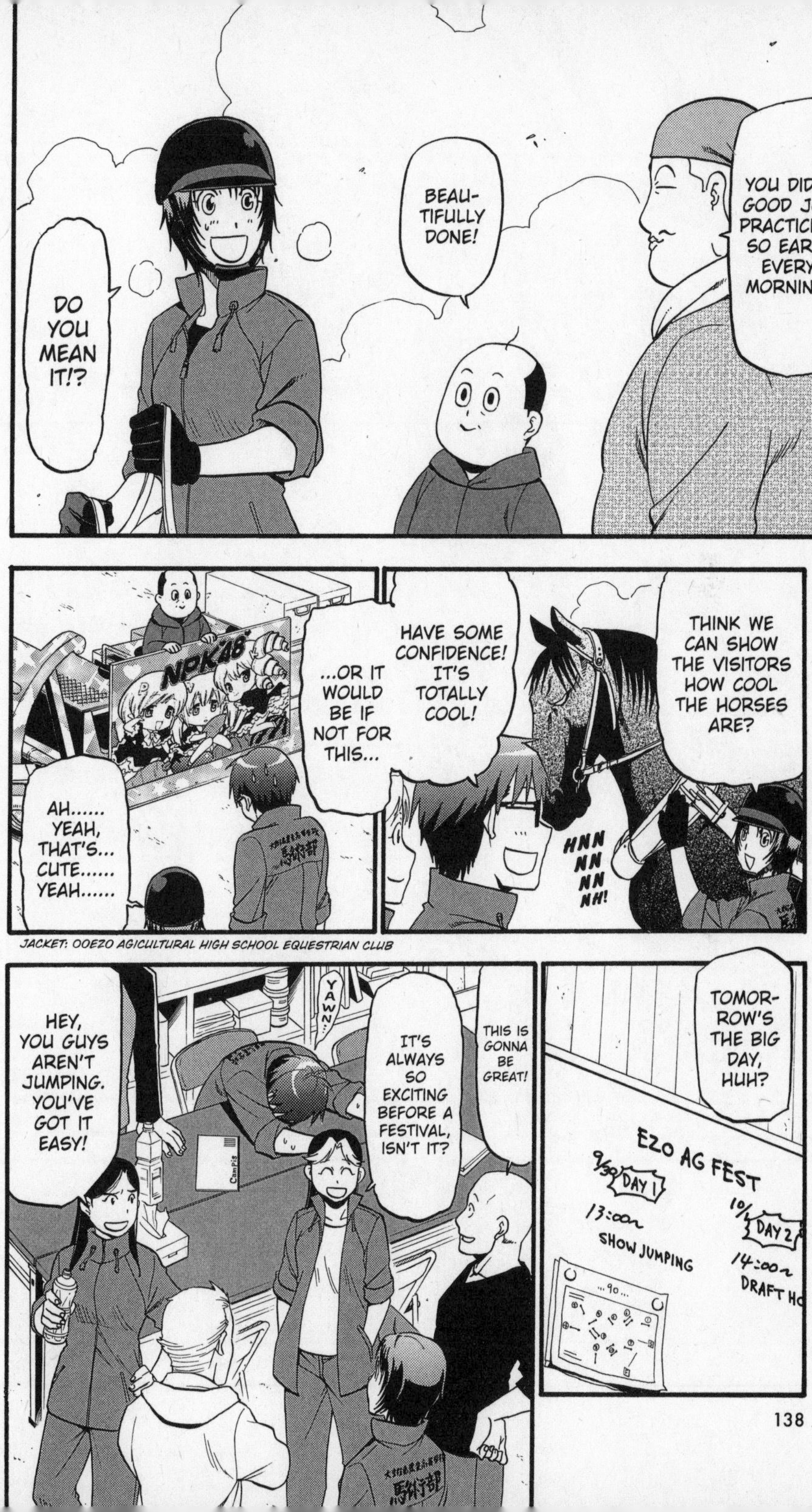
YOU DID A GOOD JOB PRACTICING SO EARLY EVERY MORNING.
BEAU-TIFULLY DONE!
DO YOU MEAN IT!?
THINK WE CAN SHOW THE VISITORS HOW COOL THE HORSES ARE?
HNNN NN NN NN NH!
HAVE SOME CONFIDENCE! IT'S TOTALLY COOL!
...OR IT WOULD BE IF NOT FOR THIS...
NPK48
AH...... YEAH, THAT'S... CUTE...... YEAH......
TOMOR-ROW'S THE BIG DAY, HUH?
EZO AG FEST
9/30 DAY 1
13:00~
SHOW JUMPING
10/1 DAY 2
14:00~
DRAFT HO
THIS IS GONNA BE GREAT!
YAWN...
IT'S ALWAYS SO EXCITING BEFORE A FESTIVAL, ISN'T IT?
HEY, YOU GUYS AREN'T JUMPING. YOU'VE GOT IT EASY!
JACKET: OOEZO AGICULTURAL HIGH SCHOOL EQUESTRIAN CLUB

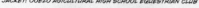

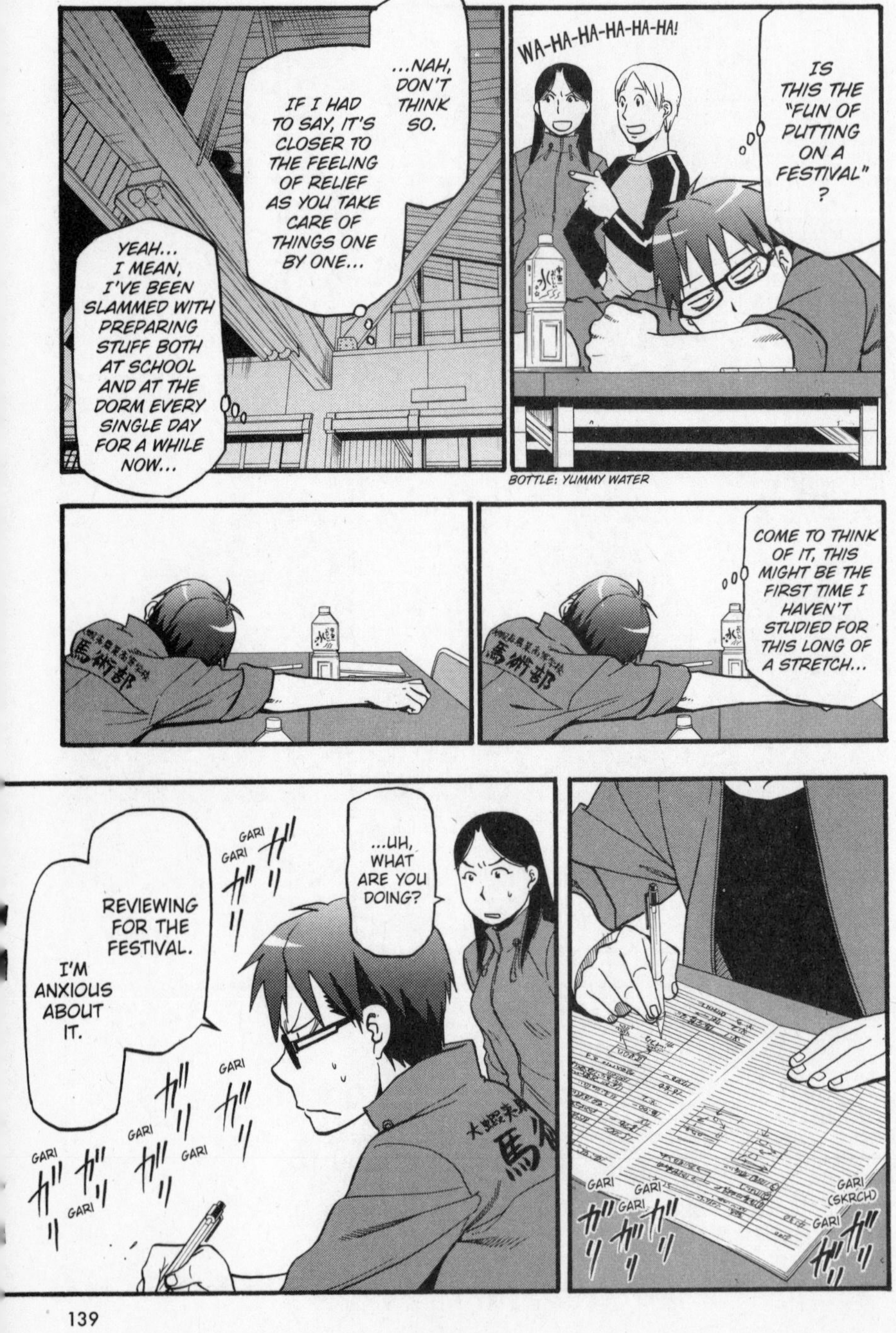
WA-HA-HA-HA-HA-HA!
IS THIS THE "FUN OF PUTTING ON A FESTIVAL"?
BOTTLE: YUMMY WATER
...NAH, DON'T THINK SO.
IF I HAD TO SAY, IT'S CLOSER TO THE FEELING OF RELIEF AS YOU TAKE CARE OF THINGS ONE BY ONE...
YEAH... I MEAN, I'VE BEEN SLAMMED WITH PREPARING STUFF BOTH AT SCHOOL AND AT THE DORM EVERY SINGLE DAY FOR A WHILE NOW...
COME TO THINK OF IT, THIS MIGHT BE THE FIRST TIME I HAVEN'T STUDIED FOR THIS LONG OF A STRETCH...
GARI (SKRCH)
GARI
GARI
GARI
GARI
...UH, WHAT ARE YOU DOING?
GARI
GARI
REVIEWING FOR THE FESTIVAL.
I'M ANXIOUS ABOUT IT.
GARI
GARI
GARI
GARI
GARI

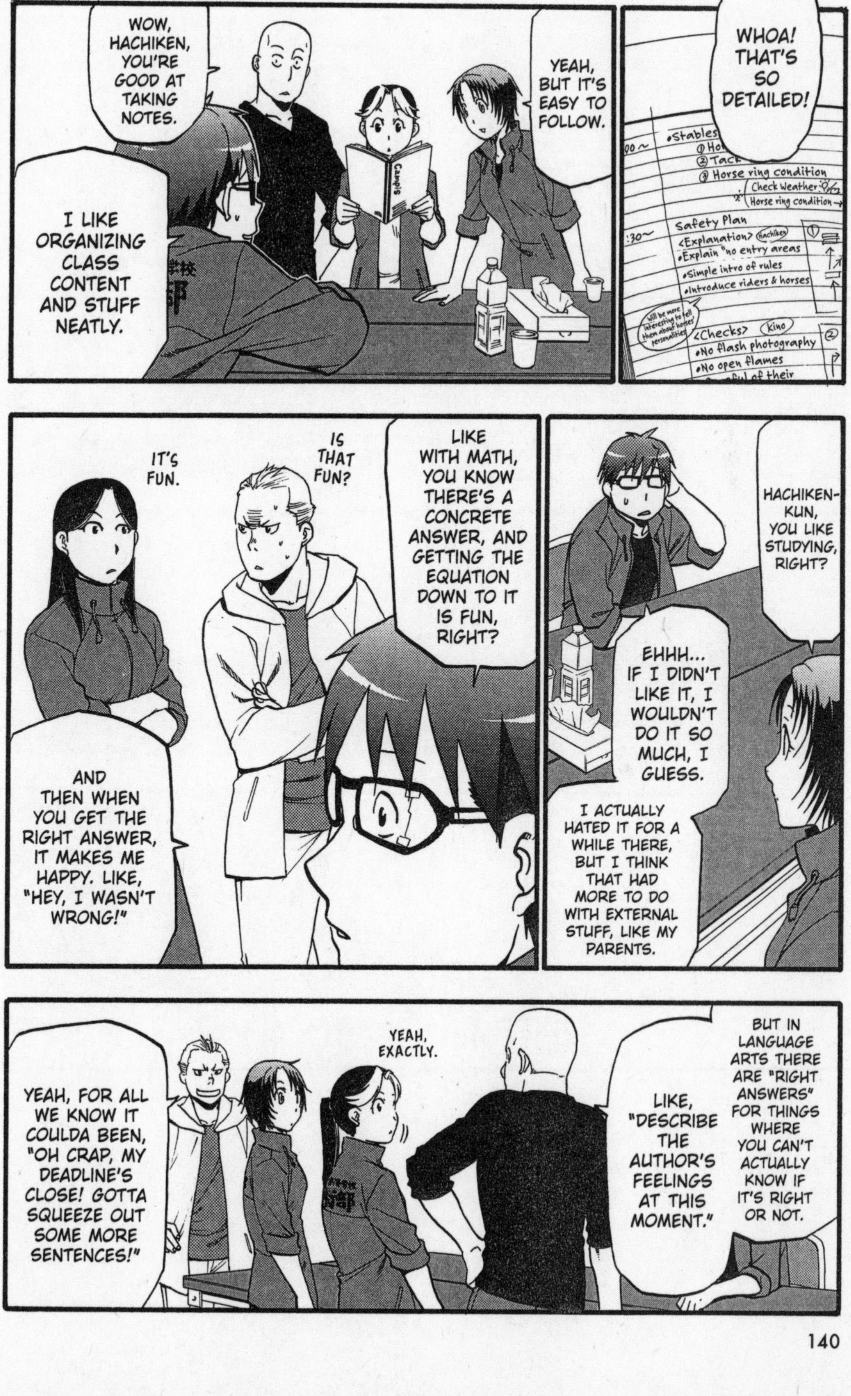
WHOA! THAT'S SO DETAILED!
•Stables
② Tack
③ Horse ring condition
Check Weather
Horse ring condition
Safety Plan
<Explanation> Hachiken
•Explain "no entry areas
•Simple intro of rules
•Introduce riders & horses
Will be more interesting to tell them about horses' personalities!
<Checks> Kino
•No flash photography
•No open flames
YEAH, BUT IT'S EASY TO FOLLOW.
WOW, HACHIKEN, YOU'RE GOOD AT TAKING NOTES.
Campus
I LIKE ORGANIZING CLASS CONTENT AND STUFF NEATLY.
HACHIKEN-KUN, YOU LIKE STUDYING, RIGHT?
EHHH... IF I DIDN'T LIKE IT, I WOULDN'T DO IT SO MUCH, I GUESS.
I ACTUALLY HATED IT FOR A WHILE THERE, BUT I THINK THAT HAD MORE TO DO WITH EXTERNAL STUFF, LIKE MY PARENTS.
LIKE WITH MATH, YOU KNOW THERE'S A CONCRETE ANSWER, AND GETTING THE EQUATION DOWN TO IT IS FUN, RIGHT?
IS THAT FUN?
IT'S FUN.
AND THEN WHEN YOU GET THE RIGHT ANSWER, IT MAKES ME HAPPY. LIKE, "HEY, I WASN'T WRONG!"
BUT IN LANGUAGE ARTS THERE ARE "RIGHT ANSWERS" FOR THINGS WHERE YOU CAN'T ACTUALLY KNOW IF IT'S RIGHT OR NOT.
LIKE, "DESCRIBE THE AUTHOR'S FEELINGS AT THIS MOMENT."
YEAH, EXACTLY.
YEAH, FOR ALL WE KNOW IT COULDA BEEN, "OH CRAP, MY DEADLINE'S CLOSE! GOTTA SQUEEZE OUT SOME MORE SENTENCES!"

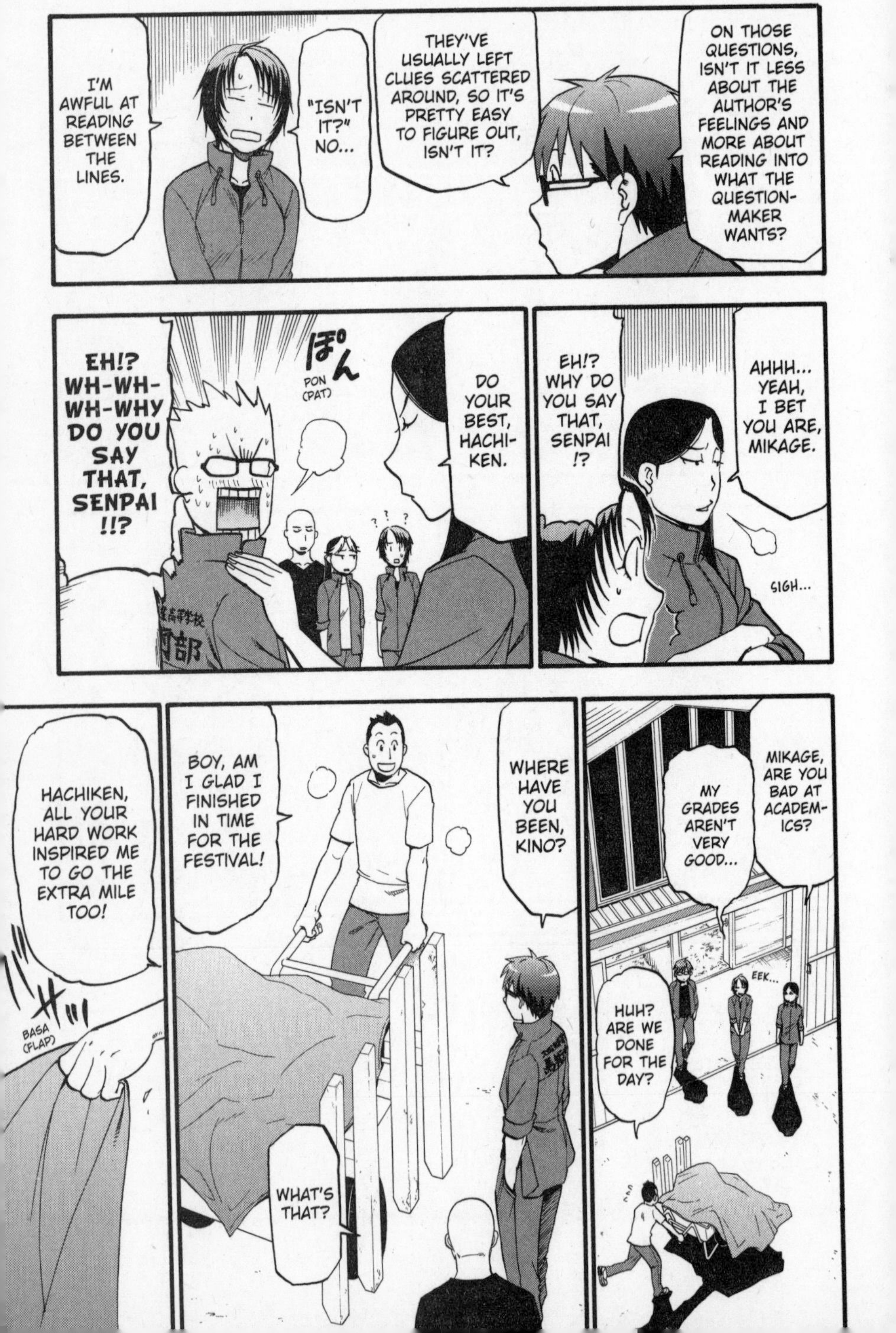
ON THOSE QUESTIONS, ISN'T IT LESS ABOUT THE AUTHOR'S FEELINGS AND MORE ABOUT READING INTO WHAT THE QUESTION-MAKER WANTS?
THEY'VE USUALLY LEFT CLUES SCATTERED AROUND, SO IT'S PRETTY EASY TO FIGURE OUT, ISN'T IT?
"ISN'T IT?" NO...
I'M AWFUL AT READING BETWEEN THE LINES.
AHHH... YEAH, I BET YOU ARE, MIKAGE.
SIGH...
EH!? WHY DO YOU SAY THAT, SENPAI!?
DO YOUR BEST, HACHIKEN.
ぽん
PON (PAT)
EH!? WH-WH-WH-WHY DO YOU SAY THAT, SENPAI!!?
MIKAGE, ARE YOU BAD AT ACADEMICS?
MY GRADES AREN'T VERY GOOD...
EEK...
HUH? ARE WE DONE FOR THE DAY?
WHERE HAVE YOU BEEN, KINO?
BOY, AM I GLAD I FINISHED IN TIME FOR THE FESTIVAL!
WHAT'S THAT?
HACHIKEN, ALL YOUR HARD WORK INSPIRED ME TO GO THE EXTRA MILE TOO!
BASA (FLAP)

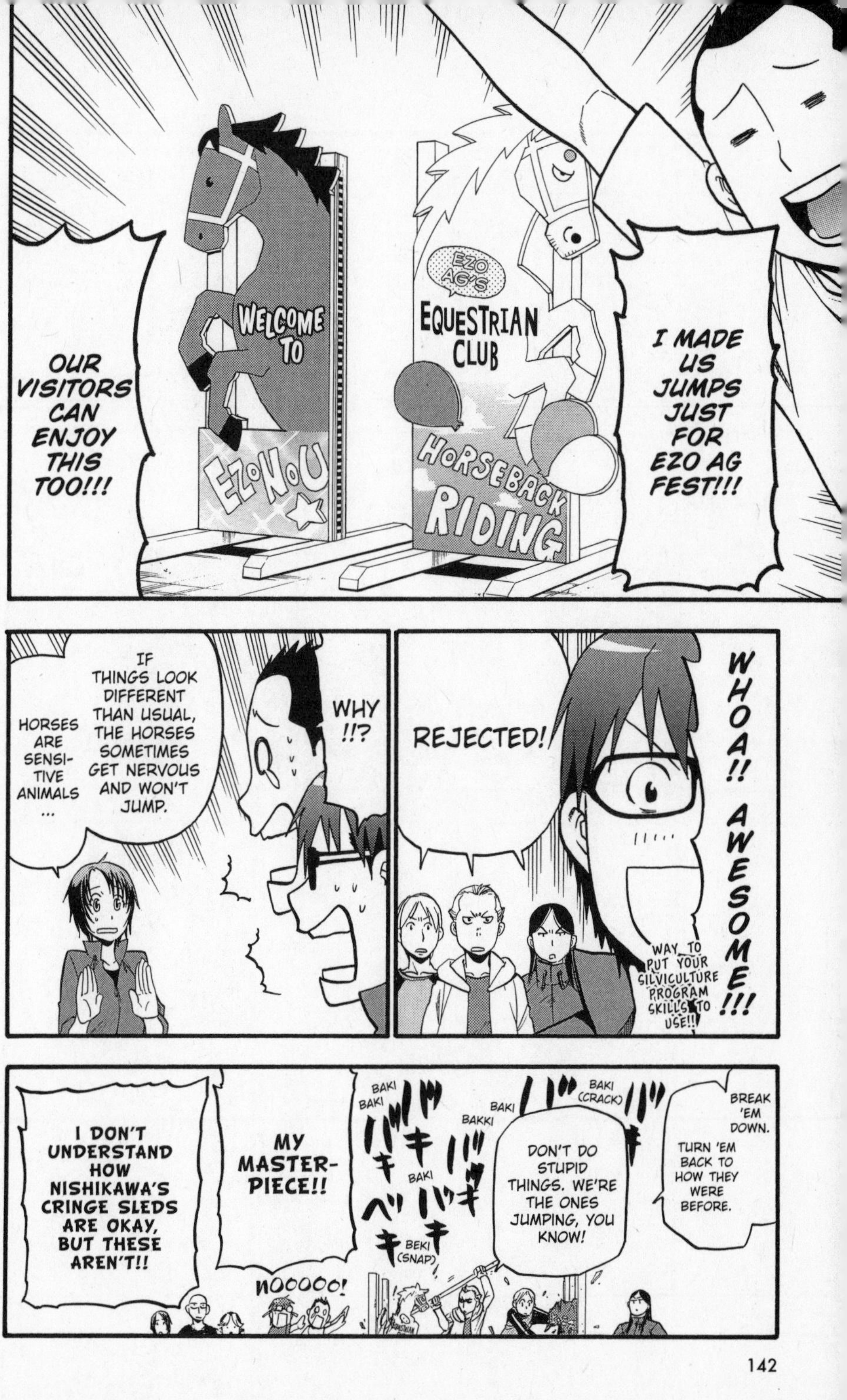
I MADE US JUMPS JUST FOR EZO AG FEST!!!
EZO AG'S EQUESTRIAN CLUB
HORSEBACK RIDING
WELCOME TO
EZONOU
OUR VISITORS CAN ENJOY THIS TOO!!!
WHOA!! AWESOME!!!
WAY TO PUT YOUR SILVICULTURE PROGRAM SKILLS TO USE!!
REJECTED!
WHY!!?
IF THINGS LOOK DIFFERENT THAN USUAL, THE HORSES SOMETIMES GET NERVOUS AND WON'T JUMP.
HORSES ARE SENSITIVE ANIMALS...
BREAK 'EM DOWN.
TURN 'EM BACK TO HOW THEY WERE BEFORE.
BAKI (CRACK)
DON'T DO STUPID THINGS. WE'RE THE ONES JUMPING, YOU KNOW!
BAKI
BAKKI
BAKI
BEKI (SNAP)
BAKI BAKI
MY MASTERPIECE!!
NOOOOO!
I DON'T UNDERSTAND HOW NISHIKAWA'S CRINGE SLEDS ARE OKAY, BUT THESE AREN'T!!

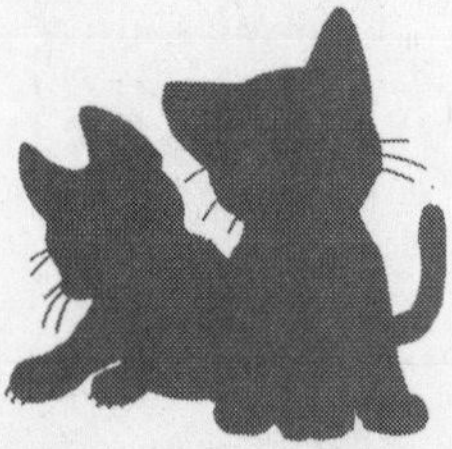

Silver Spoon

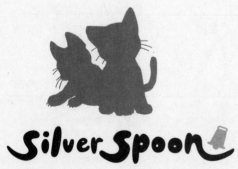

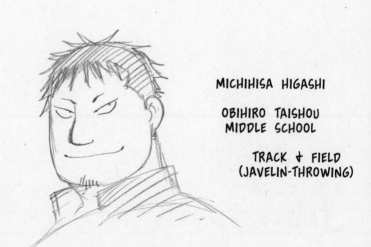

MICHIHISA HIGASHI

OBIHIRO TAISHOU
MIDDLE SCHOOL

TRACK & FIELD
(JAVELIN-THROWING)

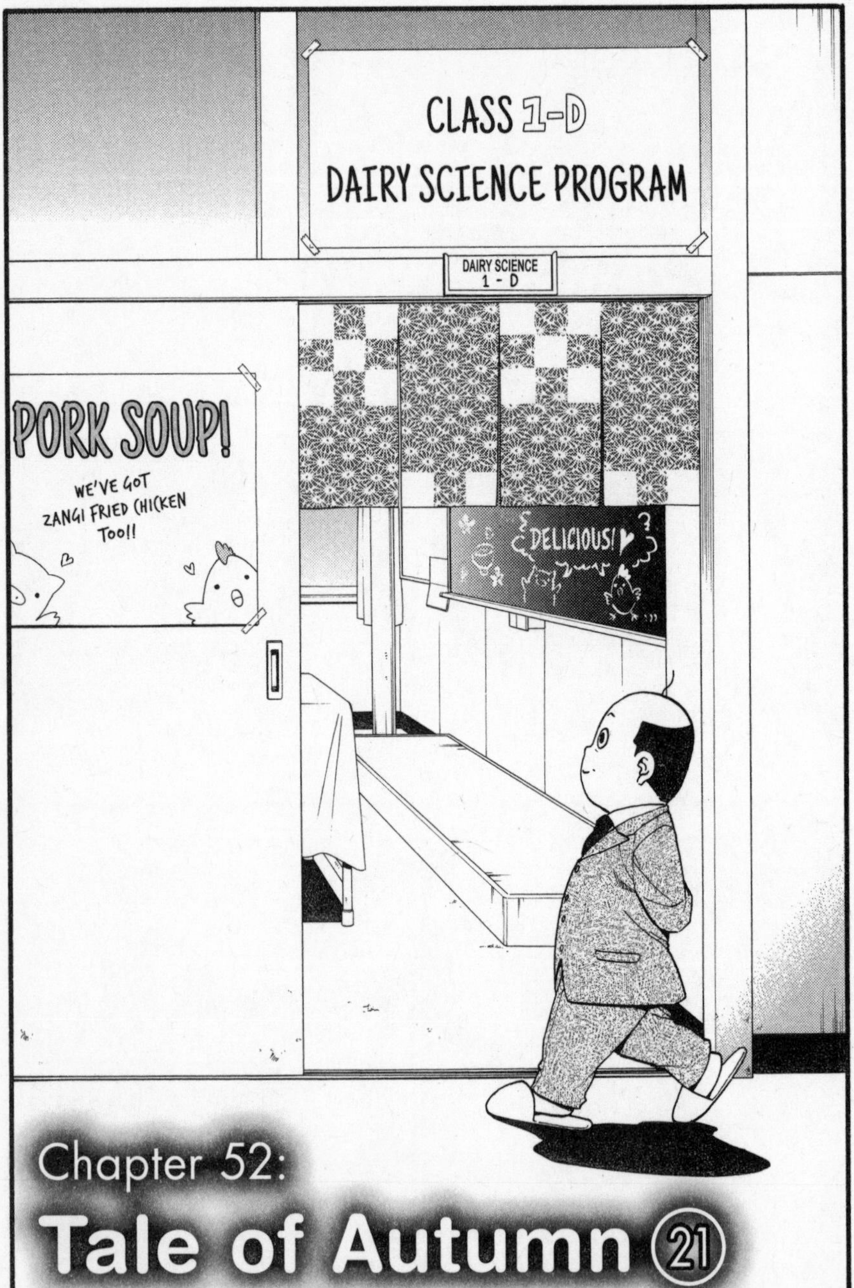
CLASS 1-D
DAIRY SCIENCE PROGRAM
DAIRY SCIENCE 1 - D
PORK SOUP!
WE'VE GOT ZANGI FRIED CHICKEN TOO!!
DELICIOUS!
Chapter 52:
Tale of Autumn 21

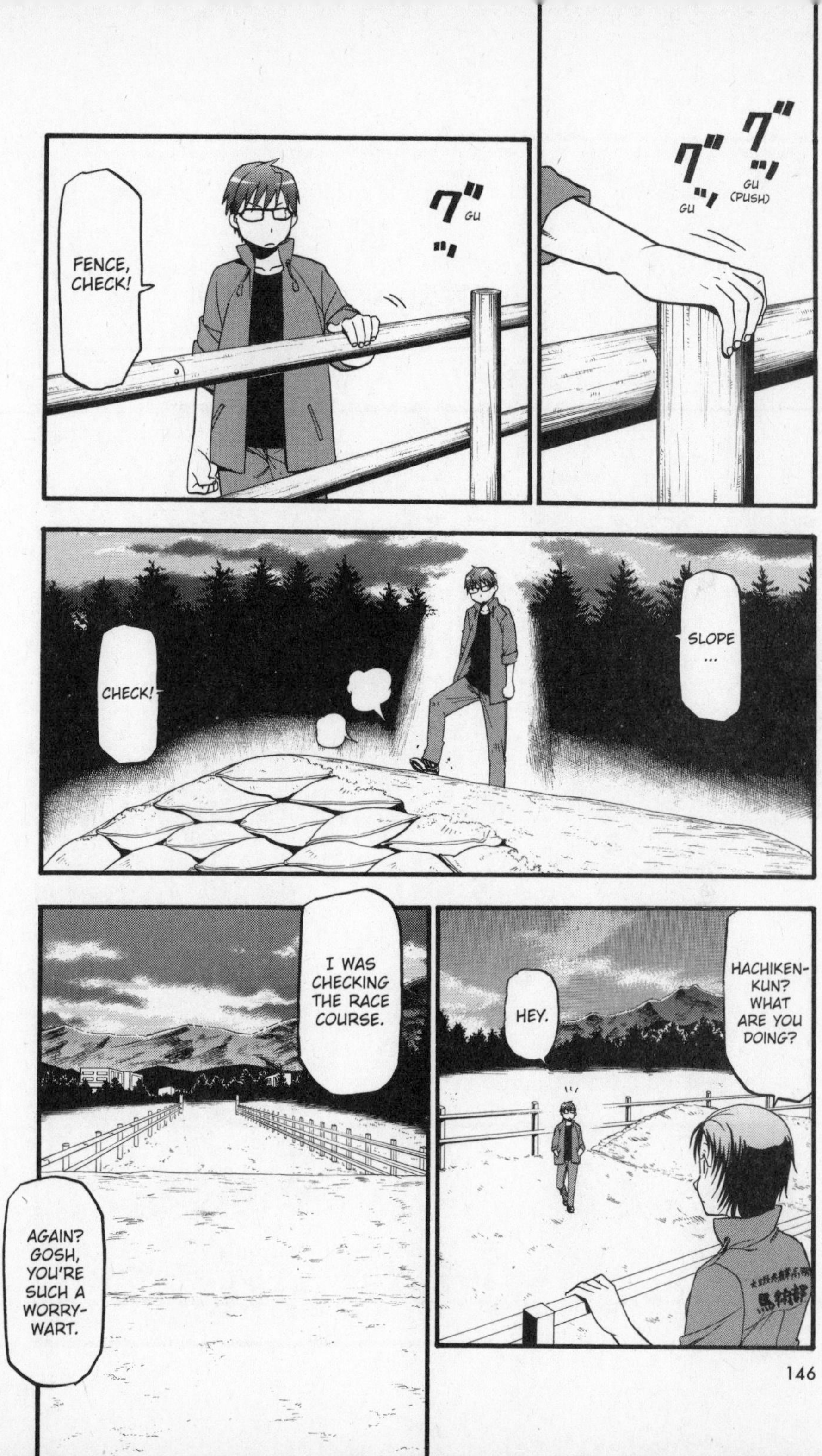
GU
GU (PUSH)
GU
FENCE, CHECK!
SLOPE...
CHECK!
HACHIKEN-KUN? WHAT ARE YOU DOING?
HEY.
I WAS CHECKING THE RACE COURSE.
AGAIN? GOSH, YOU'RE SUCH A WORRY-WART.

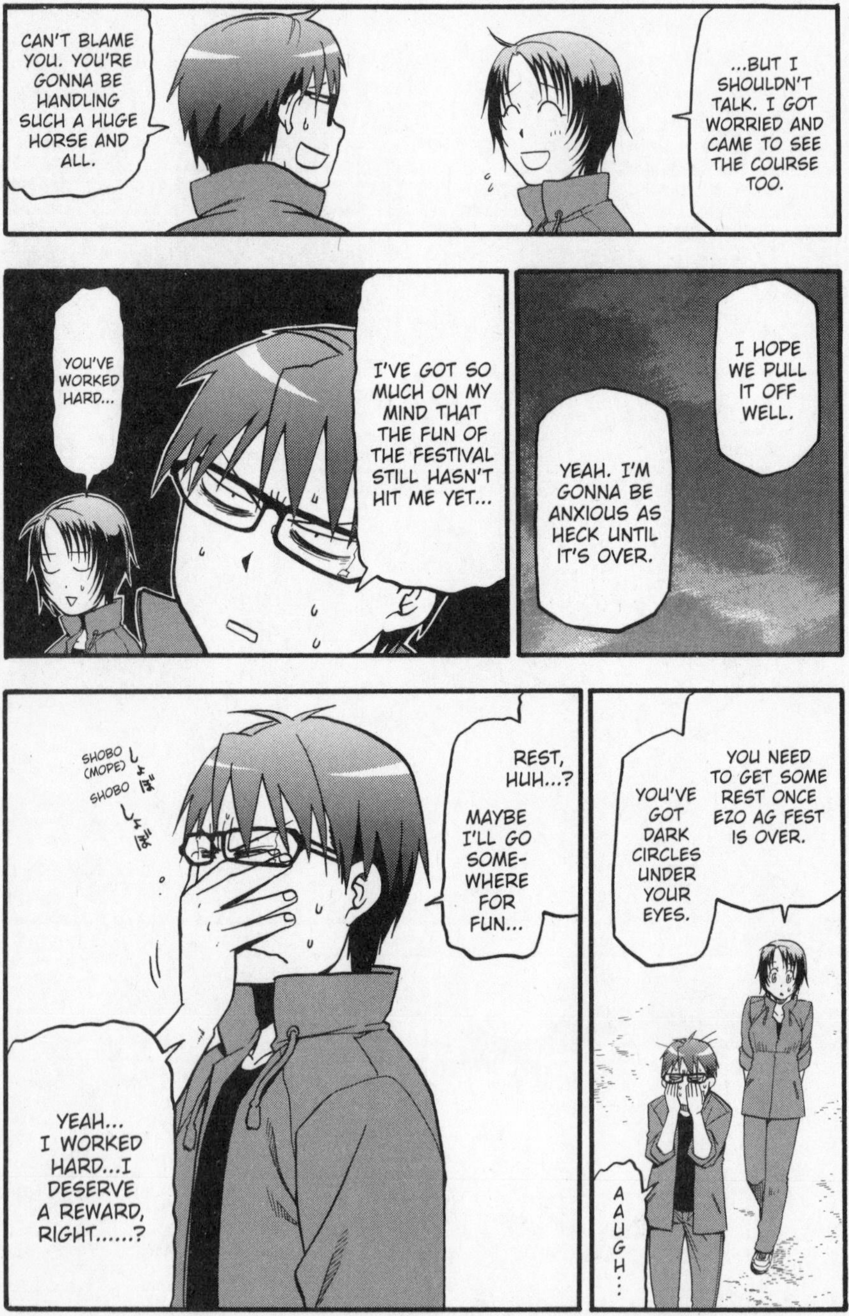
...BUT I SHOULDN'T TALK. I GOT WORRIED AND CAME TO SEE THE COURSE TOO.
CAN'T BLAME YOU. YOU'RE GONNA BE HANDLING SUCH A HUGE HORSE AND ALL.
I HOPE WE PULL IT OFF WELL.
YEAH. I'M GONNA BE ANXIOUS AS HECK UNTIL IT'S OVER.
I'VE GOT SO MUCH ON MY MIND THAT THE FUN OF THE FESTIVAL STILL HASN'T HIT ME YET...
YOU'VE WORKED HARD...
YOU NEED TO GET SOME REST ONCE EZO AG FEST IS OVER.
YOU'VE GOT DARK CIRCLES UNDER YOUR EYES.
AAUGH...
REST, HUH...?
MAYBE I'LL GO SOME-WHERE FOR FUN...
SHOBO (MOPE) SHOBO
YEAH... I WORKED HARD...I DESERVE A REWARD, RIGHT......?

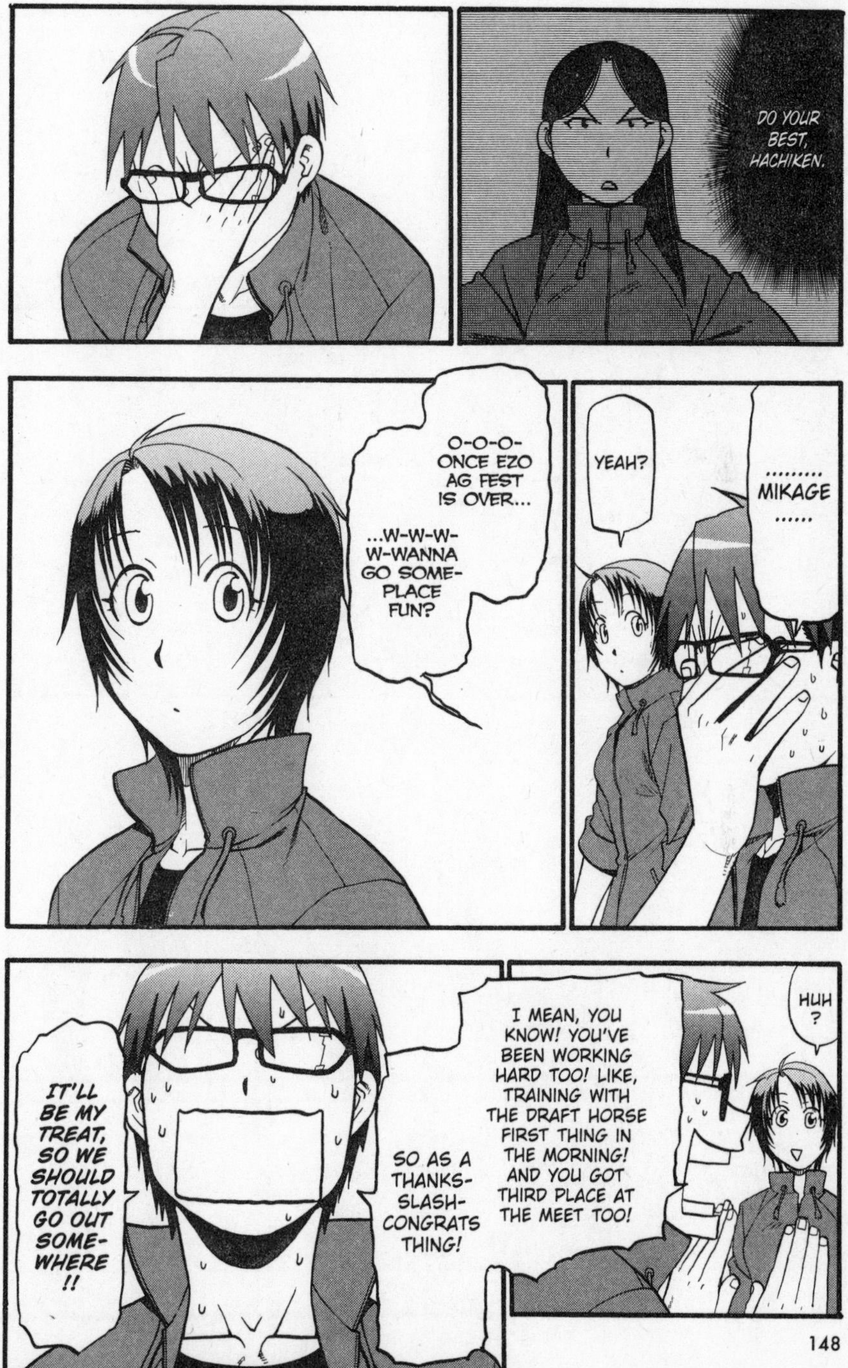
DO YOUR BEST, HACHIKEN.
.... MIKAGE ......
YEAH?
O-O-O-ONCE EZO AG FEST IS OVER...
...W-W-W-W-WANNA GO SOME-PLACE FUN?
HUH?
I MEAN, YOU KNOW! YOU'VE BEEN WORKING HARD TOO! LIKE, TRAINING WITH THE DRAFT HORSE FIRST THING IN THE MORNING! AND YOU GOT THIRD PLACE AT THE MEET TOO!
SO AS A THANKS-SLASH-CONGRATS THING!
IT'LL BE MY TREAT, SO WE SHOULD TOTALLY GO OUT SOME-WHERE!!

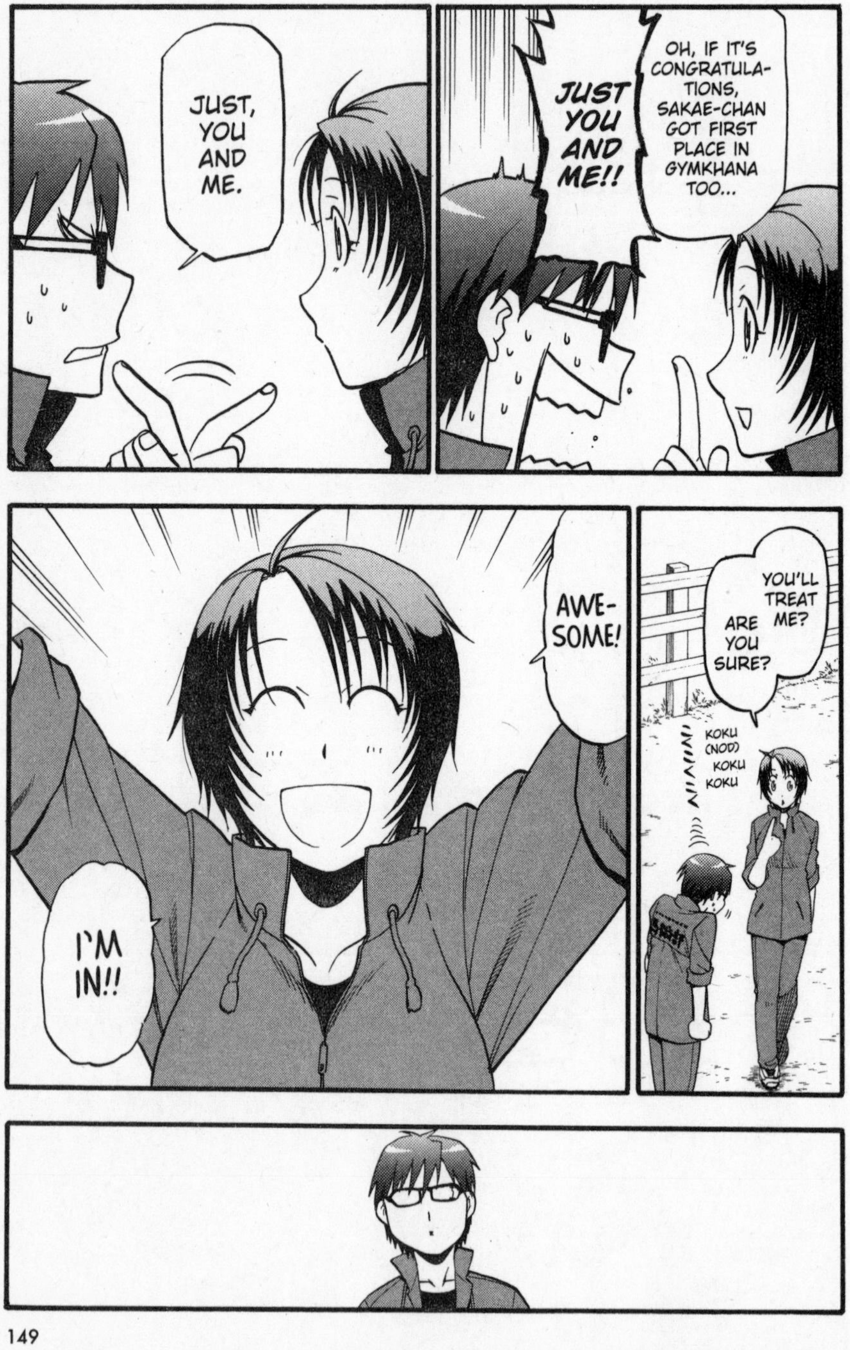
OH, IF IT'S CONGRATULATIONS, SAKAE-CHAN GOT FIRST PLACE IN GYMKHANA TOO...
JUST YOU AND ME!!
JUST, YOU AND ME.
YOU'LL TREAT ME?
ARE YOU SURE?
KOKU (NOD) KOKU KOKU
AWESOME!
I'M IN!!

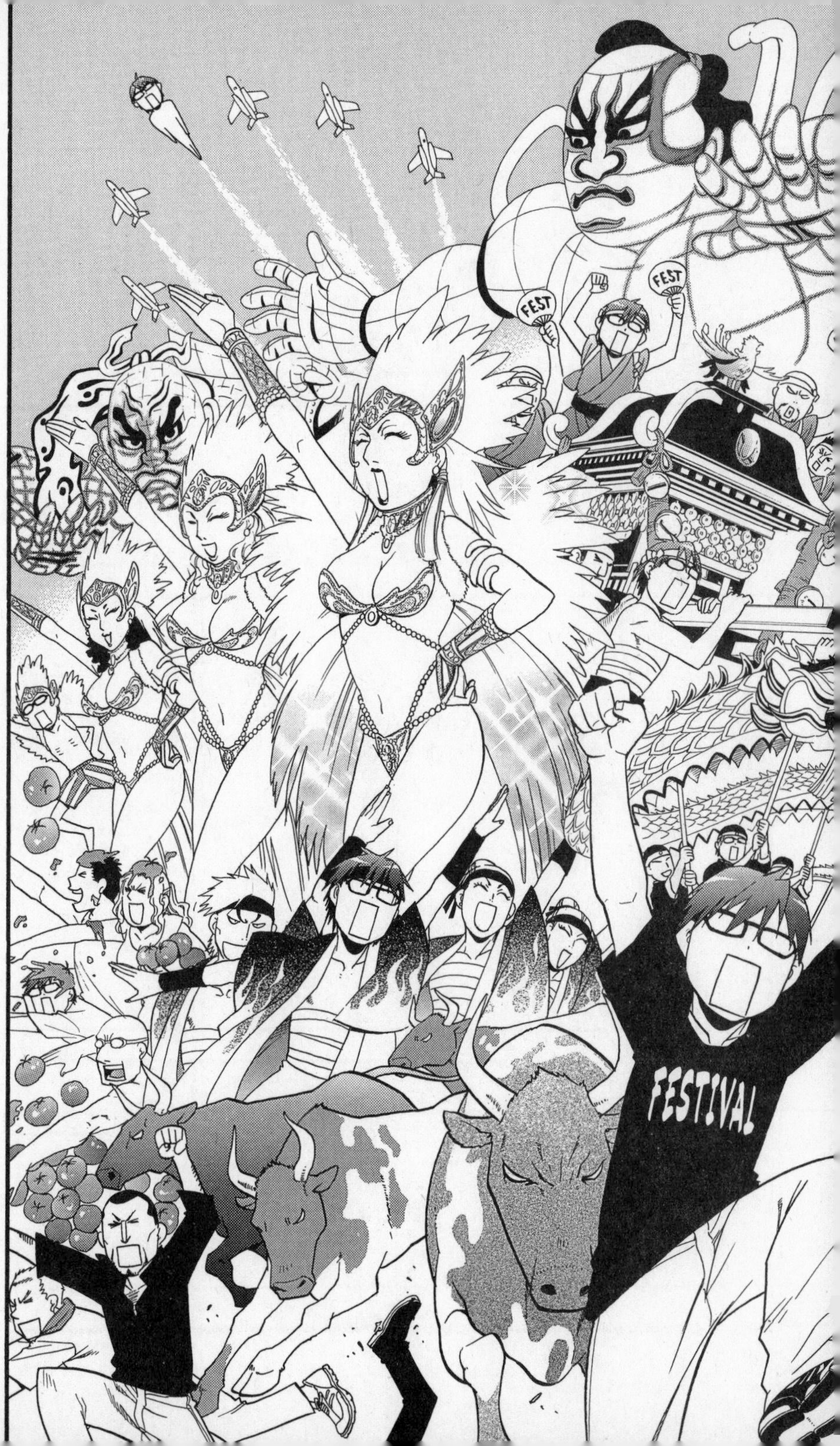
FEST
FEST
FESTIVAL

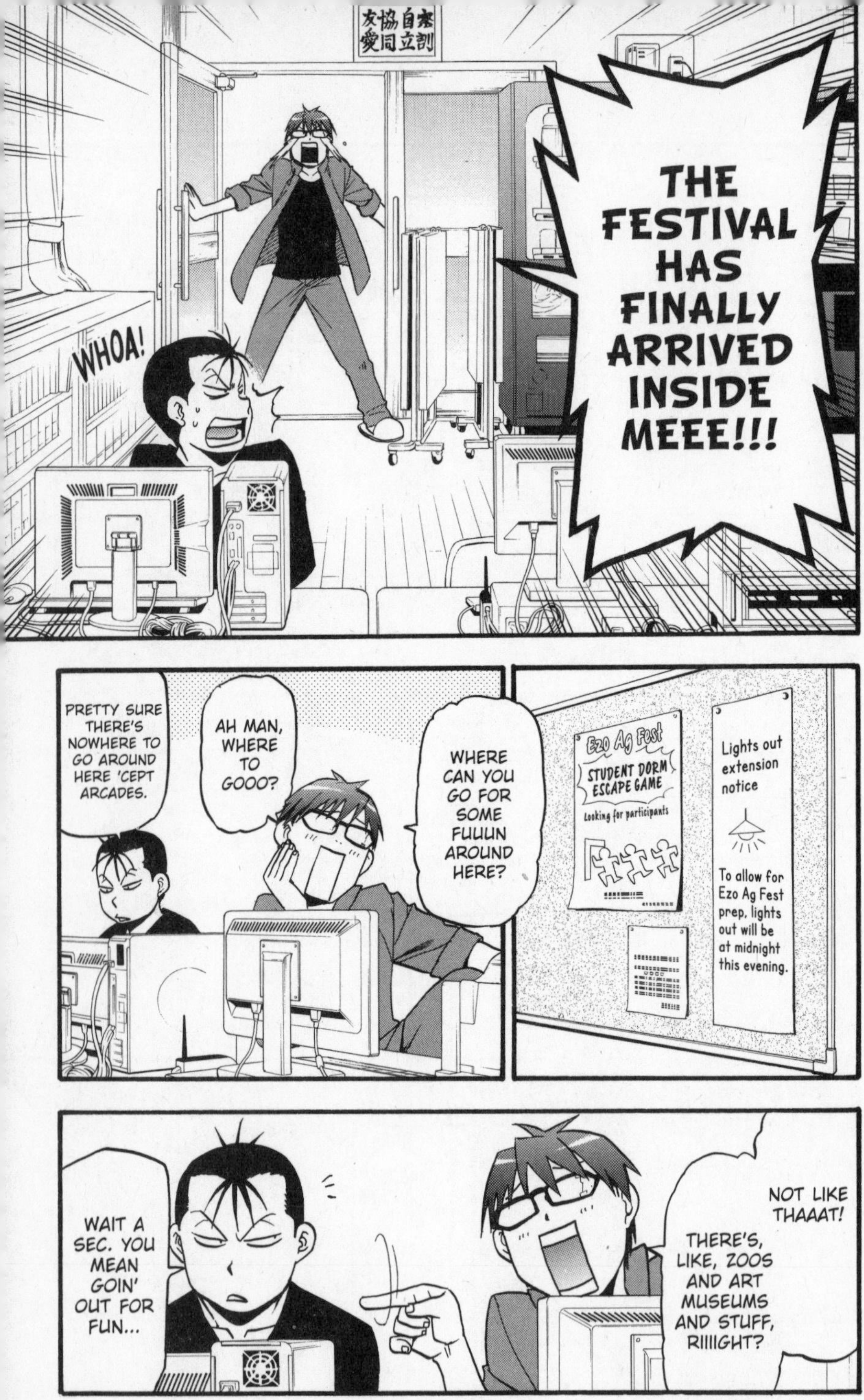
寮訓 自立 協同 友愛
THE FESTIVAL HAS FINALLY ARRIVED INSIDE MEEE!!!
WHOA!
Ezo Ag Fest
STUDENT DORM ESCAPE GAME
Looking for participants
Lights out extension notice
To allow for Ezo Ag Fest prep, lights out will be at midnight this evening.
WHERE CAN YOU GO FOR SOME FUUUN AROUND HERE?
AH MAN, WHERE TO GOOO?
PRETTY SURE THERE'S NOWHERE TO GO AROUND HERE 'CEPT ARCADES.
NOT LIKE THAAAT!
THERE'S, LIKE, ZOOS AND ART MUSEUMS AND STUFF, RIIIGHT?
WAIT A SEC. YOU MEAN GOIN' OUT FOR FUN...

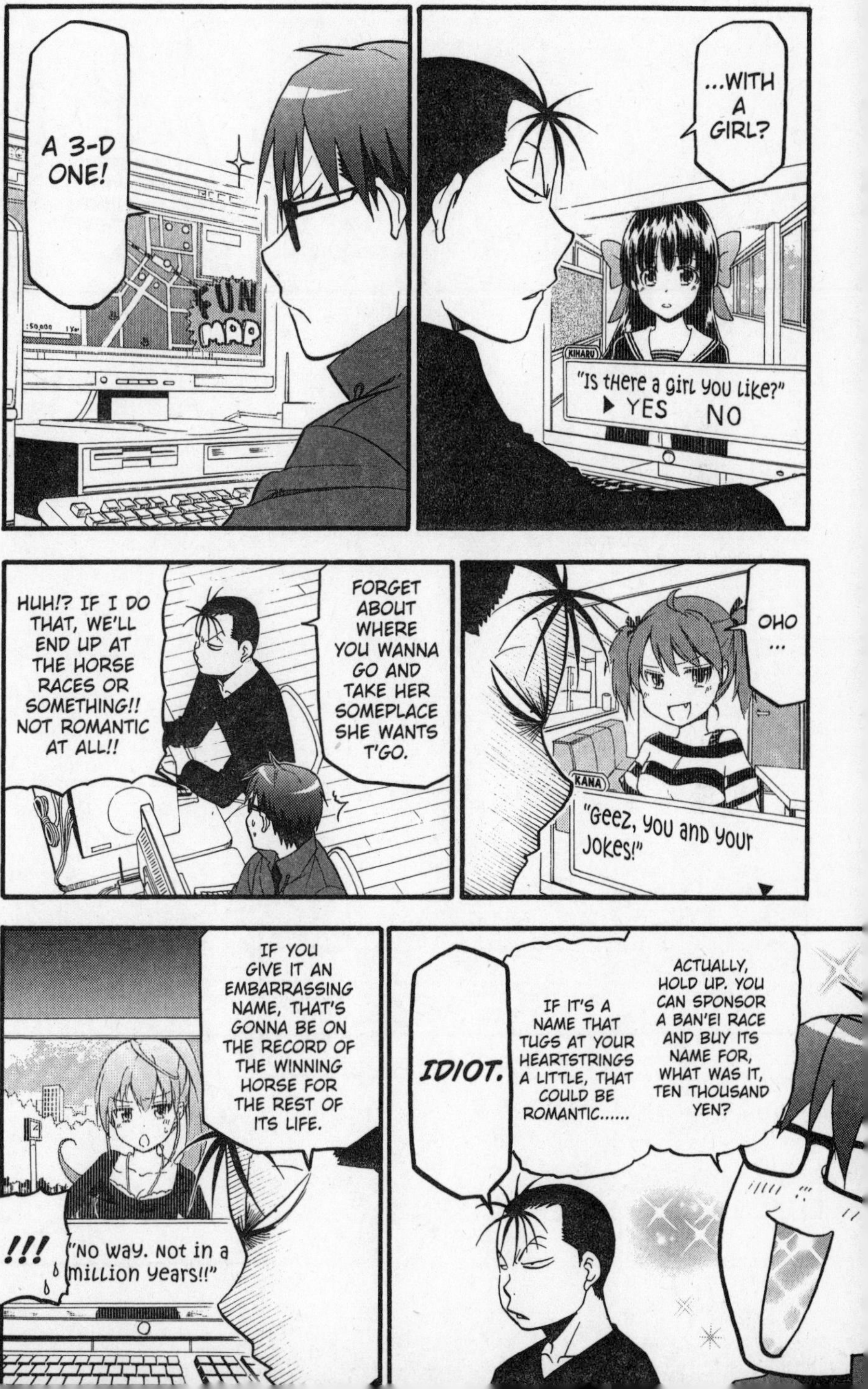
...WITH A GIRL?
KIHARU
"Is there a girl you like?"
▶ YES NO
A 3-D ONE!
FUN MAP
OHO ...
KANA
"Geez, you and your jokes!"
FORGET ABOUT WHERE YOU WANNA GO AND TAKE HER SOMEPLACE SHE WANTS T'GO.
HUH!? IF I DO THAT, WE'LL END UP AT THE HORSE RACES OR SOMETHING!! NOT ROMANTIC AT ALL!!
ACTUALLY, HOLD UP. YOU CAN SPONSOR A BAN'EI RACE AND BUY ITS NAME FOR, WHAT WAS IT, TEN THOUSAND YEN?
IF IT'S A NAME THAT TUGS AT YOUR HEARTSTRINGS A LITTLE, THAT COULD BE ROMANTIC......
IDIOT.
IF YOU GIVE IT AN EMBARRASSING NAME, THAT'S GONNA BE ON THE RECORD OF THE WINNING HORSE FOR THE REST OF ITS LIFE.
!!!
"No way. Not in a million years!!"

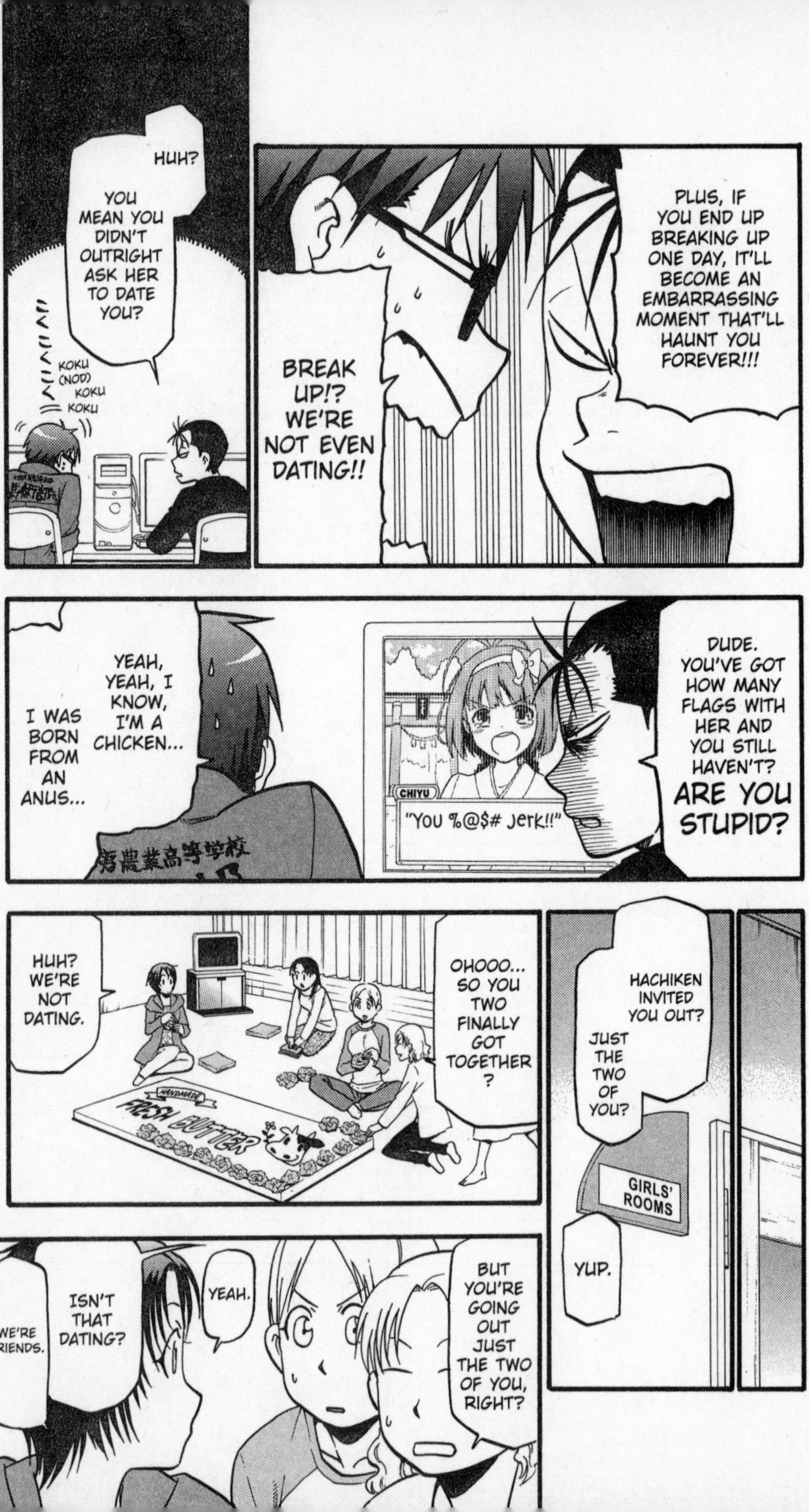
PLUS, IF YOU END UP BREAKING UP ONE DAY, IT'LL BECOME AN EMBARRASSING MOMENT THAT'LL HAUNT YOU FOREVER!!!
BREAK UP!? WE'RE NOT EVEN DATING!!
HUH?
YOU MEAN YOU DIDN'T OUTRIGHT ASK HER TO DATE YOU?
KOKU (NOD) KOKU KOKU
DUDE. YOU'VE GOT HOW MANY FLAGS WITH HER AND YOU STILL HAVEN'T? ARE YOU STUPID?
CHIYU
"You %@$# jerk!!"
YEAH, YEAH, I KNOW, I'M A CHICKEN...
I WAS BORN FROM AN ANUS...
HACHIKEN INVITED YOU OUT?
JUST THE TWO OF YOU?
GIRLS' ROOMS
YUP.
OHOOO... SO YOU TWO FINALLY GOT TOGETHER?
HUH? WE'RE NOT DATING.
HANDMADE
FRESH BUTTER
BUT YOU'RE GOING OUT JUST THE TWO OF YOU, RIGHT?
YEAH.
ISN'T THAT DATING?
WE'RE FRIENDS.

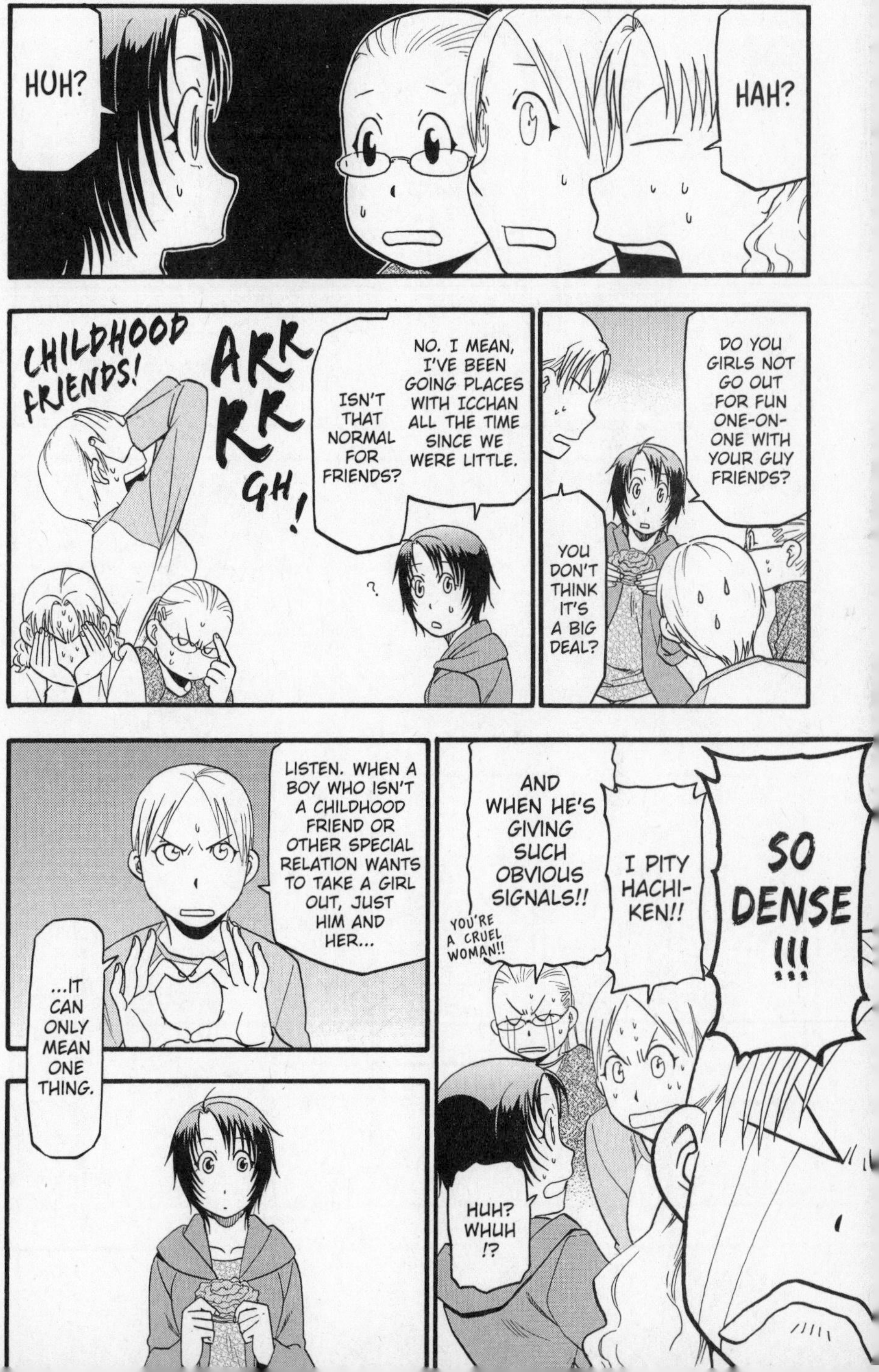
HAH?
HUH?
DO YOU GIRLS NOT GO OUT FOR FUN ONE-ON-ONE WITH YOUR GUY FRIENDS?
YOU DON'T THINK IT'S A BIG DEAL?
NO. I MEAN, I'VE BEEN GOING PLACES WITH ICCHAN ALL THE TIME SINCE WE WERE LITTLE.
ISN'T THAT NORMAL FOR FRIENDS?
ARRRRGH!
CHILDHOOD FRIENDS!
SO DENSE!!!
I PITY HACHIKEN!!
AND WHEN HE'S GIVING SUCH OBVIOUS SIGNALS!!
YOU'RE A CRUEL WOMAN!!
HUH? WHUH!?
LISTEN. WHEN A BOY WHO ISN'T A CHILDHOOD FRIEND OR OTHER SPECIAL RELATION WANTS TO TAKE A GIRL OUT, JUST HIM AND HER...
...IT CAN ONLY MEAN ONE THING.

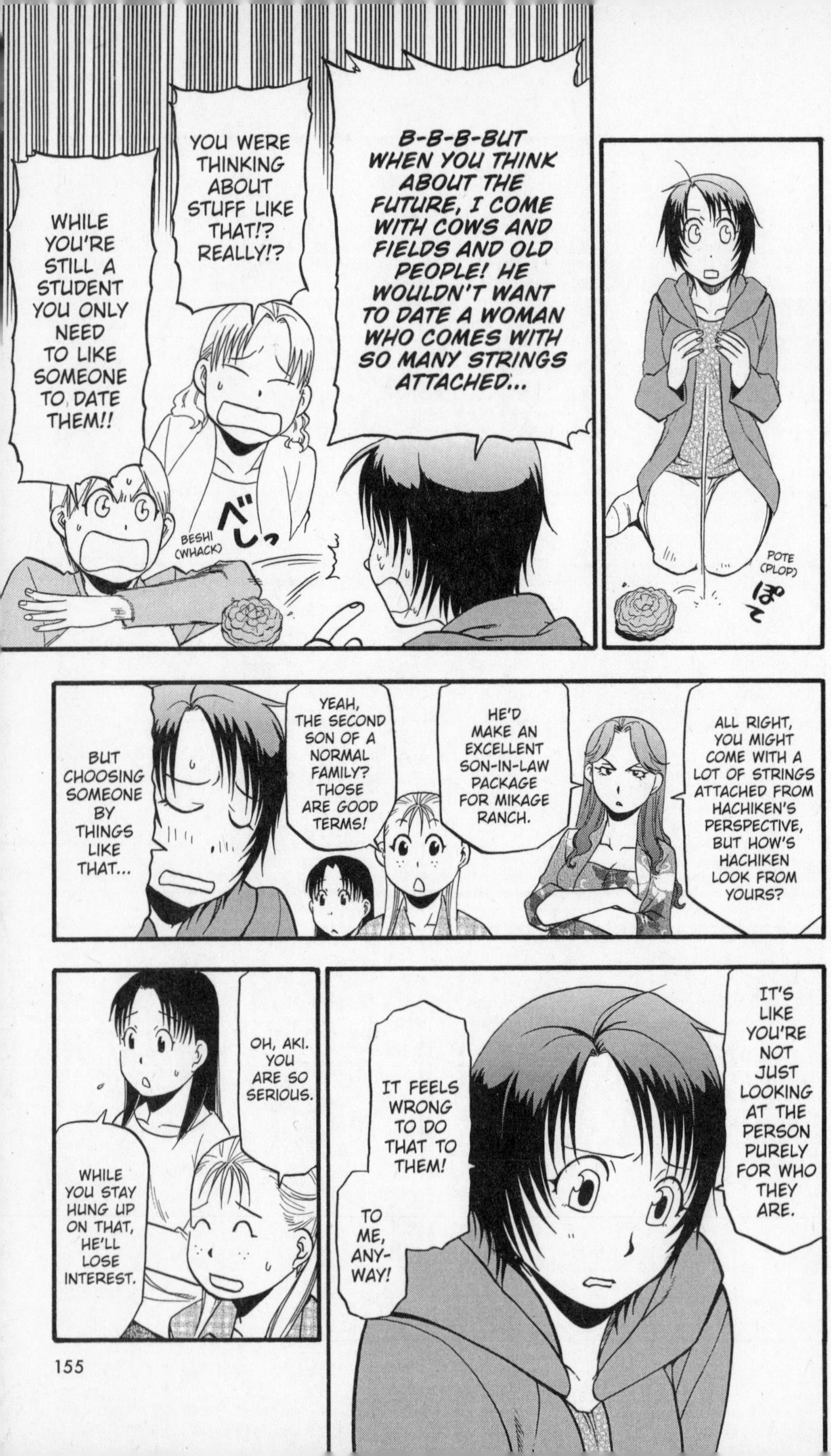
POTE (PLOP)
ぽて
B-B-B-BUT WHEN YOU THINK ABOUT THE FUTURE, I COME WITH COWS AND FIELDS AND OLD PEOPLE! HE WOULDN'T WANT TO DATE A WOMAN WHO COMES WITH SO MANY STRINGS ATTACHED...
YOU WERE THINKING ABOUT STUFF LIKE THAT!? REALLY!?
WHILE YOU'RE STILL A STUDENT YOU ONLY NEED TO LIKE SOMEONE TO DATE THEM!!
BESHI (WHACK)
べしっ
ALL RIGHT, YOU MIGHT COME WITH A LOT OF STRINGS ATTACHED FROM HACHIKEN'S PERSPECTIVE, BUT HOW'S HACHIKEN LOOK FROM YOURS?
HE'D MAKE AN EXCELLENT SON-IN-LAW PACKAGE FOR MIKAGE RANCH.
YEAH, THE SECOND SON OF A NORMAL FAMILY? THOSE ARE GOOD TERMS!
BUT CHOOSING SOMEONE BY THINGS LIKE THAT...
IT'S LIKE YOU'RE NOT JUST LOOKING AT THE PERSON PURELY FOR WHO THEY ARE.
IT FEELS WRONG TO DO THAT TO THEM!
TO ME, ANY-WAY!
OH, AKI. YOU ARE SO SERIOUS.
WHILE YOU STAY HUNG UP ON THAT, HE'LL LOSE INTEREST.

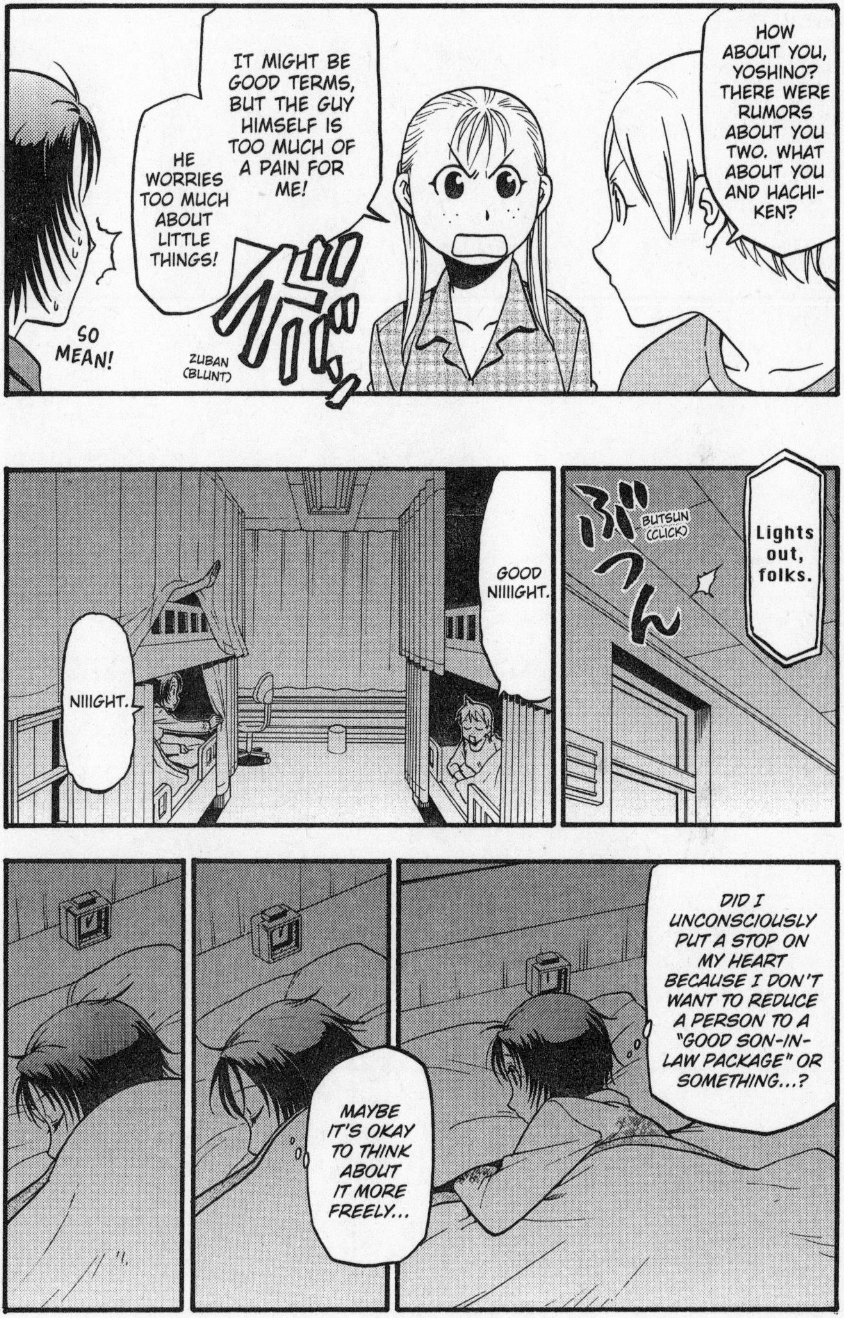
HOW ABOUT YOU, YOSHINO? THERE WERE RUMORS ABOUT YOU TWO. WHAT ABOUT YOU AND HACHIKEN?
IT MIGHT BE GOOD TERMS, BUT THE GUY HIMSELF IS TOO MUCH OF A PAIN FOR ME!
HE WORRIES TOO MUCH ABOUT LITTLE THINGS!
ZUBAN (BLUNT)
SO MEAN!
Lights out, folks.
ぶつん
BUTSUN (CLICK)
GOOD NIIIIGHT.
NIIIGHT.
DID I UNCONSCIOUSLY PUT A STOP ON MY HEART BECAUSE I DON'T WANT TO REDUCE A PERSON TO A "GOOD SON-IN-LAW PACKAGE" OR SOMETHING...?
MAYBE IT'S OKAY TO THINK ABOUT IT MORE FREELY...

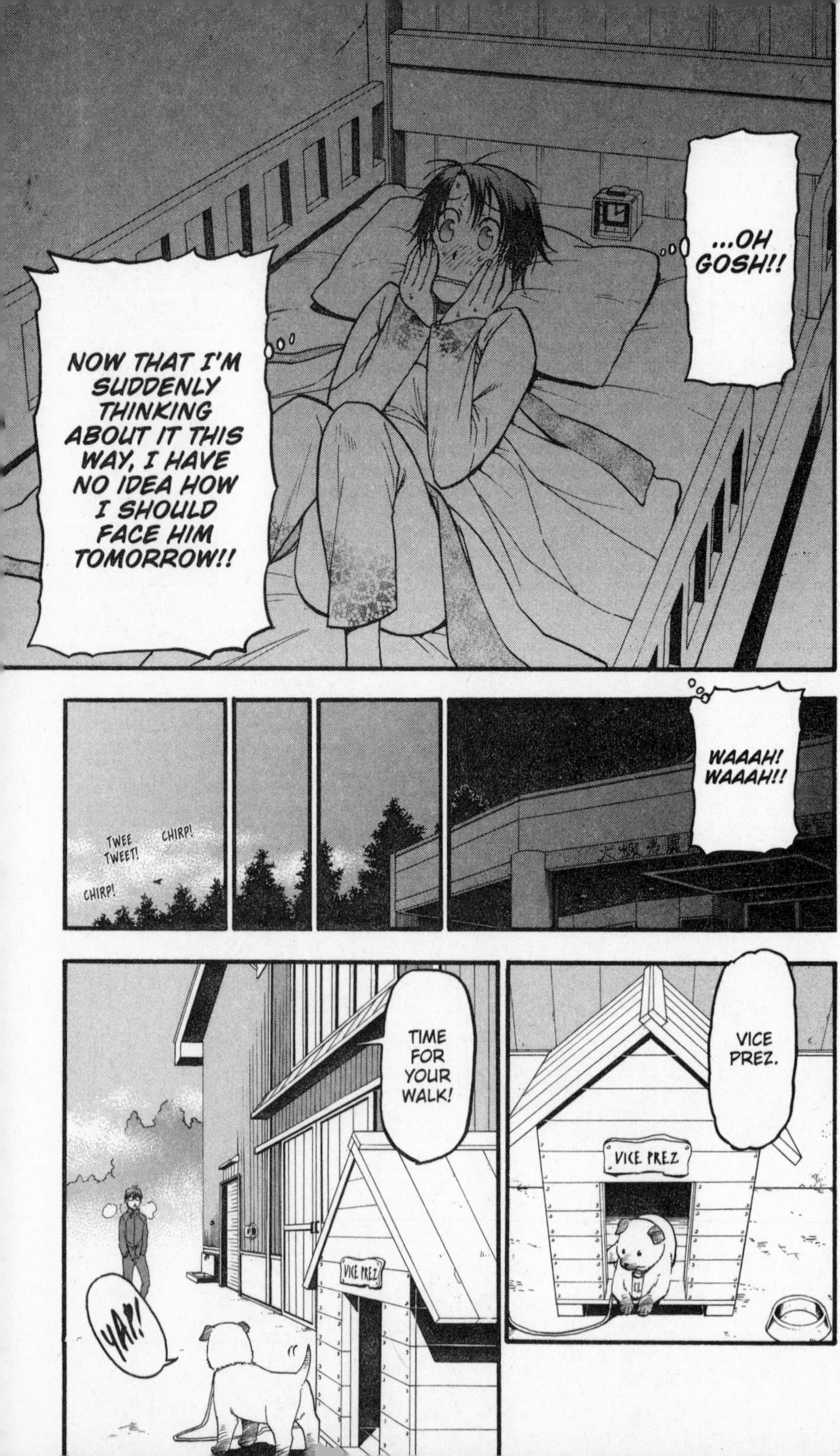
...OH GOSH!!
NOW THAT I'M SUDDENLY THINKING ABOUT IT THIS WAY, I HAVE NO IDEA HOW I SHOULD FACE HIM TOMORROW!!
WAAAH! WAAAH!!
TWEE TWEET!
CHIRP!
CHIRP!
VICE PREZ.
VICE PREZ
TIME FOR YOUR WALK!
VICE PREZ
YAP!

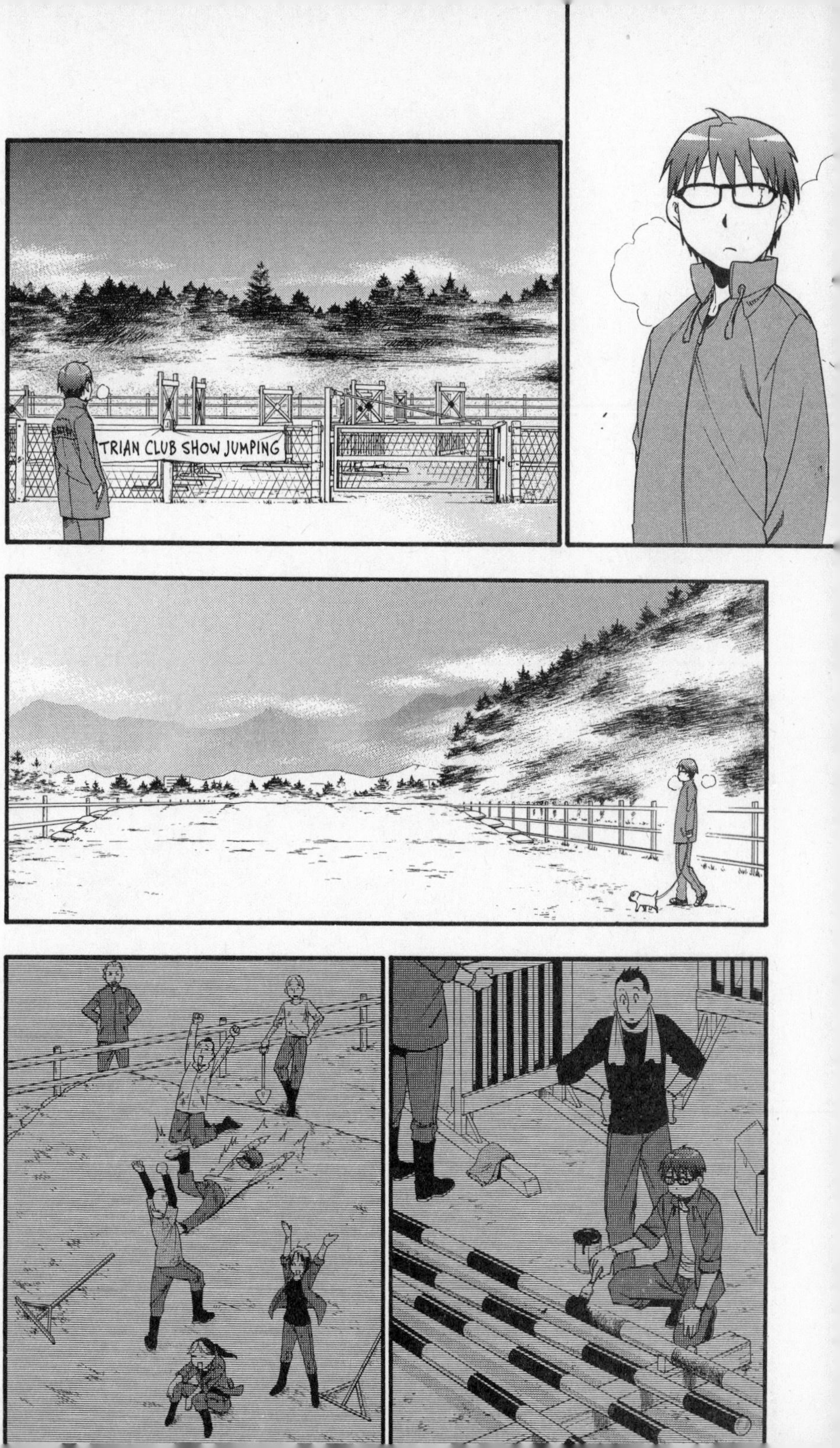
TRIAN CLUB SHOW JUMPING

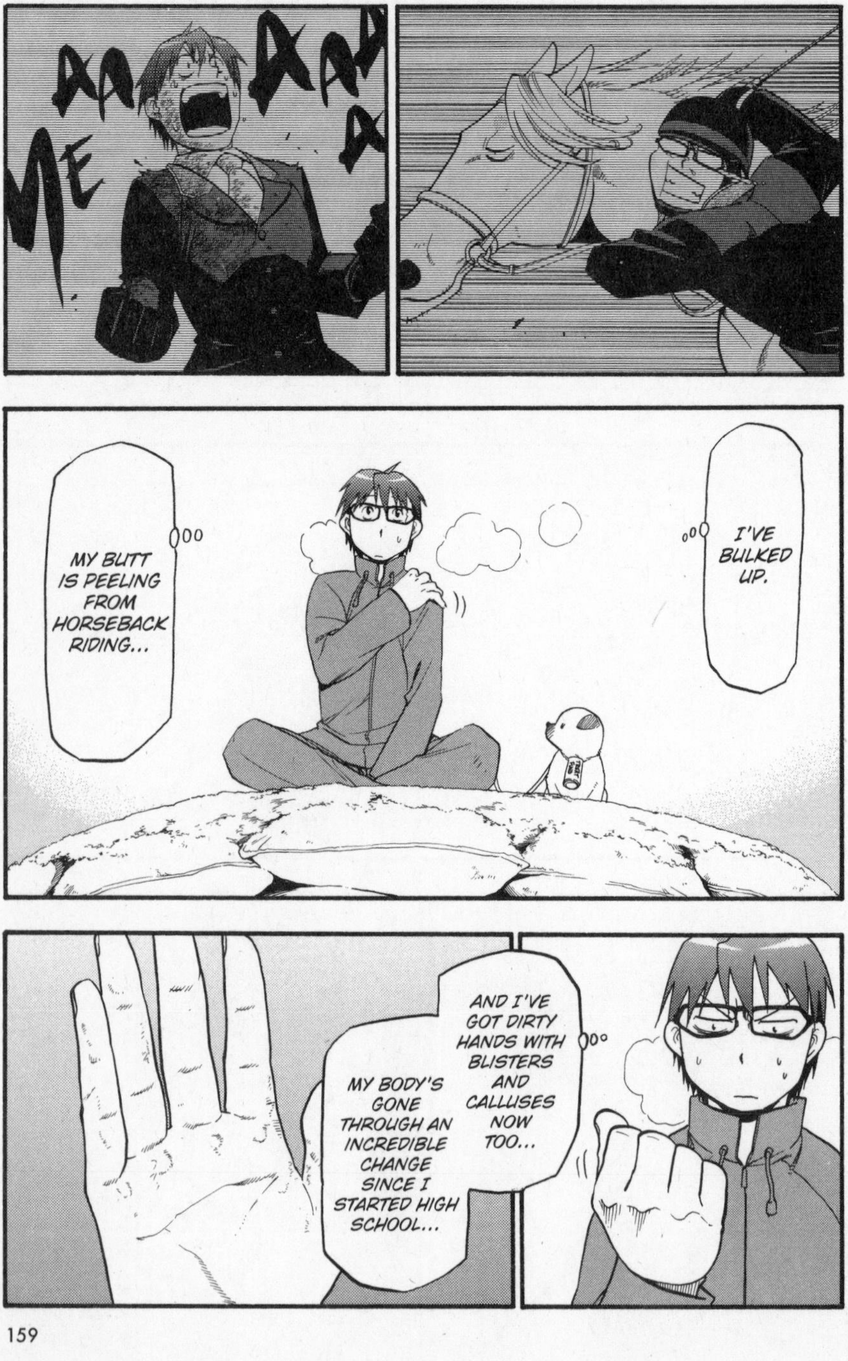
I'VE BULKED UP.
MY BUTT IS PEELING FROM HORSEBACK RIDING...
AND I'VE GOT DIRTY HANDS WITH BLISTERS AND CALLUSES NOW TOO...
MY BODY'S GONE THROUGH AN INCREDIBLE CHANGE SINCE I STARTED HIGH SCHOOL...

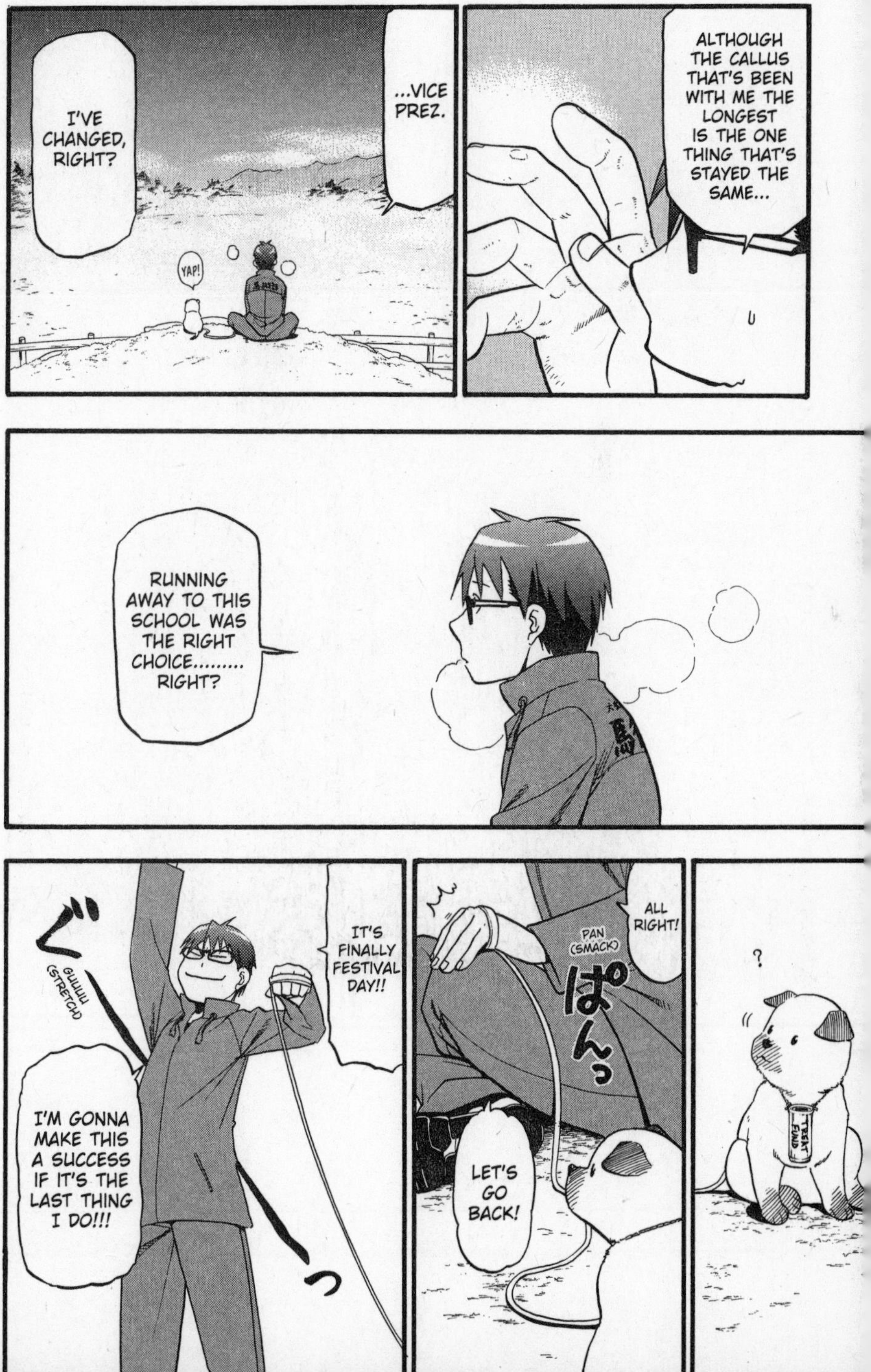
ALTHOUGH THE CALLUS THAT'S BEEN WITH ME THE LONGEST IS THE ONE THING THAT'S STAYED THE SAME...
...VICE PREZ.
I'VE CHANGED, RIGHT?
YAP!
RUNNING AWAY TO THIS SCHOOL WAS THE RIGHT CHOICE......... RIGHT?
?
ALL RIGHT!
PAN (SMACK)
ぱんっ
LET'S GO BACK!
IT'S FINALLY FESTIVAL DAY!!
ぐ
GUUUU (STRETCH)
I'M GONNA MAKE THIS A SUCCESS IF IT'S THE LAST THING I DO!!!

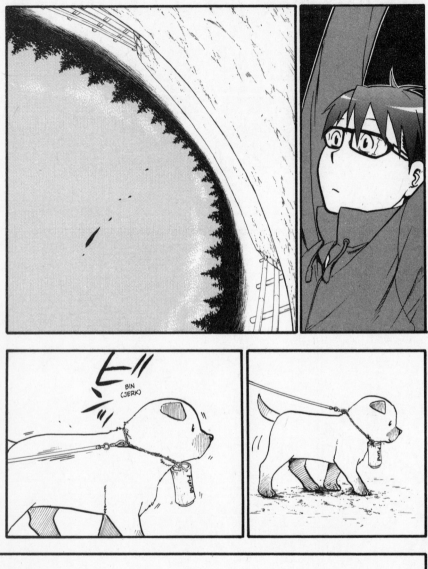

BIN
(JERK)

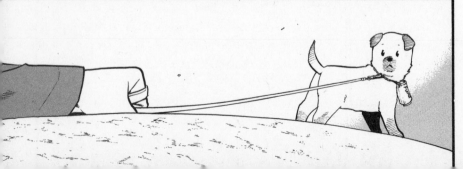

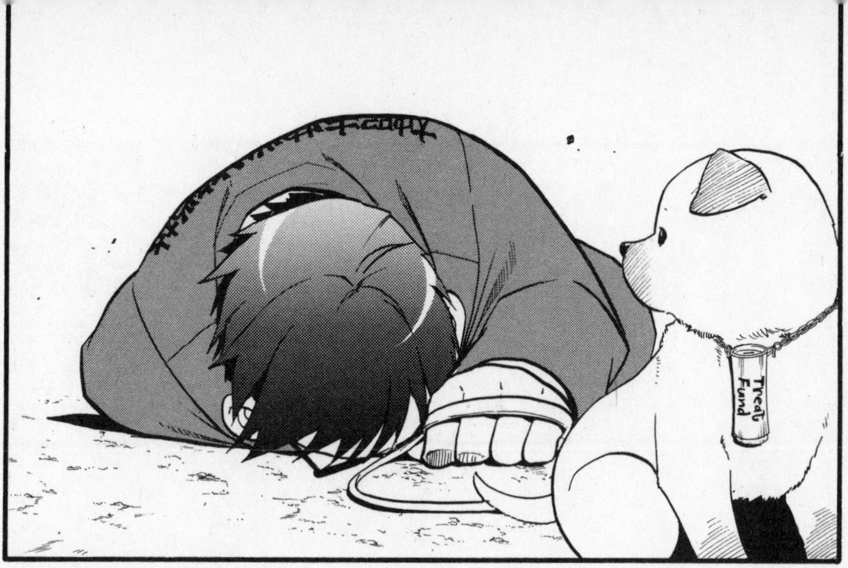
Treat Fund

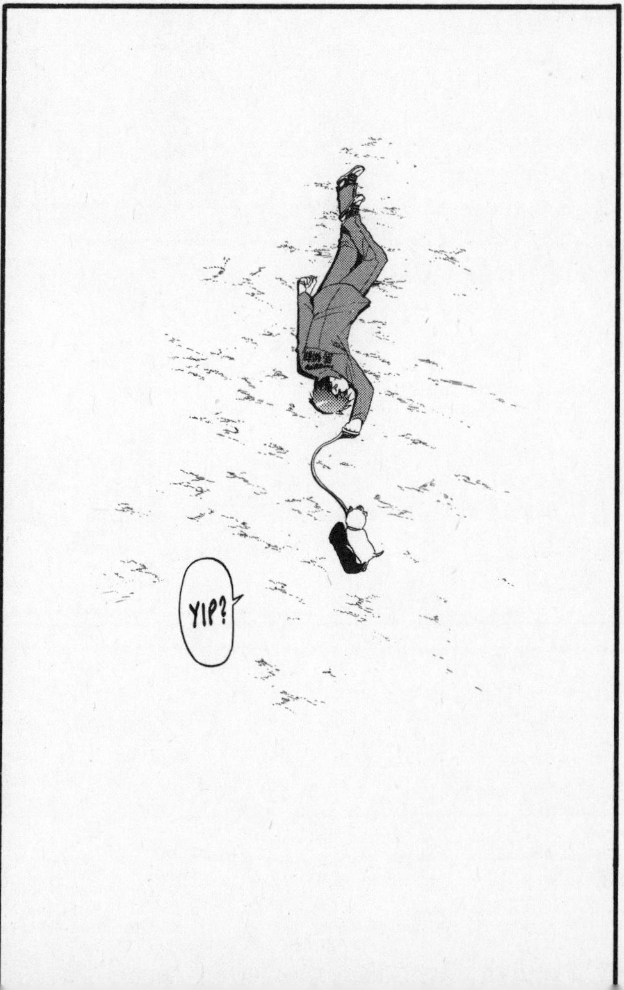
YIP?

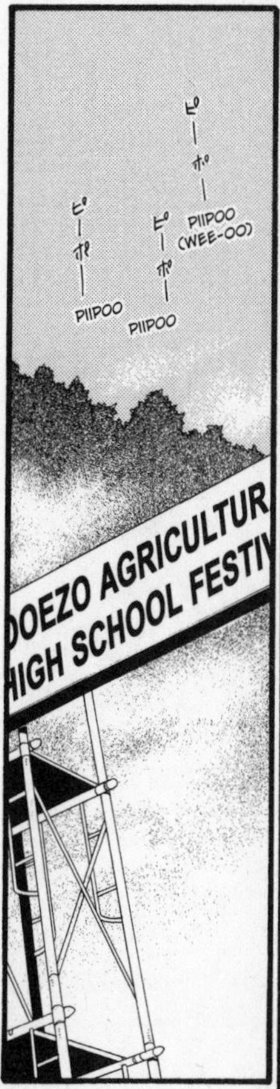
ピーポー
PIIPOO (WEE-OO)
ピーポー
PIIPOO
ピーポー
PIIPOO
DOEZO AGRICULTUR
HIGH SCHOOL FESTIV

Silver Spoon

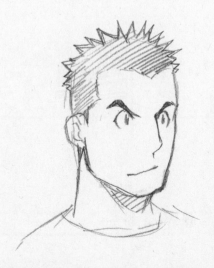

TEPPEI SHIROGANE

CHURUIMOTOMACHI
MIDDLE SCHOOL

BASKETBALL TEAM

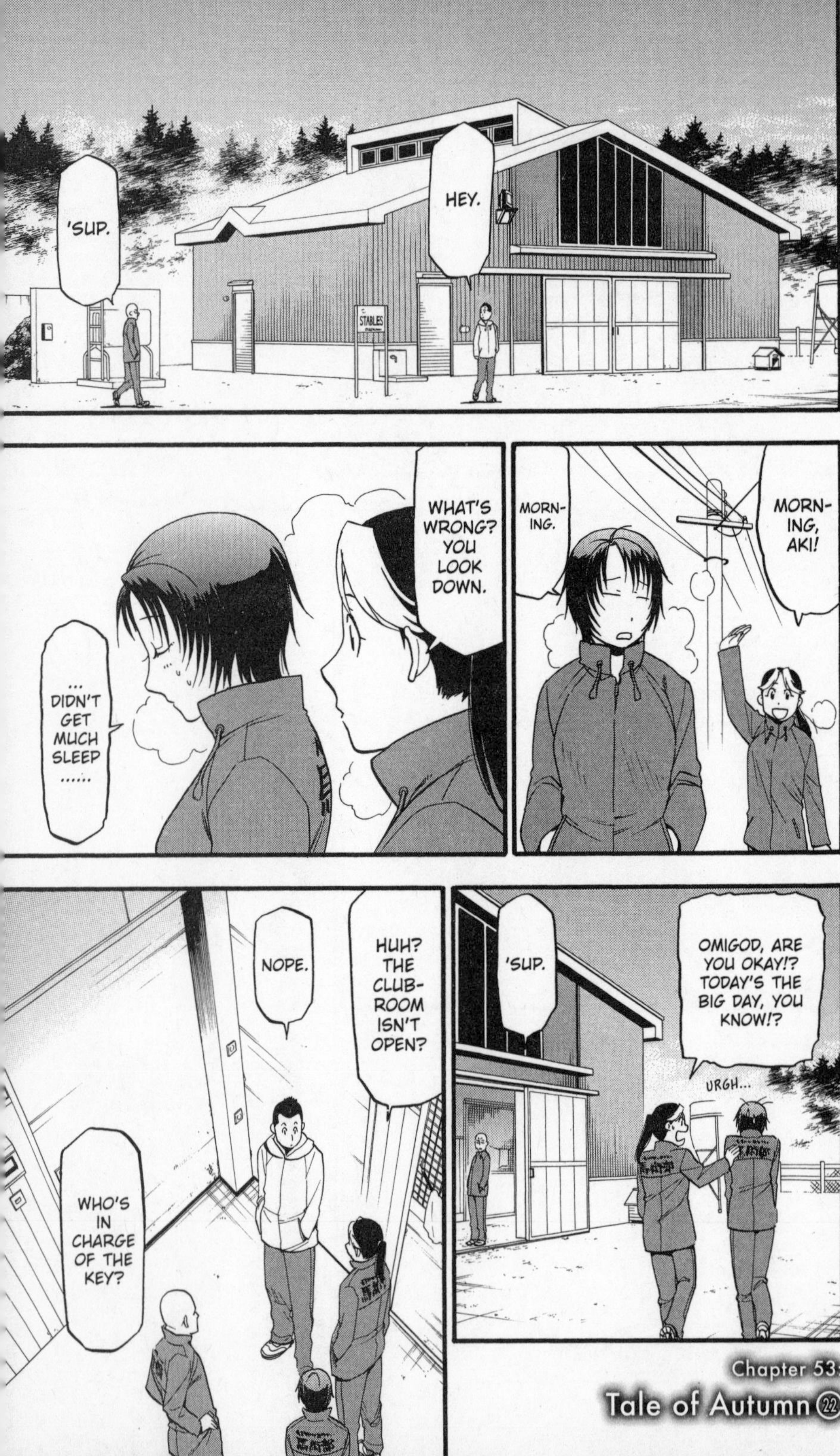
HEY.
'SUP.
MORNING, AKI!
MORNING.
WHAT'S WRONG? YOU LOOK DOWN.
... DIDN'T GET MUCH SLEEP ......
OMIGOD, ARE YOU OKAY!? TODAY'S THE BIG DAY, YOU KNOW!?
URGH...
'SUP.
HUH? THE CLUBROOM ISN'T OPEN?
NOPE.
WHO'S IN CHARGE OF THE KEY?

Chapter 53: Tale of Autumn ㉒

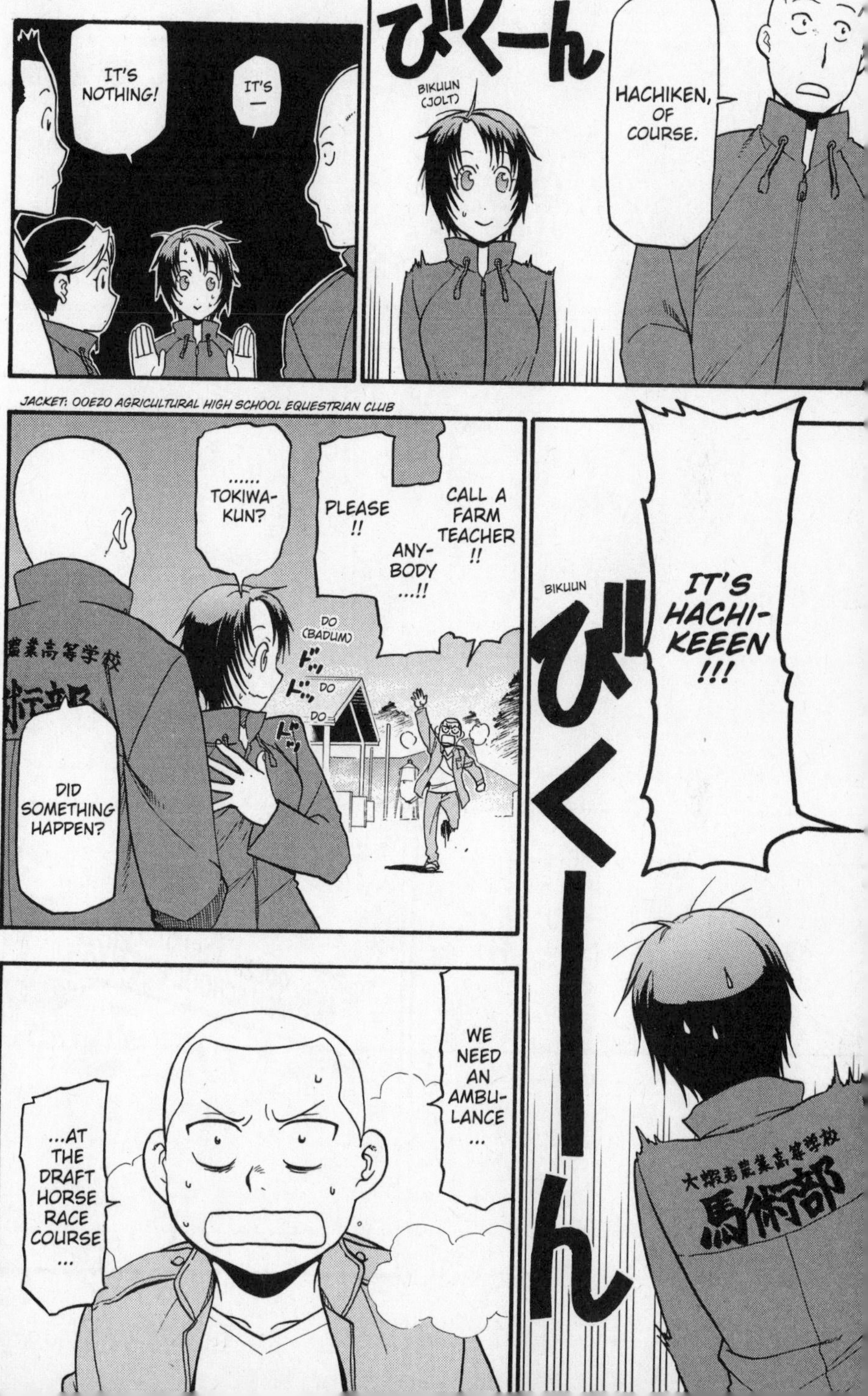
HACHIKEN, OF COURSE.
びくーん
BIKUUN (JOLT)
IT'S —
IT'S NOTHING!
JACKET: OOEZO AGRICULTURAL HIGH SCHOOL EQUESTRIAN CLUB
IT'S HACHI-KEEEN!!!
BIKUUN
びくーん
大蝦夷農業高等学校 馬術部
CALL A FARM TEACHER!!
ANY-BODY...!!
PLEASE!!
......TOKIWA-KUN?
DO (BADUM)
ドッ
DO
ドッ
DO
ドッ
DID SOMETHING HAPPEN?
WE NEED AN AMBULANCE...
...AT THE DRAFT HORSE RACE COURSE...

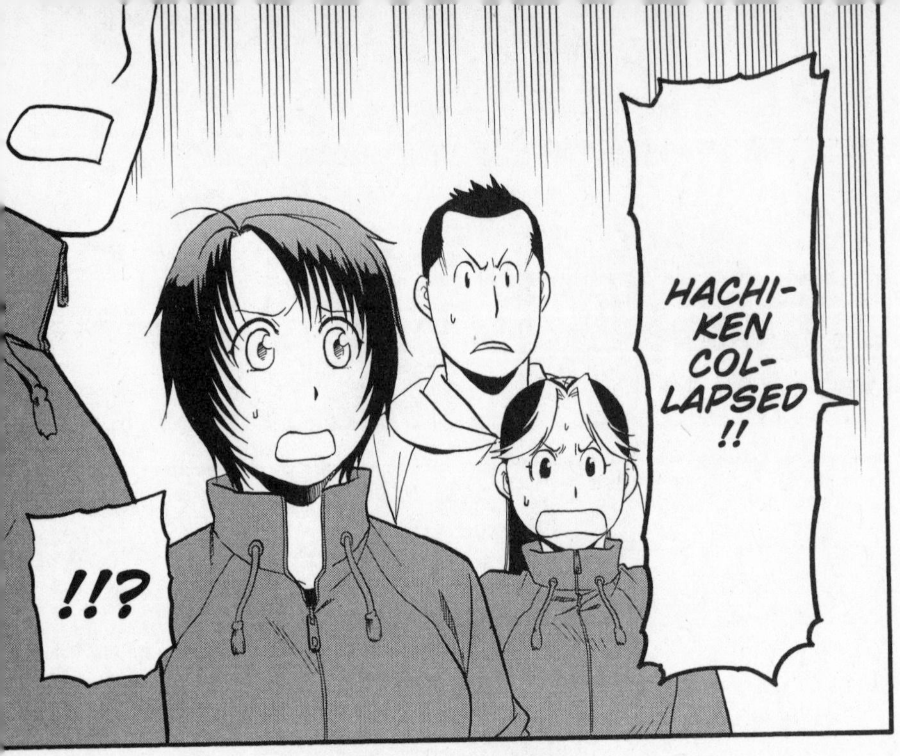
HACHI-KEN COL-LAPSED!!
!!?

Chapter 53:

Tale of Autumn ㉒

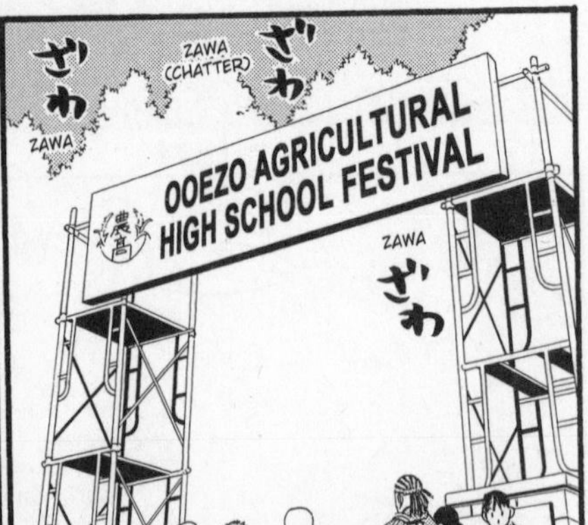
ZAWA (CHATTER)
ざわ
ZAWA
ざわ
OOEZO AGRICULTURAL HIGH SCHOOL FESTIVAL
ZAWA
ざわ

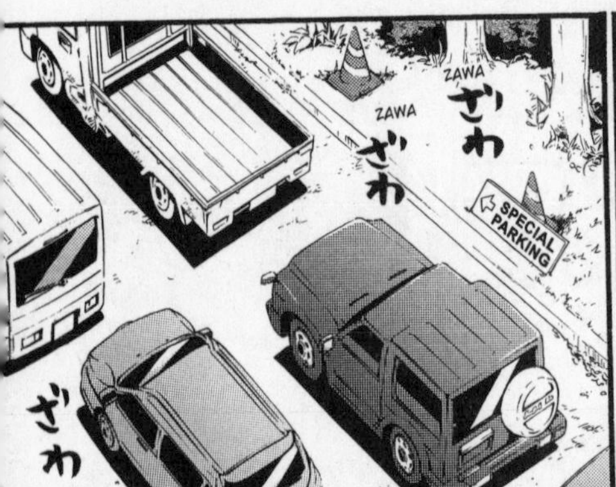
ZAWA
ざわ
ZAWA
ざわ
SPECIAL PARKING
ざわ
ZAWA

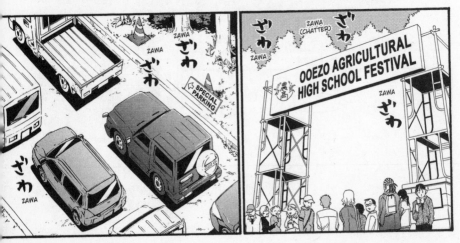

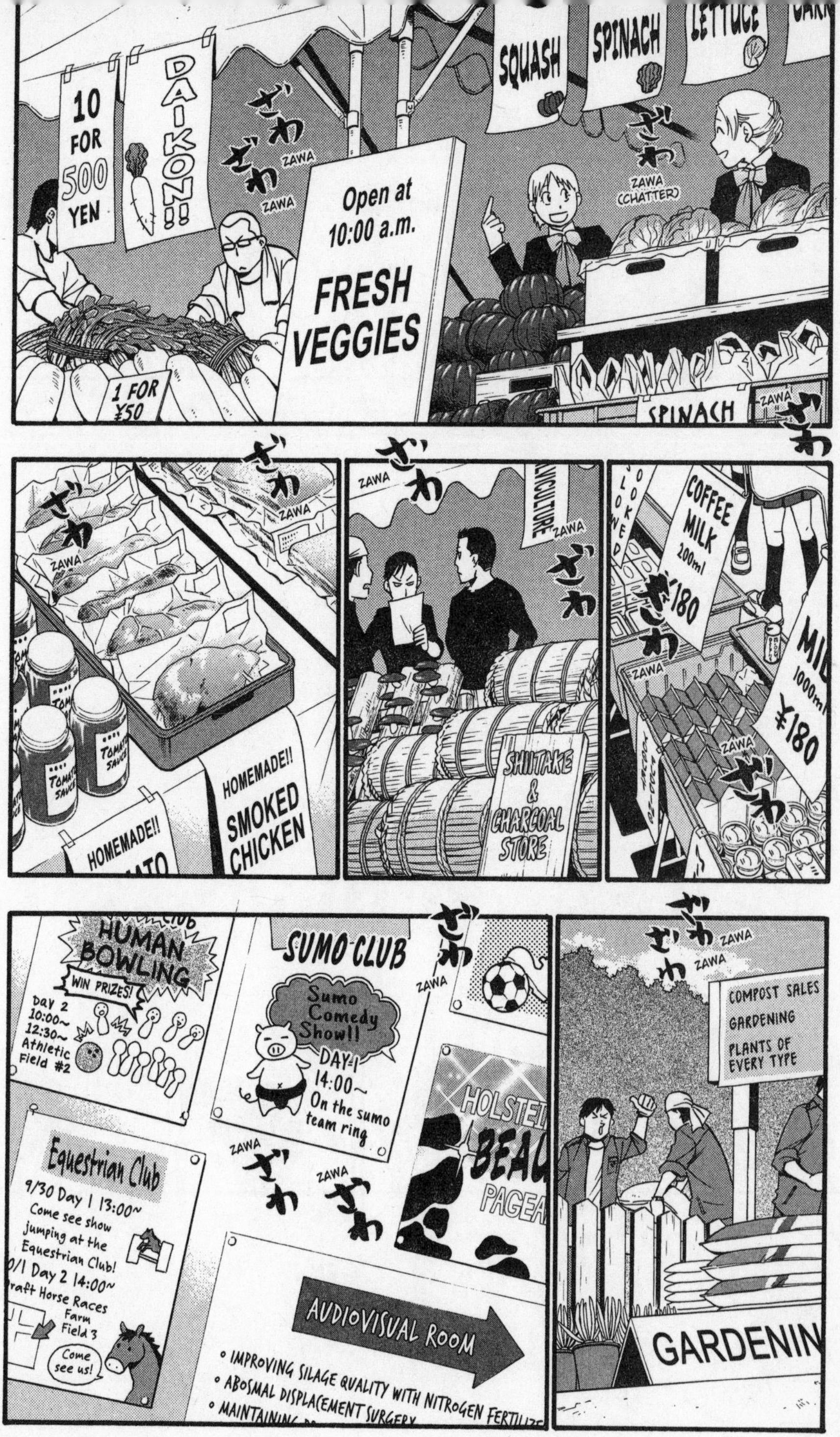
SQUASH
SPINACH
LETTUCE
ざわ
ZAWA (CHATTER)
Open at 10:00 a.m.
FRESH VEGGIES
ざわ ZAWA
ざわ ZAWA
DAIKON!!
10 FOR 500 YEN
1 FOR ¥50
SPINACH
ZAWA ざわ
COFFEE MILK 200ml ¥180
MILK 1000ml ¥180
ざわ ZAWA
ZAWA ざわ
ZAWA ざわ
ZAWA ざわ
SHIITAKE & CHARCOAL STORE
ざわ ZAWA
ざわ ZAWA
HOMEMADE!! SMOKED CHICKEN
HOMEMADE!!
TOMATO SAUCE
ざわ ZAWA
ざわ ZAWA
COMPOST SALES
GARDENING
PLANTS OF EVERY TYPE
GARDENIN
ざわ ZAWA
SUMO CLUB
Sumo Comedy Show!!
DAY 1 14:00~ On the sumo team ring
HUMAN BOWLING
WIN PRIZES!
Day 2 10:00~ 12:30~ Athletic Field #2
HOLSTEI
BEAU
PAGEA
ZAWA ざわ
ZAWA ざわ
Equestrian Club
9/30 Day 1 13:00~
Come see show jumping at the Equestrian Club!
0/1 Day 2 14:00~
raft Horse Races
Farm Field 3
Come see us!
AUDIOVISUAL ROOM
◦ IMPROVING SILAGE QUALITY WITH NITROGEN FERTILIZE
◦ ABOSMAL DISPLACEMENT SURGERY
◦ MAINTAINING

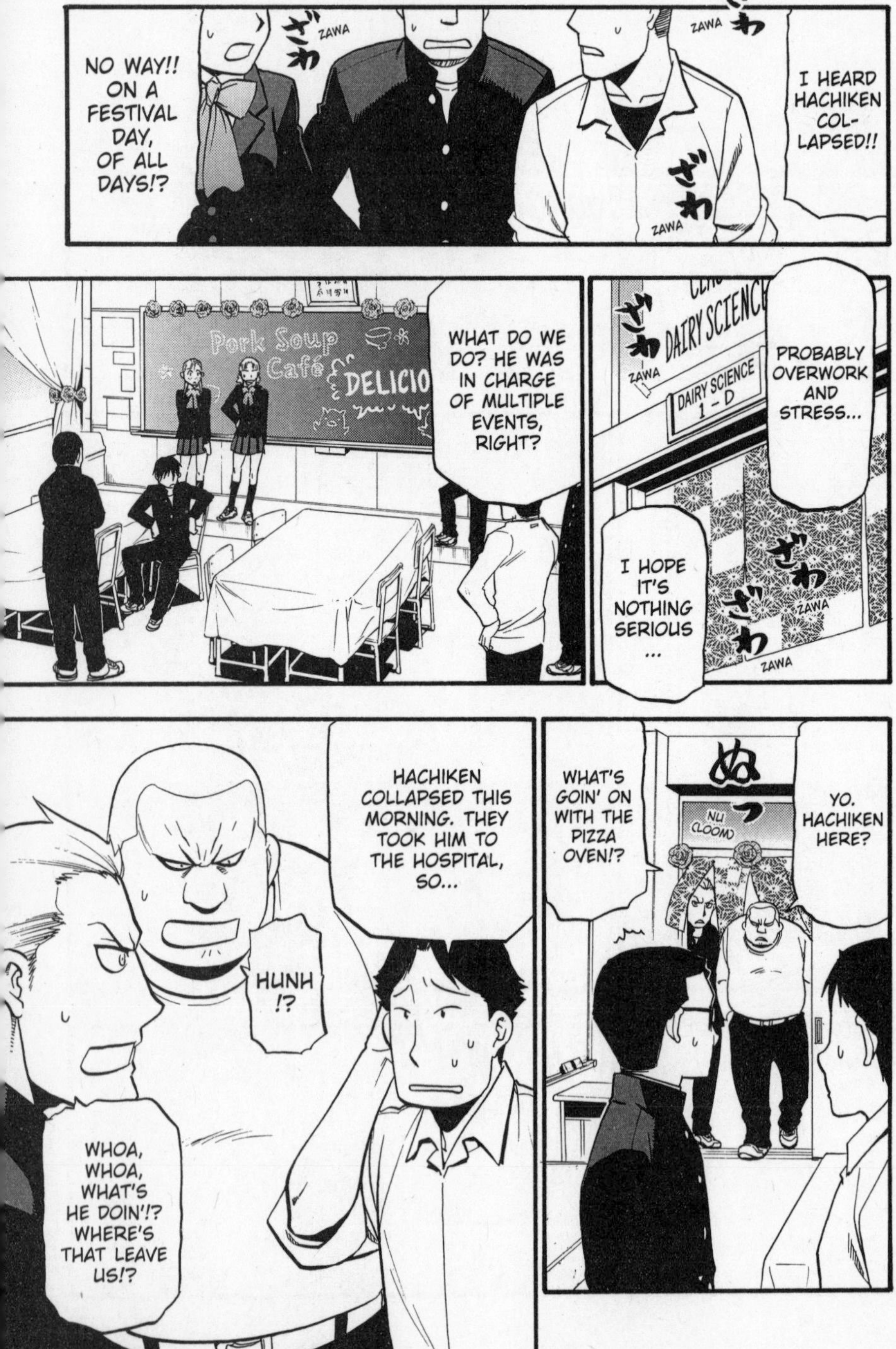
ざわ
ZAWA
I HEARD HACHIKEN COL-LAPSED!!
ざわ
ZAWA
ざわ
ZAWA
NO WAY!! ON A FESTIVAL DAY, OF ALL DAYS!?
DAIRY SCIENCE
DAIRY SCIENCE 1 - D
PROBABLY OVERWORK AND STRESS...
ざわ
ZAWA
I HOPE IT'S NOTHING SERIOUS ...
ざわ
ZAWA
ざわ
ZAWA
WHAT DO WE DO? HE WAS IN CHARGE OF MULTIPLE EVENTS, RIGHT?
Pork Soup Café
DELICIO
ぬ
つ
NU (LOOM)
YO. HACHIKEN HERE?
WHAT'S GOIN' ON WITH THE PIZZA OVEN!?
HACHIKEN COLLAPSED THIS MORNING. THEY TOOK HIM TO THE HOSPITAL, SO...
HUNH !?
WHOA, WHOA, WHAT'S HE DOIN'!? WHERE'S THAT LEAVE US!?

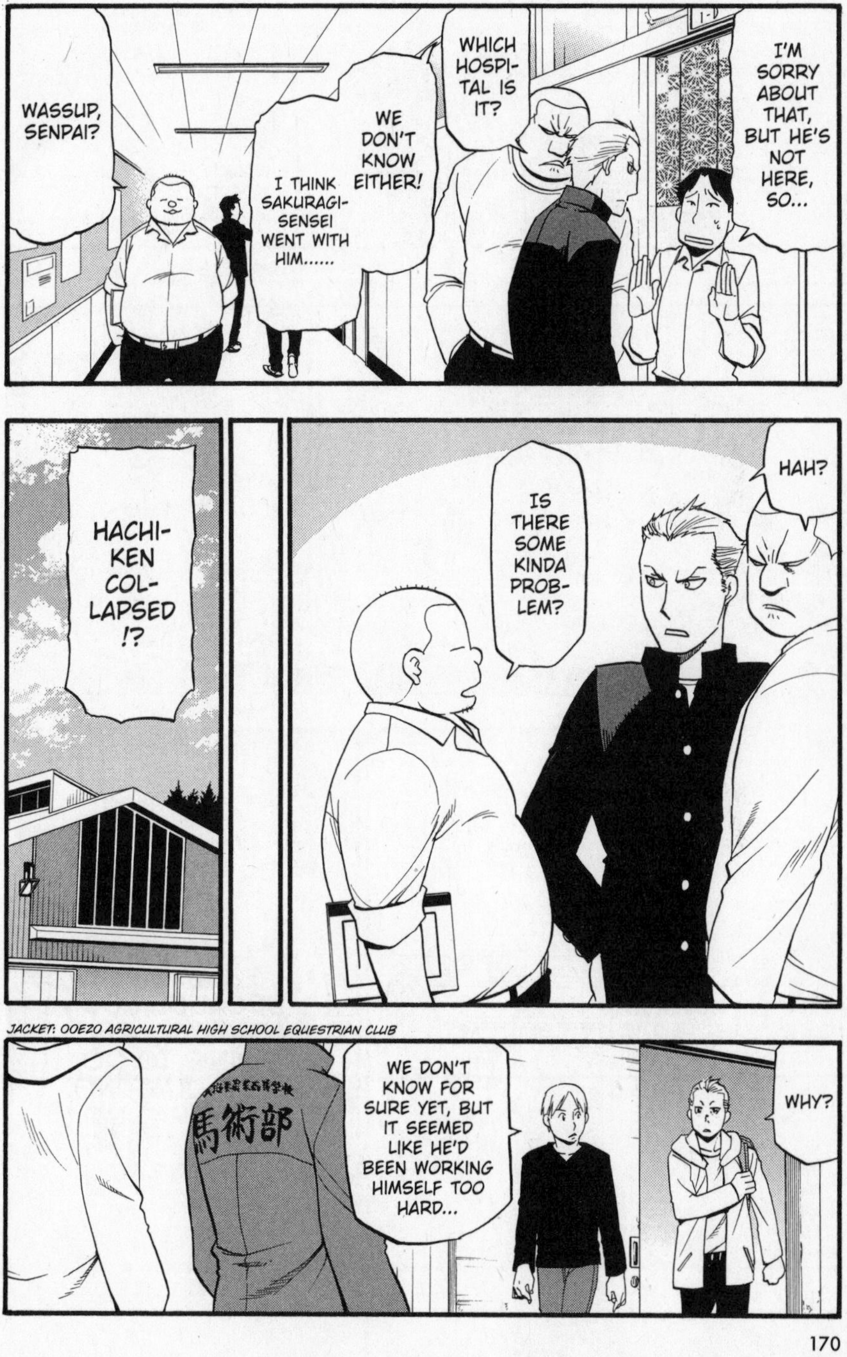
I'M SORRY ABOUT THAT, BUT HE'S NOT HERE, SO...
WHICH HOSPI-TAL IS IT?
WE DON'T KNOW EITHER!
I THINK SAKURAGI-SENSEI WENT WITH HIM......
WASSUP, SENPAI?
HAH?
IS THERE SOME KINDA PROB-LEM?
HACHI-KEN COL-LAPSED!?
WHY?
WE DON'T KNOW FOR SURE YET, BUT IT SEEMED LIKE HE'D BEEN WORKING HIMSELF TOO HARD...
馬術部
JACKET: OOEZO AGRICULTURAL HIGH SCHOOL EQUESTRIAN CLUB

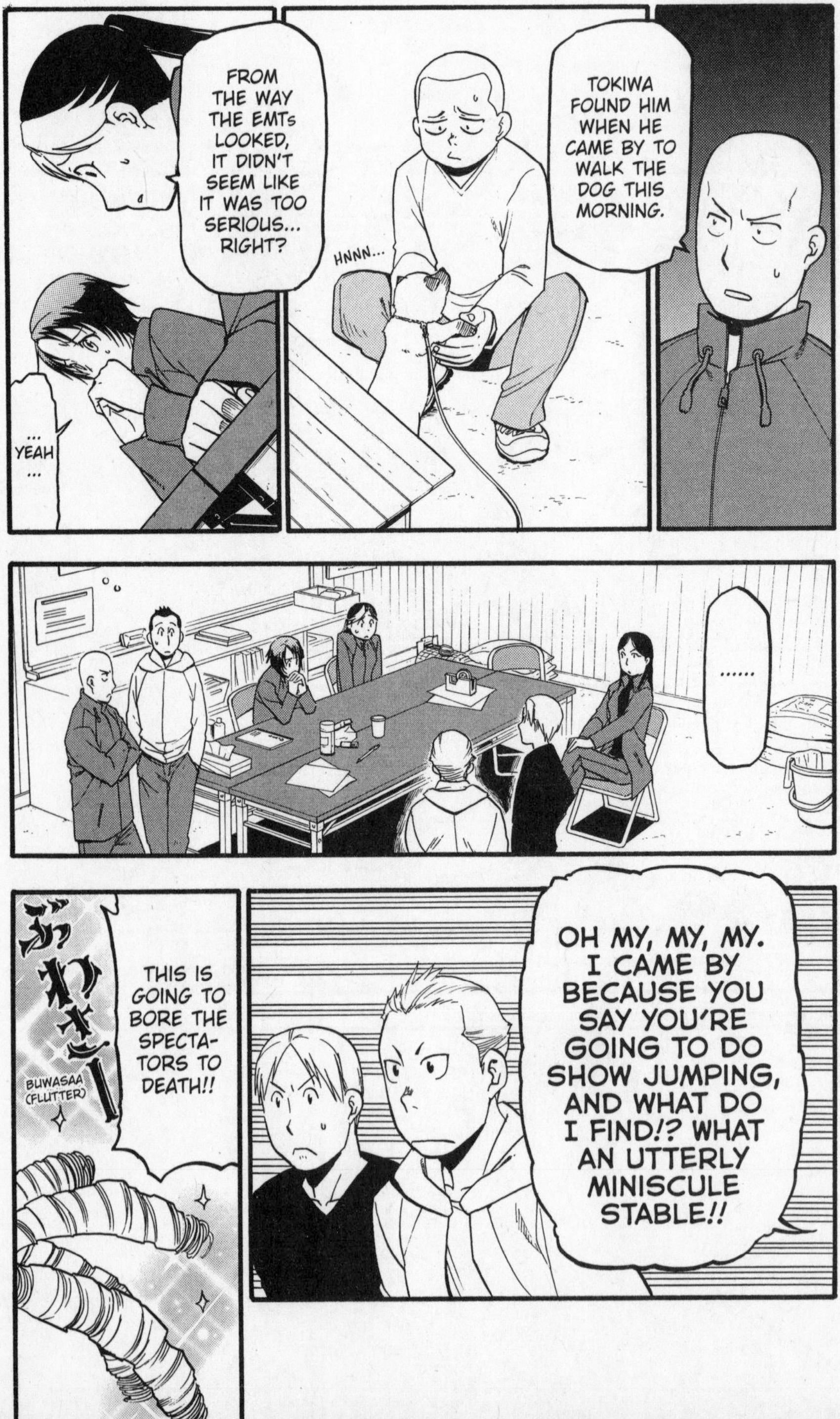
TOKIWA FOUND HIM WHEN HE CAME BY TO WALK THE DOG THIS MORNING.
HNNN...
FROM THE WAY THE EMTs LOOKED, IT DIDN'T SEEM LIKE IT WAS TOO SERIOUS... RIGHT?
...YEAH...
......
OH MY, MY, MY. I CAME BY BECAUSE YOU SAY YOU'RE GOING TO DO SHOW JUMPING, AND WHAT DO I FIND!? WHAT AN UTTERLY MINISCULE STABLE!!
THIS IS GOING TO BORE THE SPECTATORS TO DEATH!!
ぶわさー
BUWASAA (FLUTTER)

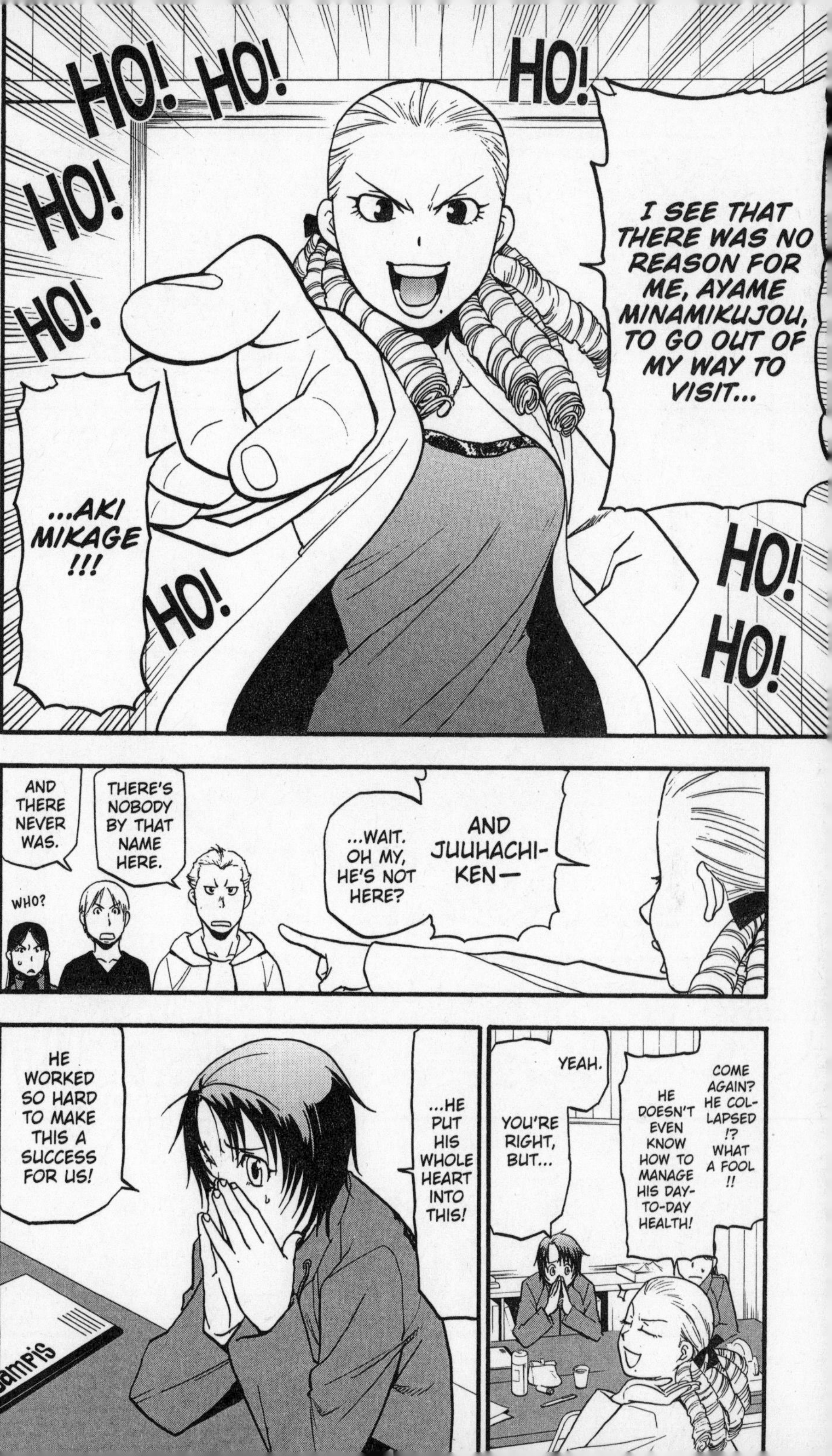
HO! HO! HO!
HO! HO!
I SEE THAT THERE WAS NO REASON FOR ME, AYAME MINAMIKUJOU, TO GO OUT OF MY WAY TO VISIT...
...AKI MIKAGE !!!
HO! HO! HO!
AND JUUHACHI-KEN—
...WAIT. OH MY, HE'S NOT HERE?
THERE'S NOBODY BY THAT NAME HERE.
AND THERE NEVER WAS.
WHO?
COME AGAIN? HE COL-LAPSED !? WHAT A FOOL !!
HE DOESN'T EVEN KNOW HOW TO MANAGE HIS DAY-TO-DAY HEALTH!
YEAH.
YOU'RE RIGHT, BUT...
...HE PUT HIS WHOLE HEART INTO THIS!
HE WORKED SO HARD TO MAKE THIS A SUCCESS FOR US!

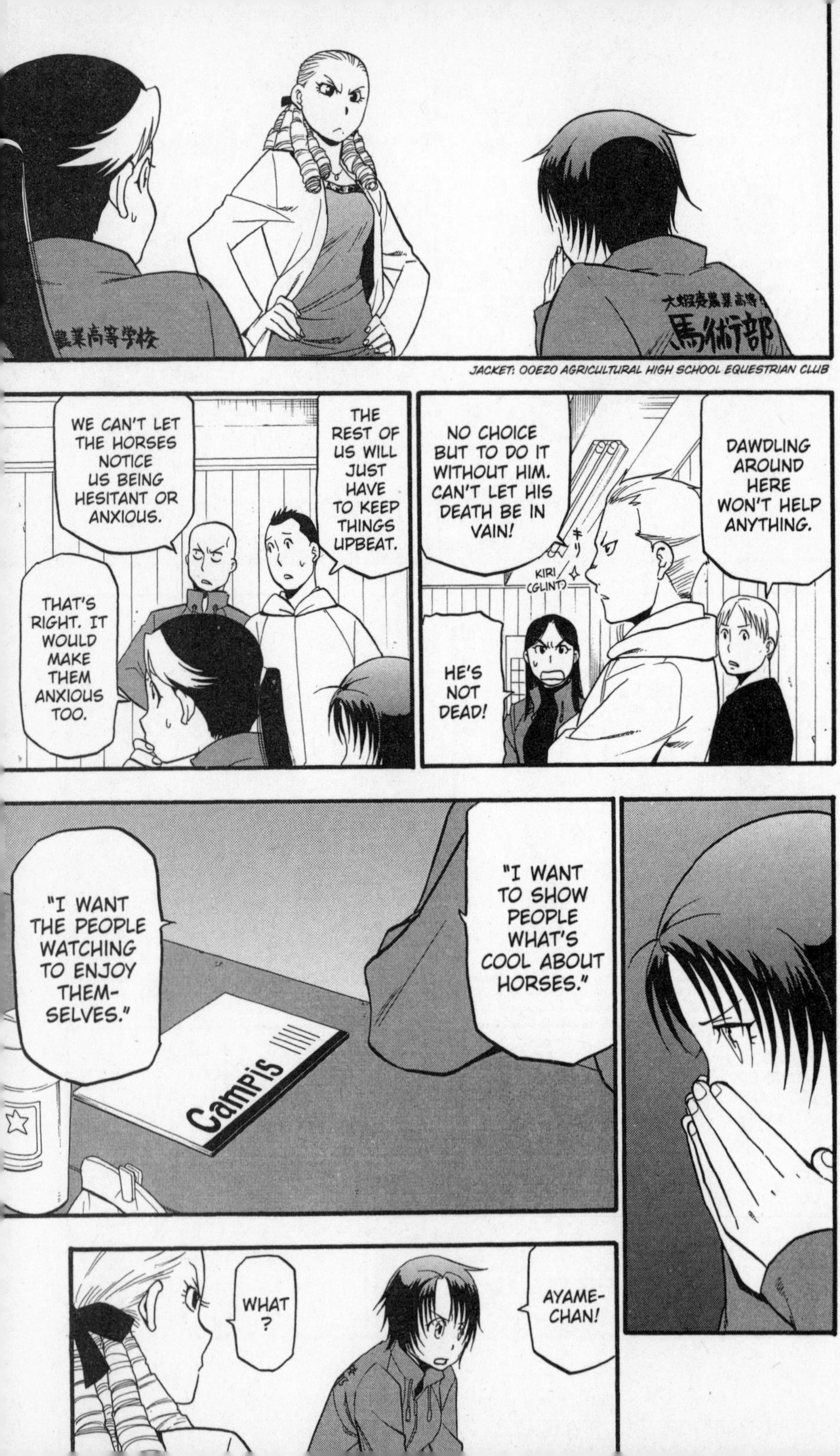
大蝦夷農業高等学
馬術部
農業高等学校
JACKET: OOEZO AGRICULTURAL HIGH SCHOOL EQUESTRIAN CLUB
DAWDLING AROUND HERE WON'T HELP ANYTHING.
NO CHOICE BUT TO DO IT WITHOUT HIM. CAN'T LET HIS DEATH BE IN VAIN!
キリ
KIRI (GLINT)
HE'S NOT DEAD!
THE REST OF US WILL JUST HAVE TO KEEP THINGS UPBEAT.
WE CAN'T LET THE HORSES NOTICE US BEING HESITANT OR ANXIOUS.
THAT'S RIGHT. IT WOULD MAKE THEM ANXIOUS TOO.
"I WANT TO SHOW PEOPLE WHAT'S COOL ABOUT HORSES."
"I WANT THE PEOPLE WATCHING TO ENJOY THEM-SELVES."
Campis
AYAME-CHAN!
WHAT?

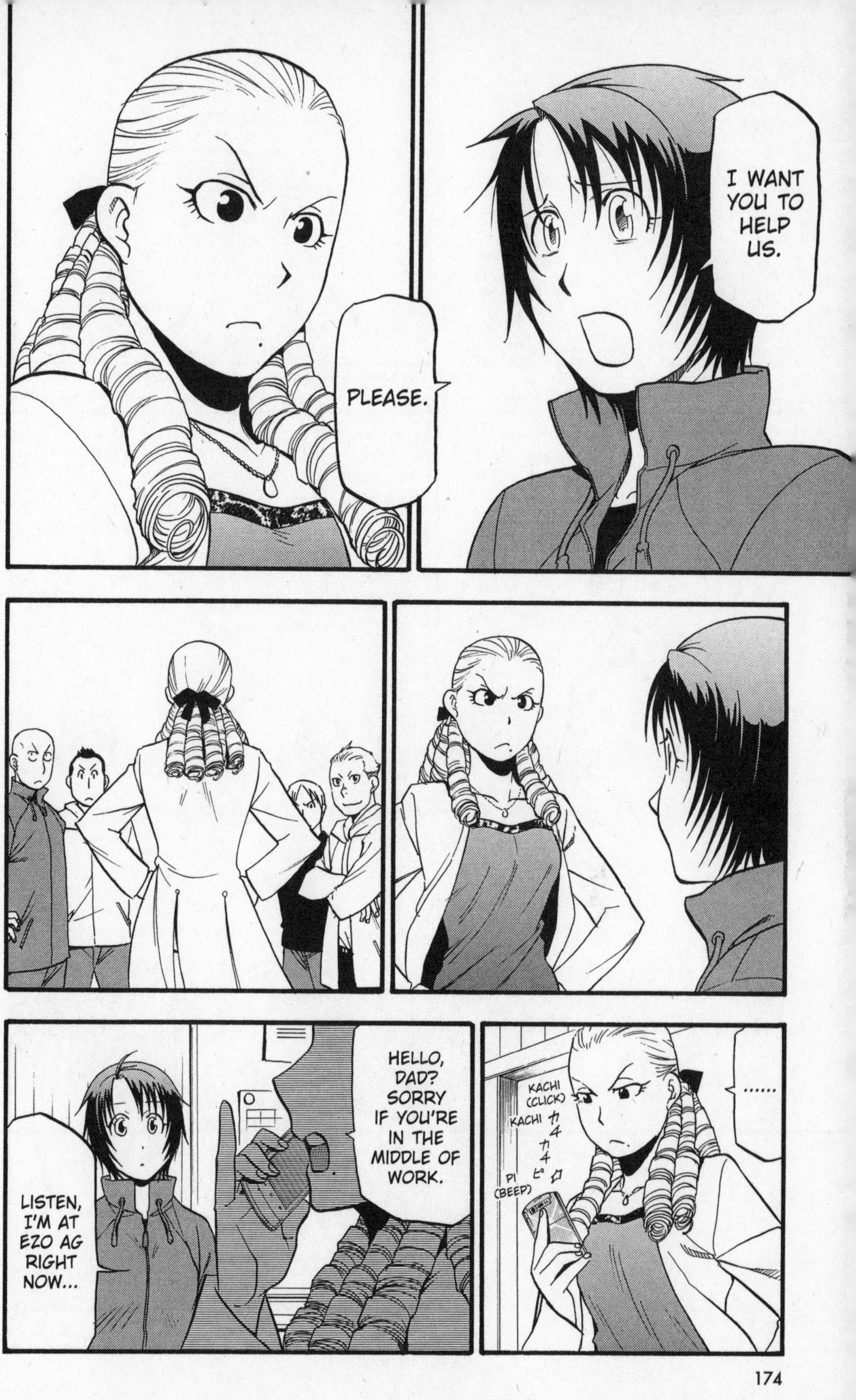
I WANT YOU TO HELP US.
PLEASE.
......
KACHI (CLICK)
KACHI
カチカチ
PI (BEEP)
ピッ
HELLO, DAD? SORRY IF YOU'RE IN THE MIDDLE OF WORK.
LISTEN, I'M AT EZO AG RIGHT NOW...

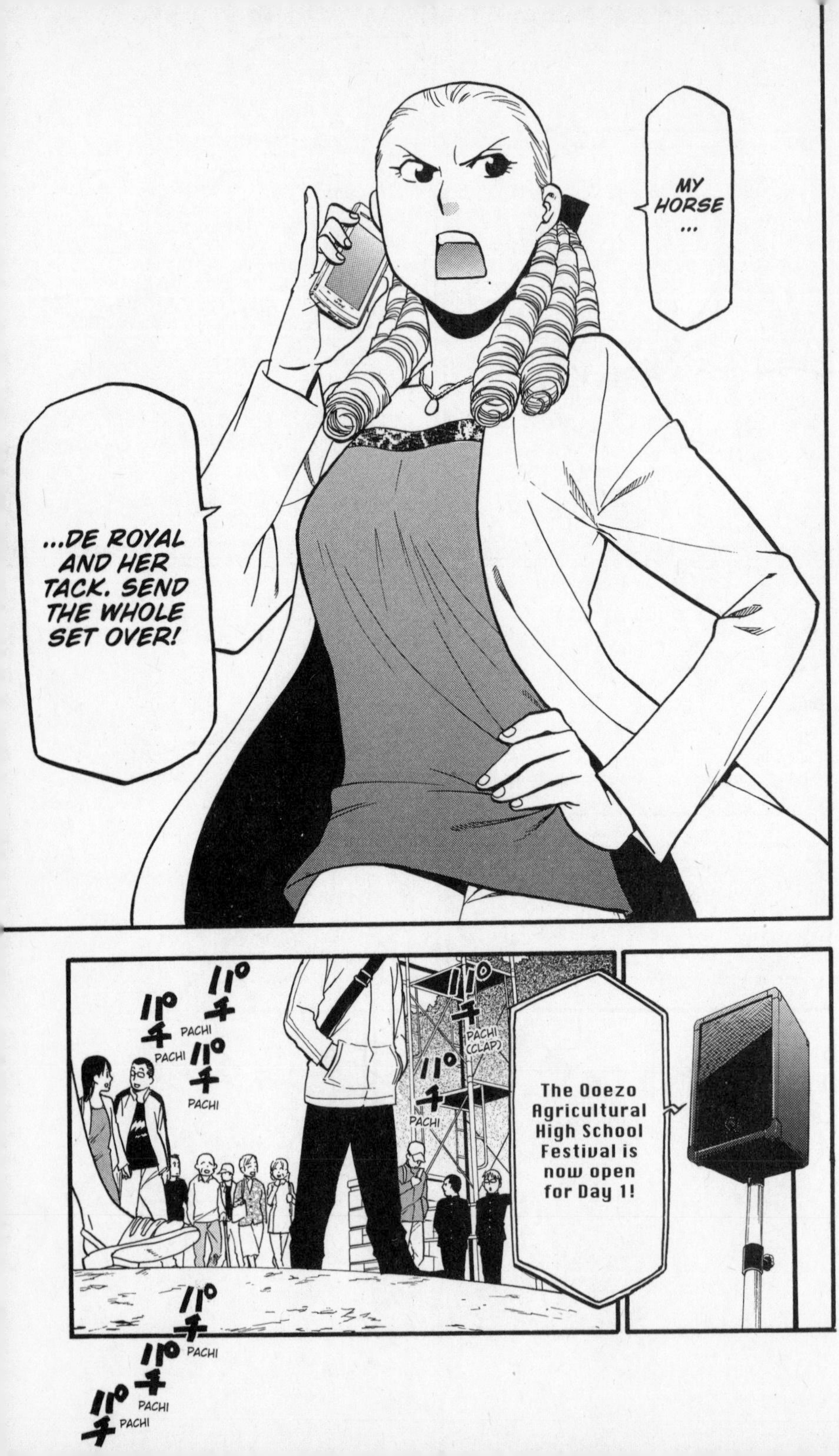
MY HORSE...
...DE ROYAL AND HER TACK. SEND THE WHOLE SET OVER!
The Ooezo Agricultural High School Festival is now open for Day 1!
パチ
PACHI (CLAP)
パチ
PACHI
パチ
PACHI
パチ
PACHI
パチ
PACHI
パチ
PACHI
パチ
PACHI
パチ
PACHI

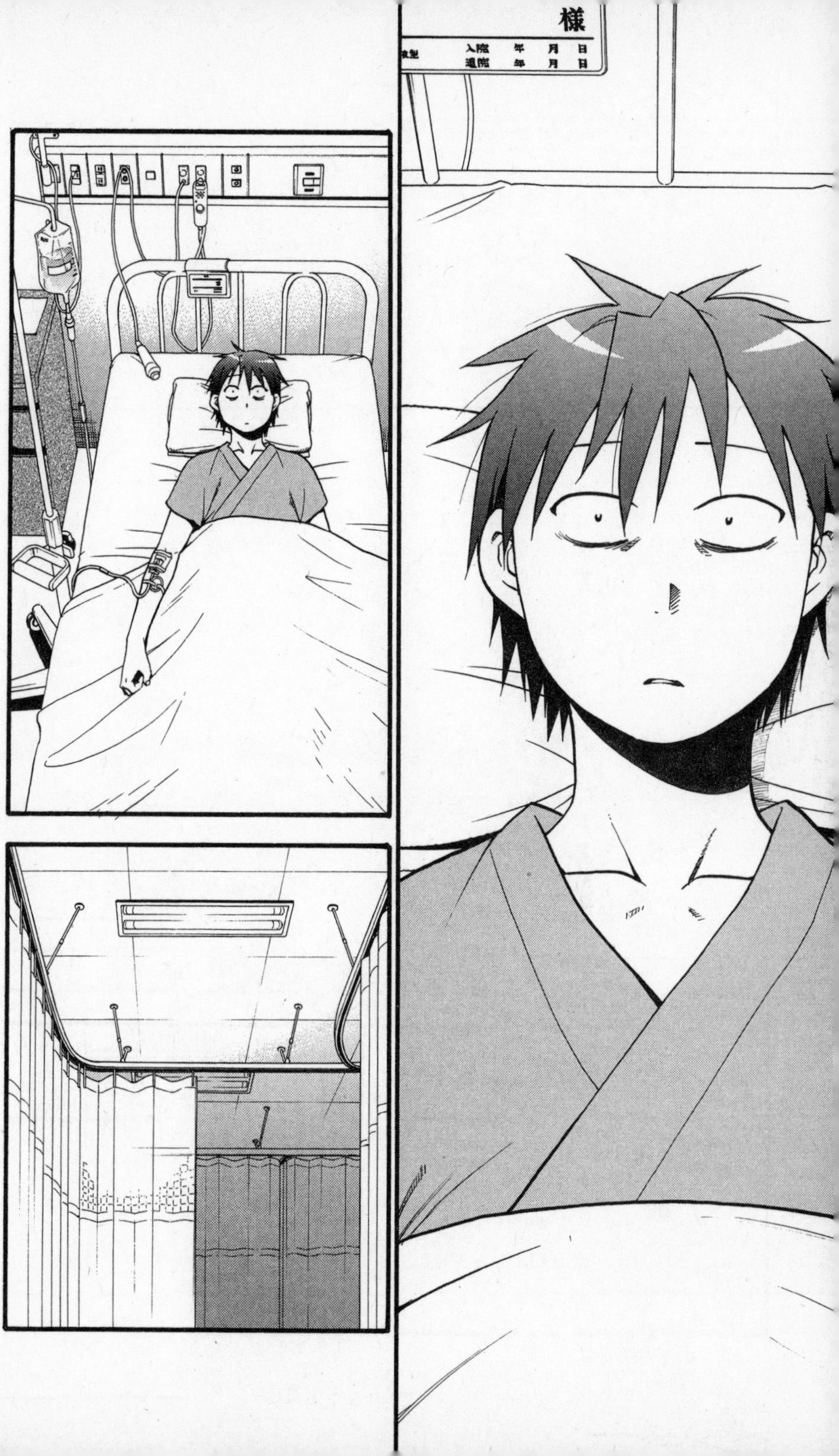
様
入院 年 月 日
退院 年 月 日

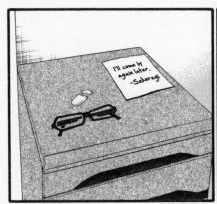

I'll come by again later. -Sakuragi
YOU'RE AWAKE?
......THE NURSE'S OFFICE...?
NO, THIS IS THE HOS-PITAL.
FURA (SWAY)
YOU DON'T NEED TO GET UP YET!

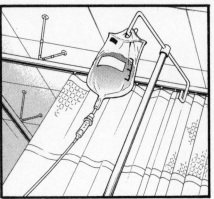

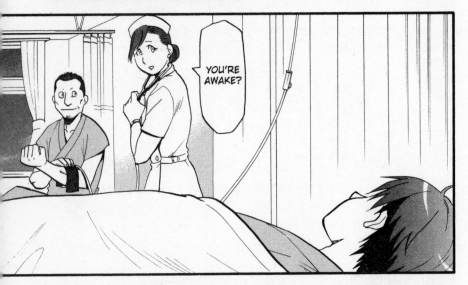

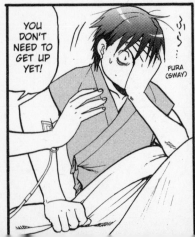

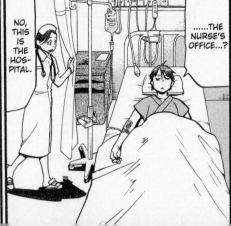

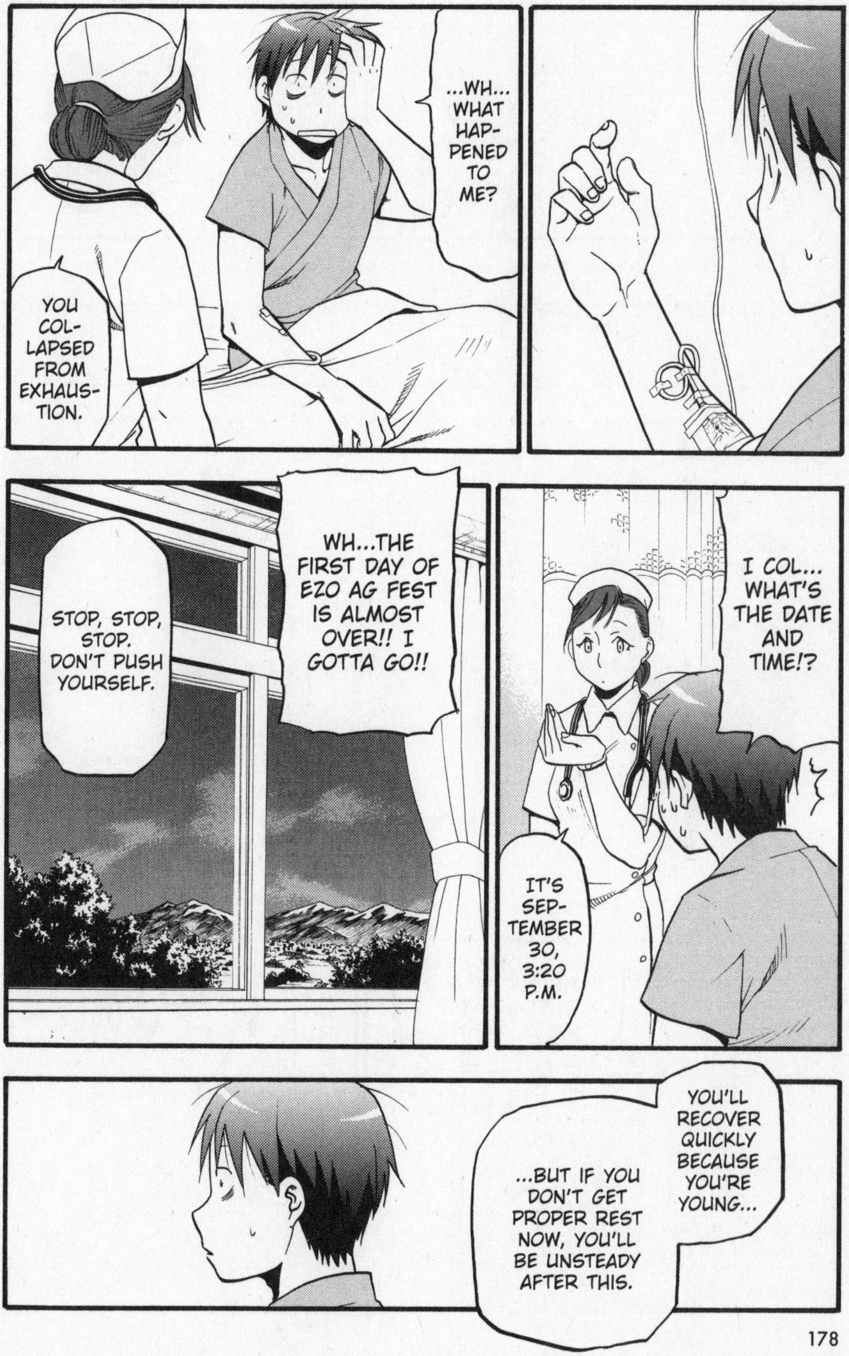
...WH... WHAT HAPPENED TO ME?
YOU COLLAPSED FROM EXHAUSTION.
I COL... WHAT'S THE DATE AND TIME!?
IT'S SEPTEMBER 30, 3:20 P.M.
WH...THE FIRST DAY OF EZO AG FEST IS ALMOST OVER!! I GOTTA GO!!
STOP, STOP, STOP. DON'T PUSH YOURSELF.
YOU'LL RECOVER QUICKLY BECAUSE YOU'RE YOUNG...
...BUT IF YOU DON'T GET PROPER REST NOW, YOU'LL BE UNSTEADY AFTER THIS.

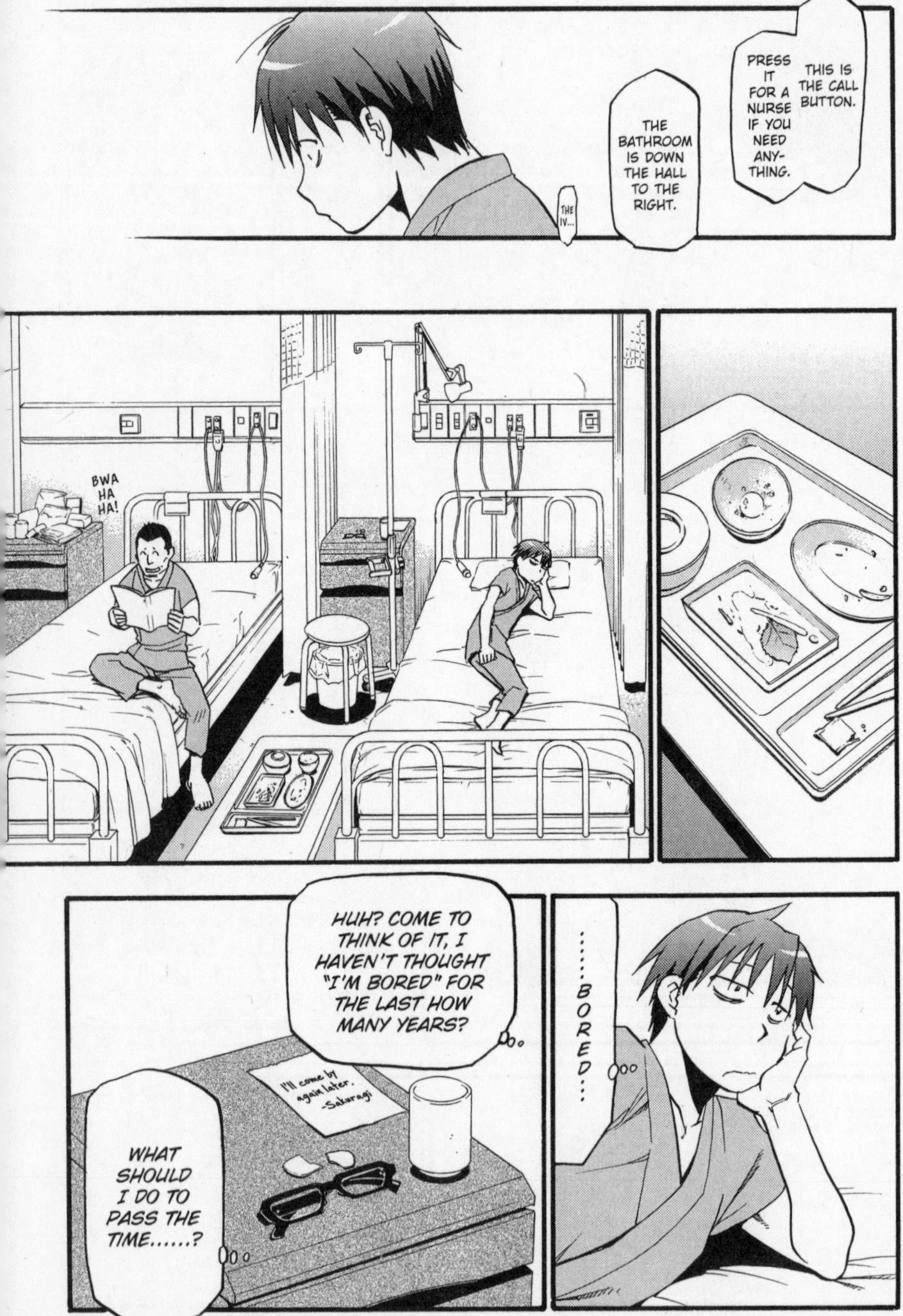
THIS IS THE CALL BUTTON.
PRESS IT FOR A NURSE IF YOU NEED ANY-THING.
THE BATHROOM IS DOWN THE HALL TO THE RIGHT.
THE IV...
BWA HA HA!
.....BORED...
HUH? COME TO THINK OF IT, I HAVEN'T THOUGHT "I'M BORED" FOR THE LAST HOW MANY YEARS?
I'll come by again later. -Sakuragi
WHAT SHOULD I DO TO PASS THE TIME......?

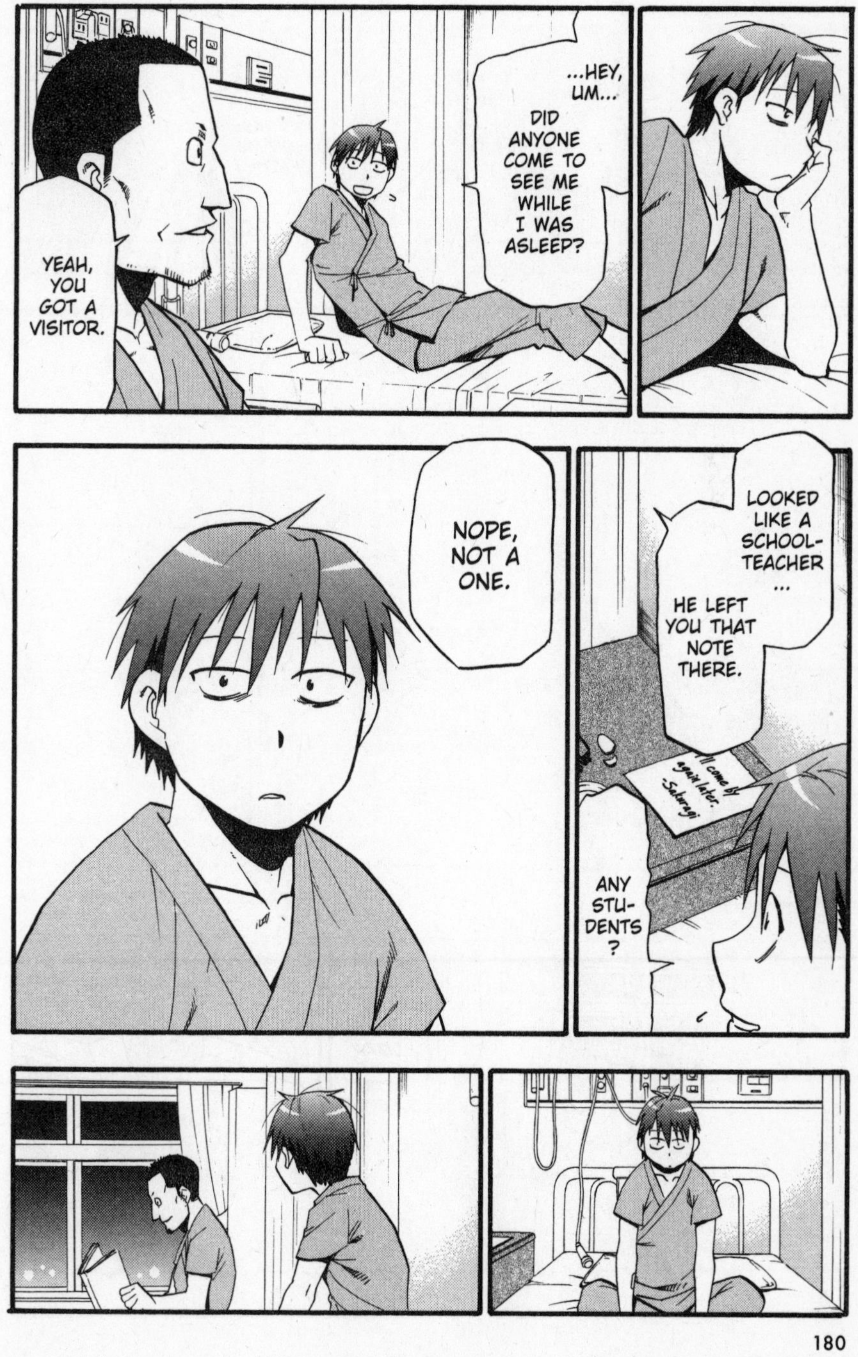
...HEY, UM...
DID ANYONE COME TO SEE ME WHILE I WAS ASLEEP?
YEAH, YOU GOT A VISITOR.
LOOKED LIKE A SCHOOLTEACHER ...
HE LEFT YOU THAT NOTE THERE.
'll come by again later. -Sakuragi
ANY STUDENTS?
NOPE, NOT A ONE.

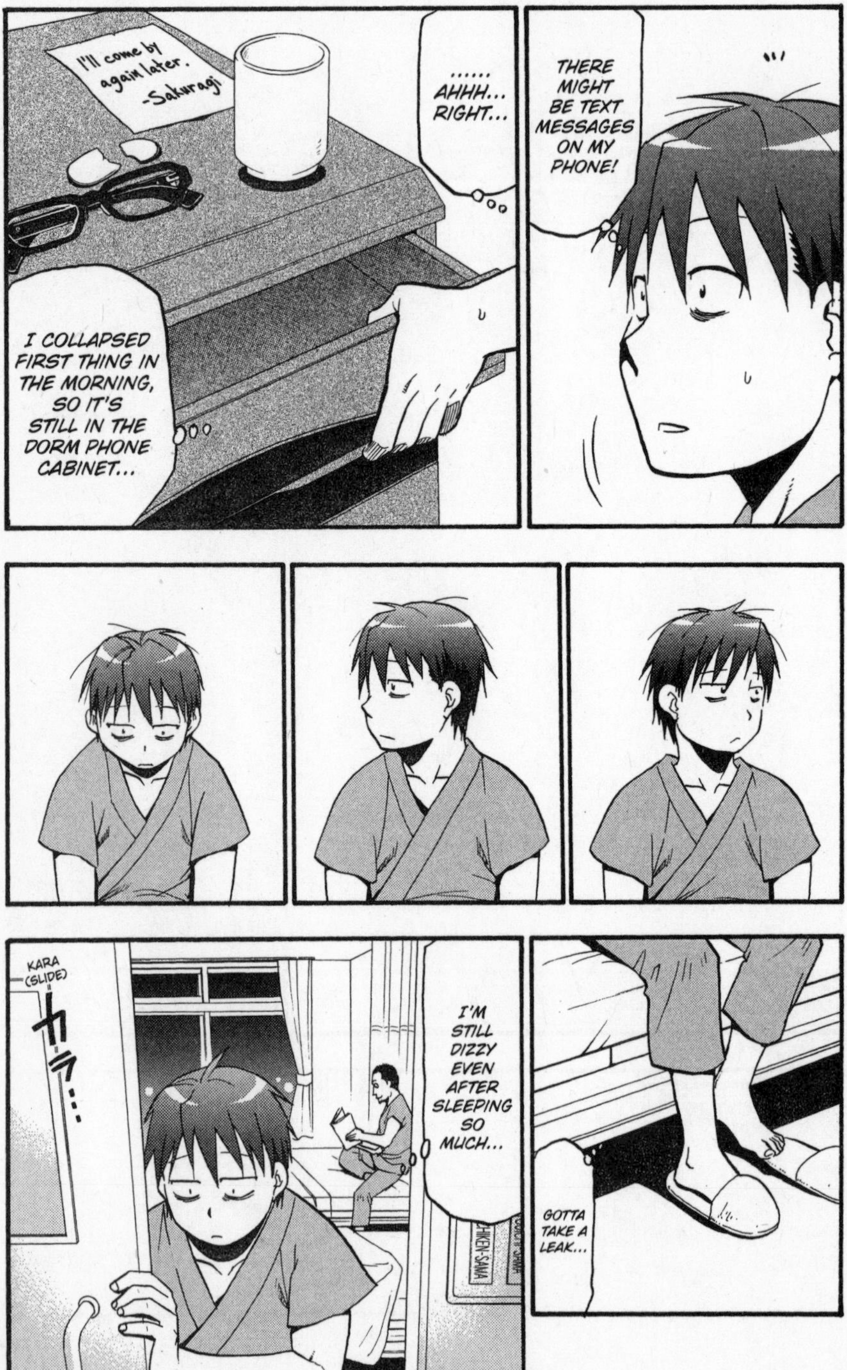
THERE MIGHT BE TEXT MESSAGES ON MY PHONE!
...... AHHH... RIGHT...
I'll come by again later. -Sakuragi
I COLLAPSED FIRST THING IN THE MORNING, SO IT'S STILL IN THE DORM PHONE CABINET...
GOTTA TAKE A LEAK...
I'M STILL DIZZY EVEN AFTER SLEEPING SO MUCH...
KARA (SLIDE)
カラ…

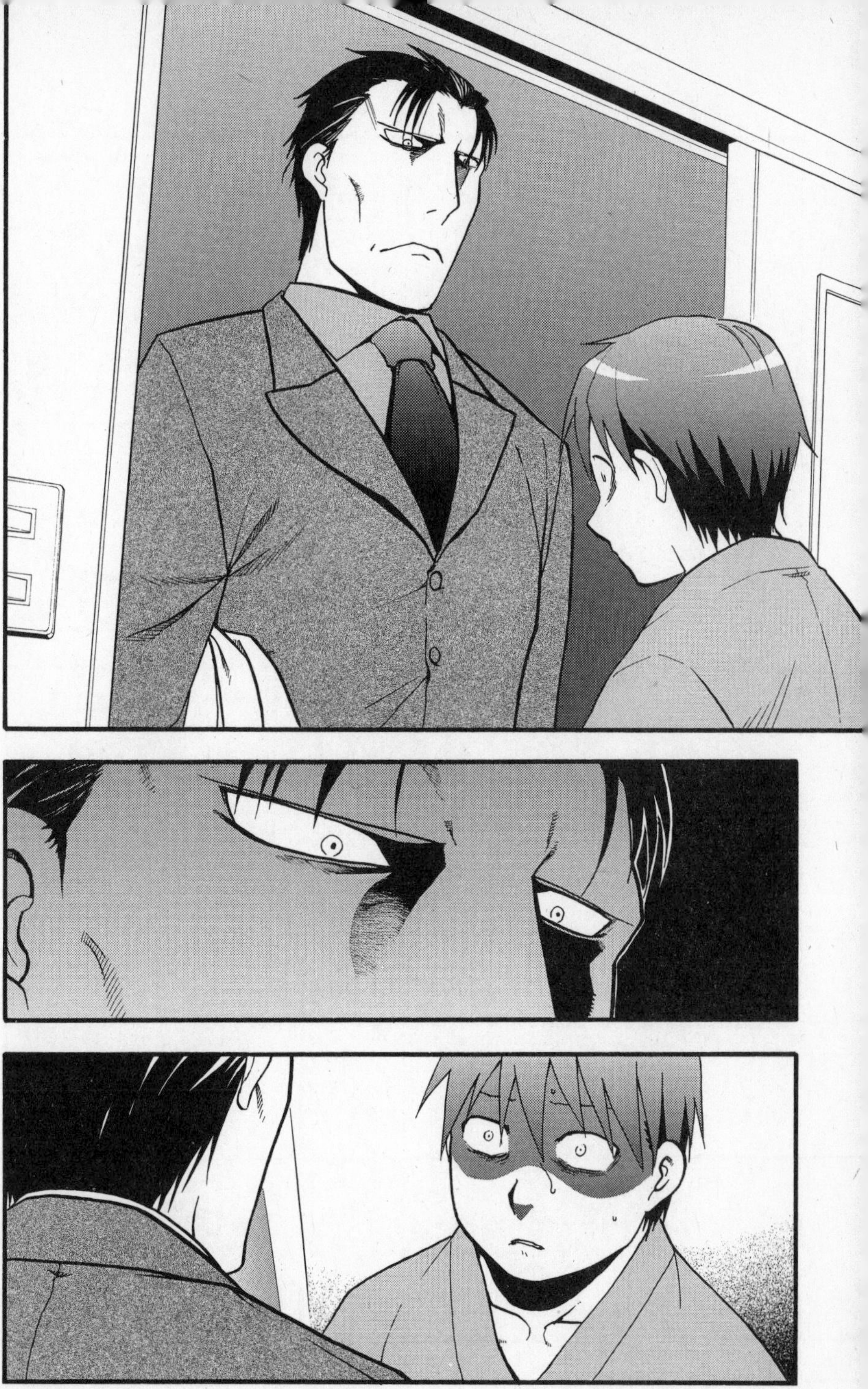

Silver Spoon 6 • END

Silver Spoon

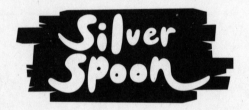

Magic Ball K

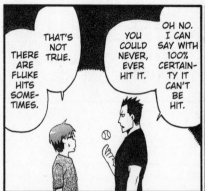

I CAME UP WITH A MAGIC PITCH THAT CAN NEVER BE HIT.
FOR REAL!?
WAIT, IT'S IMPOSSIBLE TO SAY NO ONE WILL EVER HIT IT.
OH NO. I CAN SAY WITH 100% CERTAINTY IT CAN'T BE HIT.
YOU COULD NEVER, EVER HIT IT.
THAT'S NOT TRUE.
THERE ARE FLUKE HITS SOMETIMES.
HERE GOES!
SHU (SHUP)
HERO (LOLL)
WHAT'S WITH THE SLOW BALL?
I CAN HIT THIS EASY.
WHOA. I CAN EVEN SEE THE STITCHES.
IS THIS ONE OF THOSE NO-SPIN THROWS?
RORORO
THAT'S CHEAP, YOU JERK!!!
TREAT

SFX: HERORORO RORORO RORO

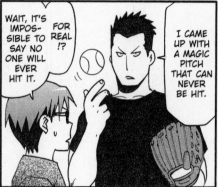

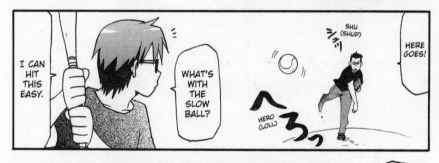

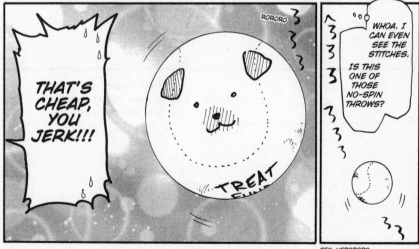

Cow Shed Diaries: "A WHAT at Tsubota-san's New Place!?" Chapter

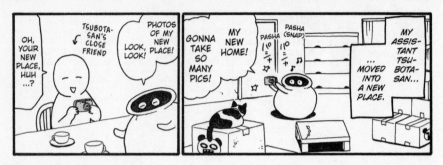

MY ASSISTANT TSUBOTA-SAN...
...MOVED INTO A NEW PLACE.
MY NEW HOME!
GONNA TAKE SO MANY PICS!
PASHA (SNAP)
PASHA
PHOTOS OF MY NEW PLACE!
LOOK, LOOK!
TSUBOTA-SAN'S CLOSE FRIEND
OH, YOUR NEW PLACE, HUH ...?
........THIS NEW PLACE OF YOURS, UH......
ZAWA (SHUDDER)
?
PHOTOS UPON PHOTOS OF A PIG BUTCHERING
JUST WHAT KIND OF EQUIPMENT DO YOU HAVE IN THIS NEW PLACE...?
DOKI
DOKI (BADUM)
N-NO!! THAT'S NOT MY NEW PLACE!!
THOSE ARE WORK PICS FROM OUR HOKKAIDO TRIP!!
PHOTOS WE TOOK FOR REFERENCE WERE MIXED IN.
DOKI
DOKI
DOKI

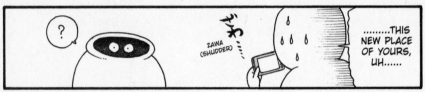

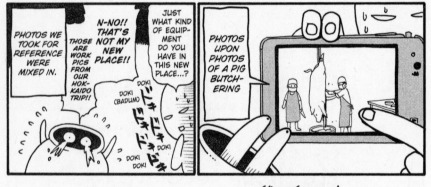

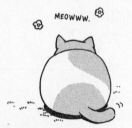

MEOWWW.

Silver Spoon 6!
I'm so glad to see you
in this volume too!

Hiromu Arakawa

~ Special Thanks ~

All of my assistants,
Everyone who helped with collecting material, interviews, and consulting,
My editor, Takashi Tsubouchi,

AND YOU!!

NEXT……

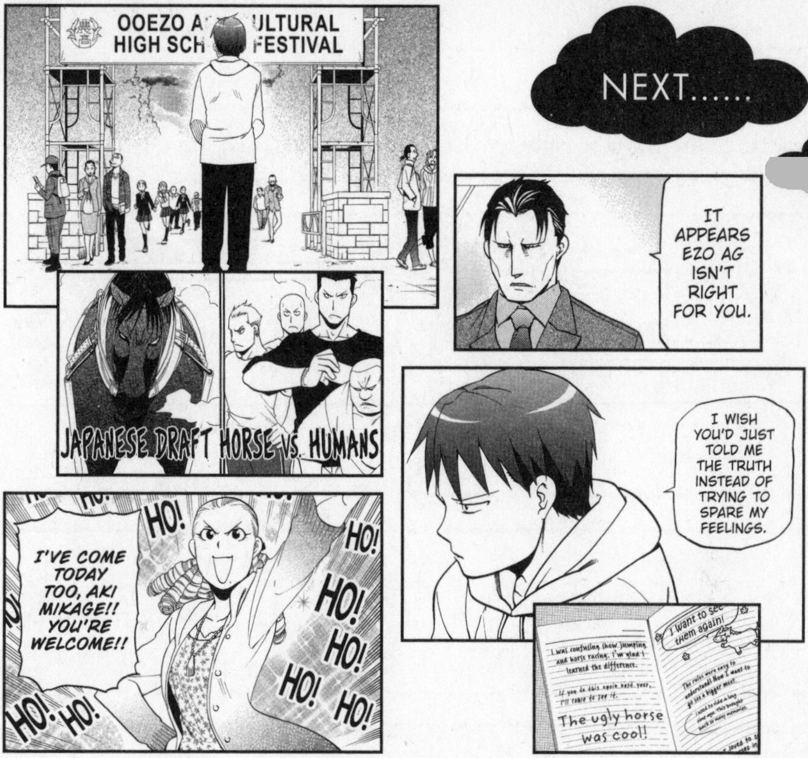
OOEZO A ULTURAL
HIGH SCH FESTIVAL
IT APPEARS EZO AG ISN'T RIGHT FOR YOU.
JAPANESE DRAFT HORSE vs. HUMANS
I WISH YOU'D JUST TOLD ME THE TRUTH INSTEAD OF TRYING TO SPARE MY FEELINGS.
HO! HO! HO! HO! HO! HO! HO! HO!
I'VE COME TODAY TOO, AKI MIKAGE!! YOU'RE WELCOME!!
I was confusing show jumping and horse racing. I'm glad I learned the difference.
If you do this again next year, I'll come to see it.
The ugly horse was cool!
I want to see them again!

He worked harder than anyone. But even so, sometimes hard work doesn't pay off. There are times you have to accept that life isn't fair. Still, someone is almost certainly watching the effort you've put in.

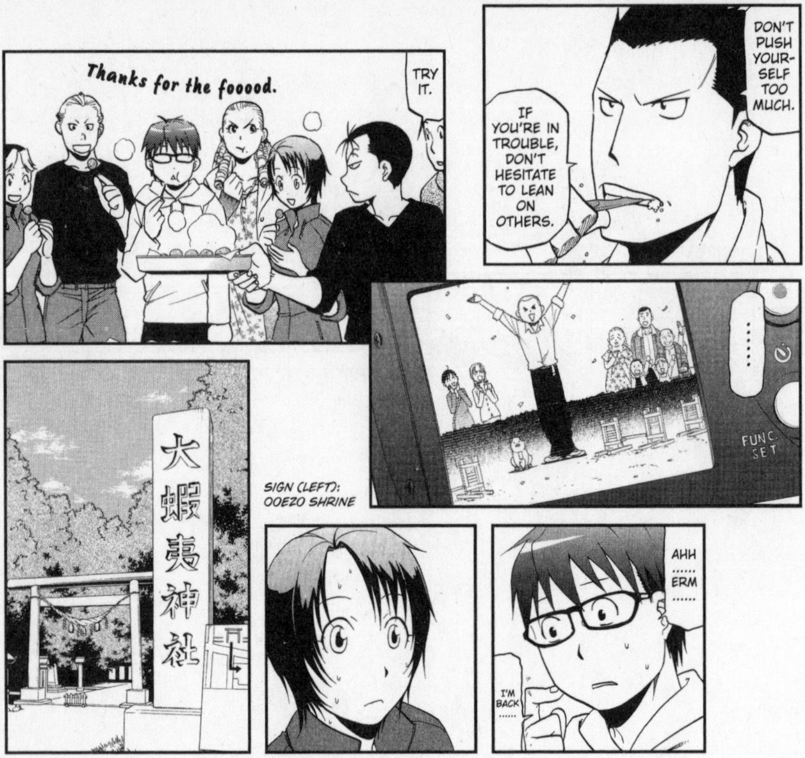
DON'T PUSH YOUR-SELF TOO MUCH.
IF YOU'RE IN TROUBLE, DON'T HESITATE TO LEAN ON OTHERS.
TRY IT.
Thanks for the fooood.
FUNC. SET
大蝦夷神社
SIGN (LEFT): OOEZO SHRINE
AHH...... ERM......
I'M BACK......

There's still plenty of reason to have faith in the world. For Hachiken, that someone is at Ezo Ag.

Silver Spoon **Volume 7 coming February 2019!!**

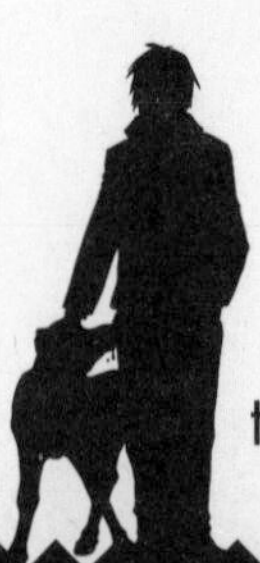

to be continued......

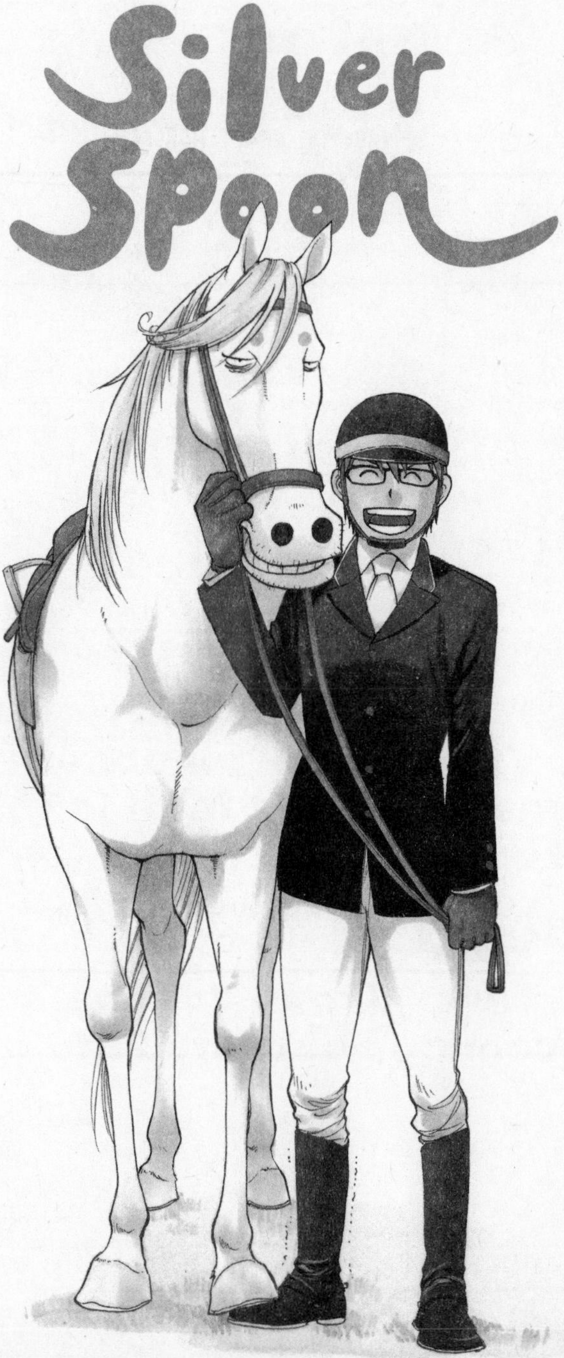
Silver
Spoon

BEWARE OF DRAFT HORSES

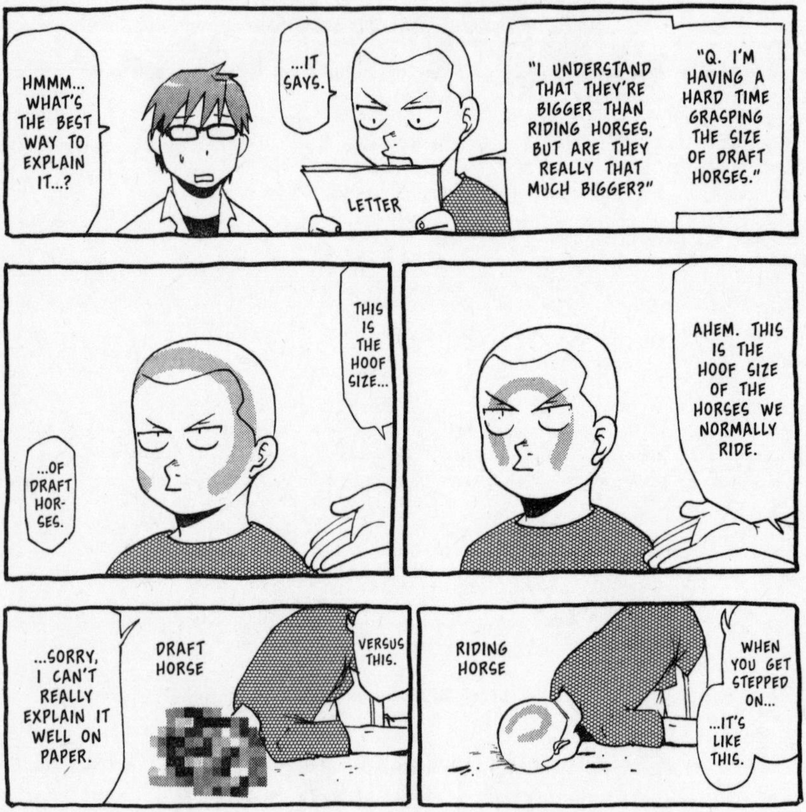
"Q. I'M HAVING A HARD TIME GRASPING THE SIZE OF DRAFT HORSES."
"I UNDERSTAND THAT THEY'RE BIGGER THAN RIDING HORSES, BUT ARE THEY REALLY THAT MUCH BIGGER?"
...IT SAYS.
LETTER
HMMM... WHAT'S THE BEST WAY TO EXPLAIN IT...?
AHEM. THIS IS THE HOOF SIZE OF THE HORSES WE NORMALLY RIDE.
THIS IS THE HOOF SIZE...
...OF DRAFT HOR-SES.
WHEN YOU GET STEPPED ON...
...IT'S LIKE THIS.
RIDING HORSE
VERSUS THIS.
DRAFT HORSE
...SORRY, I CAN'T REALLY EXPLAIN IT WELL ON PAPER.

Translation Notes

Common Honorifics

no honorific: Indicates familiarity or closeness; if used without permission or reason, addressing someone in this manner would constitute an insult.

-san: The Japanese equivalent of Mr./Mrs./Miss. If a situation calls for politeness, this is the fail-safe honorific.

-sama: Conveys great respect; may also indicate the social status of the speaker is lower than that of the addressee.

-kun: Used most often when referring to boys, this honorific indicates affection or familiarity. Occasionally used by older men among their peers, but it may also be used by anyone referring to a person of lower standing.

-chan: An affectionate honorific indicating familiarity used mostly in reference to girls; also used in reference to cute persons or animals of either gender.

-sensei: A respectful term for teachers, artists, or high-level professionals.

-niisan, nii-san, aniki, etc.: A term of endearment meaning "big brother" that may be more widely used to address any young man who is like a brother, regardless of whether he is related or not.

-neesan, nee-san, aneki, etc.: The female counterpart of the above, *nee-san* means "big sister."

Currency Conversion

While conversion rates fluctuate, an easy estimate for Japanese Yen conversion is ¥100 to 1 USD.

Page 5

The ending "-ko," is common among Japanese names for girls, so adding it to the school's name creates an instant feminine name.

Page 13

Every year on November 15 (or the nearest weekend), girls aged three and seven and boys aged three and five are dressed up for the holiday Shichi-go-san (literally, "seven-five-three"), a traditional rite of passage. While children are traditionally dressed in kimono, some are dressed in formal Western wear.

In the Japanese, the sayings Noboru and Hachiken mention are tangentially related to horses. "The clothes make the man" is *"mago ni mo ishou"* (literally, "clothes on a horse-driver"), and "the clothes don't make the man" is *"mago ni dotera"* (literally, "a padded kimono for a horse-driver").

Page 18

A Japanese trick for getting over nerves is to write the character for "person" three times on your palm and then "swallow" it. As Hachiken comments, Aki is writing a different character.

Page 21

Ayame calls Hachiken "Shichiken" because she's mixing up the number in his name—"hachi" means "eight," and "shichi" is "seven." Throughout the rest of the text, she continues to confuse "hachi" with another number. ["roku" (6), "nijuuyon" (24), "juuhachi" (18)]

Page 30

Ayame is quoting Sun Tzu's *The Art of War*. The quote is, "If you know your enemy and know yourself, you need not fear the result of a hundred battles."

Page 95

Kushiro is the most populous city in eastern Hokkaido. JUSCO (the Japan United Stores Company) is a large chain of superstores.

Page 96

Honshu is Japan's largest island and lies south of Hokkaido. Tokyo is located on this island.

Page 131
The *Mukimuki Memorial* towel is a reference to *Tokimeki Memorial*, a famous dating sim that came out in 1994. The series is ongoing, with the most recent release being *Tokimeki Idol* in 2018.

Page 153
"Flags" in dating sims/visual novels are events and choices that make a player eligible to pursue a relationship with a particular character.

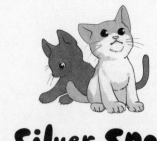

Silver Spoon

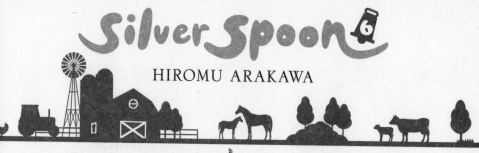

Silver Spoon 6

HIROMU ARAKAWA

Translation: **Amanda Haley** Lettering: **Abigail Blackman**

GIN NO SAJI SILVER SPOON Vol. 6
by Hiromu ARAKAWA
© 2011 Hiromu ARAKAWA
All rights reserved.
Original Japanese edition published by SHOGAKUKAN.
English translation rights in the United States of America, Canada, the United Kingdom, Ireland, Australia and New Zealand arranged with SHOGAKUKAN through Tuttle-Mori Agency, Inc.

English translation © 2018 by Yen Press, LLC

Yen Press
1290 Avenue of the Americas
New York, NY 10104

Visit us at yenpress.com
facebook.com/yenpress
twitter.com/yenpress
yenpress.tumblr.com
instagram.com/yenpress

First Yen Press Edition: December 2018

W9-CLB-886

Yen Press is an imprint of Yen Press, LLC.
The Yen Press name and logo are trademarks of Yen Press, LLC.

The publisher is not responsible for websites (or their content) that are not owned by the publisher.

Library of Congress Control Number: 2017959207

ISBN: 978-1-9753-2761-3

10 9 8 7 6 5 4 3 2 1

WOR

Printed in the United States of America